MAON: MARSHAL OF TALLAV

SONS OF TALLAV #2

CAILIN BRISTE

Maon: Marshal of Tallav

Second Edition

eISBN 978-0-9989125-5-4

Published in the United States of America

Hot Sauce Publishing
PO Box 13508
Offutt AFB, NE 68113-0508

This e-book is a work of fiction. While reference might be made to actual historical events or existing locations, the names, characters, places and incidents are either the product of the author's imagination or are used fictitiously, and any resemblance to actual persons, living or dead, business establishments, events, or locales is entirely coincidental.

Warning

This e-book contains sexually explicit scenes and adult language and may be considered offensive to some readers. Hot Sauce Publishing e-books are for sale to adults ONLY, as defined by the laws of the country in which you made your purchase. Please store your files wisely, where they cannot be accessed by under-aged readers.

Disclaimer

Please do not try any new sexual practice, especially those that might be found in our BDSM/fetish titles without the guidance of an experienced practitioner. Neither Hot Sauce Publishing nor its authors will be responsible for any loss, harm, injury or death resulting from use of the information contained in any of its titles.

For my sisters. Without them, I'd be a solitary combatant instead of fighting evil as one of the Three Aunties. The world will never know how much they owe to your dedication and fearlessness. All for one and one for all.

ACKNOWLEDGMENTS

This book would not have been possible without the encouragement and detailed editing from my developmental editor, Lea Schafer. Her advice has always been spot-on.

Kierstin Cherry, my Loose Id editor, smooths the rough places, insists I clarify and unpack so that I don't lose my readers, and generally makes each manuscript she touches better. She makes sure that what I see in my head is actually on the page. She's a wonder.

And, of course, I need to acknowledge my husband without whom I would never be able to write.

AUTHOR'S NOTE

Maon: Marshal of Tallav *takes place eight years before the events in* Shane: Marshal of Tallav. *In Shane,* Maon *was already living his happily ever after. But long before Shane found Adrianna, Maon needed someone to claim him and subdue him. Selina Shirley was a woman he never dared hope to find. This is Maon and Selina's tumultuous story. You'll find more about the universe of Tallav and the characters in the Sons of Tallav series on my Web site at http:// cailinbriste.com/. Read my blog, subscribe to my newsletter, and find the latest free downloads.*

1

S pace travel held no appeal for Selina. The CEO of the sector's leading fashion house, she'd accepted it as the necessity it was, but she'd be glad to get her feet on solid ground again. Her nose alone told her she wasn't there yet. The air filtration system on the Beta Tau station did a better job than most at removing the metallic tang of C-trol, the fuel ships ran on in hyperspace that permeated all space stations. A harsh aftertaste still clung in silvered wisps to the more mundane odors of fried foods and roasting meats that tempted travelers to part with credits before heading down world or returning to space. No, she wasn't there yet.

The strap of the portfolio slung over her shoulder slipped. A nudge and it was back in place. A trio of vacationers passed her, their excitement palpable in the pitch and volume of their voices. They hadn't noticed Selina, but who would? Hidden inside the drab, shapeless dress that constituted her armor against amorous attentions, she was perfectly content to be overlooked. No one would credit the truth. She was on her way to the Whip Hand to meet the owner and notorious sadist Randolph Meryon. The drawings she carried in her portfolio were the first install-ment of a trade she'd made. He would become her mentor while she explored sexual domination, and she would design exclusive apparel for his staff.

The underlying frisson of unease that always attended her in space was sliding up and down her spine. But the churning in her stomach, while she walked along the companionway from the private ship docks, wasn't caused by her fear of space. Her father's death over a year ago had cemented a number of things in her mind. One was the need to acquire a husband. Knowledge that she was on the marriage market would set in motion the machinations of the aristocratic mamas of Tallav—some because of her wealth and others for the connection. She wrinkled her nose. *Not going that route.*

Her Domme lessons with Randolph were the initial step in a concise plan to find her perfect husband. Emphasis on *her*. Implementing that plan was the root of her anxiety, akin to the strain of her first business negotiation for the House of Shirley.

A couple, the woman tipping along in platform heels, were cuddling and cooing while they walked toward Selina. She averted her face, seeing but not really taking in the concourse bar she was approaching. Then her gaze met a stranger's, and for an interminable moment, his eyes ensnared hers. She blinked, and the spell was broken. His lips moved in a smirk while he continued to stare at her.

Damn playboy.

When she yanked her head away, the oversize art case slipped down her arm, the strap tangling in her long dark hair. Rather than stop to fix the problem, she kept walking while struggling to release the strands that were pulling painfully on her scalp. Portfolio back in position, she sped up.

That man was the exact opposite of her ideal mate, although he was Tallavan. The string tie he wore made his Tallavan citizenship a possibility, but the badge clipped to his belt settled it. He was a Tallavan marshal. Despite his tousled sandy-brown locks that were made to comb through and pull, he wouldn't make the cut on her very exacting list of requirements. Even before he'd smirked at her, it was apparent he was a player. He'd been sitting still on a bar stool, but swagger oozed from his pores. His navy-blue eyes were full of a boldness that reached out to her and offered her more fun than she could imagine.

What the heck are you thinking, Selina? He's a snack and nothing more.

For her steady diet, she needed something less attractive, less powerful, and much more malleable. Truly malleable, not just a man who played the role to catch a Tallavan aristocrat and then left their children to nannies and tutors to raise while they flitted from event to event gambling and whoring.

The deal with Randolph couldn't have come at a better time. With his mentoring, she'd learn to recognize a submissive personality along with discovering where her preference for control would lead in the bedroom. Today was her first session. They'd had several long discussions via comm, focusing on the types of play she was interested in. Sensation play had been at the top of her to-do list. She wasn't attracted to bondage or the delivery of pain except where it enhanced the upward spiral of sexual need. Randolph had convinced her that a whip in clever hands was the perfect tool to heighten arousal.

She'd find out tonight. He required all dominants he mentored to assume the submissive role initially. To understand what you were dishing out, you had to experience it. The thought of his whip was adding its own provocation to her case of nerves. Allowing someone to use a whip on her wasn't her idea of pleasure. He'd said the effective use of a whip was more mental than physical. She could attest to that. Her mind was on full dread overload.

Steady on. You've input your destination. Now grab hold of the hyperstrand and don't let go.

Gods, she was exhorting herself with space metaphors. Maybe that was appropriate. She sure had her emotional teeth gritted like she did every time she stepped on a shuttle to head into space.

The shuttle docks were on the bottom level of the space station. Once she exited the lift and passed through entry control, she palmed the pass she'd been given. Berth 21 was to her left. Departure was close, so she hurried to the entry port. A quick scan showed three empty spots, all in the rear of the transport. With a nod to the passenger seated in the window seat, she slid into the aisle seat across from the other two vacant places. After receiving the assent of the gentleman next to her, she handed him her portfolio to slide against the shuttle wall. It fit below the large view window. Most travelers looked forward to the spectacular sight of Beta Tau while spiraling around the planet toward the spaceport. Funny how from such a great height the shifting reds, pinks, browns, and oranges of the desert planet's sands were awe inspiring, while down planet they were a nuisance to overcome.

A quick mental check of shuttle departures on her Electronic Biological CoServer showed the shuttle should start disconnecting from dock in about a minute. Where were the last two passengers? She leaned out of her seat to try to see the entry port. *Good.* Someone else was making their way on board. She settled back, and as did every other passenger who was ready to get going, she watched the pair of men amble down the aisle. The man in the lead was tall and dark. And oh sweet petunias, he was a Tallavan marshal. When they drew closer, a second marshal appeared, and a cocky half smile flashed when his gaze met hers. Again. The playboy. Selina dropped her gaze to her lap and tried to ignore the banter between the men while they settled into the two seats across the narrow aisle from hers.

"Take the window," the darker headed of the two said.

"Sure." The playboy slid past the other marshal to sit in the window seat. "Are we going straight to the club?"

"No. You eager for Randolph's challenge?"

"Eager to collect the prize."

Selina resisted the urge to stare across the aisle. Had she really heard the name Randolph?

"I don't think I'll ever get why you accept his challenges."

The playboy responded, "That isn't dropping the subject, but I'll answer you. Why does Ray Nox climb the mountains on Tallav's moon? Because they, in all their airless, soaring height, are there, a challenge to conquer. Randolph challenges, and I conquer."

"I still don't get it. But I don't get Ray Nox either."

"And you never will," said the playboy. "Just as I'll never get why you spend so much time tying women up in intricate rope creations."

Selina straightened in her seat, realizing she'd been leaning toward the pair. They couldn't be going to the Whip Hand. Could they? Clubs abounded on Beta Tau, but then they'd mentioned the name Randolph.

The tall, dark marshal grunted. "Randolph said if I can work out my Ball of Beauties, he might use it as the Whip Hand's ball drop on New Year's Eve. Put up Earth's ball drop on live vid and drop our own at the same time."

"You should think of another name. Ball of Beauties sounds dumb."

"Yeah. I'll work on that. But can you imagine crystal-studded harnesses and lights…"

The playboy laughed. "I can see you're getting transported to your happy place. So why not go straight to the club?"

"I brought special equipment in my baggage. We'll have to stop at the hotel first and wait for it to be delivered. You can spend the time checking out the staff."

"Heh."

Selina turned her head to look out the shuttle window, one finger tapping on her leg. *Damn.* Just what she didn't need. Tallavan aristocrats catching sight of her at the Whip Hand. The gossip would rabbit through the upper echelons of society, contradicting the asexual persona she presented to the world. The men had said they weren't going straight to the club like she was. If they were meeting Randolph, it would be after her appointment with him. She ought to be gone before they arrived. Randolph would help. He knew her preference for absolute privacy. Besides, she'd be masked. Stepping outside her comfort zone was giving her a case of the jitters. She took a deep breath and released it. *You're Selina Shirley. You can handle anything.*

MAON FIDDLED with the glass in his hand. From his perch at the end of the space-station bar where he sat waiting for Shane to meet him, he could observe everyone entering the companionway from the private ship docks on this side of the station. The usual eye candy passed him, rushing to explore as much as they could of the pleasures that awaited them on Beta Tau. Shane was due in on the *Adrasteia*. Maon didn't envy Shane much, but the *Adrasteia* was one sweet little craft.

"Refill?" asked the bartender.

"Yeah. But no alcohol. Something fruity."

When the bartender returned with his drink, Maon noticed a Tallavan woman heading his way. He should know her name, but it wasn't coming to him. Definitely a prude. Wearing some misshapen, baggy sack of a dress. Nice legs, but they'd look better in heels rather than the flats she wore. Shirley. That's who she was. He'd heard something about her taking over her mother's fashion house. Fuck's sake. If that was her sense of style, they'd be out of business soon.

He eyed her when she passed him, and their gazes met for a moment. He acknowledged her with a smirk. The portfolio she carried slipped, and she struggled to keep it from falling, her long sable hair snagging in the strap. Her head remained down while she swept from view. Maon chuckled.

"Are you harassing passersby again?"

"Shane!" Maon stood and grasped his friend's outstretched hand. "I can't help being devastatingly good-looking. The bane of my existence. Females dropping at my feet."

"Some bane. You up for fun?" Shane focused on the people walking past the open bar. "Randolph told me he's got the subs I need and plans for you. You're not gonna let him stretch your balls again?" He centered his bright blue gaze on Maon, one eyebrow arched.

Maon grinned. "He tries. Never wins. I have balls of steel."

"Brains of mush."

"You're jealous." Maon winked at a pretty girl passing by, letting his tousled good looks and crooked smile work their magic. One thing Beta Tau had in abundance—women, all shapes and sizes ready to have fun. And he was here to make their dreams come true.

Shane glanced at Maon and looked away in disdain. "What? Jealous! You get one girl as a prize. I've already got eight waiting on me."

"What do you do with them? Tie 'em up." Maon shook his head and paid the bartender. Both men headed toward the lift to take them to the shuttle docks. Shane seemed, as usual, oblivious to the undisguised interest the two handsome Tallavan marshals received while they strode down the companionway. Maon noticed, enjoying the attention, a slight exaggeration to his swagger while he winked and appreciated the varied reactions to his flirting. Yes, this trip was what he needed after a long stint of ferrying prisoners around the sector.

Having the owner of the top kink club on Beta Tau as one of your best friends was a definite benefit. The twins Randolph had offered as prizes on Maon's last vacation had fueled his fantasy life for months, fantasies Maon had amped up by adding in a hot Domme to put the girls through their paces. Randolph never set him up with a Domme. The prizes for winning Randolph's challenges were always subs. Not that many Dommes were willing to offer a session as a prize. Randolph said he'd never found the right one for Maon. Maybe this time.

Maon's one slim thread of hope for a long-term relationship was to find a Domme who could accept him as the switch he was and keep his cock in line. He didn't know which was harder, but combined, his requirements made that thread whisper thin. Which was why he'd stopped worrying about it. *If you can't have apple cobbler, eat the peach pie.* He was dedicated to peach pie.

Shane interrupted Maon's reverie. "You don't have to accept Randolph's challenges. They're only going to get worse. He's a sadist. He likes rigging you up and seeing you suffer. One of you has to say it's time to stop."

Maon pressed his lips together. "That won't be me. He knows I won't step back, so he'll have to be the one to call it quits. Talk to him. Not me."

"Fuck it. You—"

"No. He hasn't done me permanent damage, and he won't. Drop it. We're here to have fun, not fight."

Shane sighed, nodding. "I am going to talk to him."

"Good luck with that."

Both men showed their badges to bypass the entry control line and obtain shuttle passes. The attendant directed them to the last two open seats at the back of the shuttle. It wasn't until Maon neared the last row that he noticed the Tallavan frump he'd spotted from the bar. Up close she was quite pretty. Why the hell was she hiding in those awful clothes? He winked and flashed his panty-melting half smile and waited for her reaction. She focused her gaze on her lap, pretending to ignore him, but Maon could tell she was affected because of the muscle that twitched in her jaw. He annoyed her. Time to stop, then. He didn't like making women angry. He slid into the window seat and dropped her from his mind.

2

The G-string Maon wore was riding up and annoying him. He squirmed, wishing he could reach back and scratch. Randolph liked a show, so Maon put the friggin' thing on as well as black leather pants. Face it. Shaking his booty for the ladies was fun. One little performance and women would chase him for days. They went for his choirboy good looks and his bad-boy smiles. He chuckled. The Whip Hand was a great place to find kinky women.

First he had to beat Randolph's challenge. He winced at the remembered ache in his nuts when he considered the possibilities that Randolph would employ in his latest predicament bondage scene. No doubt about it. Randolph always devised some new method of torture. Maon sneaked his hand down to cup his balls, giving them a little stroke of comfort. Someday he'd put Randolph in predicament bondage, and they'd see who the better man was.

Like that would ever happen. Despite his ordinary, nondescript looks, Randolph, owner of the Whip Hand, had a charisma that mesmerized even the most difficult people into doing exactly what he willed. Not that Maon needed mesmerizing to take up Randolph's gauntlet. They were friends, and when Randolph had needed someone to help in a predicament bondage scene, Maon had been hesitant to assist him. After all, what was in it for Maon? He wasn't into Randolph, and he didn't like pain. When Randolph turned it into a challenge with a hot female sub as a prize, Maon's reluctance had evaporated. Now it was a given that Randolph would offer Maon a new sadistic challenge whenever Maon made it to Beta Tau. The public play space was already crowded with tourists of every stripe, from lifestyle kinksters to the merely curious. The Whip Hand was a place to indulge your fantasies or explore new possibilities. Only the serious-minded would complete the security registration that allowed them to enter the private play space and individual rooms beyond the public areas. Maon spotted Randolph heading toward him. A woman who looked familiar to Maon was following him, but she darted into the locker room before he could get a good look at her. He turned back to the scene he'd been watching.

"You ready?" Randolph asked when he strode up to where Maon was observing a younger man using a single tail to make a submissive shriek in fear. With each crack, she screamed even though the whip had yet to touch her.

"He's good," Maon said.

Randolph crossed his arms over his chest. "Trained him myself."

"What? Mind fucks or the whip?"

"Both actually." Randolph's face lit with a smirk. "We're over here." He pointed to another of the small stages around the edge of the room. "I gave Shane the main stage. He's got some plan to tie eight subs together in a ball."

As Maon approached, he noticed a woman some would call chubby, but he thought of as lush, sitting on the top step.

"Kaylee, this is Maon. Maon, Kaylee. She's generously agreed to be your prize if you win." Randolph gave Kaylee a heated look.

"Hello, Kaylee." Maon offered her his panty-melting grin. Her large brown eyes had met his when they were introduced, but the instant he smiled, they lowered.

"Hello, Sir." A smile tickled her lips.

"I look forward to spending time with you, Kaylee."

Long dark braids floated around her shoulders and brushed the tops of coffee-colored breasts held snug along with her generous curves in a midnight-blue corset. Her full plum-ripe mouth lifted in a brief curve.

Randolph gave him a tap on the arm. "Stop bragging and get onstage. Strip for the audience. Then stand over by the weights."

Maon ignored the wicked sneer on Randolph's face. "Hey, it's not my fault I cast a shadow across that Dom-master aura you lay on the ladies."

"In your dreams, prick. Now get moving."

Maon chuckled and took center stage to start his striptease. A small crowd soon built while he turned slowly, stripping off his leather pants and waggling his ass at them. He bent over at the waist and smoothed his hands along his legs, caressing his butt cheeks before peeling the sides of the thong down. With a twist, he winked over his shoulder and spun. His thumb held the G-string so his cock was pulled down but not showing. After a few more wiggles and thrusts of his hips, he whipped the scrap down and shimmied until it dropped to his ankles. His semierect cock hung long, as did his balls.

A group of lady tourists fought over the scrap of cloth when he kicked it to them. He stood, arms akimbo, shaking his head, waiting for the winner of the scramble to look his way. When she did, raising the G-string in triumph, Maon blew her a kiss with a wink and went to where Randolph had directed.

Randolph slapped him on the ass. "Time to suit up."

Maon stood stock-still when the cold chrome of a parachute collar touched his scrotum. He'd removed all his light brown pubic hair to avoid the extra discomfort of it being pulled. His balls bulged tight and heavy when Randolph locked the device around the top of his nut sac so they hung stretched below, keeping the collar from slipping off. Half-mast rose to full mast. He wasn't a pain slut. He didn't need pain as a release, but he'd discovered during these challenges, a certain amount, especially in front of a female audience, turned him on in ways he couldn't explain.

Randolph sneered at Maon's erection. "You haven't seen the weight I'm using."

Maon looked down and cringed inwardly at the four-pound parachute weight on the floor at his feet. Randolph was planning to attach it to the hook that united the three chains dangling from the collar. With it attached, Maon's balls alone would keep the parachute from falling to the ground. He'd never had his nuts stretched by something that heavy. Doubt assailed him, but he'd still try. He'd yet to fail any challenge Randolph threw at him. With Kaylee looking on, Maon wouldn't lose this time.

"Hands behind your head. Hold on to the bar." Randolph's voice was terse and commanding.

Maon grasped the cold metal of the pull-down bar, shrugging his shoulders to ease any tension in his muscles. Randolph locked his wrists to the bar. At his feet, Randolph clipped the four-pound weight to a steel cable, which went through a pulley above Maon's head, to a ring on the bar along his shoulders. A gravity node was attached to the cable a foot from the pulley. His arms slipped up when Randolph initialized the node.

"I loaded fifty pounds. Keep the bar pulled down so the parachute weight stays up in the air, Maon. It's gonna hurt otherwise. There's only a few inches of slack in the cable before it comes into play."

"How long?" Maon asked.

"Fifteen minutes."

Maon smirked inwardly while Randolph attached the four-pound weight to the parachute chains. He could do this. *Fifty pounds for fifteen minutes? Big deal!* He'd held seven times that weight in a lat pull-down for a full minute. No way he'd ever feel the four pounds hung from the collar around his balls.

"Kaylee, set the timer. If it gets to be too much, Maon, your safe word is *red*. Say it and you lose."

Maon relaxed, let his gaze travel over his audience of concerned admirers, and shut his eyes to wait out the time limit. Burning arm and shoulder muscles were nothing. No way would that bar move up.

A finger wound its way along his spine, went away, and returned to trace more patterns across his back. He wasn't ticklish. Not gonna bother him at all. Then his skin prickled. He tried flexing his shoulder blades, but the prickling turned to an itch down the middle and then all over as though bugs scurried in meandering trails over him.

Kaylee moved in front of him, chagrin covering her face. She wiped her fingers off with a damp cloth and knelt at his feet. His back itching desperately, he didn't realize she'd lifted her hand to his balls until she traced lines on them with her fingernail. If she kept it up, they would start to ache, but he could take it. Sweat broke out on his forehead. A quick glance at the time brought a groan from his guts. Thirteen minutes left.

"Shit, Randolph. You're a sadistic bastard." The exclamation burst from Maon's lips while he fought to resist the dual sensations. Air whooshed out of his lungs. While he writhed from the insatiable itching, his arms drifted up. "Agggh!" Pain slammed into him. The parachute weight was pulling the collar down. The skin on his nut sac was so taut it seemed as though it would split open. "Shit. Shit. Shit." He snapped the bar back to his shoulders. If the load had been added slowly, he could have handled it easier, but four pounds at once was friggin' hard to take.

He heard Randolph laugh. "Just say *red*, Maon. It'll be all over."

Like hell. He wanted to curl up to ride out the pain. Instead he controlled his reaction. The endorphin release would help him manage the burn from what felt like a hot poker stabbing his balls. He focused on his groin. It was Kaylee's fingernail. With each jab, his hips jerked back, jostling the parachute collar and adding to the agony radiating from his crotch. Fire from lactic acid buildup lashed across his shoulders with each spasm of his body. Sweat dripped from his torso. *Just hold on. Just hold on.* His resistance was fading. Spots were forming in front of his eyes while Kaylee continued her ministrations. His arms screamed with fatigue, but at the first sensation of added heaviness in his nuts, he would tug the bar back. Only an idiot would think Randolph's challenge would be anything as easy as holding down a weighted bar. The man's mind was wickedly cunning.

Maon chose not to watch the timer. Doing so would make time stretch immeasurably longer, the reason Randolph had set it in Maon's line of sight. At the point he was close to caving, he finally looked. One minute left. He fixated on the clock while the seconds ticked away. "Yeooow!" The scream strained his throat. Kaylee's hand was like a vise grip closed around his already throbbing balls. The dark was creeping in from the edges of his vision. *Don't pass out now. You cannot fail.*

The timer rang, his hearing faded, and everything went black.

Maon woke to find himself wrapped in a blanket, his head in Kaylee's soft lap. Across the room on the main stage, Shane was in the process of raising the women he'd tied up and formed into a sphere with gravity fields. At the moment, Maon's world was contained on this sofa and the warmth enfolding him from the woman whose fingers were threading through his hair and stroking his temple. He offered her a wan smile. "Randolph won."

"No, you won," Kaylee responded.

"Darlin', it's not a win if I can't use the prize."

Kaylee giggled. "Oh. That won't be a problem."

"No?" One eyebrow rose.

"No, Randolph gave you a dose of speedheal. You should feel fine in a few hours."

Maon gave her a mock disapproving look. "Really? A few hours? You'll be gone by then."

Kaylee smiled and stroked the curve of his ear. "You get me for three days."

A profuse grin split his face. "Well, then, we have plenty of time." He lifted his hand to her breast, scooping it up, fingers toying with her nipple. He ignored the ache in his shoulder and arm muscles. Some pain was worth it. He closed his eyes and drifted.

"Hey, mush for brains!"

Maon woke with Shane looming over him. He shifted to sit up, pulling Kaylee onto his lap. "Brilliant. That was phenomenal. Orb of Delight. That's what you should call it. Look out New Year's Eve."

Shane sat on the couch next to him. "It went well."

"You're this genius rope guy. It could be a new career. Rope guru."

"Rope guru. As if. I just like to tie things up," Shane said. He frowned at Maon. The focus of his glare turned to Kaylee, who squirmed. Shane looked away from the pair, his lips pinched. "You planning to have your balls pulled off?"

With a sheepish expression, Maon rubbed his hand along Kaylee's thigh. "Four pounds was a lot of weight. Maybe it's time I took a break from Randolph's challenges."

"Especially if you ever want kids."

"Okay. Okay. I get it. But I won. I haven't failed one of his little predicament scenes." Maon looked at Kaylee and waggled his eyebrows.

"Retire the undefeated champ." The heat in Shane's stare emphatically punctuated his statement.

With an attempt at an earnest expression, Maon said, "I'll think about it." An instant later his natural exuberance returned, and he grinned broadly. "At least I get to keep my prize for three days."

Shane sighed. "Won't be seeing much of you then?"

"I'll be around—some."

"You traveling back to Tallav with me?"

"Yep. I have another accompanist job to do."

"All right, if I don't catch you before, be at *Adrasteia's* berth at nine in four days."

"Will do." He bent his head so his lips brushed Kaylee's. "Now where was I?"

WITH A WHOLE PLEASURE planet to explore, Maon decided after spending two days in bed with Kaylee, they should spend the last day in the water dome. They drifted on air pods in the lagoon, body surfed, and played beach volleyball. They spent a few early afternoon hours in their own secluded grotto. His time running out, he brought her back to the Whip Hand.

Before heading into the club, Maon snapped a leash to the collar Kaylee wore. While he sauntered through the public venue and then on into the private area, leading her, he checked in and then scanned the crowd for old friends. He caught a flash of color. *Shit.* He came to an abrupt halt, exploring the vision across the room. Burnt-orange corset, a tiny black skirt, full latex hood with a flame feathered mask, and black leather stiletto boots. Everything about her sizzled fiery hot. The flogger and whip hung at her hip and the riding crop in her hand screamed *Domme.* The sizzle didn't stop at her accoutrements. The sight of her seared Maon. It wasn't physically possible for a woman that small to have legs that long. Or was she just perfectly proportioned? Whatever. He would suffer burns to be near her.

Maon wasn't the only one to notice her. Unattached subs were drifting toward her, hoping she would choose to play with them. His groin tightening while he contemplated her, he made a quick decision to ensconce himself in one of the elevated chairs along the back wall. Each chair included controls for the spotlight that shone down on it. With Kaylee at his feet, he set the beam on full.

"Suck my cock, Kaylee." He looked at Kaylee while she opened his pants and pulled his cock out. When she began to lick and suck, he brought his gaze up and stared at the Domme who had caught his eye. At first he imagined her mouth surrounding him, her tongue smoothing up and down the bottom of his erection, flicking the tip, her fingers stroking his balls. That required more restraint than he had to keep from thrusting and finishing quickly. No. That little fire-breathing woman wouldn't suck him off. She'd have him strapped to a St. Andrews cross, lightly flogging his erection while she pinched his nipples.

He shut his eyes and groaned. "Fuck, that's good." He jerked his eyelids open. She wasn't watching him. *Shit.* He returned to boring his gaze into her. His imagination running rampant, he almost got a hint of the fierce taste he would discover when she brought her pussy down over his face and forced him to pleasure her. He would use his tongue to tease her soft folds, tapping her clit, sucking.

His breathing kicked up a notch. With a pant, he gasped, "Fuck, Kaylee. This is moving too fast."

Kaylee was an expert at blowjobs, but he intended to hold his orgasm in check until he was sure he had the Domme's full attention. With slow breaths in and out, he fought the tingling starting at the base of his spine.

Come on. Come on. Look at me.

The Domme's gaze brushed across him and then flicked back to stare. With a cocky little half smile, he winked at her. He had her. He shut his eyes and let Kaylee's magic mouth sweep him to stomach-clenching orgasm. His cock pushed to the back of her throat; Kaylee swallowed when he came. *Fuck.* The woman knew her way around a man's dick. He relaxed into the chair, bliss oozing from his pores and a sated grin smeared across his face.

While Kaylee cleaned him up with flicks from her tongue, Maon checked to see if he still had the fire Domme's attention. *Good.* Her topaz perusal was on him. Fuck's sake she was hot. Even after his orgasm, his blood heated. He held her stare, refusing to drop his gaze. After a moment, she snapped her riding crop against her boot and turned to the small blond male who was standing meekly near her. The blond nodded when she spoke to him and followed when she approached the private room desk.

Maon smirked. Uh-huh. He'd gotten to her. While she went through the process of acquiring a room, he studied her, wondering if she would look his way again. Finally, while she was walking toward the dimly lit hallway, she paused and looked over her shoulder straight at him. He winked and smiled again, amused when she turned and strutted away.

Kaylee had finished adjusting his clothes, so he stood. "Up, Kaylee. Time to go back to Randolph. I'm sure he's missed you. You're a perfect sub even if I'm a lousy Dom."

"Thank you, Sir. It was most enjoyable to serve you. I've never been body surfing."

"Would you like me to tell Randolph you enjoyed body surfing?"

"If it pleases you, yes, I would like that."

After dropping Kaylee off with Randolph, Maon returned to the private club to sit and wait for the fire Domme to give him an opportunity to approach her.

WHAT A PRICK! A gods-damned, delicious prick. He couldn't know who she was. Selina had made certain, down to a voice modifier, that no one would discover who she was. She was Lasair. Not Selina Shirley. Randolph had told her the man was Maon Keefe, Tallavan marshal. And a man who loved to play with women. Well, she wasn't someone he could toy with. He was an idiot if he thought watching another woman give him a blowjob would make her want him. If she had him under her power, he wouldn't get off that quickly. Or at all. How would he like a cock cage? Or a chastity belt?

Lord love a duck! Who was she fooling? Watching him come was hitting all her arousal buttons. And now he was staring at her as though he knew what he was making her feel. As though he knew her nipples were hard and her clit throbbing. *Damn him!*

With a snap of her crop, she looked around her for a sub. A blond male stood a few feet away, his gaze cast to the floor except for occasional sideways peeks at her. Subs had gradually shifted in her direction, hoping to play with her. Her outfit screamed *Domme* at them, but she wouldn't be assuming that designation until she'd completed mentoring with

Randolph. For now she was Lasair. Her first assignment on her own was to practice the various techniques of orgasm denial Randolph had taught her. The blond would do. He was smaller, less intimidating, and pretty, even with the scruff of a beard he sported and his crew cut.

A brief exchange led to the blond's agreement to the scene she'd planned. Without looking, she sensed Maon's gaze boring into her. It was a pressure in the center of her back, as though he'd placed his hand there to remind her. *I'm here. I'm watching you. I want you.* Too bad. She might lust after him, but she wasn't here for lust. When the attendant gave her the key code for a private room, she stepped toward the hall. *Don't look back. Don't look back.*

Urrggh! She checked behind her. He was staring at her, and damn it all to hell, he winked and smiled at her. A growl escaped her lips when she snapped her head around. She heard the sub behind her squeak. Her voice modifier had intensified the sound, so it came out with a snap and crackle. *Focus. Get your mind on the sub.* That inadvertent growl had messed with the blond's headspace. If he wasn't feeling her dominance before, he was now. Randolph had repeatedly told her dominance was as much mental as it was physical. Satisfaction flooded her. Mental domination was definitely something she liked and might even crave if she experienced more such control. Was it possible to dominate a man mentally to a degree that physical restraint was not necessary? This wouldn't be the scene to explore that possibility. Randolph's parameters for this assignment were clear. Bind the sub because she was too new at dominance and wouldn't know him well enough to predict his reactions.

When the door swung open after entering the key code, Selina pointed and said, "Kneel by the St. Andrew's cross." The image of Maon Keefe kneeling at that cross breezed through her mind. She brushed it aside. With a sharp smile, she closed the door.

3

W hy him? When Maon had checked the duty roster he'd learned he was still stuck accompanying prisoners to the jurisdictions where they would be tried. Why? Plenty of other guys were pulling their four-year stint in the marshals before starting their hunt for a wife. Let some of them do this tedious job. Sitting on their asses was more their speed. Definitely not his. He was going to make something of himself. It'd been three years since he graduated from the academy, and despite multiple applications to be trained as a data analyst, he'd been denied every time. The window for reapplying had opened again, but his chances didn't look any better than before. If they kept detailing him to prisoner transfer, he'd never show them what he could do. On top of it, he'd pulled the assignment to accompany Cosmo Bonilla to Fed Central. That meant weeks of travel time.

Maon collected the prisoner in the transfer building, nose twitching at the wet wool smell that pervaded the facility. He'd never been able to figure out where the odor came from. A guard had told him it was the building's insulation. Bonilla had already been strip-searched and fitted with a shock collar by the prison guards. With a flick of a finger, Maon gestured for him to approach. Scans were routinely used, but Tallavan marshals were trained to be thorough. Even when shirking had obvious benefits. And they never depended on someone else's search of a prisoner.

"Strip. Place your clothes on the table." Maon and the guard with him watched while the man removed his shoes, jumpsuit, and underwear. Bonilla was large with an ample gut and covered in enough curly black hair to knit a sweater.

"Hands out." Maon snapped on steri-gloves, took a flashlight, and looked in all the hidey-holes of the human body. "Get dressed."

While he placed a chain around Bonilla's waist, he said, "I'll be cuffing you to this chain. It's synthsteel. Be advised, as a security measure, the cuffs and chain can only be removed at this prison, inside a prison transport cell, or your destination detention center. Neither I nor any other person can remove them outside those locations. Do you understand?"

The prisoner grunted with a nod.

"Good. We should get along fine. The shock collar you are wearing can be activated by any individual on the transport team and the destination receiving team. I would prefer not to have to use it. Trust me. If I activate it, your balls will end up by your tonsils."

Dressed and restrained, Bonilla offered no resistance when Maon guided him out of the facility to the prisoner transfer vehicle. From there it was a quick shuttle ride to the Tallavan spaceport and lockdown on the marshal's transport.

Maon sat on the extruded bench outside the ship's transfer cell and studied Bonilla. The drug lord had been arrested on Asturnia where he'd been hiding from a Federation arrest warrant charging him with corruption of a government official. He'd bribed a testing monitor to get his son into an elite university. In twenty years, it had been the only charge prosecutors were able to bring against him.

Bonilla raised an eyebrow at him.

Maon gave himself a mental shake before addressing the prisoner. "When the hyperspace warning comes, you'll want to lie in the bunk and turn on the safety field. The ventilation ducts wheeze on this tub, but don't let that disturb you. It's normal. Which means they can't seem to fix it. I'll be bringing you your meals. Anything you can't or won't eat?"

Bonilla grunted. "Nah, I'll eat anything. Thanks for asking."

"You're welcome." Maon frowned, his eyebrows knitting together.

"Can I ask you something?"

With a shrug, Bonilla said, "Sure. As long as it doesn't involve my business dealings."

Maon smirked. "Right. No, I was wondering why you came all the way to the Tallavan sector of the Fed to hide. The crime you're charged with carries a sentence of five years max that would have you out in two years for good behavior. Why not just get it over?"

"Timing, kid. You can't leave a business as large as mine on a moment's notice. Personnel issues, deals in progress, shoring up loyalties—all that stuff takes time."

"Okay. But why choose this sector to hide in? You didn't really think the sectors past the Sympallan Drift were as wild as the stories make us out to be? We may be more free-range than older systems in the Fed, but we're not lawless."

Bonilla snorted. "I short hopped to your sector, conducting business along the way. Gave me the time to get stuff done and avoid the Feds. Ended up here. Hid for as long as I could get away with it."

Maon didn't believe it. Not completely. The core of what Bonilla had said was probably true. The best lies were those hidden in a pile of truth. The man didn't simply end up somewhere. Bonilla had selected the Tallavan sector as his destination for a reason. If Maon could get Bonilla to talk to him about drug smuggling in the abstract, maybe he could discover what Bonilla was hiding.

"I suppose you won't tell me how long it took us to find you after you arrived?"

Bonilla smiled through a pained expression. "Sorry. That's a little too close to home."

Maon returned the smile. "Had to ask. I have to go check in with the ship's captain, but I'll be back with your supper. We can talk some more. I haven't had the opportunity to spend time with someone who's seen and done as much as you must have."

"Sure, kid. We can swap stories. Help the trip pass."

"Excellent. I'll see you later, then."

Maon hit the rungs of the ladder and scrambled up. While he headed toward the bridge, he began to formulate a plan. Once he'd seen the captain, he'd pull a download of big drug cases from the Fed database.

They could be the basis for his questions to Bonilla. These six weeks could end up being more productive than he'd thought. And maybe if Maon arrived at meaningful results, he'd be considered for a position in data analysis.

No one had told Maon to expect a crowd waiting at the detention center's transfer gate. This mob was out for blood. Bonilla's blood. Vigilante justice for lost sons and daughters was alive and howling for the guilty to pay for his crimes. Federation prison guards were trying to clear a lane for the transfer vehicle to enter the gate. Maon gritted his teeth at the sheer incompetency on display.

"Say again. I didn't copy what you ordered me to do," Maon requested over his comm.

A thin, nasal voice repeated, "Remove the prisoner from the vehicle and walk him in. Our guards will form up around you and push you through."

"That's what I thought you said. I'm not sure that's a good idea."

"Get the damn prisoner out and walk him in. We do this all the time."

Maon relaxed his jaw, wiggling it from side to side to alleviate the ache clenching it had brought on. This was Fed Central. If there was anyplace in the Fed where protocol should be strictly adhered to, it was Fed Central. So why had they allowed a crowd of this size near a prison transfer gate? It wasn't right. But beyond the disregard of proper procedure, it didn't feel right either. A cadre of guards, bulked out in protective gear, was heading toward the van.

Over the van intercom the driver asked, "What do you want me to do, sir? Shall I drive away?"

The Fed in charge snarled in Maon's receiver. "I repeat. Get the damn prisoner out and walk him in."

Fuck! Fuck! Fuck!

Over the intercom, Maon asked, "How far away is another gate we can use?"

The driver responded, "The supply gate is around the corner to the right about two blocks down."

Over the comm Maon said, "Be advised. We are pulling away and will bring the prisoner in through the supply gate."

A different, deeper voice spoke. "Marshal, this is Deputy Administrator Chavess. Do not, I repeat, do not pull away. You will escort the prisoner in through this gate immediately. I will have your badge if you fail to obey this direct order. Do you understand me?"

Between clenched teeth Maon cursed.

Bonilla, who'd been observing the situation with rapt attention, spoke. "Hey, kid. Do what the man says. Don't worry about me."

Maon snarled at Bonilla. "It's my job to worry about you."

His face grim, Bonilla said, "Do what the assholes say. It'll be all right."

The prison guards had reached the van and were pounding on the side door, a thudding beat to the surging noise of the crowd.

Fuck it. He was going to do the right thing. "Driver, back out of here."

"Sir, there are guards behind the van."

"Chavess, call your guards back. We're leaving the gate."

The sound of metal striking metal resounded from the back of the van. "My guards have orders to extract the prisoner from the vehicle. This is your last chance. Walk the prisoner in."

Maon slammed his fist against the van door. *Gods-damned fucking idiots!* Over the comm, he bit out his response. "Complying now."

Keying the van intercom, he told the driver, "We're getting out. Don't move this vehicle an inch until we're through the gate. Understood?"

"Understood."

When a prison guard thumped on the side door of the van, Maon opened it. He exited the vehicle, pulling Bonilla after him, scanning the crowd, which grew louder when they sighted the prisoner. With Bonilla thrust in front of him, Maon attempted to move quickly toward the gate, but the guard's slow movements impeded his progress as much as the force of the crowd shoving toward them did.

Was that smoke? *Shit, don't let someone have a Molotov cocktail.* Bonilla lifted on his toes to look over the crowd. Maon clamped a hand on Bonilla's wiry hair and pushed the man's head down.

"Keep down. These people are not your friends." His warning, voiced in a roaring growl, must have reached Bonilla over the discordant shouts and the whump, whump of someone beating a drum.

Angry citizens pressed harder against the guards, moving to surround

Maon and the prisoner. Tension thrummed through Maon, a hindrance to his situational awareness if he allowed it to overwhelm him. *Eyes and ears. Eyes and ears. Focus.* He understood the anger that was surrounding him. This man had profited from the drugs that had killed their loved ones. But Maon's duty was to keep Bonilla from harm, to block any attempt at revenge.

To his right, a gap opened in the guards' human barricade. Through it a man wearing an oversize coat stood, his face intensely focused on Maon and the prisoner. *Strange gear for this weather.* Maon's response was automatic the instant he recognized the assault weapon rising to point in his direction. He pulled his gun, raising his arms to fire, and bumped Bonilla hard left with his hip.

Pain exploded down the right side of Maon's body. Time slowed while he fell to the ground, head bouncing three times, impossible to stop. A face came into view. Somehow he should know that face, and he should do something. But what?

The man's hand tapped his cheek. "I like you, kid. Take care of yourself."

Maon blinked, and the man was gone. Maon's awareness sliding into oblivion, he tried but failed to grasp what was happening.

WHY WERE his eyes stuck closed? Someone was humming…

Where was he? Why couldn't he move? Too tired…

A little blue boat, his toy boat, drifted on the current of the creek that ran close to his home. He loved that boat. It was the last gift his father had ever given him before abandoning him. He'd played with that boat long past the time he should have moved on to other more mature toys.

The sun shone down, dappling the gentle flow of the water with flashes of pure light. He returned the boat to its starting point for another journey. When he released it, the sun disappeared and gloom descended. The creek churned, flooding to become a huge river, his boat out in the middle, swirling away. His arms were so heavy he couldn't reach out and grasp it. His mother would be angry. *You never do anything right. You're just like your father. You're a failure. Failure. Failure.*

Pain! Pain! Fire burning.

A voice said, "Sorry—quick check—doing well."

Sinking.

Relief.

Sleep.

A voice. Someone was speaking. Shit, he couldn't open his eyes. *Who's there?*

"Hey, buddy. I'm here."

Shane? Shane where am I? I can't move. I can't open my eyes. What happened? Am I dead?

"You're gonna be okay."

Okay? I'm gonna be okay? Don't leave me. Please don't leave me here. Sounds grew fuzzy and faded away.

The light filtering in through the window blinds was warm on his skin. A blink eliminated some of the distortion while he slowly focused his gaze on the medical equipment positioned above him. *I can see.* An attempt to lift his head failed. Too heavy to move. Panic! Was he paralyzed? The index finger on his left hand twitched, but his right hand was like a block of wood. Relief flooded him when his toes brushed the sheet covering him.

"Hey, you're awake."

Maon looked up into the face of his best friend. The smile he attempted came out as a twitch.

"The doctors said you should wake up sometime today. You've been on heavy meds for a while keeping you asleep."

He struggled to speak, his throat and mouth dry, coated with a thick scum. "Wa-ah-water."

Shane held out a cup with a straw, and Maon sipped, rinsing the cool liquid over his tongue and dabbing his tongue to the roof of his mouth. Finally he took several long pulls before he was able to say, "H-how long?"

"Eight weeks."

"More water?"

Maon drank from the cup, emptying it. He took a deep breath. "You came."

"Of course I came. I took a leave of absence. I couldn't let my best friend spend months alone in a hospital on Fed Central to recover from a gunshot by himself."

Maon blinked at the itch behind his eyes. "Thanks."

Shane's gaze dropped to his hands wrapped tightly around the bed rail. When he raised them again, Maon was grateful Shane's face showed no sign of the emotions he'd been struggling with.

"Guarding me? From the nurses?"

Shane grinned. "Maybe now that your color's coming back and you're not covered in steri-skin and hooked to life support, I'll need to."

"What happened?"

"You remember the prisoner transfer?"

Maon nodded.

"You remember getting shot?"

A shadow of confusion darkened Maon's eyes. "No. There was a crowd. Shot?"

"When you got out of the van and were taking the prisoner to the gate, you were hit by a gun blast. A PL20G."

Maon twitched an eyebrow.

"Yeah. You're lucky it didn't hit you dead-on. The doctors have had you in sleep suspension. You're getting a whole new right side. Fried your rib cage down to your hip and part of your arm."

Maon tried to lift his head again but couldn't make his neck work.

"Don't worry. They said you'd be as pretty as ever once the muscles finish regrowing. The skin's already sealed over. That's why they took you out of sleep suspension. The worst is over."

Maon's eyelids drifted closed. With that crowd? Why had he gotten out of the van? What a stupid thing to do.

"Bonilla?" He peeled his eyelids open.

"Bonilla escaped."

Maon released the breath he'd been holding in a whoosh. He grimaced when a spike of pain stabbed into his side. He'd screwed everything up.

Shane's voice was rough. "None of it was your fault. I can't believe how fucked up that transfer got. Bonilla was wearing a shock collar, and no one thought to activate it?" Shane's lips curled in a sneer. "Without that mob there, the gunman wouldn't have gotten close enough to shoot you. I've watched the vids, and it sure looks like some of the crowd went hysterical after the shooting in very convenient ways."

"I didn't see the shooter?" How could that be possible? He was trained for just that situation. Had he been caught flat-footed?

"You did see him. You had your gun up when the blast hit you. He hid behind people in the crowd until you brought Bonilla from the vehicle."

"Shouldn't have done that." What had he been thinking?

"Hindsight."

"Should have pulled away."

With a slight nod, Shane said, "Driver said you tried."

Maon grimaced. "What stopped me?"

"Claims you changed your mind."

Maon stared at the far wall. "Fuck."

"You followed marshal directives to obey Fed instructions. They'd have filed failure-to-follow-orders charges against you if you'd driven away."

"Wouldn't have gotten shot." *If I could only remember. Any way you look at it, I'm through. I let Cosmo Bonilla escape.*

"You shouldn't have been put in a position to get shot. Fed's fault. Not yours. That's how the director will see it. Don't worry."

Maon shook his head. Shane was a good friend, but it was clear. Maon was screwed. He'd failed big-time.

"You need to rest. Shut your eyes. I'll be here. We'll go home together."

Maon did, drifting off, still trying to remember.

MAON AMBLED into the doctor's office. The six weeks he'd spent in *Adrasteia's* gym on the trip back from Fed Central had been worth it. Yesterday he'd passed his fitness test. Today he'd pass his psych eval. He simply had to give the right responses. He could do that. If he could pass the fitness test despite the pain in his side, he could convince this head twister he was fine without revealing the return of his nightmares.

"Marshal Keefe." Shannon Jessop offered her hand. "I'm Dr. Jessop. I'll be visiting with you today."

"Call me Maon, ma'am." He curled his toes in his boots. Shannon Jessop. The curvy blonde bombshell that every single male in the service wanted to meet. This should be easy. He merely had to turn on the patented Keefe sex appeal.

"Thank you. Please have a seat." She gestured to a set of cushioned blue chairs off to one side in her office. After sitting, she asked, "I've looked over your records and the battery of tests you've been given. Everything points to putting you back on active duty so far." She smiled, pleasant and dispassionate.

Maon tilted his head, giving her his crooked smile. "Sounds perfect."

Dr. Jessop narrowed her eyes. "If after our session today, you feel you need more time in counseling, that can be arranged and won't affect your duty status."

"Good to know." Maon stretched his legs out and crossed his ankles, bumping the doctor's foot. "Oops, excuse me." He pulled his feet back and smiled again.

"Marshal Keefe, I recognize when I'm being flirted with, so let's cut the crap and get to the point of this visit," Dr. Jessop said.

"Yes, ma'am." Maon straightened in his chair and offered her a sheepish smile. "Sorry about that."

"Don't worry about it. Your reputation precedes you," she said with a frankness that told Maon he was truly forestalled. "I want you to think about getting shot. How would you describe your emotional reaction now you've spent time with the Fed counselor and had the opportunity to assimilate what happened to you?"

There it is. Keep cool, tell her what she wants to know, and you're out of here. "My emotional reaction? It makes me angry," Maon said, his voice bland.

"Why is that?"

Frustration surged. She had to have read this in his records. At every meeting with the Fed head twisters, they'd probed at this point. Now she was ripping aside the bandage and poking at it. Maon leaned forward, planting his elbows on his knees, and glared at her. "I'm angry at the Fed SOBs that allowed the situation to blow up the way it did. I'm angry that Cosmo Bonilla, who I came to like on the trip to Fed Central, stole months out of my life. And I'm mad at myself for making stupid decisions that nearly got me killed. Is that what you want to hear?"

"Anger is a natural response. I've read the reports, and it's clear you have a legitimate right to be angry with both the Feds and Cosmo Bonilla. Why do you believe your decisions were stupid?"

"Because they were. Getting shot makes that obvious. If I had turned the vehicle around or refused to leave it with the prisoner, I wouldn't have been shot, and the prisoner would still be in custody. I screwed up." Maon's lips narrowed to a tight line when he finished speaking. He hated the probing questions, but at least he knew the responses that would prove he was dealing with his anger appropriately.

"And yet your superiors state you acted reasonably in the situation. Which bothers you more, getting shot or failure to complete your assignment?" Jessop asked.

Maon mulled the question over before answering. "I allowed a prisoner to escape."

"You believe you failed?"

"I did fail."

"Has anyone else said you failed?"

"No." Maon scowled. "I'm sure some of them think it, though." He adjusted his position, finding it hard to sit still.

"And that bothers you?"

"Yes, I don't fail. Not on the job." With the realization his tone had sharpened, Maon took a deep breath.

"You've never failed?"

Fuck's sake, this was not going how he'd planned. Maon rubbed his temple. "Well, obviously I've failed at little things. I tried to flirt with you, and you know how far that went."

"But?"

The muscles of his face hardened. "But on the job I don't fail."

"So you're adjusting to the fact that you are capable of making professional mistakes that count?" she asked.

"Yeah, I guess you could say that." Her scrutiny and the fear he might have blown the interview sent a trickle of sweat from his armpit.

"Has anything good come from your experience? Personally good?"

"Good?" Maon considered the question. Maybe he hadn't screwed this yet. "I'll be cutting back on some of the stupid stuff I do. I just proved I'm not invulnerable." The memory of his last predicament scene with Randolph flashed across his mind's eye.

"Stupid stuff?"

Maon's mouth twitched in self-deprecation. "Yeah. I take risks in my personal life and have been known to pull crazy stunts. I'm working on my risk awareness, I guess you'd say." She should like that. Risk awareness. The Feds had ladled that on thick.

"Will that help you avoid failure?" she asked.

Maon thought for a moment and nodded. "Yeah. It probably will. Thinking that way is new to me."

She nodded. "Failure is a part of life. I'm sure you've been told that before. Risk awareness is valuable, but can go too far if you never take any risks trying to avoid failure."

Dr. Jessop's nod of approval was a small victory. "Yeah, I get that. The Fed counselor talked a lot about positive responses to failure."

"Yes. I read his notes. I agree that although you continue to deal with the trauma, you are addressing it in constructive ways."

Maon dipped his chin, focusing on his lap and the fingers he'd been curling and uncurling. He was going to make it past this hurdle. "I really am sorry for messing with you earlier. I guess it was a little defensive." Letting his risk-taking side out, he lifted his head. "Although you are the prettiest doctor I've ever met." Maon's heart rate sped up when Dr. Jessop's eyebrow rose. He caught himself before he winked.

"You seem to be doing well. If you have nightmares or anxiety attacks, please return. The post-trauma nanite infusion you received after the shooting should have already flushed from your system. The need for another infusion sometimes happens months after a traumatic event."

"Yes, ma'am."

The same pleasant and dispassionate smile graced her face. "Dr. McIntyre is available for additional counseling sessions."

Maon held up a palm. "That won't be necessary." He'd heard about Dr. McIntyre and had no wish to spend time with the old she-dragon.

"I'll be filing my completed evaluation by tomorrow. You should be returned to active duty within a few days." She stood to shake Maon's hand.

Maon rose, offering a firm grip. "Thank you, Doc." When he exited, he turned to look at her and said, "If you're ever in need of an escort, I'm available." He grinned, winked, and sauntered out the door. He'd done it. Now to prove he wasn't the total failure this last assignment had made of him.

4

Sector Chief Davis motioned for Maon to follow him. "It's good to have you back on duty."

"Thank you, sir. Glad to be back."

"This assignment shouldn't be difficult. Shipments missing. Possible embezzlement. Ordinarily we wouldn't assign a marshal. Let the local authorities deal with it. But it involves the Shirley family. Discretion and diplomacy are essential."

"Understood, sir." Maon opened the door to the conference room and waved Davis inside. Maon's jaw clenched. The rest of his career assigned to busywork stretched before him in agonizing stultification. Doomed to pander to the rich and famous; at least his charm would be useful. He was never going to be selected for data analysis if he was given cases like this. This was worse than prisoner transfer. With a roll of his shoulders, he plastered a friendly smile on his face before he entered.

The two women seated at the long dark table were the antithesis of each other. The dull government-issue furnishings were brightened by the older woman. Dressed in a flamboyant print jacket and slacks, she was decked in enough jewelry for two women. Her fingers were laden with rings, and multiple necklaces staggered down her bright blue blouse. Inquisitive eyes snapped to Maon.

The younger one looked familiar. Where had he seen her? Not Tallav. No. Sack Girl from Beta Tau. Today she wore a shapeless gray jumper over a lighter gray ribbed turtleneck. He wasn't certain, but it looked like her nostrils flared when he focused on her. *Mother and daughter. What a pair.*

Davis said, "Ladies, I'd like to introduce you to the marshal who will handle your case. This is Marshal Maon Keefe. Marshal Keefe, Audrina Shirley and her daughter, Selina Shirley."

Maon held out his hand. "Nice to meet you both."

Audrina responded palm down, fingers curled. Maon realized she expected him to kiss it, so he complied. When he turned to the daughter, he intended to do the same, but she refused to turn her hand, allowing him to take her fingertips in a weak shake. He gave her a half smile. Her head jerked to the side when she snatched her hand away. Maon bit back a chuckle. Timid little thing. If he had to do VIP duty, at least it might prove entertaining.

Sector Chief Davis settled into a seat. "I've assigned Marshal Keefe to your case because he has the skills needed to get to the bottom of the problems you've been experiencing. Keefe, I've sent you all the pertinent files. You should have all the access codes you'll need. Warrants have already been obtained, authorizing you to search the records of the different companies and individuals involved. You'll find those in the folder."

Maon accessed the information on his tablet. "Yes, sir. It's all here."

"Excellent." Davis clapped his hands together. "I understand the ladies have additional facts, so I'll leave you to get on with things." With as much haste as he could politely get away with, he rose, shook each lady's hand, and left.

As soon as the door had closed, Audrina shifted forward in her chair. "Marshal Keefe...Maon. May I call you Maon?" She fluttered her eyelashes at him.

"Yes, ma'am. That would be fine." Maon fixed an amused gaze on her.

"Please, call me Audrina." She let her gaze drift slowly down Maon's body until the view was blocked by the table.

Maon scratched the corner of his mouth, working hard not to laugh outright. "With pleasure, Audrina."

Audrina preened. "Maon, I'm not really sure why we are here. Selina is making a fuss over nothing. These things have been happening for years.

It's part of business. Katerina is one of our oldest employees. She's like family. The idea she could steal from us is ludicrous."

While Audrina had been having her say, Selina's face tensed, her lips pressing together. "Mother. Normal companies do not have the kinds of problems you have. The shipments lost over the last five years have been worth hundreds of thousands of credits. As business manager, Katerina never attempted to solve the problem. She just wrote off the expenses."

"Now dear, Maon will get the idea I'm not professional."

"Oh, Mother. Don't be upset. Creativity is your strength. Without you, the House of Shirley wouldn't exist." She sighed when Audrina turned her face away.

SELINA HADN'T WANTED to distress her mother, but this had to be investigated. If Dad were here, he would handle this, keeping her mother unaware until and unless measures had to be taken. Dad was gone, and Selina didn't have his deft touch when her mother got emotional.

The marshal, Maon Keefe—why did it have to be him?—directed his next question at her. "You've had additional shipments go missing?"

Keep it businesslike. This is one itch you cannot scratch…shouldn't even be thinking of scratching. "Yes. Three. A shipment of evening gowns for Hampton in the Sympallan Drift. Swimwear to a boutique on Beta Tau. And the samples for the new line we are manufacturing on Qingdao in the Bing Lon Sector. The Qingdao delivery had security tracking devices which were deactivated while the package was waiting in a transshipment warehouse on Tollonia." Selina scowled, locking onto Maon's navy-blue eyes. A hint of something like the rays of a star sapphire flashed from them, sending a spark straight at her. *Damn.* She dropped her gaze, fixating on the table. Maybe he'd think she was shy or one of those Tallavan women who disliked men. It didn't matter as long as he didn't discern her attraction to him and didn't connect her to the Whip Hand.

She flicked her gaze up for a moment. Maon was tapping his steepled index fingers to his lips.

"Hmm… Ladies, I'll need access to your source records. A forensic accountant may be needed, but first I want to check for patterns in your lost shipments. It sounds like this is a long-term problem. With enough data points, I'll be able to make useful interpolations."

Her gaze still focused on the table in front of her, Selina mindlessly twiddled a button on her jacket. "Our headquarters is here. In Caherna-mon. You'll receive complete access." When she realized what her fingers were doing, she dropped her hand to her lap, lifted her chin, and stared straight at Maon. "You will report your findings to me. Katerina does not know we are looking into the finances, just the missing shipments. Please be discreet with her and anyone else you come in contact with inside or out of the House of Shirley. We have a reputation to uphold. Scandal is unacceptable. Are we clear?"

Maon's body stiffened at her words; his fingers gripped and released the edge of the table. "Yes, Ms. Shirley. I hear, and I obey." He locked his gaze on hers, and when she didn't look away, he grinned. "I think we'll work well together."

Selina slowly leaned forward, offering her hand, her brow furrowing the tiniest bit. "Good. I'll expect you tomorrow morning." It was clear she'd have to be direct and to the point to discourage Marshal Keefe's penchant for flirting.

Maon took Selina's hand, keeping it pressed between the warmth of his fingers and palm. His clasp was firm but gentle as though he'd tempered his strength while exerting the exact amount of pressure that would please Selina. "Why not this afternoon? I'll go over the case file and meet you at thirteen? Or we could do lunch together?"

With a jerk, Selina pulled from his grasp. Gods, what was she thinking? He was not tailoring his actions to suit her. Nor did she want him to, except where this case was concerned. What was wrong with her? Now he was looking at her with a pleased, almost smug expression that made her nostrils flare and her cheeks, already warm, heat further.

Audrina chose that moment to join the conversation again. "Lunch would be lovely." Her fingers brushed Selina's arm when she asked, "Don't you think so, dear?"

"Mother, you may lunch with the marshal, but I'm much too busy." She flashed a glare of warning. Then she redirected her gaze to Maon. "I'm sure the marshal understands."

Maon flourished a cheerful grin. "I'd be delighted to take you to lunch, Audrina. Where would you like to eat?"

Audrina swayed in her chair. Eyes gleaming, she said, "Oh, let's go to the River Bend. If I'm going to lunch with a handsome young man, I want to show him off."

"Mother!" Selina knew her mother was just having fun, but with Maon Keefe?

"I feel the same when I'm going to lunch with a beautiful woman."

If her mother had heard the low chuckle the man had made before responding, it would only encourage further flirtation. Not what Selina wanted, but better he play with her mother than Selina herself.

When Maon rose to his feet, Selina released a quiet sigh.

"Shall I pick you up, or would you prefer to meet me at the restaurant, Audrina?" Maon asked.

"Let's meet there at twelve. I have some shopping to do this morning."

"That sounds good. And I'll see you, Selina, at thirteen or a little after."

Selina gave a curt nod and allowed Maon to escort them to the lift.

WITH A BOUNCE IN HIS STEP, Maon returned to his desk and brought up the case file on his vidscreen. The House of Shirley. He'd been wrong. This was definitely more interesting than prisoner transport. Maybe it wasn't busy-work. At least with this assignment, he'd be able to use his analytical skills. With the bots he had available to him, it shouldn't take long to discover who was stealing from the company. If he timed it right, he'd have the chance to figure out Selina Shirley. What a bundle of contradictions. He'd pegged her as shy and passive, but she had a bossy, aggressive side that was enticing.

Two hours later his EBC signaled it was time to head to his lunch with Audrina Shirley. Had any other marshals read the file or researched the House of Shirley company before handing the case off to him? Couldn't have. They wouldn't have missed the obvious red flag. For now he needed to get going. The restaurant was a short walk, but he didn't want to be late.

Although his view was partially blocked by the shimmering blue streams that created a lightfall behind the hostess station, Maon scanned the restaurant while telling the hostess he was meeting Audrina Shirley. He didn't spot her among the muted blues and greens of the leafy decor. In one corner, another larger lightfall illuminated water trickling in a gentle cascade over river rocks, the sound filling in the gaps in conversations in the room. While the hostess led him to the table, winding through pale blue linen-covered tables packed with lunching members of the landed class, Audrina stretched her arm up, fingers waving in a rapid flutter of motion. Shit, he liked this woman. She enjoyed having fun as much as he did.

"Ms. Shirley, could a man ask for a lovelier luncheon companion?" He swept her hand to his lips for a quick peck of greeting, giving an amused smile in response to the twinkle in her eyes.

"Marshal Keefe, you are such a flatterer." While Maon sat, she raised her voice. "I'm so sorry Selina couldn't join us, but this will give us the opportunity to speak plainly." She reached out and patted his hand, returning to a normal volume. "That should do. One must give the gossips a direction to head."

"Why, Audrina! You have depths of deviousness I would never have suspected."

Audrina arched an eyebrow at him. "Selina hides behind a mousy persona, but she is a catch of the first order, Marshal."

"Yes, ma'am. I'm beginning to see that." He was young, marriageable, and a marshal. All these things pointed to potential matchmaking. However, the plan for his future didn't include marriage. Matrimony was one certain failure he could and would avoid at all costs.

Conversation stopped while they placed their orders. Maon waited while Audrina looked out the window next to their table. Her face had grown solemn, all traces of the gregarious flirt gone. Without turning to look at him, she began. "Hold tight to life, Maon. It can take you places, wonderful places, and then plunge you into murky sludge that steals your breath." She turned to face him, eyes piercing him.

"Yes, ma'am. I've learned that," Maon responded. The chair's padding abruptly insufficient, he shifted his legs while his mind turned back to the failures he still struggled to surmount.

Audrina held his gaze. "Have you? Yes, I believe you have. You'll understand then that when I lost my husband, my life altered radically. I'm about to tell you a secret no one besides Selina and myself know. For the last year and a half, Selina has been the creative force behind the Audrina line of the House of Shirley. Since my husband's death. The House of

Shirley was always small. My husband and I never cared to expand beyond the Tallavan sector. When Selina joined us five years ago, she took the business farther into the Federation."

Audrina paused while their food was served. She plucked a minicuke from her salad and nibbled before continuing. "Selina left the business of the Audrina line to us—my husband and I. She brought on designers in locations throughout the Federation and established production to support the new lines. How she manages all this, including finding new talent to replace those who go out on their own once they've made a name for themselves at the House of Shirley, I'll never know." Audrina shook her head gently. A brief smile made her look younger. "When Geoff died, I lost a piece of myself that I've never gotten back. I'd come in and muck about the office, but my design concepts were dreadful. Selina worked at night, slipping me a data cube each morning. We've carried on that way ever since. I suppose this question of missing shipments wouldn't have become an issue if Selina hadn't decided to expand in this sector."

Maon swallowed his bite of sandwich and asked, "How so?"

"Well, most people don't realize that couture alone doesn't make much money. Audrina Couture always lost more than it made. The profit comes from the ready-to-wear lines that are less expensive and more"—she waved a hand in the air—"how would you say it...more practical?" she said, laughing at her own expense. "Things the average consumer wears for everyday life."

"I've seen some of your couture designs. I understand."

"Yes, well Geoff handled that part of the company while Katrina managed the couture portion. We expected to lose money and never thought much about it. Selina has the brain for business. We would have continued on, but with Selina now designing for the Audrina line, she fell in love with the *pyantha* yarns used in our signature evening wraps. She wanted to market a new Audrina professional women's ready-to-wear line that incorporated pyantha-based fabrics."

Audrina's eyebrows rose. "Really, a marvelous idea. So Selina." Her head shook back and forth the tiniest bit, and her eyes bored in on him as though daring him to suggest otherwise.

"We'd been buying pyantha fiber from the same producer for, well, forever. It's spun into yarn for hand knitting in our privately owned mill on Gallarda before being sent to Tallav. Selina discovered what she terms the abnormalities while deciding on the best location for the fabric mill needed for the new line. She insisted on an investigation. So here we are." With a sigh, Audrina picked up her fork and took a bite of her salad.

Maon, who'd finished his sandwich while listening, leaned back in his chair. "I'm glad she did." Thoughts raced through his head. The case files had already led him in a particular direction that Audrina's narrative had reinforced. He couldn't wait to delve into all the Audrina shipping receipts.

SELINA WATCHED Maon peruse the House of Shirley's Audrina offices. Creativity exploded in vivid colors, splashing across a neutral white decor, blending and complementing each other in a myriad of swatches, accessories, and garments. Vidscreens and high-tech sketch pads were accompanied by colored pencils and paper pads. His face didn't reveal what he was thinking beyond a rather bland curiosity.

Selina brought his attention back to her by gesturing to the stocky woman standing expectantly beside her. The woman's boxy business attire accentuated the tension in her body.

"Katerina, this is Marshal Keefe. He'll be looking into Audrina's shipping problem. Marshal, Katerina Donnelly. She's operations manager for Audrina."

Maon extended his hand to Katerina. "How do you do, Ms. Donnelly? I'll try not to take too much of your time."

"Ms. Shirley believes it's important, so I'll do whatever I can to assist you," Katerina responded, one shoulder lifting ever so slightly.

Maon nodded. "Thank you."

Selina's response was brusque. Inside she bristled. Katerina couldn't have made it clearer. She didn't agree that the investigation was critical. But then, if she were guilty, that was exactly the tack Selina had expected her to take. "Please give Marshal Keefe any information he requests. Have you set up a working space for him as I asked?"

Katerina's lips flattened to a thin line before she responded. "Yes, ma'am. I've made one of the intern desks available for his exclusive use, and Records is prepared to grant him secure access to the entire system."

"Excellent, Katerina. Please assign an intern to assist him." Selina turned her focus to Maon. "Marshal, please join me in my office."

"Certainly," Maon said to Selina and then addressed Katerina. "I'm looking forward to working with you, Ms. Donnelly." Arm extended, he smiled and shook Katerina's hand.

Unable to watch Maon making nice with the woman she suspected of the thefts, Selina turned on her heel and headed out the door to wait for Maon to catch up at the lifts. Before he reached her side, she punched the button to call the lift to take them to the executive offices of the House of Shirley.

Selina found it easier to be in Maon Keefe's presence if she didn't look at him and spoke to him as little as possible. The unsettled reaction that his proximity triggered was unnerving. It went back to those winks at the Whip Hand on Beta Tau. The man was so damn confident. He couldn't have guessed they'd eyed each other across the public play space. The latex hood she'd worn had hidden her face. That was a relief. Asking for a replacement marshal was impossible. If it wasn't for her standing on Tallav, her concerns would have been passed on to the local Guardia. She was stuck with him, but she wouldn't let him interfere with her personal life. No matter how attractive he was. He wasn't her type. Not in the least. Why was it taking the lift so long to move two floors?

"That's a lovely shade of gray you're wearing today."

"Thank you." Her jaw clenched.

"Does it have a particular name? Placid pewter? Faded shadow? It's very… gray."

"Not that I'm aware." *Damn the man. I'd like to…* The lift opened, and she strode toward her office, ignoring anyone who attempted to halt her. The look of thunder on her face caused most to deviate from her path. "Antoinette, please let Delia know our meeting is slipped back ten minutes. Thank you." She briskly swept inside. "Please close the door behind you, Marshal."

HE NEEDED TO stop. But she was so much fun to play with. This was not what the sector chief had meant when he told Maon to use diplomacy. Suppressing a sigh, he vowed to be good. He'd glared at his reflection in the mirror this morning and told himself in no uncertain terms, *"You will not flirt with anyone today. You are not a playboy marshal. You are a serious law enforcement official."* Yet he couldn't help noticing that, even in an outfit designed to hide any notion that a woman's body existed within, the curving outline of a hip was visible. He enjoyed the view until she turned to stare at him.

With one digit extended, she motioned him to take a seat. The gesture was one degree shy of a finger-pointing command, enough to stir his blood, at least until he focused on the chunky object he was expected to mount. The black plasti-form sculpture, pretending to be a chair, stood in front of her sleek matte-steel desk. She was ensconced in an ultra-comfortable air chair while her minions were given a seat that put design before comfort. Even the slablike furniture that made up the sitting area to the left looked comfier.

The hard edges of the room were not relieved by fashion designer clutter. Black cabinets concealed necessities. Even her vidscreen was hidden from view. The office was a cold, blank facade. With some trepidation, Maon lowered himself to sit on the chair whose designer had never imagined with six-foot-three-inch, lanky occupant. The sterility of the room helped Maon bring his mind back to the case. He wrestled his playboy persona into a cage, overcoming this odd attraction he found to the woman. Until today no female wearing a sack that hid her most basic attributes had ever stirred his cock. This woman did. It wasn't physical. Maybe a little. She was pretty. No. It was something about her that was like a siren's call to deep inside him. *Get ahold of yourself. You're a marshal. Act like a marshal.* Before Selina could speak, he said, "I had an informative lunch with your mother."

"Oh? In what way?" Her chair soundlessly readjusted when she leaned back.

"She explained how the Audrina portion of the business ran while your father was alive and who has been responsible for different aspects since his death. Including your big secret." If he'd expected a reaction from the last statement, he didn't get one. "Naturally, I consider that privileged information. It will not appear in my notes unless it becomes pertinent."

"Thank you. I had hoped Mother would return to designing again, but that hasn't happened. She still manages the runway shows and publicity appearances. Seems to enjoy those. I'm not sure we can go much longer without making that secret public."

Maon watched while Selina rubbed a thumb along the edge of her desk, her gaze unfocused. When it rose to meet his, she asked, "Is there a basis for my concern about our shipping problems? Or do you agree with my mother and Marshal Davis that I'm making too much of it?"

She wasn't going to like what he had to tell her, but there really was no way to cushion it. "The number of deliveries that have gone astray is troubling. I intend to begin data mining your information as far back as possible. At the same time, I'll focus on the latest three missing shipments. I'll want to inspect your shipping department here on Tallav. My biggest concern is that this could involve the illegal smuggling of pyantha extract."

Selina went rigid. "No." A moment passed while she crossed her arms over her chest and sat still. "No. We have taken measures to ensure that our company was never used for drug smuggling. Our special permit requires stringent procedures to make certain we don't inadvertently break the law. We keep the shipping of pyantha yarn strictly within our own hands. We purchase seed-free fiber on Gallarda and spin it into yarn in our own factory. You cannot make drug extract from pyantha fiber. But we still have to deal with special shipping permits because Federation drug detection isn't sophisticated enough to distinguish pyantha fiber from seed from extract. We are careful to keep anyone from using our yarn shipments to smuggle extract. The plant is a small operation run by trusted employees and inspected regularly."

Maon held his hand up. "I'm not saying that drug smuggling is involved. It's a concern that needs to be fully investigated. I'm sure you can understand that. I will be as discreet as possible, but you need to be prepared for the worst-case possibility."

"Yes, of course." Selina rubbed her forehead. "Please do be discreet. Keep me informed. If I can do anything, please let me know. I can't even imagine the horror my mother would experience if she learned her life's work had been used for drug smuggling. I pray you find another explanation."

"As do I. Your mother is a delightful woman. I've enjoyed meeting her."

"Thank you." Selina responded with a tight smile that did nothing to brighten her dour expression.

An overall heaviness had pervaded Maon, made worse by his inability to find the right words to say. He wanted to take his thumb and stroke away the tension in her lips. *That would be professional! You're supposed to remain detached.* The academy had reinforced that dictum regularly. Empathy not sympathy. Friggin' hard to do with a damsel in distress sitting right in front of him. He opted to respond with a tight smile of his own.

5

Maon leaned back, stretching his hands behind his head and twisting the kinks from his spine. His bots were now crawling their way through the House of Shirley data systems. Some were compiling information from the parameters he set. Others were analyzing the financial figures for discrepancies and backdating. If the system had been set up preplanned for data manipulation, those bots wouldn't do him any good. Otherwise, few people could infiltrate a secure network without leaving detectible traces. Unless they had access to some very expensive programming. Most embezzlers didn't have the credits or the knowledge to hide their fingerprints. He'd tasked one last bot to look for hidden data or the pointers that suggested fraud had been part of the system's design. He didn't expect that bot to find anything, but it paid to be thorough.

If this case was about embezzling, Selina's suspicion of Katerina was valid. Katerina didn't agree with Selina that the investigation was critical. That could mean she was hiding something. Or she resented the intrusion into her territory. Or was Selina's mistrust the result of mutual enmity? There certainly was no love lost between the two. He'd have to consider it.

Then there was Selina herself. Why the hell did that woman entice him? She was an enigma wrapped in a colorless appearance. Potent intensity had flamed through her somber deference when she pointedly told him—no, commanded him to fulfill her expectations. Did she conceal her true nature with everyone? Or just men? Or just him? He wanted to find out, but he couldn't risk his career by pursuing her. Not while he was on this case. He'd have to watch himself around her, despite the pull that was more than physical attraction. *Fuck's sake.* A glimpse of the curve of her ass had left him hoping to see more, but it wasn't until she'd ordered him to sit that his libido had truly fired. If she really let rip with her bossiness, controlling his attraction was going to be a problem. *Shit.* He'd have to restrain himself with her.

At the desk next to his, Bobbi, the petite intern with a mop of curly brown hair, his official helper, was engrossed in her vidscreen. Her current task was tracking down spider-silk charmeuse in a particular color she called sweet potato. To Maon it was orange. At a stopping point, her head popped around, and she asked, "You ready for your shipping tour?"

"Yeah, give me a minute." He pointed to his left. "Restrooms?"

"Yes, down that hall."

When Maon returned, he asked her for a map of the building. While they walked to the lifts, he brought it up on his tablet and perused it. "The two top floors are the executive offices for the House of Shirley, and this one is the Audrina line's design and business offices. Can I assume that everyone uses the shipping department?"

"Yes. Most House of Shirley affairs are conducted via hyperlink. Transport Federation-wide is too time-consuming, so it's rare for samples or product to be sent from here outside the sector. Most shipping is done by the Audrina line. Like receiving the fabric samples I just requested."

"Mmm." Maon stepped out into the ground-level lift foyer.

"This floor includes fabrication of couture pieces, our Audrina showroom, and the shipping department." Bobbi spoke with a lilting voice, every bit the young intern.

"And Audrina ready-to-wear? Where is that manufactured?" asked Maon.

"Off world on Asturnia. Although the new line will be made on Qingdao. Here we are. Let me find Ms. Donnelly. She'll have my head if I don't introduce her before showing you around."

While Maon waited, he scanned the open room. One corner held an enclosed office with opaque windows. A loading dock, doors closed, was along the back wall next to storage racks. Two large crates with gravity-field belts attached stood awaiting shipment. At a long metal table, a worker pulled yarn bundles from a bin, placed three into a red-striped bag she sealed, labeled, and tossed into a tub emblazoned LOCAL.

Bobbi walked toward him, accompanying an attractive blonde dressed in casual business attire. The woman had a delightful roll to her hips and dark eyes set dead on him. When she and Bobbi arrived in front of him, a whiff of musk feathered his nose. *Mmmm. Nice. Fuck's sake. Focus, asshole. She's a suspect, not your next piece of ass.* Old habits were friggin' hard to break. Besides, why screw your career for nice when fascinating Selina Shirley was a lift ride away?

"Marshal Keefe. I've been expecting you. Bobbi, I can take it from here." The woman looked at Bobbi and then the outer door to make clear it wasn't a suggestion. When the intern left, the woman introduced herself. "I'm Elizabeth Donnelly, shipping manager. Katerina's younger sister. Call me Liza, please."

"Yes, ma'am." Maon made certain his voice was brisk and to the point. "For now, I'd like a general overview of how shipments are handled here. We'll get to the missing deliveries after that."

"I've cleared my schedule to spend as much time as you need, marshal." She reached out a hand, her touch warm through the fabric of his sleeve.

The walk, the eye contact, and now the touch—this woman knew how to flirt. He moved his gaze to a rack with empty crates of varying sizes before responding. "Excellent."

Liza motioned to it and said, "Let's start there. Our crates are special-ized boxes provided by Federated Express to meet our requirements that garments arrive in pristine condition. The red-rimmed ones are for any shipments that contain pyantha-based items. I'm sure you know that pyantha fiber and pyantha extract, which is an illegal drug, cannot be easily distinguished from each other by custom's drug-detection equipment."

"So the packets of yarn being prepped for local delivery have that red stripe for the same purpose?" Maon asked.

"Yes, they are being readied for shipment to our handicraft workers throughout Tallav."

"Tell me how outgoing shipments are prepared."

Liza clasped his elbow and redirected him to a large crate. "Clothing is brought here from fabrication with a unique data slide. It's used to track items from packing to delivery. The slide is updated daily with the current status of the package. Each one is saved until the shipment is confirmed received."

Maon ignored Liza's touch and pointed to the red-rimmed crates on the rack next to the loading dock. "So those containers contain pyantha-based items. Interesting. You need a special license to ship anything made with pyantha, don't you?" he asked.

"Yes, it's difficult to get one. Because we oversee the entire process from mill to Tallav to customer, we were able to obtain the license." Her chest pressed forward when she slid her hands into her back pockets.

In the past he would have taken the proffered opportunity for a good, long look, but today, he was copying Shane, channeling his serious lawman persona. "Ummm. How do you prevent employees from trying to use your shipments for smuggling? I don't see any cameras."

Liza waved him to follow. "Come with me." When they entered her office, she motioned to the windows. "I can watch almost everything that happens here. The Feds preferred human visual oversight as opposed to camera. Too easy to spoof or turn off, it seems. I make unscheduled inspections of both incoming and outgoing shipments."

"So the system depends on trusting you?" Maon asked, watching her closely for any reaction.

Her throat convulsed in a hard swallow while she looked at the fingers she was tapping against the windowsill. "Yes, I suppose it does." She lifted her gaze to look at him again. "We are randomly inspected by the Federation."

"I'm sorry. I didn't mean to imply anything other than that you must be a valued employee to hold such a position of trust."

Maon found her reaction interesting. Why was she anxious? It could be the question itself, but this was an investigation into shipments that went missing after they left her department, not drug smuggling.

"Well, I'm here to look into your delivery problems. I'm focusing on the three latest. Do you have those data slides?"

"Yes. I've made you copies. Although you may see the originals if you wish." Her demeanor was now more professional and reserved.

"Excellent. Thank you. Let's sit. Tell me about each of them, please."

Liza removed a box of packing tape from the chair opposite her desk and gestured at Maon to take a seat. She added the open package to what looked like stacks of shipping supply boxes. After sliding into the desk's old-fashioned roller chair, she pulled a data cube from the middle drawer and handed it to Maon. "The first was a shipment of evening gowns. It was a special order for the family of one of the pashas on Hampton. It included five dresses with signature Audrina wraps."

"Is that a typical Audrina shipment?" Maon asked.

"Yes. We sell our exclusive designs Federation-wide if the buyer is willing to pay the shipping. Most of our buyers come from this side of the Sympallan Drift. The second crate went to Beta Tau. We supply a boutique with one-of-a-kind swimwear. That regular shipment's never gone missing before. The third was far more frustrating than costly. It contained the samples for the new fabric mill on Qingdao. The younger Ms. Shirley is expanding the Audrina ready-to-wear options. I guess Audrina was losing too much money for her." Her lips pinched together with the sour expression of someone eating an unripe pingo plum. "The bottom line is everything to her."

"So the samples were important?" Maon asked.

"Yes. They included the new yarns as well as some test fabrics. The shipment was essential for the next phase of the mill's startup. It takes nine days for a delivery to reach Qingdao, plus the time in reproducing the fabrics that were specially milled for us on Gallarda."

Maon leaned forward. "Ms. Shirley said that package was sent with a special security tracking device."

Liza crossed her arms, her chair creaking when she pushed back into it. "Yes. One was included with that shipment. Ms. Shirley had become concerned by the problem with deliveries going astray from time to time, so she requested additional precautions for it."

"I'm interested to hear your viewpoint. It seems the staff at Audrina was accustomed to losing shipments every so often." Maon sat back.

"It's part of doing business. We send valuable goods in small crates into an enormous Federation-wide shipping system. Of course things go missing. Here on Tallav, local packages rarely if ever get lost. Federated Express is the largest shipping company and least expensive solution to our needs. Besides, our deliveries are insured." She shrugged her shoulder and gave a theatrical sigh. "I don't mean to discredit her, but Ms. Shirley has spent her time in the executive suite expanding the company. She seldom bothered herself in the day-to-day working of Audrina, commanding from afar. That is while her father was alive. She doesn't understand the differences between how Audrina and a larger scale business operate."

Her lips pursed, Liza paused before continuing. "Frankly she's not one to take advice well. My sister has tried to explain things to her, but rather than let Katerina do her job, Selina... I wouldn't like to say encroaches, but she oversees everything Katerina does and has taken on responsibilities that should be Katerina's."

Maon wasn't surprised by Liza's critique of Selina. Katerina had moved into Geoff Shirley's position in the company. Selina was assuming some of her father's previous duties by managing the new ready-to-wear line. That interest came because she was the actual designer behind Audrina now. Katerina and Liza didn't know that. If pyantha extract were being smuggled via Audrina shipments, Liza would be the first person under suspicion. She had access and knew the shipping schedule. Antipathy on her sister's behalf may not be the only reason Liza would discredit Selina's request for an investigation.

"Ms. Shirley seems like a woman who prefers control," Maon said. "I'm sure she'll relax more when she grows used to running the business without her father."

"I suppose so. He was a nice man. He and Audrina always said the House of Shirley was a family, and they treated us as such. It's hard to lose that informality." Another sigh, heavy and more real this time, pulled her shoulders down.

"I'm sorry for your loss. Change is difficult, especially when it involves the death of someone you admire."

"Mmmmm." Somewhere in the slight smile Liza bestowed on him, Maon detected a hint of the woman behind the facade she wore. It disappeared when her mouth altered into a sensual pout. Without a doubt, she was a player. If he responded, she'd probably tell him anything he wanted to know about the House of Shirley. Or was he looking for a way to get around his no-flirting resolution? Like an epiphany it struck him. No. He really wasn't that attracted to her. She was what he'd always considered a one and done. And he wasn't going to continue to be the shallow guy who thought with his dick. *Fuck's sake.* Maybe there was something to risk awareness. *Think first. Assess the situation and your motivations.* With Liza Donnelly his primary motivation was to determine if she was involved in theft or his alternative theory, pyantha smuggling. He could bait the hook with sexual suggestion with no intention of ever reeling in the fish. At least not for sex. If she was guilty, he'd reel in a criminal.

"I've taken up enough of your day with this." Maon twitched his lips into a half grin when he leaned toward Liza. "Maybe I can take up some of your free time after I close out this case?"

"That would be pleasant, Marshal." She smiled back at him, biting down on one fingernail.

"Please, call me Maon. If you think of something that might be helpful, contact Bobbi or me. I'll be right upstairs." He stretched his smile the slightest bit.

"Good to know."

"And thank you for the slide data."

"You're welcome. I'll do anything you need to assist you."

THE BOTS COMPILING data from the sales and shipping records had finished by the time Maon returned to his temporary desk. It would take longer for the bots ferreting out discrepancies. He drummed his fingers while he scanned the output reports for the queries he'd formatted. It looked like Selina was right. Audrina had lost quite a few valuable shipments over the last five years. Too many to blame on shipping company failures. At minimum they should have changed delivery services. Insured or not, the delay spent replacing the missing items was bad for business.

The routing information for those deliveries was more interesting. Ninety-five percent were routed through the Federated Express transshipment warehouse on Tollonia. That included two of the three crates he was planning to track personally. Not, however, the Beta Tau swimwear shipment. Next up, a call to the local Federated Express office.

Or maybe not. He checked the time with his EBC. A few messages were queued, but none looked urgent. He pushed them to his tablet to read later. It was getting late. The ache in his side had flared as it did whenever he stayed in one position too long. He bent to the side to stretch his muscles, rubbing his palm down his rib cage. Federated Express could wait until tomorrow. He'd visit Selina to update her on how the investigation was coming before leaving. While he was slinging his jacket over his arm, Liza entered and sidled up to him. It didn't look like she had business or the investigation on her mind.

"Are you quitting for the day, Maon?" she asked, giving him the once-over with her eyes.

Maon leaned his muscular frame toward her. "Not quite yet. I need to check in with Ms. Shirley. Did you have something in mind?" He couldn't discern if her interest in him was as her next fling or to have an inside line on his investigation. But it sure made it easier to keep track of her as a suspect.

"I'm not sure," she responded, skimming a finger along his arm. Maon allowed a smile to slip onto his face.

Behind Liza, Selina walked through the door, stopped abruptly, and dropped her hand to her hip. "Am I interrupting?"

An electric zing went through Maon. He froze, his attention riveted on Selina. With effort, he relaxed, maintaining his unwavering smile. "Why, no. I was just coming to visit you."

Liza had also stiffened when Selina spoke. She relaxed when Maon brought his gaze back to her and said, "Can you wait until I finish here?"

"Sure. Not a problem." Triumph flashed across her face for an instant. "I'll be downstairs."

After Liza left the room, Selina moved closer to Maon, glaring at him. She opened her lips to speak, but then snapped them shut, pressing them into a thin line while nodding. After a moment she said, "Aren't you supposed to keep your professional and personal life separate? Especially with an obvious suspect?"

"Yes, ma'am." Maon swallowed a chuckle. *Fuck's sake, she's amazing! And she really doesn't like the Donnelly sisters.* The way her eyes sparked when she was irritated made his groin pulse. *Not now!* "May we speak privately?"

"Let's go to my office." Selina turned, heading to the lifts.

Maon obediently followed onto the lift, off, and to Selina's office.

She sat behind her desk, looking pissed off. Her glare drilled into him with the force of hardened steel. "Marshal Keefe, it was my understanding that officers of the law did not fraternize with subjects of an investigation."

There it was, the fire that made his gut drop. Maon sat in the plasti-torture chair, leaning forward, dark eyes squinting. He hated this frigging chair, but he'd endure it if she'd keep her fierce stare focused on him.

"Yes, ma'am. You are correct. My interaction with Ms. Donnelly might flip your integrity switch, but, however friendly I've been with her today, I have not been fraternizing. I prefer to consider my behavior charming and disarming. Honey is a superior investigative tool where certain types of people are concerned. Wining and dining Ms. Donnelly is not on my agenda." He quirked a smile at her.

Selina's voice was almost a growl. "Well, you need not charm and disarm me, Marshal Keefe."

The discomfort of the chair was ratcheted up by his cock straining painfully against the zipper of his slacks. Instead of releasing the explicit response that rose from his core, with a tinge of laughter, he said, "Certainly not, ma'am. I'll try to keep my naturally boyish appeal in check."

Selina's eyes narrowed. "You said you needed to speak with me."

She was getting truly irritated, so he grew serious. "Yes, I wanted to update you on what I've found. Going back five years, ninety-five percent of your lost shipments have been routed through the Tollonian Federated Express transshipment warehouse. I'm determining if those routes were the most efficient or likely ones for those orders to take. If not, I'll find out who determined the nonstandard routing and why."

"Someone here could be assuring certain shipments make a stop on Tollonia?" she asked.

"That's a possibility. The other—that a thief on Tollonia is solely responsible."

"Not likely. Is it?" With a pinched expression on her face, she brought a fist down on her desktop, eyes unfocused for a moment before she relaxed and took a deep breath.

"No. I'm sorry, but there's more. On the tour today, I noticed a couple of things. One employee was working in the shipping department as well as Ms. Donnelly. I'll look at staffing and hours in that department to check how often that happens. It's possible an employee could be using times when Ms. Donnelly is absent. It's also possible that Ms. Donnelly is behind the losses. She would find it easier with her knowledge of freight schedules that the packers would not have in advance. The real trick would be hiding the pyantha extract on the premises, waiting for a chance to slip it into a crate. It wouldn't be easy for anyone but Ms. Donnelly. She has her office. Although the extract could be hidden in another place on-site and brought to the department when an opportunity presented itself. I'll need to set up a concealed vid system soon, but it may be more watching the chickens after the fox has moved on."

Maon shifted, searching for a more comfortable position. The intensity of the ache in his side was increasing. It was joined by a return of the heaviness in his chest he'd felt when last he delivered bad news to Selina. It was pure reaction to her distress. Something he would have felt for anyone in the same situation. It wasn't personal. No, it—

"What next?" she asked.

Maon ducked his head, flushing his train of thought away before returning his focus to her. "Tomorrow I also intend to speak with Federated Express about the last three losses. Two of those include pyantha fiber products. The shipments lost through Tollonia were almost all red-marked pyantha crates. I've looked at your sales records, and that's an extraordinarily high percentage, considering the shawls are included in only ten percent of your orders."

"You're thinking drug smuggling. Aren't you?" Her eyes pleaded with him to deny it.

"Yes, it looks obvious at this point," Maon said, speaking softly while shifting his weight to favor his side. "I'll be able to tell you more after I get the results from the data mining I've set up for overnight." A grimace cracked his effort to repress his response to the pain along his ribs.

Selina's forehead creased. "Are you okay?"

"I'm fine." Maon resisted the urge to rub the ache. "The chair's a little rough on an old injury. It's nothing." He leaned toward her, the desk blocking him from taking her hand. "I'm going to get to the bottom of this is as quickly as possible. I should finish up with your records sometime tomorrow. After that, I want to inspect your mill at Gallarda and then the Federated Express warehouse on Tollonia. Maybe include a stop on Beta Tau first, and after Tollonia, if needed, Qingdao or Hampton. Not sure about the last two. Depends on what I find."

Selina stood and moved around her desk to perch on the edge in front of him. "I'd like to go with you."

Maon tightened his hand into a fist and grunted, his gaze steady on hers. "Why?"

"Except for Tollonia, you're stopping at places I need to visit anyway. Your trip will be much quicker if you allow me to provide private transport for the both of us." Selina held his gaze. It was obvious she was prepared to argue her point until he agreed.

Shit, her eyes had that do-as-I-say look that made his spine go quivery. He hadn't been looking forward to traveling economy class on a big liner. But being in close company with Selina Shirley was a danger he should probably avoid. *Crap.* If this were a test, he'd failed because there was no way he wouldn't take her up on the offer.

Besides, she could be helpful. She knows the plant and its routine since she's the one who's overseeing its expansion. This case was important to him and Selina, but on Gallarda the operation was small potatoes. The cartels had been ignoring it for that very reason, but they wouldn't be averse to him shutting it down. It's much more likely the House of Shirley employees involved were packing things in and preparing to run.

So, he'd go with Selina, but he still needed to keep things professional. A necessity he'd have to exert himself to maintain, but once the case was over, he was going to discover who Selina Shirley was under her drab clothes.

"You'll have to allow me the freedom to set our schedule." Maon wasn't sure if she'd agree, but it was nonnegotiable.

"Of course. Your investigation will be top priority for this trip."

Maon relaxed his shoulders, helping the now stabbing pain in his side to ease up. "Sounds like a plan. You make the arrangements. We'll leave for Beta Tau day after tomorrow."

The smile Selina gave him at his concession sent sparks to his groin. He imagined those pretty little teeth marking his skin. *Fuck's sake.* Almost four days in transit and then Beta Tau. Shit, he could spend more than a day on the *Adrasteia* and not see Shane. Selina probably had a ship the same size or bigger. It would be rough, but it would give him more time to observe and solve the riddle of her magnetic pull. From a distance. Because, despite his inexplicable attraction to the woman, he needed to show the powers that be that he could maintain a professional demeanor. Screwing up now wasn't an option. This case was his opportunity to escape the downward spiral of his career. Damned if he'd be a failure again. And letting Selina down was even less of an option.

6

Maon woke, soaked in sweat, clawing to fight his way out of the suffocating enclosure of his dream. He'd been trapped in a pit, unseen figures staring down at him, pronouncing judgment while they sealed him in.

"Failed."

"Just like his father."

"Disgrace to the marshals."

"Never did anything right."

"Complete failure."

"Failure."

"Failure."

His hand slung out, knocking into the lamp on the bedside table when he fumbled to turn it on. Gulping great lungfuls of air did nothing to assuage the panic clamoring in his brain and chest. The light in the room grayed out while black narrowed his vision to a tunnel. *You're hyperventilating. Control your breathing.* When he did, the tendrils of terror dissipated.

Dr. Jessop had told him if he experienced stress problems, he should get another post-trauma nanite infusion. But Maon wasn't reliving the shooting. This was the old nightmare from childhood. Growing up, his mother's verbal attacks had turned his every success into failure. She'd been impossible to please, and the stress of the struggle to gain her approval had bled into his dreams. Instead of the peaceful sleep of a normal boy, his nights had been ravaged by terrifying images of being buried alive as a failure. Why was that nightmare back, haunting him? If he went to Jessop now, they would know how messed up he was. They could furlough him or even start discharge procedures. He'd be damned if he'd let bad dreams end his career as a marshal. His job was one aspect of his life his mother couldn't belittle, and he was determined to prove his worth by becoming a well-respected marshal. He needed this investigation to turn out well. Who knew when another fluff case would involve something as serious as drug trafficking.

Why, why did the friggin' dreams have to come back now? They had stopped at the age of thirteen when he'd decided to emulate his father and be the most successful ladies' man on Tallav. Funny, the nightmares were all about failing, becoming like his father. All he had to do to get rid of them was to embrace that failure. He'd stopped struggling to do better, refused to care what his mother thought. Given up. Except he'd found a loophole, one that, had his father embraced it, would have saved Maon from his mother's scorn. If Maon never married or had children, he wouldn't destroy another person's life. He wouldn't fail as a husband or father. He wouldn't do that to his own family, his own son, like his father had to him. His father's charm and flirtatious manner had come down to Maon in full measure. No woman had ever instilled a desire for monogamy in him. The certainty he couldn't keep his wedding vows made him an adamant bachelor. Divorce was one failure he would avoid.

The plan hadn't changed, so he couldn't understand why the dreams had returned. An internal voice kept insisting he was worried about his job. *Not going there.* The case he was on had the potential to put him back on track and maybe even ahead for a change. *No negative thinking. Positive responses. Yeah, tell your subconscious that.*

His body resisted when he dragged himself from the bed, got a drink of water, and replaced the damp sheets with dry ones. The room, like the entire apartment, was stripped to essentials with no personal details except those necessary for his comfort and pleasure. Vidscreens focused on the news rather than slide shows of family and friends. Others might look at his private space and think he was a cipher. Maybe he was. Maybe the true Maon

Keefe was still waiting to be constructed. If he'd died on Fed Central, his life would have been totally lacking in accomplishments. Fuck's sake, he hadn't even gotten the data analyst slot he craved. His own fault. No one took him seriously because he never acted that way. Always joking or pulling pranks. Lots of good-time friends, but only two that really cared about him.

If he'd died, Shane and Randolph were the only people who would truly miss him. Even they couldn't say more about him than he was a fun guy. Most people would remember him as the guy who liked to fool around and let Cosmo Bonilla escape custody. He'd joked his way out of attempting anything difficult, and he'd still managed to fail. He'd be damned if fear of failure held him back anymore. Nightmares or no nightmares, he was not going to let failure be his epitaph. He'd work this case and become the best friggin' marshal the service had ever seen. He ignored the churning in his gut.

Settled beneath the sheet once more, he shut his eyes and turned his thoughts to something appealing—the little flame Domme he'd noticed at the Whip Hand before his injury. He knew nothing more than what he'd seen of her that day, so she made the perfect fantasy escape. It took a while before he realized the Domme of his imagination was no longer wearing a hood. Her face, now visible, was that of Selina Shirley. If only. His mind drifted into sleep while he imagined what she would do to him after she cuffed him.

SELINA LOOKED up when Maon entered her office. It was a battle to combat the distraction caused by the slow, easy swing of Maon's pelvis when he walked toward her and flashed that seductive half smile of his. "Hello, Marshal. What have you learned?"

"That's what I like about you. Get right to business. None of that polite chatty talk for you."

He dipped his chin and lowered his gaze. A short pause later, he looked up at her through his lashes. Selina fought with herself not to order him to drop his gaze again. He was that sexy with that submissive stance. Damn him. He knew how to play with her. And that was what he was doing.

Playing with her. She could show him what it meant for a man to submit to her. But that wasn't what they were here for, so she clamped down on the lascivious thoughts running through her head.

With a casually breezy air, she settled back against the soft leather of her chair and said, "Marshal Keefe, polite palaver may be your forte, but it is not mine. Please tell me how things stand with your investigation." She winced inside. Did she just say *polite palaver*?

Maon's lips quirked before he cleared his throat and shrugged his shoulders, donning his marshal persona. "Yes, ma'am. I'm sorry to say that someone within the House of Shirley is behind the redirection of the missing shipments."

All thoughts of sexy Marshal Maon Keefe blew from her mind. Her stomach dropped. "Damn."

Maon nodded. "I'm sorry. I know that's what you feared, even while hoping you were wrong. I contacted Federated Express. They are initiating an investigation into the three lost crates. Plan on it taking up to two weeks. I don't expect much from them."

A frown creased Selina's forehead. "You said one of our employees was implicated. How did you arrive at that conclusion?"

"After examining the data I pulled from your system overnight, it was clear someone at Audrina had to be purposefully changing shipping routes. Transshipment through Tollonia isn't needed for crates headed to the Perseus or Bing Lon sectors or inside the Tallavan sector. The only shipments that should go through Tollonia are those dispatched to the Sympallan Drift or to the rest of the Federation via the Drift. Yet lost deliveries meant for the three sectors located this side of the Drift were all shipped by way of Tollonia."

"I see." Selina dropped her gaze to the dull gray of her desk. He was right. It would be a waste of money to ship packages through an indirect transshipment point.

"Yeah, I haven't figured out who yet, but I will by the time we reach Beta Tau. The records showed the changes were made by an anonymous account. I have a fine-tooth search combing out system inconsistencies. When it completes, I'll be able to tease out who created that account. The marshals will send in a team to set up monitoring devices while we're gone. Although, as I said before, I don't expect the offender to do anything while I'm still investigating."

"I assume you'll arrest this person immediately." Selina grimaced. She did not want her mother anywhere near when that happened. Selina would insist on it and that she be able to comm her mother to break the news.

"Probably not."

Selina jerked her head up to stare at him. "Why not?"

"We'll keep an eye on whomever. Obviously. But there's no sense spooking any confederates. Once we know who's behind rerouting shipments from Tallav, we can track their communications. Determine who's involved on Gallarda before we get there. That will make that portion of my investigation easier. Before moving on to Tollonia, I hope to have those two stops on the pyantha-smuggling route ready for marshals to take down. But that would have to wait until I'm sure I can gather evidence against the leader of the operation."

"Should we skip Beta Tau and go directly to Gallarda?"

Maon shook his head. "No. As far as the smugglers are concerned, we're still tracking lost shipments. That means Beta Tau since it's the closest of the three delivery points. After that they'll assume we're heading to Qingdao and Hampton rather than our true destinations of Gallarda and Tollonia."

"Subterfuge." She smirked. "I like it."

Maon responded with a smirk of his own. "I assume that you've got things ready to leave tomorrow?"

Her words were quiet but determined. "Yes. I do. Spaceport shuttle at six."

She returned to staring at her desk. This was going to be hard on her mother. Even if Selina couldn't say who it was yet, she should prepare her mother by telling her there was a turncoat among them.

Maon seemed to guess her thoughts. In a soothing voice, he asked, "Do you want me to speak with your mother?"

Selina's eyes blinked rapidly while she fought to maintain her emotional control. "No, I'll do that myself. Thank you."

"Six, then."

Selina dipped her head. "Berth F11."

∽

ALMOST FOUR DAYS had passed since Maon had boarded the corporate space dart Selina hired for their trip. Space darts were known for their speed. Sleek and fast, the dart could be as luxurious as possible, but it was still cramped. Besides the engines and functional sections, the area for people accounted for a little less than a third of the entire ship. The pilot had a bunk behind the bridge. The remainder was taken up with two cabins, a bathroom, and the lounge. Cramped quarters made observing Selina from a distance impossible. The pilot had become Maon's new best friend while he worked hard at avoiding her on the small craft. The fact that she seemed to be ducking him helped.

On Beta Tau, they headed their separate ways. She intended to accomplish some House of Shirley business, and Maon planned to visit the swimwear boutique and the Federated Express offices. Those offices were on station, so Maon hadn't even shared a shuttle to the surface with Selina. He'd been on the bridge, making a comm call to the marshals' office on Beta Tau when she'd left. His stop at Federated Express had been brief. The package had been found and sent on to the shop. With his task completed, Maon headed to the Whip Hand to talk to Randolph.

At a shiny, ebony table in one of the private niches available in the club's dining room, Maon sat, sopping up the last of the prime rib juice on his plate with a dinner roll. Randolph relaxed in the seat opposite him. This was the first time Maon had seen Randolph since he'd been shot.

While catching Maon up on the latest club gossip, Randolph examined him. "You look thinner, but not much worse for wear. You should have some dessert," Randolph said.

Maon looked up from his plate. "Chocolate cake?"

"Sure. Chocolate cake." Randolph cocked his head to the side, smiling slightly. "I talked Fern at Glencove Academy into sending me her recipe. Told her you'd been shot and needed some TLC. The cake my pastry chef creates tastes just like the one she always baked for you."

Maon grinned like a little boy getting a treat. "She didn't bake it just for me. She made it for all the students."

"Yeah, but you're the one she always brought an extra slice."

Maon chuckled. "Her chocolate cake was the best in the universe."

After signaling the waiter and ordering the cake, Randolph returned to pondering his friend. "You're sure you got shot? You seem fine."

Maon reached out to fiddle with the napkin he'd laid beside his plate. "Huh. There's fine, and then there's fine." With a shake of his head, he continued. "Physically I'm almost back to normal except for this nerve in my side. It got entrapped or something when the muscle tissue was regenerating. If it doesn't settle down, they'll fix it. Until then it hurts. It's okay, though."

When Maon paused, Randolph asked, "So what's not?"

Maon shifted in his seat and came close to speaking before dropping his head, his fingernails seeming to require his scrutiny.

"You'll talk one way or another, so just start somewhere."

A thin smile slid onto Maon's lips when he glanced up. "Yes, Sir."

"I'll smack you later. Talk." Randolph settled back, his eyes focused on Maon.

Maon gave a short, hollow laugh. "It may surprise you, but I had plans for my life. Nothing grandiose. Make a career of the marshals, spend as much time as I could with beautiful, bossy women, and have fun with my friends."

"That's how I'd describe your life." Randolph's brow wrinkled. "How has that changed?"

Maon's smile was rueful. "The last two haven't. Womanizing and playing games seem to be the only things I'm good at." He wiped his nose with his fingers and studied the far wall. "I think I blew my career with the marshals."

"You think or you did?"

Maon huffed out a breath. "I've been relegated to fluff duty since I came back. It's dead-end work. Even prisoner transport was better than this. I wanted to be an analyst, but they'll never trust someone who made the bad choices I did on Fed Central."

"Have you talked to Shane? I find it hard to believe your career is over for getting shot."

"He says I'm fine. That they're letting me ease into work." Maon shook his head in disagreement.

"Isn't that possible?"

Maon's voice grew louder, and his chest thrust forward when he responded. "Sure, it's possible. But it's equally possible they can't figure out what else to do with me. Do you realize how long it took to get something on Cosmo Bonilla? And I'm the one that let him escape!"

The waiter approached with Maon's cake, looking to Randolph to determine if he should interrupt. With a wave, Randolph signaled him to leave the dessert. Maon scooped up his fork, holding it in a grip tight enough to whiten his knuckles, and took enormous mouthfuls while staring at the plate.

Randolph sighed. "Look. I get it. In your place, I'd be worried too. You hate that you might have fucked everything up. Hate to lose. You've proven that often enough. Hmmpf. There's gotta be something you can do to make them sit up and take notice of you."

Maon grimaced and waved his fork. "There is a chance I can redeem myself. This case for Selina Shirley's company has turned into more than fluff."

Randolph crossed his arms. "There you go."

"Yeah, but I have to play straight. No womanizing on the job. Shit like that is why I'm not taken seriously. Which didn't bother me before. I sort of worked to not be taken seriously. Preferred it. Getting shot has… I don't know. Left me feeling… Well, like maybe it's time to grow up. Don't tell anyone I said that." Maon scowled.

"That's not a bad thing. Give the marshals your best shot. If it doesn't work out, you'll find something else. I expect you'll be fine no matter what you think. Meanwhile, you're on Beta Tau at the Whip Hand." A chuckle rumbled up from Randolph's belly. "It's where grownups come to play."

Fork held up, Maon licked the last of the chocolate frosting from it. With a wince, he acknowledged Randolph. "You're right." He plunked the fork on his plate. "I'm on Beta Tau at the Whip Hand. And in serious need of getting my mind off Selina Shirley's assets."

"Is that gonna be a problem?"

"Yeah. It is. It doesn't really make sense. I mean, she's pretty and all. But she hides under some of the ugliest clothes I've ever seen. It's hard to tell if she even has curves. But when I'm around her, my dick takes over."

"Huh. Sounds like you need a woman."

"Yeah. Probably. I haven't had sex since I got shot."

"Fuck. That's been months. Maybe that little orange-corseted Domme you got your skirts in a whirl over the last time you were here will show up tonight."

What the hell? Maybe Randolph was right, and all Maon needed was to spend time with a hot woman. If that turned out to be the little flame Domme... A vibrating thrum ran through him. "What does she call herself?"

"She goes by Lasair."

With a nod and a grin, Maon repeated him. "Lasair. That sounds about right." He rose and thumped Randolph on the arm. "Thanks. I'm gonna head to the locker room. You gonna be out on the floor?"

"Not till later. Enjoy yourself," Randolph said, smirking.

Maon grinned, turned, and walked away. Despite the pep talk from Randolph, his usual swagger was missing. His guts still churned. How could two women as opposite as Selina Shirley and Lasair both turn him on?

Inside the locker room, he nudged the door of the cubby he'd chosen until it snicked shut. Sans shirt, boots, and socks, Maon was ready to enter the public play area of the club. For some reason, he was nervous. He slipped his way through the door and found the closest possible empty chair. This early in the evening, most of the stages weren't in use. During slow times, Randolph would make sure at least three of the eight small stages were active. Maon had his choice of watching a laser etching, a plasti-spray mummification, or a sensation play scene. The chair reformed around him when he slumped to watch the young woman who was alternating squeals with moans. Her Dom had strapped her slender limbs to a St. Andrews cross and was selecting items from a tray next to him. The Dom's choices seemed random, but he was building toward something. The sub was enjoying herself, which the smiles accompanying her cries proved. No words were spoken, but it was obvious from the pair's rapport they knew each other well.

Maon had played with a lot of women, but never long enough to form a close relationship. When a dalliance headed that direction, he'd always ended it. *Leave before anyone gets hurt.* That was his motto. Funny. Living life that way hadn't been lonely until now. Elbow on the arm of the chair, he leaned his head onto his fist. *Fuck's sake. You're one morose son of a bitch.*

More people filtered into the play area. Soon, activity surrounded him.

A tall, buxom switch he'd played with before approached him. "Hey, Maon. I haven't seen you in a while." She smiled, finger twirling in the curls of her long auburn hair.

Maon raised his head, returned the smile, and responded, "Eva. No, I've been busy. But I'm not now."

"Mmmmm. That's nice. I thought we could spend time with a spanking bench. I could spank you, but it looks like you need to work off some frustration." She bent at the waist and gave him a direct look. "What d' ya say?"

If anyone could snap him out of his funk, Eva could. She was an easy-going woman who never asked for more than he could give. His dick was shouting at him to get a move on. "Public or private?" he asked, his eyes gleaming.

"Public, of course." When she grabbed his hand, her cold fingers made his blood heat. Nothing was better than spanking a cool bottom until it was red and hot to the touch unless it was letting a sexy woman spank him. He allowed her to drag him across the floor to the stage with a spanking bench. It had been occupied while he'd sat brooding, but they were next in line.

Maon pulled her next to him on a love seat. He skimmed her hair back so he could nibble on her neck and earlobe, sliding his fingers up the peek-a-boo shirt she wore to cup her breast. She giggled while he whispered the silly banter he was known for. Even on autopilot, he could make a woman happy. A splash of orange caught his eye when he moved his lips around to her nape. It took a moment for it to register, but when it did, he snapped his head up to look. Sure enough, it was Lasair, the flame Domme. He followed her with his gaze while she walked toward the bar and ordered a drink.

"Hey! Maon!" Eva grabbed his chin and turned him to face her again. "I lost you."

With a rueful grin, Maon attempted to pay attention to Eva, but his focus kept drifting to watch Lasair.

Eva twisted to find out what was distracting Maon. "Oh, I see. I really have lost you."

"No, sweetie." Maon pulled her into a kiss, trying to regain the earlier mood.

Eva drew away and smiled. "You want to meet her?"

Unsure if Eva was serious, Maon flicked his gaze back and forth, judging her sincerity.

"Really, Maon. Do you want me to introduce you to her?" Eva asked.

Air locked in his chest as Maon forgot to breathe. "Sure," he responded, hoping his voice hadn't sounded as strangled to her as it did to him. Then his lungs began working with a whoosh.

Eva laughed when she patted him on the cheek. "You have it bad. Don't you?" She grabbed his hand and pulled him up. "Come on. I never thought I'd see the day Maon Keefe was smitten with a woman."

Not quite resisting, Maon allowed himself to be drawn along by Eva. "I'm not smitten. I'm in lust."

"Uh-huh. Whatever." When Eva reached the bar and stopped beside Lasair, Maon hung behind her, his heart pounding and his diaphragm making breathing difficult again. "Hey, Lasair. I've got someone who wants to meet you."

Lasair turned to face Eva, brushing her gaze over Maon for a moment. "Hello. Is this the switch you were telling me about?"

"Yes. This is Maon." Eva yanked on Maon's hand to get him to stand beside her. "Maon, this is Lasair."

"Hello, Maon."

If he hadn't already been finding it hard to speak, the sound of Lasair's voice took his own away completely. Her hood was fitted with speech modification. Instead of that of a normal woman, the tones that curled through him, winding along his spine straight to his nuts, were deeper and imbued with the snap and crackle of a fire. The attempt to dazzle her with his patented smutty-boy half smile went down in flames. His body quivered as though he'd been turned out of an aspic mold. His mind was on hiatus. An attempt to smile ended up more dopey and lovelorn than provocative.

Lasair smirked at him. "Were the two of you looking for someone to play with together?"

Eva sneaked her hand to Maon's side and gave him a pinch. "Snap out of it, doof."

Maon jumped, stumbling to get words past his lips. "Ummm. No…I…"

With a roll of her eyes, Eva said, "Maon was going to spank me, but when he caught sight of you, he turned fourteen. I don't play with boys." She slid her fingers along Maon's arm and then waved at Lasair when she departed.

Maon glared at Eva's back, shedding his adolescent reactions. He plastered his proven panty-melting smile on his face, more muscle memory than actual cockiness.

"Mistress, I would like to get better acquainted. If we're compatible, I'll try my hardest to please you."

Lasair pursed her lips. "I see. First, I am not Mistress. You will call me Lasair. Second, if we play, you will please me or you will be punished. Third, you're wearing too much clothing. Strip the pants off."

The slut in Maon came roaring back. His fingers shook, he was so giddy with the possibilities before him.

Selina led Maon toward the club's private area desk. Satisfaction pulsed through her veins. At last, this damnable, tantalizing man would be in her power. Eva had called him a switch, but his submissive side had flared to life in front of Selina. Confident, swaggering Maon Keefe had frozen, unable to voice even one taunt or suggestive insinuation. That was different. Different from his professional and club personas. The smart charmer and playful flirt had deserted him, leaving him vulnerable. Perhaps she'd written him off too quickly. Maybe he was the one, the Tallavan male who met her qualifications for marriage.

After completing the process of obtaining a private room, Selina immersed herself in her Lasair identity. The play space she'd chosen was her favorite because it reminded her of centuries-old film noir. The darkness was lit from a vidscreen showing a window with a flashing neon sign outside dimmed by a sheer curtain. A spotlight shone down on a spanking bench and another over the bed, itself a piece of art. A distressed baroque headboard and footboard added shabby elegance to the room while the deep red crushed-velvet spread and pillows contributed gaudy flamboyance. Leather straps were anchored to each bedpost, awaiting attachment to the worn brown cuffs slipped over the finials. All this was reflected at odd angles by random mirrors set flush in the walls and ceiling. When she walked inside, she turned to Maon. "Shut the door."

When he completed the task, he stood before her, shoulders back, hands behind him, gaze lowered. He seemed to tower over her, all strength and physical prowess. His excitement was evident by the bulge in his briefs. A succession of activities to pursue with him flowed through her mind. She moved closer and blew a stream of breath across his chest. His muscles flexed. She lifted her chin. This close to him, she could gaze directly into his stormy eyes. She held him in a locked stare until she was certain. He wanted to be hers. With her. Under her control. *So be it.*

"Lie down. Let's talk first."

Maon complied, lying on the side of the bed closest to the door.

"Scoot over more. Give me room to sit next to you."

As he moved, she watched the play of muscles in his abdomen and thighs. The urge to touch accosted her, but she ignored the itch in her fingertips.

"Are you comfortable?"

Maon shimmied on the bloodred coverlet, putting his hands behind his head. "Yes, Lasair. Thank you." A smile played across his lips, and it was clear he had regained his usual self-assurance.

"Good." A full minute passed while she quietly observed him. Relaxed now, he watched her in return. At last, she said, "Eva said you are a switch. How would you describe yourself?"

"I'm a switch only in that I will top someone if they ask me to. My preference is to bottom, although I'm not really submissive." Maon had dropped his smile. His eyes narrowed as though he were expecting a negative response.

"Bottom. Submissive. Let's not quibble over nuances. While you are with me, you will submit to me. That is a requirement for us to play together. I prefer not to use bondage. My submissives must maintain control of their bodies. If I tell you to keep your hands behind you, then you will keep your hands behind you. Can you do that?"

"I love a challenge, my lady. Failure is not an option for me." Maon's navy eyes gleamed with an intensity that told her this was a core value. He did not like to fail.

"And if I devise a test you cannot win? What then?" she asked, her curiosity aroused.

The muscle in his jaw twitched. "I won't fail."

With a gentle smile, Selina stroked his arm. "Failure is a hard limit, then. Don't worry. I won't let you fail. I may bind you to probe beyond your limits to see where I might stretch you. I will learn the extent of your boundaries. We will move past them from time to time."

She reached for a bottle of oil on the bedside table and poured some of the scented liquid into her hand, rubbing her hands to slicken them.

"You're talking about playing more than once."

Selina paused before answering, surprised that in less than ten minutes, she'd broken one of her own rules. No relationships, even short-term, until she knew what she wanted. She should back up, but something inside her pressed her to move forward. Discover what this was she felt for him, and then, tell him who she was. She didn't want the right man to slide through her fingers. The sleekness of his skin, warm and slippery with oil, brought a brief smile to her lips.

"Yes. I am. I'm not here for fun and games. I'm looking for my perfect submissive, and you might be that person. After we are better acquainted, I will want a monogamous relationship. Does that interest you?" Selina waited with apprehension while Maon considered his response. His nostrils flared when he inhaled deeply.

"I don't do long-term relationships. Well, I haven't, but maybe it's time I did. May I touch your hand?"

"Yes," Selina breathed.

He reached out to clasp her. "At heart I'm a man slut." His eyelids drooped, and he looked at her through his lashes. "I'm not sure it's in me to settle down in any relationship. I flirt by default with all women. Most times it's purely innocent, but often it's not." His thumb brushed back and forth across the tender skin between her thumb and forefinger.

Selina closed her hand over his thumb, trapping it in her grip, her fingers tingling wickedly. "I can handle your waywardness. A male chastity belt is one possible solution." When Maon winced, she smirked at him. "It's time I learned more about your body. Scoot up. Grasp the straps attached to the headboard. Make sure you're comfortable. You will keep your hands on the straps until I tell you to release them."

WHEN MAON EASED himself up on the bed, the leather was cold beneath his palms, but the straps warmed as he gripped them. When he was ready, he nodded at Lasair. The warmth of her hand while she smoothed it over his abdomen, up to his sternum, and over his chest was like a balm, fingers healing the ache of tension that had been building in him for too long. Then she pinched his nipple. Maon's eyes, closed in contentment, snapped open, and his body jerked in response.

"Do you like pain, Maon?" Flames seemed to flicker in the topaz depths of her gaze while she waited for an answer.

"No, I don't." Maon's voice was a rasp while his mind flickered through the possibilities beneath her question.

"You allow others to spank and flog you. The predicament scenes Randolph devises for you always involve pain. Are you sure you don't like it at least a little?" Her words were like a scalpel she wielded to cut him open, to find the truth of who he was.

She'd seen one of his bondage scenes. "My pain tolerance is high. If a friend needs the release of flogging someone, I can offer that to them." Lasair's eyes gave him no hint to her thoughts. Did she like to make men writhe in agony? He couldn't tell. "Enjoyment for me is unnecessary. I'm not a masochist. I can stand a significant degree of torture, but I don't like it. And I certainly don't crave it. Randolph and I? His scenes are challenges. There's always a prize, which I always win."

Lasair's nostrils flared at his last statement. "Hmmm. I'm not a sadist like Randolph, Maon. I don't enjoy inflicting pain without equivalent pleasure. Any pain you experience from my hand will be used to heighten your pleasure. Pleasure I will control completely."

The throb in Maon's groin, which had waned while they talked, returned in full measure.

"Close your eyes and keep them closed." Lasair's voice crackled over him. The brush of feet on carpet and the scrape of cupboards opening and closing met his ears. The mattress dipped, and the heat of Lasair's body reached out to him. A rustle and *ting* of metal sounded when she dropped items to the bed. His imagination ran through a list of possibilities while he considered how she might combine pain and pleasure.

He nearly jumped again when she placed her hand at the base of his throat, fingers curled around his neck, clenching and releasing. "More pleasure than pain today. If you need me to stop anything I'm doing, say the word *salt*. I will stop, and we will discuss the problem. Is that clear?"

"Yes. To stop I say *salt*." His body shuddered while he exhaled.

"Anxious?"

Maon heard the smile in her voice. "Yes. To begin." Was the spicy scent coming from Lasair or something she'd brought to the bed?

"Sweet man, we already have begun."

Cold metal contacted his thigh, sliding up to the edge of the leg hole in his briefs. "You won't need these." With quick snicks of her shears, she parted the fabric. When both sides were cut through the waistband, she lowered the flap she'd made. A stream of air blew on his cock from base to head. The precum that was leaking chilled. Her hand followed the path her breath had taken. Again, Maon had to restrain himself from jerking. He was already close to being overwhelmed with arousal, and she'd barely touched him.

"I'm not sure how long I can last, Lasair. It's been months for me." Maon groaned the words.

"Months?"

"An injury. Line of duty. Oh shit—" His ability to speak fled when she stroked him.

"We must do something about ending that dry spell." Her hand left him just when the tingling started in the base of his spine.

He whimpered. "Yes, please."

"You ask so nicely, but I have a few other things I want to try. Can you be patient a little longer?"

His lungs expanded when he sucked air into them in long drafts. "Yes, Lasair."

"First the bit of pain I promised." Already on edge, his nipples pebbled hard when she flicked them with her fingernail. "You have beautiful nipples, Maon. Perfect for clamping." She twisted and pulled his right nipple in her fingers. A sharp, aching spike radiated from it when she attached a clamp. He clenched his butt but had no real trouble absorbing the brief stab. Soon she had his left nipple secured, and while the pain from it evened out, a warm liquid dribbled down his body. Drizzles fell on his cock, which rose to meet them.

While her hands smoothed the oil over his body, massaging his muscles in circular motions, Maon relaxed. He undulated his hips in a slow, thrusting motion, the movement setting off twinges from his nipples. His cock ached for her touch. "Darlin', you're killing me."

"Am I?" Lasair laughed—a low, sultry sound that sizzled and fried his senses.

"Please, stroke my cock." He was already reduced to begging.

"Yes. I can't wait for you to come either." With those words, she cupped her hand over his balls, between his legs, and drew it up over his cock, spreading the warm oil. Another laugh seared him when she encircled him with both hands, stroking his length in a continuous stream of sensation. The tingle that had been stamping its feet at the base of his spine exploded, and his cock hardened to synthsteel.

"Ahhh. I'm coming." While his whole body strained toward orgasm, his cock was sucked into the heat of a velvet mouth. By the time his cock finished jetting its load, Maon could not move or think. Hands, once again smoothing over his body, barely registered. Lips brushed across his. The drag of Lasair's latex hood wasn't as pleasant. Fuck's sake. Who was this woman? He wanted to know, but she wasn't sharing that information.

"Open your eyes and release the straps," Lasair whispered next to his head. After a moment, he complied. Topaz jewels, twinkling in a sea of black accented by the different shades of orange feathers on her mask, studied him. "Time to remove the clamps."

Maon winced but held himself still while she removed them, pausing between them to give him a chance to recover. She delivered a kiss to each nipple.

"May I pleasure you, Lasair?"

Her gaze met his when she raised her head. Her broad smile was larger than the hole in her latex mask. "You already have given me pleasure, sweet man. Perhaps next time I will permit you to touch more than my hand."

"Next time?"

With a chuckle, she ran a finger down his chest. "Yes. Next time. I will contact you. I travel throughout the sector, but for now we will meet here when our schedules allow."

"That could be quite a while. What about vid chatting?" The need to deepen his connection with Lasair surprised Maon. A woman whose real name he didn't know. For fuck's sake. This was crazy. But compulsion drew him on.

"I'm sure we can arrange something." She patted his chest. "I'll leave you now. You'll want to shower. You're dripping with oil."

Maon wanted to reach out and hold her when she rose from the bed. She hadn't granted permission to touch her, so he stopped himself. He took what satisfaction he could from watching her graceful body while she walked to the door.

"Clean the room." She slipped out.

As rapidly as he could, Maon placed the items they'd used in the bag hung on the back of the door. He stripped the coverlet and remade the bed with one he pulled from a drawer. He wiped the excess massage oil from his skin with the dirty spread, realizing that the spiciness he'd smelled earlier had come from the oil. After sliding into his pants, he gathered the soiled coverlet, the bag, and his ruined briefs and rushed down the hall to drop them in the supply room.

When he dashed into the public area, Lasair was nowhere to be seen. After a hurried shower, he found himself again unable to locate her by scanning the club. When he passed the maître d' for the dining area, he asked about Lasair. On hearing she'd left, Maon sprinted out the club's entrance. She was gone. All hope he could follow her and discover who she was left him. Now he would have to wait until she commed him. He dismissed the idea of cajoling her info from Randolph. That wouldn't happen. Randolph didn't disclose member information even to his friends. Especially to his friends. Maon looked at his bare feet with a sigh and returned inside to finish dressing.

Randolph caught him. "How you doing? I saw Lasair take you to a private room."

"I don't know. She's friggin' amazing. Thinks she can reform me. Maybe she can." Maon's head shook while his mind's eye replayed their time together.

"Would that be so bad?" Randolph asked.

"No, that woman could keep me busy all by herself." Maon laughed, fingers splayed wide across his chest. "Don't you go telling tales and ruin my reputation."

"Never, my friend. Women come to the Whip Hand hoping to rub up against your reputation. But if she turns out to be the one who finally collars you, I'm happy for you." Randolph slapped him on the shoulder.

"Be back soon as I can," Maon responded.

8

Maon had wandered around the main Beta Tau dome between the club and the spaceport, scanning busy restaurants and hotel lobbies for anyone who looked like Lasair. When the evening wore on, he gave up and settled on a stool at a beach bar. The beach being a patch of sand dedicated to volleyball off the back of the open-air bar. He let his gaze wander over the bikini-clad women fiercely competing for each point. By the time his fourth Long Island tea was empty, he was cheering for everything.

A hand smacked his arm, startling him. "You're drinking!"

Maon beamed at Selina. "The little gray mouse has come out to play!" he hollered. All the stools at the bar were full, so he clambered down. "Here. Sit. Bartender, I'll have another and one for the lady."

Selina caught the bartender's eye. "No, none for me, and he's had enough." With her arms clamped firmly around Maon's upper arm, she pulled him after her. "Come on, Maon. Time to catch a shuttle back to our ship."

Maon patted her hand. "Yes, ma'am. Are we going to play there?"

Selina tried rushing him along, but he wouldn't be pulled faster than a slow walk. "No, we are not going to play. We are going to bed."

"Oh!" Maon waggled his eyebrows. "Bed! Good call."

Selina slapped the arm she was holding. "Not together. Me in mine. You in yours."

"That wouldn't be nearly as fun." Maon's words were slightly slurred, and he was weaving. A spicy scent caught his attention. Fierce and sensual. He followed it until his nose was nuzzling the hair on the top of Selina's head. "You smell good." The fragrance reminded him of the time he'd spent with Lasair. It was almost the same. "You smell like her."

"How do I smell?" She yanked on his arm to pull him toward the tram stop when he drifted the other direction.

Maon rolled his head to look directly into Selina's face. "Hot. Sizzily. An' your eyes are kinda like hers." An expression crossed Selina's face that puzzled him for a nanosecond before his brain flitted in another direction.

"This is our tram." Selina steadied him while they climbed on board.

"We're going to bed," Maon announced, winking at the other passengers who were gawking at them.

"We're going to the spaceport."

The sigh Selina released when she sat drew Maon's attention away from smirking at the tourists and back to her. "You're not wearing gray or brown. That is a color."

Selina rolled her eyes. "Yes. It's puce."

"Puke. It's called puke?"

Selina glared. "Puce. Not puke. Puce."

"It would be less confusing if you called it pink. Because it is. Pink." Maon nodded as though the controversy was settled.

Selina eyed him. "How did your day go?"

Maon leaned his head on her shoulder. "Perfect. They found the shipment. And I'm in love." The shoulder Maon was leaning on tensed. Massaging it with his hand, he said, "Soften up."

"With her?"

"Who?"

"The woman who smelled good?"

"Yeah." Then he snuggled down on her shoulder. "I'm in love, so you have to stop trying to seduce me." With that, his eyes closed, and he fell asleep.

∽

SELINA WASN'T sure who she was more exasperated with, Maon or herself. She should have left him to make his own way back to the dart. He hadn't seemed like someone who drank to intoxication. Why had he chosen tonight? And what was this business about him being in love?

The trip from the tram to the shuttle dock and finally their berth at the space station had exhausted her. It had taken all her patience to get Maon into the bunk in his cabin rather than shove him to the floor. Instead of helping her, he'd used the opportunity to let his hands wander. The bed had a safety field; the floor didn't. With the pilot set to leave early the next morning, she didn't expect Maon to wake until they were well on their way to the hyperpulse point. That meant he needed to be in his bunk. And she could sleep in.

In her own quarters, the duffel bag she'd brought on board before returning down world to find Maon sat on the floor by the cupboard. She pulled out the pieces of her Domme outfit and laid them on the bed. The mask with its red-orange feathers stared at her with blank eyes. She picked it up, placing it in front of her face before turning to look at herself in the mirror inside her clothes cupboard.

You screwed up. You should have told him who you were.

She dropped the hand holding the mask to her side, continuing to stare at herself. Tomorrow. She'd have to tell him tomorrow when he wasn't drunk. He would be angry. Angry enough to break it off? She didn't want that. The scene they'd shared was so perfect. She wanted more. More of him. At least more of his sexually submissive side. Things were such a tangled knot in her mind. She wanted a man like Maon, but she needed a man who was submissive at all times. Someone she could completely control, who would always do what she told him to do without question and without putting her needs before his own.

Someone Maon Keefe definitely was not. A fling with him while she looked for that man seemed wrong somehow. Maon's reputation said he was the ideal dalliance. But the Maon she'd had under her control seemed to respond with a need for something deeper. *Blast.* It was all moot until she exposed herself as Lasair to him.

With a long sigh, determined to stop rehashing the problem, she leaned over and opened the bottom drawer that held the locked case where she stored her Lasair costume. When she was setting it next to the clothing, the door to her quarters swished open. She turned. Why didn't the pilot comm her? She froze.

Head hanging low, Maon was slumped against the door frame. "I came to apologize. I've behaved despic—" His words stopped when he looked at her bed. "What…why? That's Lasair's costume."

Damn. Her voice shook. "Yes. It is." She remained frozen in place despite the urge to grab the costume and hide it.

"Why do you have Lasair's clothes?" Alcohol was interfering with Maon's logic process, but realization would come. When it did…

"You're Lasair?" he barked. "You're Lasair." He held his head, his fingers tangling in the tawny brown strands of his hair.

"Maon…" Selina attempted to speak, but Maon raised his head and stared straight at her. The liquor in his system seemed to burn away, replaced by anger. Fury poured from him in an onslaught of words.

"Why, Selina? Is this a game you play with your submissives? Never let them know who you are while they bare themselves completely to you? Or was this payback for my teasing? Wasn't I respectful enough, Ms. Shirley? Throw me a little hope and then snatch it away? Is that your plan? I have no fucking idea."

"Maon, please…" Her plea to be allowed to explain died on her lips, overwhelmed by his barrage of accusations.

"Did you request me for this assignment? Give me an on-the-job mind fuck? Have I not been sufficiently subservient? You've made it clear you can't stand the sight of me. Are you planning to finish my career? Ha! Too late. I've already done it in all by myself." Maon turned his back on Selina, swaying when he slammed his hand against the wall.

Selina went to him, wrapping her arms around his torso. "No…" The force of his breathing made it hard to remain clutched tight to him. Was it anger or pain roiling through him? Or both?

When he whirled around, she got her answer. Face suffused with a yearning hunger, he clasped her head and brought his mouth down to hers in a crushing kiss. No tenderness. No submission. It was as though he were pouring out all his need for her. Was it to show her how he still felt? Or was he trying to rid himself of every feeling he'd ever had for her?

When he broke the kiss, he took her by the shoulders and pushed her away. "Lasair and I are done. I'll complete this case like the professional I am, but when it's over, I never want to see you again."

Shaken, Selina tried to stop him, but he brushed her off, slewing toward his own cabin. The door slid shut with a slap of finality. Repeated attempts to get him to respond failed. Eventually Selina left him alone. Lasair's costume still lay out. Her fingers plucked at the pieces while she listlessly stored them away. She fell on the bed, trying to sort out where she'd gone wrong and how she could fix things. "Damn it all to hell!" She hit the blanket hard with her fist.

Maon groaned when he rolled over, but the sound sent pain crashing through his already throbbing head. *What was I thinking?* He stayed away from alcohol because it dulled the senses. Wisps of memory threaded through the steel drums banging between his ears. Lasair. He'd been celebrating finding someone who might understand him. Selina had showed up and helped him home. And then...

Fuck. Last night's discovery in Selina's cabin came flooding back to him. Selina was Lasair. Why had she hidden that from him? He'd accused her of all kinds of things, the alcohol having obliterated his self-control. Anger still churned inside him. Who'd have thought, he, philanderer extraordinaire, would find himself in a position to have his trust betrayed. Philanderer, yeah, but liar he was not. Women knew what to expect when they were with him. Hiding her identity from him was the same as lying. Did she grasp that being with her violated service regulations? Sure, she must. Hadn't she suspected him of that very thing with Liza? *Screw it!* Time to crawl out of bed, fix his head, and confront her.

His plan was to go straight to the bathroom once his cabin door swished open, but he couldn't prevent himself from looking in Selina's direction. She sat in one of the three chairs fastened in place to the deck around the small plasti-form table that served as the dining and work area of the ship. Fingers tightly gripping her handheld, she was reading when he interrupted her with his entrance. For an instant their gazes locked. Selina looked as though she wanted to say something, but hesitation lost her the opportunity.

Inside the bathroom he leaned against the door, struggling to get control of the anger that had flooded him at the sight of her sitting calm and composed. And fuck it all to hell, his cock was hard. He slammed his fist against the plasti-steel panel, wincing when the throbbing in his head intensified. Meds. He needed meds. He used the toilet, washed his hands and face, and exited back into the miniscule lounge.

Selina stood waiting, holding a steaming cup of coffee in one hand and two small green pills in the palm of the other. "Something for your hangover and some coffee?" Her gaze never met his.

He stared at her for a moment before he reached out to take what she offered. "Thanks." After washing the pills down with a long swallow, Maon grunted. "Sit."

With slow, controlled movements, she did what he asked, waiting quiescently. He sat across from her. Silence engulfed them while he fiddled with his cup, grasping at composure. Finally, his voice gruff, he said, "I'd like you to explain why you didn't tell me you were Lasair."

Her gaze flicked to his briefly. Her eyes, along with her nose, had reddened. Gods. She was going to cry. He wouldn't let her play on his sympathy. She had lied to him. A flush of pain hardened his anger.

In a monotone, Selina answered, "I don't know. I should have. I'm sorry."

Maon's jaw went rigid. "There has to be a reason."

Lids sealed, Selina drew a breath deep into her lungs. "I—"

"Look at me while you speak."

With a quick nod, she said, "All right." She brought her gaze up to meet his, eyes dry, tears no longer threatening to fall.

"Lasair has always been a secret. Very few know. Randolph. Maybe some other club staff. That's how I wanted it when I began exploring"— she swallowed hard, coughed, and continued—"exploring domination. I didn't intend to start anything even short-term."

The table was impervious to her fist thumping down. "Damnation, Maon. I wasn't trying to hurt you or use you. I would never do anything to harm your career. You've been in my head ever since the first time I saw you at the club. And then you walk in the door of the marshals' conference room. My one chance to get someone to solve the problems the Audrina line is having, and bam. It's you. I don't know how you manage it, but you irritate me. You fluster me. You drive me crazy. And..." The rush of words tumbling from her mouth slowed when she softly said, "I can't get enough of you."

Arms crossed over his chest, Maon raised an eyebrow. "Let me understand. You're attracted to me. So rather than come out and say that, you decide it was better to pretend you're someone else and play a scene with me. A scene in which I lay myself open to you, give you my trust, and go away believing I've made a real connection. A scene in which you didn't trust me enough to tell me who you were. Is that what you're telling me?"

"Yes. But please. I didn't expect that we would connect on such a fundamental level. I was testing the water, and if things seemed right, I would reveal myself. But I was so swept up in being Lasair that I waited until it was too late to say anything. You'd have been angry, and I wanted to figure out a better way of telling you."

Soft brown eyes pleaded with him to understand. Conflicting emotions warred inside him. Lasair had enticed his sexually submissive side, but this vulnerable woman got to him too. The room had gone unbearably warm. A tightness in his chest urged him to take her in his arms, to comfort her, but the ugly knot in his stomach warred with that idea. He had to get away from her. Clear his mind.

"I don't know what to say." He stood to escape.

Selina jumped up and grabbed his arm. "Please. There's no excuse for what I did. Please understand. You scare the hell out of me."

Maon spun on her. "I scare the hell out of you?" He grasped his forehead, shaking his head. She was scared? Hell, he was scared. He couldn't do this right now. He was losing focus.

"Selina. We need to set aside this incident and our personal feelings. This case is far more important to me than you probably realize. I have to concentrate on it. Until it's completed, we will treat each other like cordial professionals. There's never been an us. There may never be an us. But we'll figure that out when doing so won't destroy my career. Understood?"

Selina nodded, looking at her hands. "Yes. I understand."

Maon tipped her chin up and gazed deep into her eyes. "Okay."

～

SOMETIME DURING SELINA'S tossing and turning last night, the dart had made hyperspace. Two days to Gallarda and then another twelve hours until they docked. Messages were queued, awaiting her response, but they could wait. Her mind was too much of a jumble for business. Besides, her replies wouldn't go out until they exited hyperspace.

In the half hour since Maon had laid down the rules for their relationship, Selina had sat at the lounge table, attempting to get some of her ideas for the fall Audrina line on paper. Her electronic drawing board was too cumbersome to bring on the dart, so she relied on the ever-faithful fallback, a pad and colored pencils. She usually found drawing relaxing, but so far, her attempts had been pointless. Nothing flowed. Instead, her mind kept returning to the last conversation she'd had with Maon. His words infiltrated her brain, around thoughts of skirt lengths and large floral prints. *"There's never been an us. There may never be an us."*

Why was she fixated on those words? That was her plan. A short fling. There was never supposed to be an us. Yet whenever his words played in her mind, her throat tightened. Fling or no fling, us or no us, she owed him respect for his position as a Tallavan marshal.

While she was mentally affirming her plan to do everything Maon asked her to do, the door to his cabin slid open. The somber look on his face made her inner tension tighten another notch.

He sat opposite her, one hand on the table before him, navy-blue eyes dark. "I've gone through my messages and have news that may distress you."

Selina nodded, chewing her bottom lip. His voice was composed, impersonal. Was she imagining a hint of sympathy in his expression? He couldn't completely suppress his innate kindness. He'd said he would focus on the case, so this was about the investigation. This she could handle.

"The person working with the smugglers on Tallav is Liza Donnelly."

"Liza Donnelly." Selina had tried not to let her enmity to the woman color her thinking, but to learn Liza was behind the smuggling wasn't a bombshell. Her mother would be heartbroken. The Donnelly sisters had been with the company for a very long time, and Katerina Donnelly was as much her mother's friend as an employee. Liza Donnelly, though. Her mother would find that believable—sad but believable. Audrina thought

Liza's wild party days were behind her. She hadn't told Maon because she'd wanted him to reach his own conclusions, but the main reason Selina had suspected Katerina of embezzling or theft was the older sister's need to cover up Liza's often costly mistakes. She'd been wrong. Katerina would be devastated.

"That doesn't seem to surprise you."

"No. She had the access and knowledge required. We've never gotten along. She disliked me from early on. Before I took a position at the company, she was a little freer with letting me overhear what she thought about me. *Spoiled brat* was one of the nicest things she said."

Maon made a noncommittal grunt.

"I didn't like her. She didn't like me. She ran the shipping department with a tight fist. It would be hard to imagine anything going on that she didn't know about. But drug smuggling?" Selina shook her head. "I never saw that coming. Will you be arresting her?" she asked.

"She's under surveillance. We'll arrest her as soon as I finish on Gallarda and Tollonia."

Maon's finger tapped a rhythmic pattern on the table. "I plan to spend the rest of our trip to Gallarda studying drug-smuggling patterns this side of the Drift. This operation running through Audrina is odd."

It couldn't be more obvious. Maon didn't wish to devote any more time than necessary with her. His once bright and engaging personality was muffled, completely subsumed by a dull professional demeanor. No, he'd been businesslike before without seeming lifeless. He'd teased her about being a gray mouse, but that had been a facade, not the real her. This solemnity came from inside him, and it was her fault.

"If I can do anything to help, please tell me. Otherwise, I'll stay out of your way." It was the only olive branch she had to offer. She attempted to smile, wanting him to smile in return, but the muscles of her face didn't seem to be responding properly.

"Thank you, Ms. Shirley. If I need something, I'll ask." Maon gave her his half grin. This time it wasn't cocky but sad.

As his cabin door swished behind him, Selina rested her elbow on the table and pressed her mouth against her knuckles. Ms. Shirley. Her insides remained tightly clenched. *Damn.*

9

Shortly after arriving in the Gallarda system, Maon sat, leaning against the head of his bunk, sorting through his message traffic. The last two days had been the longest of his life. The tiny dart made getting away from Selina impossible. Her scent seemed to permeate the ship. He'd left his cabin door unlocked, half hoping she might come to him and command him to pleasure her. That hadn't happened, so he'd used his own hand to find release from his near constant arousal. When he wasn't indulging in lust-filled daydreams, his mind drifted to figuring out the enigma that was Selina Shirley. The knot in his stomach slowly loosened. Before they left this dart, he would make sure she knew his feeling toward her hadn't changed. He wanted her in his life, and it wasn't just for the sex. Insane as that would sound to anyone who knew him. Her bossy vulnerability had taken hold of him. She was someone he could see being with for a very long time. Someone he'd never imagined, because he'd never met anyone like Selina Shirley.

A message had come in from the marshals' headquarters on Tallav. The marshal charged with watching Liza Donnelly reported that she continued following her normal routine. She and her fellow smugglers must still feel safe from discovery. The next message wasn't as encouraging. The Gallardan marshal who was keeping an eye on the House of Shirley's pyantha mill informed him the plant manager was missing. Without notifying anyone, he had missed work two days in a row. His home appeared empty. His wife and children were also gone.

Maon scratched his jaw. Could the Gallardan have gotten the wind up and fled without telling Liza? If he was the head of the operation, was he leaving Liza holding the bag?

In twelve hours, they'd make dock on the Gallardan space station. An hour or so later, they should be down world. It was time to take action. In a message to the marshals on Tallav, he ordered Liza Donnelly's immediate detention in protective custody. If the smugglers were running, he wanted Donnelly available to question and serve as a witness if needed. In a second message to the Gallardan marshals, he requested an investigation into the disappearances of the mill manager and his family, including a determination if they had left Gallarda.

The door to his cabin pinged. When he opened it, he found Selina carrying a tray with a sandwich and what looked like potato salad.

"I thought you might be hungry. Sorry. This isn't typical breakfast fare."

"Thank you. I'm famished, and it looks good. Let me take that." With the tray in one hand, he asked, "Are you eating too?"

"Yes. I am." Selina's hair fell across her face when she moved to leave.

"I'll eat with you." Maon trailed after Selina. He missed the little spitfire she had been before their blowup. He'd overreacted, and this was the result. He couldn't blame the alcohol for his anger or for the savage way he'd kissed her. He'd gone from fiercely hot to brutally cold in seconds. No wonder she didn't want to look at him. And yet she was reaching out. And fuck if he didn't want to take hold of her and kiss away her unhappiness.

He was a first-class dick. The booze hadn't helped. From the first, it was clear she wasn't a manipulator or schemer. Even her attempts to appear shy and retiring failed miserably. She couldn't sustain a false front for long. When she had been Lasair, they had reached an immediate connection because the emotions she was feeling and projecting were authentic. He still wished she hadn't hidden from him, but he could understand any woman guarding herself against him.

Somehow he needed to explain how he felt without igniting the passion that could flare so easily between them. A fine line to walk. *Yeah, I want you. I want us. But we have to put that on hold until the case is resolved. Stop stalling.*

When they were both seated, he stretched across the table and laid his hand on hers. Beneath his own, her fingers twitched. "Selina, I need to apologize for treating you so harshly. I've been going over what happened. My reaction was...it was wrapped up in my own anxieties. If you haven't lost all hope in me, I'd like to get to know you better." That was nice and bland. It didn't come close to how he felt about her. *Get to know you better?* Ha! "I want to know if you watched the Mr. Muffles vids when you were little. I want to know your plans, your dreams. I want to know what drives you."

Her hand tightened into a fist under his. The need to keep distance between them forced him to pull his hand back. He let it hover in midair before he dropped it to his side of the table.

She was bossy without being a bully. She hid her beauty and tender heart, but those qualities awaited someone willing to look beneath her disguise. She was so much more than she let the world see, and he wanted to know her, deeply, truly, the real Selina. With a crushing heaviness, he brushed those thoughts aside. It had to wait. But would she wait?

"I still need to focus on this case, but it's getting hard not to wrap my arms around you when you look so dejected all the time." *Fuck's sake. Way to be detached.*

Selina raised her gaze to his and, with a hesitant smile, nodded. "Thank you. Talking would be a good idea. I will do everything I can to help you, but since you seem to like bossy me, maybe I'll let her back out."

Oh hell. Maon waggled his eyebrows, unable to contain an impish smirk. "I like bossy you."

Selina grinned at her plate.

Maon's crotch tightened. He chewed a forkful of potato salad until it was less than mush. Selina's next comment saved him from the flirtatious remark he'd been trying to avoid making.

"What have you heard about the case?"

Right. The case. "Well, I've sent orders to go ahead and detain Liza and put her in protective custody. The plant manager on Gallarda and his family are missing."

"Missing? As in possibly killed?"

It struck Maon as odd she'd immediately assume he'd been murdered. "That's a remote possibility, I suppose. But it's much more likely he's fled to avoid arrest. I've asked the marshals on Gallarda to look into the disappearance. They should have more information when we get down world."

"Hmmm."

"It will be early evening before we can go to the mill, but I want to head there as soon as possible even if it is past regular work hours. It should make searching easier if the workers have left for the day." Maon took another enormous bite of sandwich.

"A night watchman will be on duty, but I have the access codes for the entire plant," Selina said.

"Mmmph." It took a moment for him to swallow. "Good. I wanted to interrogate whoever is working this end of the smuggling route. If it turns out to be the plant manager, that may not be possible now. I want to expose the brains of this operation. It's definitely not the head of any of the cartels. Maybe someone branching out on his own, but that doesn't make any sense either. The setup is small and carefully planned, but I can't see how they are making a profit. If they are, it's got to be too small for anyone but petty criminals. Which makes me think House of Shirley employees like Liza."

"Maybe she will know."

"Perhaps. This setup is not like typical drug smuggling. Smugglers don't send their product through customs and risk detection. Fools with their personal stash try that. It's puzzling." Maon finished his sandwich and stood to discard his tray. "I want to head for the shuttle docks the minute we're snugged into our berth. Can you be ready to leave?"

"Yes. Not a problem."

"Terrific. Consider taking a nap. It may be a while before we go to the hotel."

"Sure."

Their eyes met. Thoughts clothes-pinned themselves to a line strung between them. Nap. Bed. Us. Together. Naked. *Fuck's sake.*

Selina's gaze dipped to the rod rigidly filling his pants. She looked up, cocking an eyebrow.

Maon pointed toward his cabin door. "I-I'll just…" He waved his finger toward her door. "You can... Oh, for..." He bolted for his cabin. Shit. This was going to be harder than he thought.

BY THE TIME the dart docked, the Gallardan marshals' office notified Maon that they had located the plant manager's family. The wife had taken the two children to visit their grandparents. James Short had not been found. His wife said he'd intended to work long hours while they were gone to prepare for a vacation the family would take later in the spring. After questioning her, it was apparent she knew nothing about pyantha smuggling and didn't believe her husband did either.

Impatient to inspect the mill and its offices, Maon notified the Gallardan marshals he would head to the plant that night before checking in with them the next morning. Any new information should be sent directly to his EBC once he was down world.

From the shuttle's window, Maon studied the world below. The district around the spaceport was upscale compared to the rest of the city that comprised Gallarda's largest urban area. The original colonists had scratched out a living using the fibers of the pyantha plant to spin thread, yarn, and rope. The ability to grow pyantha was rare in the galaxy and unique to Gallarda on this side of the Sympallan Drift. The discovery that pyantha seeds could be distilled in *sturnilium* to create a highly hallucinogenic extract had changed the planet from a placid agrarian society to a drug-growing haven.

Millions of credits were made from the extract distilled on Gallarda, but little came into the hands of workers who tended the pyantha fields or the hydroponic warehouses where all food on Gallarda was grown. Cartels ran the large-scale operations that shipped extract throughout the sector. If someone was running a boutique production through the House of Shirley, it was time to find out.

Down world, Maon tossed their overnight bags into the back of the maroon air car Selina had rented. He spent a few minutes sliding his hand along the side of the car even though the lines of this particular sedan were sedate rather than racy. Still, it was an air car. On Tallav cars had wheels and ran on roads. That was sensational. Especially at high speed. But an air car was something he'd had few opportunities to drive—fly. Under his breath, Maon said, "This is gonna be fun."

Selina frowned at him over the roof of the car. "Maybe I should drive. You're like a kid who's been handed the keys to a candy store."

"No way. I'm the marshal on this case. I get to drive," Maon responded, opening the door to climb in. Once Selina was strapped in, he began raising and lowering the car.

"Are you finished playing around?"

"I'm not playing around. I'm getting a feel for the vehicle. What if we end up in a high-speed chase?"

Selina rolled her eyes. "Air cars don't go at high speeds."

Maon raised his eyebrows and gave Selina a smirk. Teasing her felt natural. She made the perfect straight man to his comedian. He'd have to try his favorite jokes out on her. "Don't worry. I'll keep her low and slow."

After the initial fun of driving an air car, the ride settled into monotony while they passed warehouse after warehouse dedicated to hydroponics. Selina explained that the mill was located close to the pyantha fields, which were all well outside the city and its food farms. When warehouses were replaced with field after field of pyantha, golden stalks swaying in the breeze, Maon began restlessly thumping a thumb on the steering wheel.

"That's it." Selina pointed to a conical-topped tower that stood above the pyantha fields. When they drew closer, Maon saw that the silo was attached to a building. A much larger area next to that was taken up with a construction site.

"Damn," Selina said. "Losing those samples is nothing compared with how far behind we are on construction of the new section of the mill. This has to be the most corrupt planet in the Federation."

"Top ten at least," Maon commiserated.

"They still haven't finished pouring the synthsteel piers and walls. Everything they do requires another inspection and another bribe paid."

An old battered air car stood next to the main entrance. "The security guard's?" Maon asked.

"I assume. Let's head inside."

After Selina opened the front door with her access code, Maon asked her to take him to the manager's office first. "Stay out in the hall. No need to add your DNA to the room. It doesn't look like crime scene techs have been here yet." Before entering, Maon pulled a can of steri-coat from his pocket and sprayed his hands and the soles of his boots to keep from contaminating whatever he touched. The office seemed ordinary, pictures of family, an older model vidscreen, and a large jar of candy on the desk. The contents of the drawers were insignificant. He'd have to check the techies' report, assuming they'd already been here. The document hadn't been in his download when he arrived in system. But would they have found anything? Except pyantha? Probably nothing here to find.

Selina was leaning against the wall, talking with the security guard when Maon left the office. The man eyed Maon, nodded, and said, "Marshal. Tom Shankle. Anything I can do, let me know." Maon scrutinized him. Gray-haired but still fit-looking, he was shifting from foot to foot as though he'd rather be anywhere else than speaking to a Tallavan marshal. The guard turned his attention to Selina. "I'll be outside taking a turn through the construction area. I thought I saw someone nosing around at night out there. The workmen messed up the security cams and lights. They haven't worked the last couple of days."

"Thank you, Tom." As soon as the guard was out of earshot, Selina asked, "Anything?"

Maon shook his head. "No. I have some bots preset to analyze the local data system. If you'll show me to system access, I'll get those running. We might have information by the morning."

"Sure." Selina led him down the hall, unlocked another door, and waved him in. "The access granted on Tallav will give you data access here too."

The brief contact, when Maon slid past Selina into the tiny room, jiggered a prickle of pleasure at the base of his spine. The room held just enough space for a gel tower, a small table, and chair. The vidscreen on the table was integrated with a keyboard and scripting pad. Maon popped the data cube he'd brought into the slot on the pad and initiated his searches. Behind him, Selina said, "I never would have thought of you as a data dink."

The chair scraped the floor when Maon turned and winked at her. "I prefer to call myself a data crunch. Much more manly than data dink. Dinks play with the hardware. Crunches know how to use it to their advantage." He stood and waggled his eyebrows at her. "On to shipping, and then we can get back to the city."

Maon surveyed the area. The setup was smaller than on Tallav. They had no dedicated shipping staff. The drying-room workers handled the mechanicals that bundled the finished yarn into skeins. Skeins went straight into bins that were loaded into larger crates to be sent on to Tallav. A generic data slide with an incremented lot number was attached to each crate and handed off to a Federated Express shipment courier. How could anyone ship pyantha extract out in one of the containers unless everyone in the drying room was involved?

With his arms crossed over his chest, he pursed his mouth and nodded. He caught a small smile flitting across Selina's lips.

"I see that smile," Maon said when he approached her. "You've figured it out too, huh?"

"No. You'll have to dazzle me with your powers of detection."

The sexy little smile she flashed froze him in place. Dazzling was going on, all right, but he wasn't the instigator. Fuck's sake, she was incredible. "Uh. First, I need to ask the guard who stays late after the workers leave."

"Okay."

She smiled again. How was he supposed to keep his mind on solving this case when a mere smile from the woman had him wishing she'd rip his clothes off? He pulled himself back from the brink of saying something he shouldn't.

"Come. Prepare to be dazzled." He gave her best comic grin and raised his hands, wiggling his fingers.

Selina bit her lip, but the chuckle she was attempting to restrain slipped out anyway. "After you, brainiac."

10

Selina looked at Maon when he started the air car for their return trip to the city. For a moment inside the drying room, Maon had gotten that same goofy, lovelorn look he'd had when he'd first met Lasair. He'd covered it by continuing to joke around, but it had happened. It wouldn't take him much longer to put the pieces of this case together, and then she was going to explore this connection between them. Lasair was going to put him through his paces and see what came of it.

He leaned back in his seat with a cocky smile, one hand holding the steering wheel.

"Okay. You look like a cat who figured out how to get cream from the cooler. I heard the guard tell you who stays late at the plant. What does it mean?"

"Elementary, my dear Shirley." With a pause, he glanced at her, raising one eyebrow in question.

She rolled her eyes. "I've read Sherlock Holmes. If you're hinting that your powers of observation are greater than mine, I'd like to see you analyze a competitor's runway show."

"Could it be a lingerie show?" he asked. His face was solemn with a hint of a grin at the corner of his mouth.

Selina glared at him. "What did you learn?"

Maon's repressed smile flashed into view. "I was expecting the plant manager to be the person who made a habit of staying after maintenance and cleaning had left. The guard confirmed that for me. The best time to hide pyantha extract in an outgoing crate is after hours. Fewer people around."

"That makes sense," she said.

The air car zipped along the road, the only vehicle in sight, past hydroponic warehouses laid out on either side in regimented rows that went on for endless miles. Everything neat and orderly. And monotonous. Even the refuse Dumpsters were positioned in the same location between the buildings. Maon kept his gaze fixed on the empty road ahead, driving in automatic mode while they sped through the buildings on a straight shot toward the city sprawl. Most of his attention seemed focused on his conversation with her.

"Outgoing crates are loaded with three bins filled with skeins of yarn. The shipping rack had two empty crates and one crate with two bins in it. It sat open, waiting for the third bin to be added before shipping."

"So the manager was adding the pyantha extract to one of the bins in an unfinished crate. That would be easy if no one was around. But couldn't anyone do that? What about the guard? The guard is there all night."

"True, it could be someone else. But it's the plant manager who's missing. And he would have access to the shipping information once the crate was sealed. Remember, he'd have to tell Liza when to expect the shipment with the pyantha extract." Maon paused, running his hand across his mouth. "Hmm. Unless every crate included it. If every crate had extract, then maintenance, cleaners, workers, and the guard could do it." Fingers drumming the steering wheel, Maon stared off into the distance. "No, Liza would have to inspect them all, and that would look suspicious. It had to be someone who could tell Liza the next batch of extract was on its way and the shipping manifest information. I wouldn't be surprised if the manager handled outgoing inspections himself too. I'd also be interested to learn who began the policy of shipping yarn in three-bin crates and allowing partially filled crates to remain open."

"I'd like to know that too. It's a violation of our established security procedures."

She was discovering that Maon was more complicated than the adventurous flirt she'd been with on Beta Tau. He was smart and analytical. For some reason, he believed his career with the marshals was in jeopardy. From her perspective, he'd uncovered a smuggling ring that had been operating under her nose for some time. Maon didn't treat her case like the courtesy duty that Sector Chief Davis considered it. No, Maon had dug into it and found a criminal enterprise. The Marshals Service should be glad to have him. Maybe a man who could think for himself wasn't a bad thing long term. If he minded his own business and not hers, maybe. Something to consider.

Selina shifted her body to face Maon. "Do you think—"

Before Selina could ask her question, the *bzzztttt* sound of a stinger beetle whizzed past her ear, followed by a *thunk* when the upholstered seat back burst open. Selina would forever remember that sound, the noise a bullet made speeding past you. Padding spilled out of the fifty-millimeter perforation where her shoulder had been moments before. While this registered, a stream of air rushing in through a hole in the car's windscreen blew her hair into her eyes. With one hand pushing the hair from her face, she stared at the jagged cracks zigzagging out from the hole. The next instant, Maon shouted at her to get down, grabbing her head and forcing her toward the floor of the air car.

Selina resisted, shoving up against the pressure of Maon's palm, trying to shake off the fingers tangled in her hair. *What's happening? Why is the windscreen cracked? Why should I get down?*

Oh gods! The plasti-glass windscreen shattered, raining in glittering shards around her, and another lump of padding exploded from her seat. *Somebody's shooting at the car. How can that be? Someone's trying to kill us, kill me. Who?*

Her elbow cracked into plasti-steel when her body slammed against the car's door. She cradled her throbbing joint to her stomach. *I could die. Here on Gallarda. In an air car.* The harsh noise of someone breathing rapidly reached her ears. It took a moment to realize she was the person hyperventilating, and the thudding sound was her own heartbeat. Maon was shouting something at her, but she couldn't understand him.

As her body shook, she curled up and tried to bury herself in the foot well on her side of the car. *Stay down. Maon will save you. Oh gods. What if he was shot, killed? Please don't let him die.*

Maon's evasive driving flung her around, so she careened like the ball in a gravity court match. Just when her stomach decided it had had enough, the vehicle slammed to a stop, the force of the landing throwing her up and toward the front of the vehicle. The back of her head cracked against the dashboard panel. Pain radiated through her skull. She heaved a breath, trying to keep the contents of her stomach from coming up. *Why did we stop?* Steel fingers latched onto her shoulders, pulling her from her spot on the floor. *No, don't make me move. Please let me stay still. Please.* The hands were insistent. She looked up. Maon, fury suffusing his face, was yelling at her to move.

AS MAON STRAINED to force the air car to respond to his evasive maneuvers, a shot took out the front controls. *Shit.* They would have to land, but they'd be sitting ducks for whoever was shooting at them. Where could they hide to wait for help? The solution was obvious, with miles of warehouses in all directions. Below and to his right was a cluster of large Dumpsters. It was the closest potential hiding spot for the car, but the bright maroon color of the vehicle made discovery inevitable. With skill born of necessity, he landed the faltering car, partially hiding it amid the Dumpsters. Leaving the vehicle and finding shelter was paramount.

After grounding them, the shooter could be coming to finish what he started. They were a good twenty minutes from the city's outskirts. He sent a comm message, including their location, to the marshals and the local emergency line. "Shots fired. Officer needs assistance." Then he scanned the warehouses on both sides of the alley. Each building had two sets of double doors. It would take too long to reach the two farthest away.

Selina was on the floor of the car, whimpering and shaking. Had she been hit? No, no blood. He latched onto her shoulders and attempted to pull her up into his arms. Rather than allow him to help her, Selina yanked herself back to cringe in a huddle.

"Selina. Selina." She wasn't listening. No time to comfort her. He had to get her away from the car. When he grabbed hold of her again, Maon shook her.

"Selina. We have to move. Now!"

Her face turned up to stare at him, eyes wide and pupils dilated. With a desperate tug, Maon hauled her up and across his seat. When he had her out on the pavement, she stood shakily. Afraid she might collapse at any moment, he scooped her up and positioned her over his shoulder. He skirted around the vehicle, heading toward the door closest to the disabled air car. With a wrenching twist, he tried the handle, but it was locked. His training kicked in. Having taken it in the shorts enough times during situational-awareness simulations, he had the sense to override the adrenaline pumping through his system and the tunnel vision it brought. A quick scan of their surroundings showed no hint of the shooter that had been targeting them. Nothing. After setting Selina down, he struck the door of the warehouse on his left with his foot until it broke open.

"I'll be right back. Stay here unless someone shoots again. Run into this building and hide if that happens." His gaze fixed on Selina. Did any of what he'd said register with her? Her eyes were still wide with fright, but her shaking had slowed. If he could get his hands on the shooter, he'd kill the fucking bastard firing at her.

"Yes. Stay, shooting, hide." The words came out in an inflectionless croak.

"Good girl." Maon patted her cheek before dashing across the alley to the warehouse on the right and reaching into his jacket to pull out a leather case. It was a good thing the door locks were standard and he'd brought his lock pick. This wasn't what he thought he might need it for, but he was friggin' grateful he had it. He set and pointed the small device at the lock and waited while it looped through a series of entry codes. With a clicking sound, the lock opened.

Maon ran back to Selina. The hum of a vehicle reverberated in the distance. If it was the shooter, Maon hoped that he searched the warehouse with the broken door before looking elsewhere. With one arm, he grabbed Selina around the waist, pulling her tight against his ribs, and sprinted to the open entrance. After whisking her through, he locked it again.

Inside, the smell of fresh-turned earth pervaded the building. Ceiling-to-floor racks of plants marched in orderly columns toward the far side of the cavernous building. The racks and columns were all connected by various size pipes. Whatever the small bushy plant being grown was, it must be near to harvest. The tops were close to brushing the lighting fixtures that formed the top of one level and the base for the next level up. Each column was almost a solid wall of vibrant green highlighted by the downward-focused light. Beyond the range of the grow lights, the warehouse was dark. To one side of the door they'd entered was a control room. Parked near were automated wheelbarrows. Empty now, but probably used to remove organic matter for composting in the Dumpsters in the alley.

When he realized his hold on Selina was squeezing her tightly, he loosened his arm. "Selina, are you hurt?" Maon asked. Face still pale, she didn't look as bad as she had when he'd pulled her from the car. She had some color to her cheeks, but she retained the terrified expression of the hunted.

"I'm okay." It sounded like she was trying to convince herself. "I hit my elbow, and my head throbs. But I'm okay. Tell me what to do." Her right arm cradled in her left hand, she straightened, determination setting her jaw.

He clasped her to him, stroking her back. "It's going to be all right. I've got you. I won't let him hurt you." He wouldn't allow this beautiful woman to be harmed any more than she already had been. Whoever the bastard after them was, he was a dead man if he continued to pursue them. Selina shuddered. A sob escaped her while she clung to him.

Maon's lips resting on the top of her head, he said, "We've got to move to the other side of this warehouse and try to cross the alley to another. We need to get as far away from the car as possible. Can you walk on your own?"

She straightened, tipping her chin up to look at him. "Yes. I'm okay. Really."

"Good. I sent an emergency message on my EBC to the marshals' office. Help is on the way. Our last resort is to try hiding." He said it, but it wasn't a good option. The racks of plants had no space for a person to climb in and conceal themselves amid the foliage. A methodical search would quickly expose someone trying to hide. "Follow me. Stay close."

The columns of racked plants went straight across to the other side of the warehouse, but no door showed at the opposite end of the aisle. Maon headed right, looking down aisles until a set of double doors came into view at the other end. He glanced over his shoulder to check that Selina was keeping up. "This way. You okay?"

She was panting, but she still managed to answer. "Terrific. Keep going."

"We'll rest soon."

Except for the sounds of their own footfalls and ragged breathing, the warehouse was eerily quiet. Compared to most planets, Tallav was sparsely settled and as close to earthlike as possible. Maon had grown up hiking and camping in woods teeming with wildlife. Walking in the midst of all this vegetation and not hearing a slight rustling of wind or the sound of night insects and animals was creepy. A forest stilled when a predator was stalking, and the weird silence of this place made it seem like eyes were watching them, that someone was about to pounce on them from hiding. *Calm the fuck down. You're going too fast for Selina.* He slowed and said over his shoulder, "Almost there, sweetheart. You're doing great."

Selina didn't answer, waving a hand at him, too winded to speak.

Once he was closer to the doors, Maon sprinted forward, letting Selina catch up and slump to the ground at the end of the aisle. Lockpick out, he soon had the lock released. He cracked a door open and listened, but other than something rattling against a pipe, he heard nothing. A quick check of his messages showed that the marshals were responding and sending in the local police. The warehouse number was posted beside the exit, so he included their new location in his update. Marshal Gage commed Maon, informing him he was close to their position and would pull up in front of the double doors in a couple of minutes. *Thank the fuck.*

Relief lasted only an instant. On the far side of the warehouse, a sharp *thud* and the sound of twisting metal screeched. Someone was battering their way inside. *Shit.*

He commed Gage. "Shooter is breaking into the other side of the warehouse. Send additional backup to that location. Hyperspeed to pick up Selina."

"Selina, sit here. Keep the door cracked. You're looking for a black air car. The driver will hold his badge up for you to verify who he is. When you've identified him, run and get into the backseat as fast as possible. I'll be right behind you."

"What are you going to do?" She looked toward the racket coming from the other side of the warehouse.

"I'll make sure we don't get shot."

It didn't seem possible for her eyes to get any wider, but they did. "Be careful."

"I will."

He wanted to snatch her to him, reassure her, and kiss her senseless, but he couldn't allow the shooter to get another step closer to her.

"Now watch for the marshal." Maon pivoted and with slow, soft steps walked along his side of the warehouse, pausing to listen and peek down each aisle before crossing. At the fifth column from the double doors, he stopped. Something had scraped against a rack. His heart hammered. This bastard was not getting past him.

A quick glance showed Maon the back of a man heading the opposite direction, toward the aisle that led straight to Selina. With a dash, Maon reached the next aisle, turned, and aimed at the man who was holding a gun pointed at him.

"Tallavan marshal! Put your weapon down and surrender."

The gunman responded by shooting. Maon had expected that and dodged behind the next column of plant racks while he spoke. The assassin did the same on his end. How bright was the guy stalking them? Would the solid appearance of the plant racks give him a false sense of security? Maon squatted and fired a pattern of shots that should hit anyone hiding behind the racks. No return fire. Had he found his target?

Selina hissed at him. "Gage's here."

Maon worked his way back to the double doors and dashed to the car, climbing in beside Selina. As soon as he was inside, the door slammed behind him, and the marshal took off.

11

Maon heaved a sigh of relief, circling his arms around Selina and holding her down against the seat. When she yelped in pain, he repositioned himself to avoid putting pressure on her elbow. "Sorry, sweetheart. Stay down until I tell you to get up." Selina's body was shuddering beneath his hands while he rubbed along her back in even strokes. The spicy, hot scent that was distinctly Selina soothed him. She was here. She was safe. Well, safer.

"Where are we headed, Marshal?" Maon directed his question to the massive uniformed marshal driving the air car.

Voice gruff, the marshal said, "Call me Gage. I'm taking you to the Federation enclave. In a few moments, we'll be rendezvousing with more marshals and a Fed drug-enforcement team. They'll send someone with us as an escort. The rest will continue on to the crime scene. The local police are cordoning off the area as we speak."

Maon lifted his head to glance over the dark leather bench seat and out the front windscreen. A mass of marked and unmarked air cars with swirling emergency lights was ahead. "The shooter is armed and dangerous. He may be shot. He stopped returning fire, but he might also have fled. I didn't get a good look at him."

Maon waited while Gage passed the information on to his superior.

When he was finished, Gage asked him, "How about you two? Are you injured?"

Slices of sharp pain stabbed Maon in the side whenever he moved now, but that was his old injury, nothing new. Otherwise he seemed fine. "Ms. Shirley has hurt her elbow and may have a concussion. I'm okay," Maon said.

"The enclave has a medical facility that is set up to handle trauma," Gage said.

"Thanks."

"No problem. You're safe to sit up now."

Maon lifted himself off Selina. When his weight shifted off her, she attempted to rise but couldn't quite manage while holding onto her elbow. Hands around her waist, Maon boosted her onto his lap so her good arm was against his chest. He brushed the hair from her face and cradled her to him. The shaking stopped.

Her body burrowed into him while she nuzzled his neck with her nose. "I'm cold." Her voice was almost a whimper. Two emotions warred inside him, anger and compassion. He wanted to strangle whoever had done this to her; at the same time he needed to comfort and care for her. His body tensed, hardening into battle mode again. That gunman had come so close to killing her. With conscious effort, Maon relaxed. Selina didn't need a hard-ass. Her arm was in pain, so he rubbed her thigh. The fabric of the latest rendition of ugly dress bunched under his palm. Soon, he was stroking bare skin. Not much later, he was caressing. She was so friggin' smooth. Except for the brief minutes he'd held her hand at the club, he'd never touched her in an unbusinesslike way. During that scene, she hadn't let him put even a finger on her in a sensual way.

If it weren't for the situation, he would have rejoiced to have her on his lap, letting his fingers trail over her while the warmth and weight of her body sank into him. He buried his nose in her hair, inhaling the fiery scent of her. Eyes closed, he ached with a longing he'd suppressed ages ago, killed by the daily verbal punches his mother had landed with devastating effect. *You'll never amount to anything. You're just like your father. Unreliable. No one can trust you. You should be sterilized to keep from passing on your pathological defects. You should never have been born.* Yet somehow that desire that he might one day find someone he could take care of, that hope, had resurrected. Selina was the focus of that dream. He had to avoid screwing up his chance with her. But even this hungering yearning was better than returning to a life where sexual release anesthetized his emotional needs.

Gage's deep voice broke into Maon's thoughts. "We're almost there. We'll stop at the clinic first."

Selina stirred against him. "Oh!" When she straightened, she said, "Thank you, Marshal Keefe. Ummm, I can sit on the seat now."

Maon winced, not wanting to let her go, but recognized that propriety required he act professionally. "Yeah. Sure. Let me help you." When he helped Selina slide onto the spot next to him, he regretted the loss of her body tucked against him. With a shrug, he let the mantle of Marshal Keefe fall back on his shoulders. Selina's actions reminded him of his own rule. Nothing personal until the case was completed. His teeth ground in a grimace. The case, which had seemed close to completion, had just exploded into something bigger. *Fuck.* Someone had tried to kill Selina, and he had no clue who, unless the plant manager was also an assassin with sniper training. Highly unlikely. It had the stink of cartel, but why take notice of this piddly-ass operation now after it had spent years funneling small amounts of extract off planet? If the cartels took any notice, it would have been to squash the setup long ago. None of this made sense.

Marshal Gage opened the air car's door, and Selina allowed him to help her out, letting him guide her through the entrance of the medical building into the triage area of the trauma unit. Staff were ready and waiting for them with a hover chair. A female nurse took over from Gage.

"Ms. Shirley, if you'll sit here, I'll take you to an examination room," she said.

"Thank you." Apprehension flared inside Selina. With a glance over her shoulder, she found Maon.

"I'll wait for you here," he said. His steady gaze calmed her. Why was she behaving like such a ninny? Maybe all trauma victims turned to mush. She seated herself and let the nurse guide the hover chair down a short turquoise hallway.

In the exam room, the nurse provided her with a patient gown, helping her remove her clothes and put it on so her elbow was not stressed. Why did she need to change? Her elbow and head were injured. Couldn't they give her some nanites and meds so she could go somewhere and sleep? After she stretched out on the exam table, the nurse raised the head so Selina was sitting up, propped her bad arm on a cold pack covered by a towel, and put her other arm in the medical analysis unit. Selina barely noticed the machine sample her blood.

"Your vitals are good, considering the excitement you've gone through tonight," the nurse said.

A tight smile was Selina's only response. She didn't want to be reminded of the assault or what she'd felt while sitting on Maon's lap. To distract herself, she let her gaze travel over the room. Most of it was done in a neutral palette of tans and light grays, but the wall facing the exam bed was a baby blue with a large picture of a pyantha field. The plant was easy to recognize after driving past fields of it. But she hadn't seen beyond the monotony of those acres of plants they'd driven past to discover the loveliness the artist had captured. A lapse on her part. The launch of the new line of clothing needed to introduce the average consumer to the pyantha plant itself. It was usable for more than airy shawls. Natural beauty and durability were essential marketing elements. She'd have to discover who the artist was. Her perusal of the decor ended when another woman entered.

"Hello, Ms. Shirley. I'm Dr. Graham. I'll be examining you today."

"Hello, Doctor."

Dressed in crisp white, the middle-aged doctor exuded efficiency. "Let's talk about your elbow first. Do you have any numbness or tingling in your hand or arm?" She placed her fingers on the pulse point of Selina's wrist.

"No, not at all."

"Good." She gently lifted Selina's elbow from the towel, examining it without moving the joint. "Can you bend your elbow?"

"Not really." Selina demonstrated, wincing. "It hurts when I try."

"Hmmm. How about flipping your hand? Yes, like that."

"That hurts too, but not as bad."

"Okay. I need to do a scan to be sure, but it looks as though you've broken the tip of your elbow. I'll splint it whether it's a fracture or a bone bruise. You'll be wearing a sling for several days. Before we get the scan, let me look at your head and check you for other injuries. Lean forward."

As Selina complied, she went a little light-headed. The doctor's fingers were working their way over her scalp until she hit the spot that hurt. Selina jumped.

"Found it. There's a good-sized knot here, but it's only a contusion. The skin isn't broken." The doctor used a small penlight to check Selina's eyes.

"I feel woozy when I move my head."

"Hmmm. We'll be doing a complete body scan to make sure you have no internal injuries. I understand you were thrown about the foot well of the car."

"Yes. Thrown about describes it perfectly. After I hit my elbow, I couldn't hold myself steady."

"Let's take a look." The doctor removed the gown from different portions of Selina's body while she did a visual inspection and palpated areas, asking Selina if this or that hurt. "You'll be sore over the next few days. I'll be giving you some painkillers to deal with that. First let's do the scans, and then I'll decide exactly how to treat you. Sound good?"

"Sounds good." It didn't sound good, but Selina had nothing left with which to resist. She was tired. She hurt. And more than anything, she wanted to crawl onto Maon's lap, have him wrap her in his arms, and let him take care of everything.

"Okay, the tech will be right in."

It had taken two hours before Selina was released, wearing a sling to support her splinted arm. Her eyes were hooded and sleepy. The events of the day alone could account for that, but the painkillers she'd been given added to her sluggishness. Maon encircled her waist and guided her out to the air car waiting to take them to their guest rooms. By the time they'd made the short trip to the enclave visitor quarters, Selina had conked out and didn't wake when Maon scooped her up and carried her inside. With help from the desk clerk, he got Selina into her room. It was a tricky balancing act to pull back the covers and settled her on the bed. He removed her shoes and tucked her in.

As he dimmed the lights, he looked over at her, thankful that her injuries were minimal. A cracked elbow and a mild concussion. The doctor had dosed her with a dual set of nanites. One set would manage any problems coming from the blow to her head. Those nanites had the added benefit of helping her other bumps and bruises. The second set carried the resources and instructions for knitting her fractured bone back together. A chilling shiver ran down his spine. What if she'd been shot? He stared unfocused as a vision took shape in his mind of Selina lying in a pool of blood, body broken. The muscles in his shoulders tightened. He needed to hit something, preferably the bastard that had been shooting at her. No one was going to hurt her if Maon could help it.

After removing his jacket, he folded it and threw it on the desk. The room wasn't fancy, but it was clean and above all, safe. He placed his firearm on the side table and removed the shoulder holster, setting it atop the coat. It was a surprise that he'd been allowed to keep his gun. A discharge of a weapon investigation would probably catch up with him the next day. With the gun, he was twitchy, on edge. Without, who knew? He flexed his shoulders before dropping into the cushioned comfort of the recliner. While it adjusted to him, he sighed, a long, slow release of tension. With flicks of his feet, he pushed first one and then the other of his boots off, letting them thud to the carpeted floor.

Eyes shut, he couldn't sleep. Why had someone shot at Selina? How did they know where to find her? Who was behind it? It had to be bound up with the smuggling running through her company, but he couldn't understand why anyone would kill her now. Maybe before she'd asked for an investigation, but once the marshals were called in, killing Selina wouldn't stop them from continuing to probe. On the contrary, it would probably amp up the investigation. Was this revenge on the part of the plant manager or someone else involved in the smuggling?

When he'd waited on Selina at the clinic, he'd briefed the feds and marshals on the case and the attack. The shooter had been wounded but managed to escape the cordon set up by the local police. That wasn't a real shock. Investigators had found evidence he'd used an air scooter to establish himself on a warehouse roof from which he could aim down the roadway. A sniper weapon had been left behind on the rooftop. They surmised that the gunman had gone after Maon and Selina on the scooter when they'd landed the air car in the alley. A blood trail had led from the ware-house they'd hidden in. It ended outside where the assassin had fled on the air scooter. By morning the suspect should be identified from his DNA. Maybe that would clear things up.

His eyes open, Maon leaned forward, repositioning his gun to within easy reach. When he settled back, he closed his eyelids. His attraction to Selina had been growing daily, but it wasn't the purely physical affinity he bore for most of his dalliances. True, with some of those women it went beyond that to a friendly affection. With Selina, it was so much more. This was unexplored territory for him, and he was without map or prior experi-ence to guide him. He wanted to tear the man who had tried to kill her limb from limb. Nothing clean and antiseptic like a sniper's takedown. No, pound his fists into the guy's face until it was pulp. His mind slowly unwound, and he drifted toward sleep, his exhaustion smothering the jumble of emotions jangling to keep him awake.

A NOISE AWAKENED HER, but she wasn't certain what it was until she heard the muttering groan again. Disoriented at first, Selina remembered that she was on Gallarda in the Federation enclave's visitors' quarters. Her hands gripped the covers against her chest as she looked toward the sound. It was Maon. He was asleep in the recliner by the room's window. In the dim light, his face was contorted in misery. Distress resonated from the indistin-guishable words he was mumbling.

She twitched the blanket back and sat up. "Maon, wake up. Maon." No effect. Afraid of what he might do if she woke him too abruptly with that gun lying on the table next to him, she stood and crept closer, calling his name. Beside him, she reached to move the firearm away, jumping when Maon's hand flew out and landed heavily on her arm.

"Oh!"

With a wide-eyed stare, Maon asked, "What are you doing?"

"Uh, I was moving the gun. You were having a nightmare. I didn't want you to shoot me when I woke you up." Selina swallowed, the muscles of her throat tightening. "That's all."

Maon blinked. An expression similar to the one he'd worn during his nightmare crossed his face. He snatched his hand away. It landed in a fist on his thigh when he turned so Selina could no longer see him. "Sorry. I... Sorry."

Selina sank to her knees beside him, placing her palm over his tightly clenched fingers. "Were you dreaming about the attack?"

Maon pulled free and plunged his head into both his hands. "No. Not the attack."

Although he didn't seem to want to talk about it, Selina pushed a little more. "Oh?"

Maon looked at her, heaving a sigh and taking her hand in both of his. "It's a nightmare I have every so often." He drew the back of her hand to his mouth, letting his lips brush her skin. "I'm in a pit, and these people are sealing me into it. They keep telling me I'm a failure. It's like the final punishment for hopeless losers. To be sealed away so you can't hurt anyone else." He dropped their joined hands to his thigh. "I used to have the dream when I was a kid, but it stopped after I grew up. Ever since the shooting on Federation Central, I've been having it again."

Selina stroked his leg. "You're not a failure. You know that, don't you?"

Maon gave a rough laugh. "I haven't done much right lately."

"What do you call saving my life?"

"Well...yeah, but first I—"

"First you shut down a smuggling ring using my company to transport drugs."

Maon offered a small smile. "You're not going to let me have a pity party, are you?"

"No. I'm the one who deserves the pity party. I'm the one who was shot at." Selina dipped her chin, staring at him with challenge in her eyes.

Maon ducked his head in penitence, but not before he shot her a heated look and his sexy half smile. "Yes, ma'am."

He brought his hand toward her, hesitating before stroking her cheek. She should pull back. For his sake. She should. But she couldn't. When he swept his fingers behind the nape of her neck and pulled her toward him, she didn't resist. His lips brushed hers with a tenderness that didn't match the intense desire that burgeoned inside her. She took control of the kiss, deepening it, ransacking his lips, tasting him, reveling in the texture of their entwined tongues and the sharp edge of his teeth.

The connection between them was powerful. She'd survived a terrifying murder attempt because this man had saved her. Exhilaration skimmed through her, increasing her need for him. His hand stole up under her skirt, grasped her by the waist, and dragged her to straddle him. She broke the kiss, lifted up, and then ground down against the steely rod beneath his slacks. Maon shuddered. His eyes were closed, but his hands were busy opening the clasp of her bra, scooping her breasts into his palms, and gently squeezing them.

He opened his eyes, revealing pupils blown wide and a look of agony and wonder and raw need. "I want you, Selina."

She pressed into him, continuing to rock against his erection, and claimed his mouth again, overwhelmed by the taste that was pure Maon Keefe as they slid their tongues together in a tangle of exploration. His hands had left her breasts and were scrabbling up her thighs to find the hem of her dress.

With a gasp, she pulled back, staring into the deep navy of his eyes. "We shouldn't."

His voice harsh with want, he said, "No." His body said something else with its thrusts against her.

Just one more kiss, and then she would stop, but as though her pelvis had a mind of its own, she rocked to meet him each time his hips lifted. Reality rushed in on her. If she kissed him again, she wouldn't have the willpower to end this exchange. She owed him better than seducing him and destroying his career.

"I should get more sleep." She slipped off him and stood, her good arm clutching the damaged one so she wouldn't touch him while she did. The fist of her good arm clenched, she broke eye contact, pivoted, and moved toward the bed, her body rigid with the need to do the right thing. She climbed into bed, her back toward Maon, and fought to slow her breathing. The ache in her head had returned. The bottle of pain pills stood on the bedside table. She reached for them and swallowed one dry. With her eyes closed, she awaited the sleep the medicine guaranteed.

12

Selina was initially lost when she opened her eyes. Then she registered where she was and that Maon was gone. She checked the time. It was past noon. A rare late sleeper, she was surprised until she considered her exhaustion of the night before and the pain meds. And that Maon's nightmare had woken her, making it hard to get back to sleep. *Hell.* It wasn't that he woke her, but what they had done after.

Maon. Where had he gone? A tendril of panic inched along her spine. She accessed her EBC and found the message Maon had left at 10:50, saying he'd be at marshal headquarters and would check on her later in the day. How much later had he meant? Why had he left her by herself? Was it truly secure here? On bare feet she padded to the room door and tabbed the entry security vid. A man was sitting outside on a wooden chair. She stiffened, petrified until her brain decoded what her eyes were seeing. He was a marshal. Sent to guard her. She was safe.

Legs wobbly, she stumbled back to the bed, slumping and wrapping her arms around her torso. *Sweet Mother above. Get a grip.* Eyes shut, she worked to control her breathing until she felt not quite calm, but better. She returned Maon's message, telling him she was up, and then headed to the bathroom to take a shower.

With the controls set to rain, Selina let the water trail over her in warm rivulets before finally pumping extra-large dollops of peachy-scented gel from the dispenser. The fruity foam washed away the sticky layers of sweat, grime, and terror, soothing her nose and skin as well as her need to be in control again. She'd fallen apart when the shooting began. Her mind had deserted her at the same time her body had rebelled, turning her into a quivering mass incapable of thought or action. It was humiliating to acknowledge that confident, steady Selina Shirley had needed someone not only to tell her what to do, but to make her do it.

This was not how she saw herself, nor how she wanted others to see her. She'd rigidly applied self-control to banish any personality traits that didn't adhere to the person she was determined to be. Self-sufficiency was her goal in all aspects of her life. It was maddening to realize that with all her effort, her mind and body had betrayed her, and she'd reverted to a little-girl persona who needed her daddy to take care of her.

Her father. Tears itched to fall. She missed him so much. He'd bolstered her throughout her growing-up years with his wealth of sound advice conveyed with good humor and love. His business acumen provided a backstop for her early forays into expanding the House of Shirley. At first, she'd blamed her mother for his premature death. But it hadn't been long before Selina had recognized that, just like her mother, she had relied on him, believing him invincible. His nature was to be more concerned for his loved ones than for himself, so he'd ignored the signals his body had been sending him. Selfishly accepting all he had freely given, she hadn't considered his needs. They'd never crossed her mind.

Her determination to rely on no one but herself had taken a serious blow yesterday. If she was truthful, it wasn't so much that she'd fallen apart and needed help. If it had been someone other than Maon, it wouldn't have been as problematic. Maon. Her shoulders tensed despite the warm massage of the shower. The attack had demonstrated that he'd lay his life down for her, and that she would let him do it. She could not become involved with a man who would give his all for her because she was selfish enough to take and take and take. To avoid becoming a manipulative, dependent female, she'd have to look for a partner who was essentially helpless, one she had to look after because they insisted on it. One whose needs couldn't be put aside. The submissive side of Maon tempted her, but he had too much of the protector in his makeup. That made for an excellent marshal but, for her at least, the worst kind of husband. He'd proven he would be there when she needed him. He didn't realize he couldn't expect the same from her. She had to end things before it got to where she brought him harm.

She had no other choice but to distance herself from him as much as possible. It was time to take the understanding she'd gained by her forays into femdom and find herself the perfect husband, a round-the-clock submissive. Someone who would accept the structured life she would establish to meet his needs and stick to raising their child. Surely such a man existed on Tallav.

THE REACTION to his arrival at the Gallarda Marshals headquarters confused Maon. The day before, they'd treated him with open friendliness. Today, solemn faces greeted him. Gage rose from his desk, flashing a smile that came closer to a grimace, and flicked a finger for Maon to follow him. In the interrogation room, Gage pointedly shut off the vid and audio monitors and disengaged the view wall that allowed those next door to watch interrogations. When he turned to Maon, he said, "Take a seat."

Maon eyed Gage for a moment. Whatever was going on, Gage was obviously not happy about being chosen to give him the news. "Has something happened on the case?"

"Yeah. But that's not why we're here." Gage shrugged his right shoulder and, staring at the table, said, "Sit. Please."

Maon pulled out a chair and set it to the side of the table before sitting. As soon as he moved to sit, Gage followed suit. Eyes focused on Gage, Maon waited for the blow to fall.

Gage kept his gaze on the table where his hand lay splayed out. "I figure you have the right to know what's happened on the case before you get cut out of the loop."

Maon's stomach fell. He was being taken off the case. If the big boys were taking over, he'd expect Gage to express anger or a little sympathy. Instead he was acting like he'd been ordered to kick Maon in the balls.

"The shooter was ID'd as a member of a system drug cartel. Guy who did their wet work. Vid shows him arriving from Beta Tau before you. His body was found early this morning." Gage glanced up at him. "No, your shot disabled him. He'd been carved up with a knife and dropped onto the verge of the road that runs through the center of the city. Someone was sending a message. We're not sure if it was the cartel he works for or a rival."

Maon's brow creased while he considered the information. How many players were involved in this? With a mental thrust, he pushed his thoughts aside when Gage continued to speak.

"The other big news—we found the plant manager."

Now this was news. Maon shifted forward in his seat.

"When the construction crew set up this morning to pour synthsteel into the forms, they discovered his body crammed into the bottom of one. The medical examiner says he'd been there a couple of days. No security vids from that period. Seems the system was turned off."

The table wobbled when Maon slapped it. "Shit. The guard said the workers had been turning the vids off. He also said he thought he'd seen someone out there at night."

Looking uncomfortable, Gage shifted in his chair. "Yeah. Well, this sucks, but I'm not supposed to discuss the case with you. You're ordered to return to Tallav immediately."

Maon absorbed the news. "Why?"

"Didn't say." Gage's lip curled. "This morning the chief commed Sector Chief Davis. The comm clerk told us his report did everything but seal your coffin. He claimed you'd ridden in on your high horse, ordering his staff about, shooting a local citizen, and holing up in Fed enclave visitors' quarters with a potential suspect."

"Shit," Maon said.

"Fucked up," Gage agreed. "Davis set him straight that Ms. Shirley wasn't a suspect, but the chief here is still charging you with inappropriate behavior." Lips pressed together, he shook his head. "Listen, I'll make sure the official reports are accurate, but you're going to have to deal with that accusation. I can emphasize Ms. Shirley's mental state after that attack and the unknown nature of the assailant. Make out it was protection duty."

Maon scowled, shifting his hand from the table to his lap, the kiss playing over in his mind. "It was protection duty. I slept in the chair with my gun on the table beside me."

Gage held his hands up. "Hey, I don't care if it was or wasn't. Either way, you don't deserve to be penalized. You saved that woman's life, and from my perception, uncovered a long-standing drug operation. Maybe they have to pull you from the case, but anything else is crap. I promise, we'll take good care of Ms. Shirley."

Maon had been thinking of grabbing some breakfast, but his appetite was gone. He stood and tapped Gage on the upper arm. "Thanks. I guess I need to get my gear in order."

Gage got to his feet and said, "Fiona's booked you on a flight to Tallav. You've got time to stop by the ship you came in on and pick up your stuff. If you want to talk to Ms. Shirley before you leave, have Fiona hook you up through comm."

Maon's eyebrows rose slightly while he nodded. "Thanks. I do want to tell her I'm going. Look me up when you get to Tallav."

"Will do." Gage flashed a regretful smile and slapped Maon on the back when he left the room.

Maon pressed his thumb and forefinger to his eyes. He wouldn't change anything about the way he had behaved toward Selina. He let his hand drop and rolled his shoulders. The Gallardan chief could shove his opinions up his ass. The man hadn't even talked to Maon before sending on that report. *I've got nothing to prove. My actions and the facts will speak for themselves.* Starting now, he'd play everything by the book. Cross his *t*'s and dot his *i*'s. They wanted to see how a professional Tallavan marshal conducted himself? He'd show them. He strode from the interrogation room to the bull pen where the marshals, seated at their desks or standing about, turned to look at him.

"Where's Fiona?" Maon spotted a young woman with red hair waving at him.

"That'd be me."

"I need to make a comm."

"Sure thing. Follow me." Maon trailed her down a corridor, noting that the instant his backside was out the door, conversation resumed inside.

Fiona set up the call and excused herself from the comm room.

Selina's image came on-screen immediately. "Maon."

Before she could say more, Maon said, "Ms. Shirley. I'm calling to tell you I'm leaving for Tallav this afternoon."

"What?" she interrupted, her voice uncertain.

Maon reiterated, "I'm leaving for Tallav. The sector chief is sending a team to investigate the attempt on your life. The case has his full attention. He'll have his top men here as soon as possible. The Gallardan marshals are experts on the criminal class here. They identified the shooter and his affiliations. They've stepped up monitoring of others within the cartel."

"I see." She brought her hand to her throat.

Fuck's sake, this was harder than he'd thought it would be. Guilt stabbed him for abandoning her. She was so beautiful, but despite his desire to drink her in, he had a hard time keeping his gaze focused on her. "I requested a protective detail on you before I left this morning. A marshal is outside your door. If you need anything, let him know."

"Yes. I know. I saw him." Her gaze swung to the left, fixed on something off-screen.

Maon's chest tightened. "Don't leave your room for now. I'm sure the station chief will want to speak with you soon. He'll fill you in on all the details. Follow their advice, and you should be fine."

Her gaze returned, drilling him through the vidscreen. "I don't understand why you're leaving. Won't you need to brief the new team?"

The back of his throat ached. He swallowed twice before saying, "The marshals here have been fully briefed. They have all my data and reports."

"What if I said I need you here?" She winced. "I-I mean…"

Maon brought his hand to his chest in a futile attempt to rub away the pain crushing him. "I can't." He swallowed hard. "I'm sorry to leave so abruptly, but I have orders to return, so I have to go."

"Oh. Well." Confusion flitted across Selina's face, but then her expression settled into her all-business demeanor. "Thank you for all your hard work. My mother and I are both very grateful that you took us seriously. I'll be sure to tell your superiors how impressed we are with you." Selina slowly trailed off, weakly voicing more platitudes.

In the pause, Maon said, "Thanks. Good-bye," and quickly ended the comm.

With nothing else he could do, Maon found Fiona again to obtain the details of his flight to Tallav and the location of his luggage abandoned in the air car last night.

Once he arrived at the space station, he boarded the dart, packed his remaining luggage, and had it sent to baggage. He soon found himself sitting in an economy class seat, the type that reclined to form a bunk. Already Maon missed the small cabin on the dart.

He watched the vidscreen that showed their commercial liner undocking from the Gallardan station. When undock completed, the view changed to one of Gallarda. From 400 kilometers away, the vast fields of pyantha weren't visible. Neither was a topaz-eyed beauty who stirred within him the desire to protect as strongly as a need to submit to her. He'd never felt like this for any individual. Even those he was protecting while a marshal hadn't generated this gut-clenching fear. Yes. Fear. He was afraid of losing Selina Shirley. He was coming to consider her his personal miracle. She was this beautiful, unattainable princess, and he was the underling who should be forbidden from ever approaching her. Yet, somehow, his fairy godmother had sprinkled him with magic dust and brought him to Selina's attention.

He sneered at the romantic drivel running through his mind. Yeah. Now all he needed was to crash a royal ball and sweep her off her feet.

13

Pain pierced Selina's jaw for the second time while she paced back and forth in the short span of the reception area at the Federation Interplanetary Trade Bureau. She needed to stop clenching her teeth. It wasn't like her to get worked up over a delayed meeting. In truth, she could have handled waiting on the trade representative if the rest of her life wasn't messed up.

After Maon's call, she'd berated herself. She'd said she needed him. What was wrong with her? More proof that she couldn't curb her need to rely on a man. She would not be that woman. It was obvious. She could have nothing more to do with him. What was the saying about ending not with a bang but a whimper? The ending to their almost relationship had been a whimper. But she'd refused to shed tears. Wasn't this what she wanted? Then no regrets. Maon was out of her life. Time to get back on course, but since then, the feds and the marshals had dealt her setback after setback.

The answers the marshal outside her door had given her were evasive. Wait for the chief to contact her. Waiting wasn't her strong suit. Frustrated, she'd commed marshal headquarters and been given the runaround until finally she was forwarded to Marshal Gage. He'd filled her in on the new developments and told her the chief was working on an action plan for dealing with her situation. She'd asked what the hell that meant, but Gage hadn't seemed to know other than she was to remain in her room under guard for the near future.

The brief period she'd spent stewing over that information had been interrupted by a call from an import-export agent from the Fed's trade bureau. He was calling to request a meeting to discuss her revoked pyantha license. *Damn.* Waiting for Chief Fiddle About to get his action plan in place so she could go where she needed to go was no longer an option. With the meeting scheduled for early afternoon at fourteen, she'd opened her room door and informed the marshal he had five minutes to get her transportation, or she'd be walking to the Federation Trade Bureau. With no desire to anger her further, the marshal had an air car and backup ready within the time limit. She'd acknowledged his assistance with a sharp nod, irritation tamped down. At last something had gone her way.

The pain in her jaw interrupted Selina's reverie. She relaxed it, moving it from side to side, and strode to the reception desk. Fourteen had come and gone. For the third time, she asked how long she was expected to wait. The receptionist narrowed her eyes and flattened her lips in a line as though she needed to redraw the barrier of acceptability that Selina insisted on crossing. With snip in her voice, she told Selina that Mr. Kowloon knew she was here and would be with her as soon as possible. Selina stiffened and prepared to return to pacing when a yellow button on the receptionist's panel lit.

The receptionist pinched a smile at Selina and said, "Mr. Kowloon is available now." She rose and led Selina to his office, knocked, and opened the door. "Ms. Shirley, sir."

"Thank you, Ms. Potselm." He held out a hand to Selina. "Ms. Shirley, thank you for coming in."

Selina shook his hand, letting her former frustration bleed away. She couldn't let her irritation show. "Of course." Kowloon's attire was much as she would expect a low-level bureaucrat to wear, synthetic fabrics in drab colors. The only odd element was the dark-brown-striped Nehru jacket. It had been almost a century since anyone had worn them, but he had obviously dressed to impress her. He made a pronounced display of adjusting his cuffs. She quashed her amusement. Mr. Kowloon would be manageable. She liked offbeat people. *And who knows? Maybe it's time for a revival of the Nehru jacket.*

When both were seated, Kowloon said, "The revocation of the House of Shirley pyantha license, I think you'll agree, was inevitable with the smuggling problem that has come to light."

Selina nodded. "Yes. When I requested an investigation into missing shipments, theft was my chief concern. The Audrina segment of the House of Shirley has always been a family-run business. Most Audrina employees have been with the firm for many years. To discover that two of our most trusted staff were involved in this scheme is..."

Kowloon shifted forward to interrupt, his eyes glittering. "It must have been devastating. I'm not privy to all the details. Yet. But the news vids are saying that a body has been found at the plant."

Selina blinked when the impression registered that he wanted to gossip with her. "Yes. I was told this morning that James Short, the plant manager, was discovered in one of the construction forms."

"And you were shot at?" Kowloon's eyebrows rose.

"Yes. But I've been told not to discuss the investigation. I'm sure you understand."

Kowloon leaned back, crossing his arms. "Naturally. Police matter. These things happen on Gallarda more often than I like to acknowledge. Unfortunately, the serious nature of the violation of your license means you must go through a complete recertification process."

Selina furrowed her forehead. The ultimatum was expected, but now that Kowloon had said it, she didn't believe he'd stick to it. "I'm sure you understand that the time involved would be catastrophic to our plans to expand our use of pyantha fiber in our clothing lines. Security oversight procedures for the new plants here on Gallarda and Qingdao have been vetted by bureau officials on Tallav. The Gallardan expansion included upgrading and merging security of the older section of the plant with the new. If we expedited arrangements to upgrade our Tallavan facility, a temporary revocation would suit both the Federation and the House of Shirley. Getting our mill up and running on Gallarda means more jobs outside the pyantha extract trade."

Kowloon relaxed, dropping his arms while Selina spoke. Her conciliatory tone was having the hoped-for effect. "You make some good points. I hadn't considered that you were already in essence going through a recertification." Kowloon nodded. "Yes, Ms. Shirley. I believe I can work with you under those conditions. Expansion of legal trade on Gallarda is a priority of the bureau. I'll pass on my recommendations to the office on Tallav. I can't guarantee they'll agree, but it seems likely to me."

"Thank you. I appreciate your assistance. It's been a pleasure meeting you. You've been very helpful. Perhaps when we hold the official plant-opening ceremony, you or other members of the trade bureau would like to attend," Selina said.

"The pleasure has been mine. I'm sure the bureau would welcome sending a contingent to the opening." He shook his head, a sad smile on his lips. "It's unfortunate that things like this have to happen. Will you be staying on Gallarda long?"

Selina twisted her lips in a wry grin. "I have no idea. The chief marshal is creating an action plan to deal with me, which I am yet to be privy to."

"Let's hope there are no more attacks!" Kowloon's eyes widened.

"Thank you. I agree wholeheartedly."

PLEASED THAT THE appointment with Mr. Kowloon had gone so well, Selina directed the bodyguard accompanying her, Marshal Pickering, to take her to marshal headquarters. If only the meeting with Chief Fitzgerald went as well. When she entered the bull pen at marshal headquarters, she noticed that no one would look directly at her. Eyes were quickly averted when she looked at anyone.

"Is there someplace I can wait to meet with Chief Fitzgerald?" she asked Pickering.

"Yes, ma'am." He led her to a conference room that reeked of stim smoke and stale café. "Have a seat. I'll have Fiona see if you need anything." He left without awaiting a response.

Selina eased into a battered chair that squeaked when she sat and skidded on its rollers. Planting her feet to avoid touching any of the tatty furnishings, Selina stopped the chair's movement. A tap sounded at the door, and a sunny-faced redhead poked her head in.

"Ms. Shirley? I'm Fiona. Would you like something to drink? We have the usual canned stuff, or I could get into the chief's stash and make you some coffee."

"Coffee would be wonderful, Fiona."

"Right. I'll be back in a moment. Cream or sugar?"

"Both please. Two sugar." Selina smiled cordially.

"Right."

While Selina waited for Fiona to return, she assessed the damage to her plans for the clothing line. She gripped her forehead, a stress headache niggling at her temples. Her plate, already too full, was now running over with more problems than one person could handle. Someone would have to remain on Gallarda and deal with the situation here. At least until the new mill manager they'd hired was on the job and the plant had successfully begun production. Maybe Katerina would agree to come, but with the arrest of her sister, who knew? Selina needed to visit the plant manager's family and offer her sympathies. His involvement in the smuggling was likely, but her parents were adamant that Shirleys took care of their employees and their families.

Fiona opened the door, carrying two steaming cups of coffee. "Here we go." She placed a cup in front of Selina and then sat in a chair. "I made a full pot and brought some to the chief first. He said I should keep you company. I figure we can have a little girls' natter."

Selina took a sip of her coffee, closing her eyes and smiling before returning her focus to Fiona. "Sounds good. You're from Tallav. How'd you end up on Gallarda?"

Fiona's chuckle was accompanied by a roll of her eyes. "My mum and dad are in service to the Phelans. It was expected for me to follow along." She shook her head. "I had other ideas. Wanted to live. Travel farther than the next village on from the estate. Dad thought a visit to Cahernamon would cure me, but it only made me want to explore off Tallav. The marshals take on female clerical staff, so I applied." With a rueful grin and another self-deprecating eye roll, she said, "I expected something a little more glamorous than Gallarda."

"You've traded one agricultural planet for another," Selina commiserated, sipping from her cup.

"Yeah, not as picturesque either. But it has a few perks."

Selina raised an eyebrow.

Fiona gave her a nod. "The marshals stationed here don't have much for female companionship. I figure I have a decent chance of hooking me a third or fourth son. If I did, he could stay in the marshals, and we could find a planet to our liking."

Selina took another sip. "Sounds like a plan. I haven't dealt with anyone other than Marshals Gage and Pickering, but they both seem like good men."

Fiona swallowed a swig of her own coffee before looking into her cup. "Oh, Pickering has a girl back home. And Gage... Well...he fits the bill but can be standoffish. Doesn't say much when I chat him up."

"Maybe he's shy around women. Sometimes the first conclusion you have about a person is the opposite of the truth. Shy people are often considered stuck up," Selina offered.

"Well, and you're the picture of that being true. All those men are treading on pop berries, worrying about you taking their heads off. You could yell *boo* down the hall, and they'd all jump out of their chairs."

Fiona's merry eyes and smirk made it clear she'd enjoy watching Selina do just that, but Selina couldn't figure out what she'd done to cause that kind of reaction. "Where did they get that impression?"

"Rumor mill says you demanded the chief fire Marshal Keefe. Which I didn't believe was right, because Fitzy likes to stir up a tizzy in a piss pot whenever possible," Fiona said.

"I'd only spoken with Gage and Marshal Keefe after the attack. Why didn't Gage squelch the rumor?" Selina asked.

"He grunted his objections when he first heard the gossip, but no one paid attention. True or not, it was too juicy to pass up. The Aunt Minnies had to natter on." Fiona shook her head and drank from her cup. "Never you mind. I'll set things straight." Her eyes got that blank look that meant she was receiving a comm message. When her eyes refocused, she said, "The chief is ready to see you. If you feel like lowering your guns on anyone, he'd be the perfect target. His replacement will be here in two months, and we're counting the days."

"Thanks, Fiona." Selina rose and followed Fiona to Fitzgerald's office.

Fiona announced Selina. Fitzgerald rose from behind his pristine desk and approached her, hand held out. "Ms. Shirley. It is such a pleasure to meet you." Even, white teeth beamed at her from the midst of a light brown mustache and short beard. With one hand, he clasped Selina's while the other hand patted it. "I have heard so many fine things about you and your family. It is indeed an honor."

Selina pulled her hand out of the overly long handshake. "Thank you. May I sit?"

"Oh my. Yes. Yes. Please do. Would you like another cup of coffee? Fiona, more coffee. Oh my. Yes."

"Chief Fitzgerald," Selina began.

"Oh, please call me Edward." He looked at her with an air of expectancy, but she didn't reciprocate the offer.

"Edward, can you explain why I was being held in my room practically a prisoner?"

Fitzgerald's hands rose palms forward. "Oh my. No. No, not a prisoner. Indeed no. It was for your own safety while I determined the nature of the danger."

"And have you determined the nature of the danger?"

"Oh my. Yes. That is a work in progress. Indeed, in progress. An official team should arrive in...let's see...yes...four days and thirteen hours. They will, needless to say, be assuming lead in the investigation when they arrive." Fitzgerald clasped his hands and looked at her, his mustache wiggling.

Selina deepened the scowl on her face. "Does this mean you intend to keep me in my room until then?"

Fitzgerald straightened and puffed his thin chest out. "Oh my. Yes. Indeed, yes. I understand your appointment today was vital, but we can't have you traveling about by air car, visiting places of business. Too dangerous. Much too dangerous."

"If that's your position, I have no reason to remain on Gallarda. Please have a shuttle available to lift to the station. My luggage is packed and ready. Please allow Marshal Gage to accompany me," Selina said.

"Oh my. No. No, you mustn't leave. No. Indeed, no."

"May I ask why?" Selina responded, voice stern.

"The Tallavan team will want to speak with you. Most assuredly. No. Indeed no. You must be here when they arrive." Fitzgerald was blinking rapidly, his ears tinged pink.

"I have made my statement. I have nothing additional to it. If I do, I will do so to Sector Chief Davis. Directly. Please make whatever arrangements are necessary for my departure."

At that moment, Fiona tapped on the door and stepped in with a tray of coffee. "Ah, Fiona," Selina said. "You're clerical staff here. May I assume that you are responsible for making travel reservations?" Fiona nodded with a quick glance at Fitzgerald. "Excellent. I'll need a shuttle available at the spaceport to take me to the station. Please inform Marshal Gage that I'd like him to accompany me."

"Yes, ma'am. Sir?" When Fitzgerald didn't respond, Fiona ducked from the room.

Selina held Fitzgerald with her unwavering gaze. "Thank you for your concern, Edward. But it's clear this is best for everyone. I hope to provide a good report to Davis of my experience here."

"Oh. Yes. Indeed, yes. We've done our utmost in this difficult circumstance. Please allow us to assist if we can do anything else before you leave." He showed his precise little teeth once again, but the smile was not cheery.

With a flutter of her fingers at the marshals, Selina breezed through the bull pen. Her mother would be proud. Outside she climbed into the car that Marshal Gage had waiting. That was quick. Must have been Fiona. Selina smiled.

"Is my luggage loaded?"

"Yes, ma'am."

"Excellent. Thank you, Gage."

"You're welcome."

"I have one stop to make before the spaceport. I wish to offer my condolences to the widow of James Short. Would that be possible?"

"Yes, ma'am. I believe she's been asked to remain home during the investigation. I can take you there."

"Perfect. Thank you."

Relieved to be finally on her way, Selina positioned herself so she could observe Gage's face in the rearview mirror of the car. After a bit of rambling, one-sided, polite chat, Selina said, "Fiona's a nice girl." Gage grunted in response. "She assumed you were standoffish, but I told her you were shy around women." He rolled his shoulders without speaking. "That's what I thought. Some advice. Look at her when she's talking to you and respond to her with a word or two when she pauses. She's perfectly happy to carry the conversation, but she needs to know you enjoy being with her. Understand?"

"Yes, ma'am." He rolled his shoulders again. "Thank you, ma'am. I'll work on it."

Selina smiled. Under her breath she said, "You do that." Maybe Fiona could have her happily ever after. For herself, she was going to concentrate on an acceptable ever after.

14

Maon steeled himself. On the trip home from Gallarda, he'd mentally prepared himself for this meeting with Sector Chief Davis. The man was fair, but Maon had also heard Davis could be a stickler with those that liked to color outside the lines. Maon hadn't needed Shane's input this time. What Shane would advise him was evident. *Tell the truth.* That was what Maon intended to do.

When he walked to the lift in the lobby of marshal headquarters, Davis was waiting. He turned and greeted Maon. "Maon. I should apologize. I gave you the Shirley assignment to ease you back into work. Seems I put you right in the thick of it. I'm glad you handled it well. Back up in the saddle and all that. Getting shot at again wasn't part of the plan, though." He chuckled and slapped Maon on the back while they entered.

"Thank you, sir." Maon blinked slowly, drawing in a deep breath through his nose, then releasing it, attempting to keep his relief from showing. Davis wasn't angry with him. Although the chief still might chew him out, Maon hoped he wouldn't receive a formal reprimand. After entering his office with Maon, Davis moved around to sit behind his desk, gesturing Maon to a chair opposite. "Have a seat. I bet you're wondering why I didn't let you stay on Gallarda and assist the team."

Maon nodded. "Yes, sir."

"Two reasons. There was a perception on Gallarda that you had crossed boundaries with Ms. Shirley." Davis looked straight at Maon.

Maon struggled to maintain eye contact. "Sir, I never—"

"I'm sure you didn't. Your service record shows you're by the book. That makes me certain you followed the letter of the law. The spirit of the law…I'm not so sure about."

"Sir."

"Let me finish. You have a reputation as a ladies' man. Tell me. Infatuation, indiscretion, or something more?" From the stern look on Davis's face, Maon's response was crucial to the man's opinion of his worth as a marshal.

But the answer was there, waiting for him to acknowledge fully that what he felt for Selina Shirley was something he'd never felt before and couldn't label. It came from deep inside him.

"Something more, sir." A muscle in Maon's jaw tightened.

Davis pursed his lips and nodded. "Well, then. Let me tell you what you're going to do. No contact while the case is still active. After that, give it a month, time for people to focus on the next little kerfuffle. Can you do that?"

Maon raised his chin higher. "Yes, sir. Not a problem."

"Good. I'm putting a notice of warning in your file. If you keep your nose clean, it will be pulled in three months." Davis tapped his fingers against his desk.

"Thank you, sir." Maon ducked his head for a moment.

"Now the good news." Davis chuckled when Maon brought his head back up. "You did an excellent job handling the Shirley case. I'll be honest. I thought it was an employee theft problem. You proved me wrong."

"Thank you." Maon forced back the grin that threatened to spread across his face.

"I never would have pegged you for a data dink, but you've shown your talent. After some initial training, we'll be assigning you to one of the system planets as a data analyst. How does that sound?"

Maon beamed. "That sounds very good, sir. Data analysis has been my goal since the academy."

"Excellent. You can access your schedule for the details. I understand you have a medical issue that needs attended to."

Maon's brow wrinkled. What did Davis mean? Not trauma counseling?

"The nerve in your side. Several days are allotted before your training begins to take care of that. But even before that, I need you to finish some work on the Shirley case."

"I thought I'd submitted complete reports."

"You did. No, Liza Donnelly has agreed to confess all, but only if she confesses to you." Davis's expression was pinched, eyes narrowed.

"Me?" Maon's mouth fell open.

"Yes, you. She says she trusts you."

"Hmm."

"Get yourself settled today. I've set up the interrogation for tomorrow at nine at HQ examination room three. I'll attend, as will the system drug-enforcement chief."

Davis tapped his fingers against the desk. Maon read that as his signal the meeting was over. He rose from his seat. "Thank you, sir. I'll be there."

Maon was light-headed, his legs a little weak when he walked to the closest bathroom. Inside he leaned against the door. An analyst. They were making him an analyst. He'd done it. Caught between laughing and crying, he brought his fists up. "Yes!" And then he did laugh.

He felt the door push against his back and moved away from it. A marshal stopped, held the door open, and cocked a quizzical look at him. "You okay?"

Maon grinned broadly. "Better than okay," he said, took hold of the door, and brushed past the other man.

MAON HADN'T BEEN certain what to wear when taking someone's confession. He assumed the regulars had a protocol, but he wasn't a regular, so he opted for slacks and shirt as he would on any ordinary day. Sleep hadn't come easily last night. He'd been too tangled up in a miasma of thoughts about events on Gallarda, his relationship with Selina, and what he would learn from Liza Donnelly. *Time to find out.*

When he entered the interrogation chamber, Liza was already sitting slightly reclined in the cushioned examination chair. Her arm was encased in the biometric analysis unit, and her head had been positioned and restrained so that the analysis cameras could monitor her right eye and full face. The blue ambient lighting mediated the anxiety the restraints caused, as did the scent that was diffused through the ventilation system. The room's configuration could change, depending on the person being interrogated and their willingness to confess. This was Maon's first time in the room conducting an interview, although he had been present for several on the opposite side of the viewing panel.

Maon settled himself on the padded metal stool. The lumbar support had been raised to accommodate his torso. When seated, he could look directly into Liza's face without blocking the cameras. Liza blinked up at him and gave him a slight smile. The mild relaxant given to her when the analysis nanites had been injected into her bloodstream was working.

Maon took her hand in his, giving it a slight squeeze. "Hello, Liza."

"Hello, Marshal. What's new?"

Maon didn't miss the sadness that flooded her eyes. "I've been to Gallarda and back."

Liza attempted to turn her head, but the restraints prevented her. Maon squeezed her hand again. "It's all right, Liza. You're going to tell me your story, from the beginning, and I'm going to listen. Okay?"

Liza smiled weakly and said, "Yeah."

"First I need to ask you one more time. Do you freely agree to waive your privilege against self-incrimination and to have legal representation present?"

"Yes."

"Do you acknowledge that anything you state during this interview can be used against you in criminal proceedings, and that you have not been coerced into making this confession?"

"Yes."

Maon patted her hand. "Start from the beginning. What sent you down this path?"

With a sigh, she began. "It seemed like easy money, and no one would be hurt."

She pressed her lips together, blinking rapidly.

"A Gallardan I'd met on a trip to Beta Tau had introduced me to using pyantha seeds as an aphrodisiac. Chewing one or two seeds doesn't get you blissed out like bliss beads do. There's no risk. It makes you feel hornier and makes the sex amazing. He gave me a small packet to take with me.

"Later I met a sheik from Ma'a Alheyaht. I told him about the seeds. He offered to pay me to send him packets on a regular basis. I knew it was illegal, but he offered a lot of money for enough for him and his friends to use with their harems. I asked James Short, the manager at the Shirley Gallardan mill, what he thought about it. He said he would help. He put the bags of seed into yarn shipments and told me when they were coming. I'd set aside those shipments for inspection and wait until the shipping room was empty to open them. When an order that included pyantha shawls was due to go out, I'd pack the seeds into it and then contact the Federated Express clerk on Tollonia we'd found to work with us. I opened a second House of Shirley shipping account. He'd switch the shipping data slide to one using the secondary account, which directed the delivery to the sheikh. The clerk assumed we were stealing not smuggling."

"What is his name?" Maon asked.

"Milakh Canzione. Is he okay?"

"We'll find out. Was anyone else involved? Anyone else working for the Shirleys?"

"No. Just James and I." A tear rolled down her cheek. "I don't know who killed James. It doesn't make sense to me. We've been doing this for years, and no one ever threatened us."

"When was your last shipment exchange?"

"The evening gown order to Hampton. The other two lost shipments you were looking at, those I had nothing to do with."

Maon furrowed his forehead. "The samples to Qingdao were sent after the Hampton shipment. Correct?"

"Yes. I remember because it had special handling. It was shipped a couple of days later."

"Okay. For the record. Were you responsible for the death of James Short?"

"No. I wasn't." Liza's eyes darkened. Her chin quivered.

"Were you responsible for the attempted murder of Selina Shirley?"

"No, I was not. I wouldn't do that."

"I didn't think so, Liza, but it was necessary to ask." He squeezed her hand. "Have you or anyone working with you or for you ever illegally shipped pyantha extract?"

"No. Just bags of seeds."

"How much seed did you send per shipment?"

"We shipped one ounce at a time. That's a lot of seeds since they're small and lightweight."

"Did you ever ship more than that?"

"No, if the sheikh needed more sooner than usual, we sent an extra order."

"What is the name of the sheikh?"

"Sheikh Gunther Al-Chadun," she responded.

"Gunther?" Maon looked at her with a slight smile.

Liza lifted her shoulder in a small shrug. "Family name, I think."

"And he's a citizen of Ma'a Alheyaht?"

"Yes, that's what he told me, and that's where we shipped the pyantha seeds."

"Is there anything else you wish to tell me?"

Liza's forehead wrinkled. "No, I've told you everything."

"Liza, in a few minutes, your attorney and the prosecutor will sit down and explain your legal jeopardy. Do you have any questions for me?"

"No. No questions. I wish you'd caught us before James was killed. Please find out who did that." Lower lip trembling, Liza blinked back tears.

"The marshals service will do its best, Liza." He patted her hand. "Okay. The tech will get you out of this rig. Take care."

Maon had been invited to join the debrief in the interrogation room's viewing space to discuss Liza's confession. He entered the hall, closing the door behind him, and turned the handle on the unmarked door next to it. Sector Chief Davis and the drug-enforcement chief, Brewer, were seated in dark plasti-form chairs on a raised platform. Maon paused when he opened the door, allowing the prosecutor to exit before moving inside to stand before them.

"Good job, Keefe. You handled that just right," said Davis. "My assistant informed me that the Tollonian, Canzione, was found dead in his apartment before our investigation began. An apparent suicide."

"Marshal Keefe. Brewer, system chief for drug enforcement. We haven't met before," Brewer said.

Maon regarded the heavyset older man. He'd heard of Brewer, but they'd never been formally introduced. "No, sir. We haven't."

"Your interview with Donnelly has provided the info we needed to wrap up this investigation. I'm glad we waited for you to get back rather than attempt a hostile suspect interrogation. Give us your take on what you've learned today," Brewer said.

Maon looked down for a moment before raising his head to look at Brewer. "Well, it looks to me that Donnelly's petty crime ring drew the attention of a larger drug-smuggling syndicate. The samples shipment must have been stolen as proof that the House of Shirley was expanding their use of pyantha fiber. A new pyantha fabric mill on Qingdao must have raised hackles since it is a jumping-off point for smuggling via the Drift to the broader Federation."

Brewer nodded and gestured to Davis. "That was our take. It's our guess that someone believed that Selina Shirley had discovered the ring and was taking over and expanding. Whoever that someone is, they started killing people on very little evidence. I'll never understand why criminals make things harder on themselves by eschewing the simple for the complex."

Maon winced, rubbing a hand over his chest. Liza Donnelly's regret would be doubled when she learned that her grand plan to avoid detection hadn't been necessary. Two deaths and her own imprisonment resulted from her misunderstanding of the law. "It's unfortunate that Donnelly didn't realize that pyantha-seed smuggling of an ounce or less is a misdemeanor. She could have had the sheikh order a shawl or even yarn for repair and added the seed to the shipment. Now she faces prison for repeat counts of grand theft and must live with the death of two people involved with her."

Brewer pursed his lips to the side and looked away from Maon. "Hmm." With a glance toward Davis, he said, "It looks like we have enough to wrap up this case. We'll turn over the Short and Canzione murder investigations to the local authorities. An official announcement of Donnelly's arrest, along with a leak of pertinent details to the press, should remove any danger to Ms. Shirley. We'll continue protection detail until then and advise her to hire a bodyguard after that."

Both men rose and stepped down from the platform, ending the meeting. While Maon held the door for them, Davis exited, patting Maon's shoulder. "Again, good job, Keefe. Consider your month of no contact with Ms. Shirley starts now." He smiled and gave Maon another pat on the arm before leaving.

Maon brushed his hand up to smooth his hair while his mind rummaged through possible scenarios with Selina. Before he knew it, he found himself back at his apartment.

15

In the three and a half weeks since he'd returned to Tallav, Maon hadn't had any downtime. After hearing Liza Donnelly's confession, he'd been scheduled for immediate outpatient surgery to deal with the trapped nerve in his side. With speedheal he'd been back to work in two days.

The period of initial data-analyst training had been a breeze. He was going to pass faster than any previous student. Not a surprise. He'd already read the pertinent manuals and courseware over the shoulder of a friend who'd gone through the training last year. The duty station request form was sitting in his EBC, awaiting his decision on where he preferred to be assigned. Before he filled it out, he wanted to discuss it with Shane. Finally, Maon felt more like his old self and with some spare time to fill, he was looking forward to facing Shane in the gravity court. Maon grinned while heading to the court he'd scheduled for their match. It would give his pain-free side a good workout, and he loved when he beat Shane.

Shane was already there. After a backslapping hug, they began play, interspersing the game with conversation. Soon the smell of sweat and hot male bodies permeated the white cube. Maon was attempting to go two up on Shane. His gravity ball record against Shane was 216-215. Maon rarely got two games ahead of him.

Maon hit a shot toward the upper left corner. The ball ricocheted off the back wall to the ceiling and then dropped. "Rumor has it you've been given a new posting."

Shane met the ball and hit it high into the same corner, grunting a noncommittal response.

Maon returned Shane's shot with a slam that popped the ball up high. "No one seems to know where to. So give."

Shane leaped, stretching his six feet seven inches to slam the ball back down, making it fly in even higher. "Nothing big," Shane responded.

"Crap," Maon yelled, attempting to reach the ball with a leap of his own. When he missed it by inches, Shane laughed.

Shane bounced the ball, preparing to serve. "Your news is bigger. Did I not tell you your career was fine?"

"You did. But you have to admit it wasn't leading to a data-analyst position."

"You would have got there eventually." Shane served, and Maon dodged left, pumping the ball away from him in a curling throw that set the ball flying in an unpredictable direction after it hit the back wall.

Shane got his racket on the ball, but his return set up an easy shot for Maon. "Finding a drug-smuggling ring and saving Selina Shirley's ass..." He handled Maon's return and sent the ball spinning to the lower right corner. "That's what did the trick." Maon ran toward the ball, barely hitting it with the rim of his racket. The ball dropped to the floor.

"My point." Shane held the ball and looked directly at Maon. "No one believes the Gallardan chief's report. What a fucking prick." Shane served hard, high and center.

"Yeah." Maon deflected a shot to the upper right with a backhand swing. "Are you going to tell me or not?"

"Rebecca O'Bannon," Shane hollered when he jumped to make an overhand cannonball that came flying straight back at Maon.

Maon, unable to get under the ball, ceded the point. He waved his racket at Shane and said, "That's not what I asked. Wait. What about Rebecca O'Bannon?"

"I'm escorting her to the Marshals' Banquet." A low serve took Maon off guard.

He chased down the ball and bounced it to Shane. "Really. She asked you?"

"She did." Shane served low and hard again. Maon caught the ball in the gravity hole of his racket and sent a soft shot ricocheting off the back wall, ceiling, and sidewall that then petered out and fell abruptly. Shane's plunge to reach it failed, and his racket clattered to the floor.

"Wow. And I don't just mean that impressive dive." Maon smirked. "Stop avoiding the question. What's your new assignment?"

Shane rolled over, sitting up and resting his arms on his knees. With his own smirk, he said, "Beta Tau."

"You're kidding." Maon reached and offered Shane a hand up.

"No. Beta Tau," Shane said, fetching the ball. "They have an opening for a data analyst. If you apply and get it, we could go together after the banquet." Maon caught the ball when Shane said, "Your serve."

Maon tossed the ball in his hands, staring at the back of the court. Beta Tau. That could be ideal. Shane cleared his throat, and he returned his attention to the game.

THE ANNUAL MARSHALS' Banquet was a combination of dinner, recognition ceremony, and boring speakers. If the participants stayed, there was dancing afterward. Maon had been told to attend. While he studied himself in the full-length mirror in his bedroom, he flicked lint off the shoulder of his jacket. He wasn't inclined to dress up, but his mother had insisted before he went to the Marshal Academy that he purchase an evening suit. The new vest he'd bought to replace the black brocade was a fiery red orange. His black bolo evening tie was held in place with a miniature gold marshal's badge.

Fuck's sake, he looked fine. Selina ought to appreciate his homage to her. During the time since they'd left Gallarda, she hadn't once attempted to contact him. Unable to call her himself, he had hoped to explain his restrictions when she called him. But she hadn't. Well, his month wasn't quite up, but tonight he would find out where he stood with her. She could be the single Tallavan woman who not only understood him, but could also keep him in his place. He'd finally admitted to himself that he longed for a wife and children, a family. If she was his only hope, he would not lose her without a fight.

His date should be arriving below to pick him up. The cold black metal of his pistol was a reassuring presence in his hand. Strapping on his service weapon had become a ritual that was both comfortable and comforting. He checked the charge level of the cartridge. Full. After securing the gun in his side holster, he ensured the extra cartridges were also fully charged. Now he felt like a marshal. Like a man capable of handling all that life threw at him. Not a nerve-soaked suitor hidden inside the formal armor of a Tallavan aristocrat. Taking one final look in the mirror, he smoothed his vest and jacket back in place. He was ready.

An older dark-blue sedan had pulled up to the front of his building when Maon exited the automatic door. A uniformed driver jumped out and moved toward him. "Marshal Keefe?"

"Yep. That's me," Maon responded.

"Madame is waiting in the car for you." The driver returned to the vehicle and opened the back door for Maon.

"Thanks," Maon said when the driver shut him in. He turned his attention to the woman in the seat next to him, a big grin settling on his face. "Audrina, you will without a doubt put every other lady to shame at the banquet. You are beauty itself."

Audrina giggled, smoothing the turquoise chiffon of her gown, and tilted her head so her diamond earrings showed to best effect. "I knew there was a reason I asked you to accompany me this evening. I'm the one who will be envied with such a good-looking charmer at my side." She reached out and patted his hand. "Have we flattered each other sufficiently for tonight?" The merriment wreathing her face communicated her enjoyment of the banter.

"A gentleman always assures the lady receives the final compliment. So I must say, your eyes are like two of the fairest stars in all the heavens." While he spoke, Maon focused round, soft eyes on her, his mouth faltering with a tremulous smile.

"Oh my, stop the calf eyes. I recognize Shakespeare when I hear it." Audrina laughed. "Dear boy, you are such fun." She grasped his hand. "How have you been?"

Maon squeezed. "Good. I'm being reassigned to Beta Tau as a data analyst. It's the position I've always wanted."

"Marvelous! Hmmm. Beta Tau. I'd hoped you'd be assigned to Tallav. I won't hide the fact that I thought you and Selina would make a perfect match." After a quick glance at Maon, Audrina turned and looked away, shaking her head.

"Then I won't hide the fact that I agree."

Audrina faced him. "Do you? Then why haven't you done something about it?"

"The chief on Gallarda reported me for improper conduct toward Selina." When Audrina's brow furrowed, he said, "I spent the night in Selina's room in a recliner, guarding her after the attack."

"What's improper about that?"

"Nothing. If I'd done so from a chair outside her door." Maon grinned ruefully. "I was ordered not to contact Selina for a month after the case was closed out. It's a few days shy, but even so, I intend to speak with her tonight. I assume she'll be there."

Audrina nodded. "She will. She's bringing a date. Filip Patinka. If it were me, you'd have him beaten hands down, but Selina..." She lifted her shoulders in a genteel shrug. "Selina has been dating every milksop she could find among the aristocracy. She's treating it like she's hiring an employee. She seems to have settled on Patinka. She's installed him in her apartment to see if they suit physically."

Maon clenched his fist, ready to hit the car door but caught himself, drawing in a slow, steady breath and relaxing his hand. "I don't understand Selina. We had a shaky start. That and the job made me back off after we left Beta Tau. It seemed to make things better between us. We were talking and getting acquainted without anything physical. That last night on Gallarda, she helped me deal with my own screwy issues. Even teased me. When she returned to Tallav, she never tried to call me, and I couldn't call her. Fuck, I just don't get it." He scrubbed a hand over his face. "Sorry, excuse my language. I shouldn't take my frustration out on you."

Audrina rubbed his arm through his coat sleeve. "Speak with her. Perhaps it's a misunderstanding."

Maon grimaced. "Oh, I intend to speak with her." With effort, he forced Selina to the back of his mind and focused again on Audrina, allowing a smile to return to his lips. "Meanwhile I intend to enjoy the company of one of my best girls."

"You're such a flirt."

WHEN MAON and Audrina moved into the reception room at the Bellmount Club, she waved at friends. Maon held her elbow and leaned in to whisper in her ear. "Would you care for a drink?"

"Yes, please, dear. I'd like a Manhattan. I'll be over there with Mary Beth Hayden."

"Coming right up." Maon made his way through the milling crowd, heading toward the bar. The understated elegance of the club was complemented by women in jewel-toned evening gowns and men in more muted evening suits, sporting splashes of the same jewel tones in their choice of vest and tie. While he stood waiting his turn to order from the bartender, a physically fit, middle-aged man approached him.

"Maon Keefe?"

"Yes, sir," Maon responded with a genial smile.

"This probably isn't the best place to do this. I was sent an invitation to the banquet and decided it was time I spoke with you."

Maon's forehead wrinkled, the smile leaving his face. The man looked familiar, but Maon couldn't remember him. "What is this concerning, sir?"

The man gave a choked laugh. "You don't recognize me. I guess that's to be expected. It's been many years." His dark-blue stare fixed on Maon. "I'm your father, Maon."

Maon's eyes widened, and he took a step backward.

The man held a hand in front of Maon. "Please. Before you say anything. I realize we can't talk here. I'd like to tell you what happened twenty years ago, and why it's taken so long to contact you. That's all I'm asking. If you can do that, here's my card. Contact me to arrange a visit. Your aunt and I both would like to speak with you."

Maon took the proffered card with numb fingers. The shock of being blindsided by the person he'd longed for as a boy and came to loathe in later years reawakened buried emotions. That hatred had turned to indifference once he'd outgrown his adolescent angst, but vestiges of anger spilled out from somewhere deep inside. Between gritted teeth, he said, "I'd like to hear what you have to say, because frankly whatever excuse you have for abandoning me can't begin to make up for the pain you caused me and my mother." He pointed the card at his father. "You will hear from me."

His father's shoulders slumped, and he shook his head. "I'm so sorry, Son. I'll await your call." Maon stared at him while his father turned and slowly walked away.

After taking the two Manhattans the bartender handed him, Maon worked his way back through the crowd to Audrina.

"Maon, I was telling Mary Beth how you saved Selina's life." When Audrina looked up at him, the smile on her face froze. "My dear. What's happened? Are you well? You've gone pale."

Maon pushed her drink toward her, and she took it, searching his face for clues. "I've just met my father."

"Isn't Johnathan Keefe your father?"

"Yes." Maon grimaced. Fingers wrapped rigidly around his glass, he drank the cocktail in two rapid swallows.

Mary Beth quietly excused herself.

"But what do you mean, you just met him?"

"I haven't seen him since I was six. That was when he left my mother and me." Maon stared at his shoes, wishing he could be almost anywhere else but here with his emotions on display for all the crème of society.

"My dear, I don't know what you've been told about your father, but it's my understanding he didn't leave your mother as much as she rejected him. Has no one ever told you how he's cared for your aunt all these years?" Audrina asked, her voice soft, making it hard for others to overhear.

"Do you plan to drink that?" He pointed at Audrina's Manhattan. She handed it to him, and he tossed it back in one long gulp. With both glasses in hand, he shoved them toward a server, who took them from him.

She pursed her lips. "Come here," she said, pulling him toward the corner. "Your aunt was hurt in a terrible car accident while your father was at the wheel. She's been through years of medical procedures, and he has cared for her through it all. He's the kindest, dearest man. I had no idea your mother had kept him from you." She grasped his arm. "Oh, my dear. I'm so sorry."

The floor seemed to shift under Maon's feet. "Audrina, I need to leave."

Audrina bit her lip. "No, no, you can't leave."

"I can't stay, Audrina. Can we go?"

"Oh. I'm not supposed to tell you, but..." She shook her head. "You're getting an award tonight. A big one. You have to stay."

Maon slumped. "What?" It was just a Purple Heart.

"Go splash some water on your face and catch your breath. I'll wait outside, and when you're ready, we can go sit at our table." She gave him a boost on the elbow toward the men's room.

Inside Maon faced the mirror. He didn't really look different, but since the shooting on Fed Central, his life had been nothing but drama. And now this. His father, after years of abandonment, wanted to meet with him. Hell. Audrina was waiting on him. He took a deep breath and adjusted his tie.

Maon walked from the bathroom to find her right where she said she'd be. Embarrassed that he'd gotten so emotional, he ducked his head when he approached her. She reached out with both hands and clasped his arms.

"You're looking much better." She regarded him in much the way he always imagined a mother should.

"Thank you, Audrina. Sludge sluiced off for now." He leaned down and kissed her cheek, grateful for her kindness.

She squeezed before letting him go. "People are taking their seats. Escort me in." She held out her hand and hooked her arm around Maon's when he offered it to her.

"Yes, ma'am."

With a sharp rap to his arm, she said, "You do not say 'yes, ma'am' to your date."

Maon gave her his half smile with a note of chagrin added. "Yes, oh beauteous flower."

Audrina lifted her chin. "That's better."

16

Selina paused her pacing to calm her temper. Her bedroom had seemed to shrink once Filip moved into it. The restful colors of sand and sea that had gone into the decorating of the room did nothing to ease her tension. They were already late for cocktails at the Marshals' Banquet, but Filip was asking her yet again if wearing a string tie was overstepping. "Filip, I'm sure they'll take it as the tribute you mean it to be. We're late. Please finish." Filip left the dressing room with a tie in either hand. Selina snatched one and clipped it around his neck. "There. You are very dashing."

He smiled at her, big brown eyes happy at the reassurance. "Thank you, Lina. You always know what to do."

Selina sighed. "Yes, I do. Come. The car is waiting."

Filip followed her, picking at a speck on his jacket sleeve. "You did make sure I'm having the chicken. Not the fish. I can't abide the fish they serve at these functions. Not that the chicken's much better, but I can at least choke it down."

Selina refused to allow the sigh that pressed at her to escape her lips. He'd continue prattling about the fish if she didn't affirm, for what must be the thousandth time, that he was indeed getting the chicken. "Yes, Filip. I double-checked that you'll be getting the chicken."

"Did you ask about the paprika?"

"Yes. There will be no paprika."

"Thank heavens. I'm sure I've told you before about the dreadful incident with the paprika on the chicken at Des Nuerdes."

"Hmmm." Selina was already putting her reactions on automatic. Their driver assisted them into the car. "I don't believe I've heard the paprika story." She had, but the story was long enough to take the entire trip to the banquet without requiring her to pay attention. She settled back into the leather seat while the car moved into traffic.

The pattern of the lace overlay on her gown included small holes, one of which was positioned over her thigh in the perfect spot for her to insert and remove her right index finger. This she did repeatedly, not paying attention to the finger or to Filip, who was deep into his paprika story.

Tonight was it. Most Tallavan aristocratic women entered society at a younger age, primarily to sample the men who were presenting themselves as potential spouses. She had eschewed the rounds of parties and dinners, focusing on expanding the House of Shirley. When her presence at the few charitable events she'd attended over the years was required, she'd dressed to be overlooked. She'd managed to escape the attention of all but the most desperate gold diggers.

Tonight would be her big reveal. Society would see the real Selina. Most wouldn't recognize her in flaming colors. She had no need to shroud herself in monotony anymore.

In the last month she'd taken her mousy persona on a round of parties, working her way through a series of men who outwardly fit the parameters for the perfect spouse. Looks hadn't even made the list. Nor had a charming personality. A complete lack of interest in her business had been in the top three. Submissive, happy to remain on the estate for extended periods of time without her, capable of raising children—all had been part of the mix. But even that last wasn't absolute. She could keep their children with her in Cahernamon.

Most of her potential candidates hadn't fit for one reason or another. Then she'd met Filip. He was happy to be pampered, giving Selina complete control over his life. He'd been trained by his mother to be the perfect Tallavan aristocratic husband. Good manners, devotion to aesthetics, and shallow thinking were his in abundance. He was someone she could trot out at society functions, capable of dealing with even the highest echelons of society. Otherwise she would ensconce him at Ettington, her family estate.

Filip broke into her thoughts. "You know how everyone can see everyone at Des Nuerdes?"

"Yes. No privacy at all," she said. And Filip was off again, describing the horrors of everyone watching him while his face grew absolutely purple from the excess of paprika.

Gods, she was going to have to ask Randolph what she was doing wrong. Filip couldn't shut up about himself. But self-centeredness was a key ingredient in the makeup of her perfect husband. Filip was entirely self-involved. He was quite possibly the neediest man alive. His thoughts were for himself unless she specifically called his attention to something she needed. He always obeyed promptly, but inevitably, he'd work her around to what he wanted with delaying tactics and flattery. It was usually easier to let him have his way.

Yes, Filip had met the requirements. He was submissive. She just needed to learn how to discipline him better, to direct him into proper behavior. She would move forward with plans to marry him. The sooner the better. *Get it over with and don't look back.*

To do that, she needed to stop thinking about Maon Keefe. Marshal Maon Keefe. Forgetting him would be the hardest thing she'd ever done. So far she was finding no success. It was probably this dinner that kept him alive in her thoughts. Once she made it through tonight, he'd be a thing of the past. She'd marry Filip and that would be that. Gods, how was she going to survive the next few hours?

Tonight she would no doubt have to introduce Filip to Maon. She'd perceived jealousy on Filip's part when they discussed Maon and the purpose of tonight's dinner. Filip wouldn't act out. At least she hoped he wouldn't. Maon was another thing. It was probably impossible to hope Maon wouldn't have something to say about Filip. Mocking taunts at the very least. Why couldn't she stay home in bed?

Too late. The car pulled up to the front entrance of the Bellmount Club. When she exited the vehicle, the flutter of nerves in her stomach was not a surprise. This evening was chock-full of anxiety-inspiring possibilities.

Never one to prefer the limelight, she'd always allowed her mother to take center stage at any parties or events they'd had to attend. Overheard remarks that she was such a mousy thing compared to her mother hadn't bothered her. But this was her moment to come out in society, the phoenix reborn in a blaze of fire. The goal was to make their jaws drop, their eyes widen, and the gossip begin. Selina had risen from the ashes of Audrina, and the modifiers were now young, bold, vibrant, and new. While she entered the Bellmount Club, messages were going out to the appropriate members of the press and industry, detailing the changes at the House of Shirley.

All that had her on edge, but the vast majority of the silkworms spinning away in her stomach were caused by one man. Maon Keefe. There really was no point in continuing to deny it. Tonight would be the first time they'd been in proximity since Gallarda. The fire opals dangling from her ears were clicking together in a syncopated beat to that of her heart. If only she could wave her palms to dry their dampness. She had to keep her composure.

Whatever remarks Maon directed at Filip she hoped went over his head. Filip wasn't bright, but he could be catty when he believed himself slandered. Wouldn't the gossip newsies love a verbal fight between her date and the hero of the hour? *Gods.*

They strolled into the reception area, which was nearly empty. Most of the dinner guests had already made their way into the dining room. Even so Filip made certain they spoke with each of the small groups remaining. He seemed determined to be the center of attention, the trophy who'd finally allowed himself to be caught. He tittered when she looped her arm through his and insisted they move along. While she forced him to a faster pace down the hall to their destination, he played the indulgent lover, understanding she was eager to show him off. Outside the open doorway, she released him.

Ready to get the encounter with Maon over, she headed toward the front of the dining room to her reserved spot with her mother and Maon. She assumed Filip was following but didn't care. This was her moment to make the most of the fabulous dress she wore. At a stately pace she walked through the tables with what she hoped was an enigmatic smile playing along her lips while her gaze roved over the crowd. A susurration of voices followed her progress. With a slight dip of her head, she acknowledged acquaintances until at last Maon was before her.

By now her fingers were tingling, and she was a little dizzy. *Breathe, you silly goose.* Maon was exactly as she remembered him, except more. His presence hadn't filled a room like it did tonight. Tall, masculine, muscular. She'd experienced those muscles sitting on his lap and had stroked them at the Whip Hand. His sandy-brown hair was slightly tousled, and his evening suit was stunning, accentuating his broad shoulders and narrow waist. Then he smiled at her, that sexy half smile that felt like he'd gently pinched her nipple, sending sensations straight to her clit.

Once she reached her seat, Selina was about to ask if Maon had worn the bright orange vest for her when Filip interrupted. After a brief flurry of introductions, she had found herself seated with Filip between her and Maon.

Filip was repositioning the table service with jerky movements of his fingers.

"Filip?"

He ignored her to continue fiddling with the silver.

"Filip, what's wrong?"

His shoulders sagged, and he looked at Selina with large mournful eyes. "You should have told me what color you were wearing so I could have matched you." His lower lip trembled in a slight pout.

"I'm sorry, Filip. It didn't even occur to me. I have no idea why Marshal Keefe's vest is orange. Only my mother and I knew the color of my dress, and I didn't tell him."

"Naturally you wouldn't. I shouldn't make such a big deal out of it. It hurt me. That's all. But you didn't understand what you were doing."

Selina rolled her eyes when he looked away toward her mother. Filip and her mother were involved in a polite but caustic ongoing war. Maybe Selina was crazy to keep Filip with her, but for now, he made a fine barrier between her and Maon.

AS PEOPLE FILTERED into the room, Maon watched for Selina. When he finally spotted her, his whole body grew hot. She seemed to glide through the cream-colored linen-covered tables. It appeared she was the only one to have discerned the color scheme for the night. Upon entering the room, the picture of fiery beauty, the floral arrangements on each table burst to life as though her presence ignited the oranges, yellows, and red oranges of the flowers.

He was not alone in admiring her. The men looked at her as though they'd discovered a jewel in their midst. The women were in obvious lust for the gown she wore. A Selina original. It had to be. Red-orange lace covered her from shoulders to hips, tempting hints of skin showing through on the yoke and arms. A froth of fabric flames licked up the lower half of her skirt. The goddess of fire had appeared among them.

His attention never left her while she made her way to the table where he sat. Everything about her was perfect. Her dark brown hair was no longer mousy but ablaze with red highlights, swept up in a spiky froth that made her neck look long, slender, and graceful. The dress hugged her body, highlighting the inward curve of her waist and the outward flow of her hips. Her topaz eyes smoldered, and a tiny spark of flame glinted from one eyebrow. Not caring that his pants were bulging with the beginnings of an erection, he rose to meet her, drawing up when a short man in a dark green evening suit interposed himself.

"Lina, we're right up front here," the man said. When Selina didn't answer, he searched to discover what had caught her attention. His perusal of Maon went from face to tie to vest and back.

Maon's squinted, inspecting Selina's date. "Hello, I'm Maon Keefe. We haven't met."

"Marshal Keefe. Delighted to meet you. I'm Filip Patinka." He smirked and gestured to Selina. "I'm with Selina."

Selina interrupted before Maon could unleash the denigrating remark that was forming on his lips.

"Marshal Keefe. It's good to see you again," she said, her face impassive except for a brief flare of her nostrils. It was satisfying to know he affected her. When she leaned to say hello to her mother, he stared at the spot below her ear where he yearned to kiss her. How had he gone this long without claiming her lips with the hunger for her he felt in his soul? A tug on his sleeve broke his reverie. "Why don't you all take your seats," Audrina said.

Maon went to assist Selina, but Filip beat him to her chair. When she sat Maon caught his first look at the back of Selina's dress. It was open in a low V. How she kept that dress from falling off, he had no idea. He smiled to himself; getting her out of it looked easy. His fists clenched tight. *Get a grip, Keefe.* With wooden steps he returned to his own chair and dropped into it.

In a hushed voice, Audrina said, "Something else, huh?"

"She truly is."

"Certainly Selina, but I meant Filip."

Maon turned to consider Audrina. The glint of malicious humor in her eyes steadied him. He may have to suffer under a need for restraint with Selina, but that didn't have to stop him from letting Filip make a fool of himself. "An absolute treasure."

Maon twisted in his seat, left elbow on his chair back. "Patinka. Your family owns all the mortuaries. Right? Or am I mixing you up with someone else?"

The smile Filip forced to his lips stoked Maon's need to torment the man. "Yes. My mother's family has extensive holdings in bereavement services."

"Was it kind of macabre growing up? I mean, did you spend a lot of time around dead people?" Maon asked, as solemn as possible.

At that point Audrina added, "I've heard the funeral industry is quite profitable. Does your family own internment estates as well?"

Filip glared at Maon and squirmed. "Why, yes, Audrina. We do."

Maon would have continued, but he saw that the other three members of their table were heading their direction. *Crap.* With a sharp glance at Audrina, he surreptitiously gestured for her to look.

"Oh dear," she said. Headed their way was his father, and coming through the door, his mother, not a hair out of place, escorted by Chief Fitzgerald from Gallarda. Why hadn't it occurred to Maon that if his father had been invited, his mother would have been too? He wasn't surprised she hadn't contacted him.

As his father found his designated chair next to Selina's, he introduced himself. "I'm Johnathan Keefe. You must be Selina. You won't remember me, but I recall you hiding under the buffet table at one of your mother's parties when you were a tiny thing."

Selina gave him a wide smile. "Yes. Were you the man who kept sneaking me food?"

With a subdued chuckle, Johnathan's gaze went unfocused for a moment. "One of several who couldn't resist helping you subvert your parents' request that you stay in bed."

He glanced across the table at Audrina. "Audrina. You look as lovely as ever."

"Thank you, Johnathan. You're looking well."

Johnathan nodded at Maon. "Maon."

Maon met his father's dark blue eyes and bobbed his head in response. "Father." He grasped Filip's elbow and said, "Filip, this is my father, Johnathan Keefe. Filip Patinka, Father."

As Filip and his father acknowledged the introduction, Fitzgerald and Maon's mother arrived at the table. Maon and Filip stood, and Maon introduced the pair. His mother pointedly ignored Johnathan's polite greeting.

Flustered, Fitzgerald said, "Ms. Keefe, I believe this is your appointed seat." He gestured to the chair next to Johnathan.

"It is impossible for me to sit there. You must switch seats with me."

"Oh. Yes. Indeed. Certainly," said Fitzgerald.

Once they were settled, the table was quiet long enough for everyone to become uncomfortable. Maon had been watching his father's reaction to his mother. She was snide as usual. If he'd wanted to, his father could have risen to the bait and verbally sparred with her. Instead of anger his face was shadowed with sadness, his gaze fixed on his hands.

With a halfhearted laugh, Maon said, "We're a lively group." Selina's gaze popped up to watch him. "Selina, you are ravishing tonight. Did your fairy godmother wave her magic wand and turn you into the princess we see before us?"

Audrina patted his arm. "Oh, Maon. That's a Selina original."

"You're coming out of the clothes closet?"

Selina glanced around the table before answering. "Yes. The Audrina line is now called Selina. Notices have been sent out. The first runway show will be at Beta Tau's fashion week in about a month."

Amid the congratulations, Maon watched Selina. Her cheeks were slightly pink from being the center of attention. Where was Lasair in the woman before him? Did Lasair's mask make Selina bold? No, he'd seen Selina deal with situations in a forthright manner. It must be the acknowledgment of her design talents. That she was a brilliant designer was clear. Her bashful response was nothing like her mousy, faux, timid persona. That guise elicited a teasing reaction in him. This Selina he wanted to kiss and encourage, lavishing her with the praise she deserved.

When conversation again died, Maon turned to Filip. "Filip, you are utterly dashing tonight. That string tie is quite a bold touch."

Filip preened, lifting a hand to flutter at his neck. "I consider it a sort of tribute to the marshals. Not that I would ever place myself on the same level."

"You didn't attend the academy, then?"

"No." Filip shook his head with a pained expression. "Mother said I wasn't suited."

"Ah, well then. Speaking of suits. That is a lovely shade of green you're wearing," Maon said, smiling solicitously. "Did Selina pick it out for you?'

Selina lifted her chin and narrowed her eyes at him. He lifted one eyebrow at her and continued. "I learned so much about colors while I was working on the House of Shirley investigation. Tell me, Selina. What color would you call that green? Limp leaf? Maybe wilted cabbage?"

Filip looked at Selina, his face perplexed. "Um, Selina, didn't they call it fern?"

Before Selina could respond, Maon said, "Yes. Yes. Flaccid fern. I thought I recognized it. Perfect choice, Selina."

Filip pushed his shoulders back and smoothed down the strings of his tie. "I take pride in my dress. Being well-dressed is the first sign of leadership, my mother always said."

Maon gave him a meaningful smile. "And mother is always right. Am I right?"

Filip responded with a snarky little laugh.

Maon brought his fingers to his temple and flicked them away. "What was I thinking? We have two mothers here with us. Selina's and my own." He took hold of Audrina's hand and kissed it. "You, my dear, are nothing if not inherently accurate."

"Darling, you're too kind," she responded, eyes agleam with merriment.

As he looked past Audrina to his mother, his eyes went flat. "It should go without saying you are always right, Mother."

She lifted her chin at him, all platinum-blonde aloofness. "Your charm never worked on me."

Fitzgerald said, "Oh my. A woman who cannot be flattered and knows her own mind. How remarkable. You would make an astute addition to the interrogation unit on Gallarda. Indeed. Yes."

"Perhaps, Edward. But it's more I'm an expert on the methods of the delinquent I deal with most often."

"Oh my. Well, yes, Felicity. Maon can be a bit of a knave, can't he?" Fitzgerald said with an abrupt laugh, his gaze flitting to the others at the table.

"More than that." Her humorless consideration shifted to Maon.

"Oh, come, Mother. Your name means great happiness. Let's try to be happy tonight. Shall we?" Maon asked.

"I'm here because I was asked to be here. I'd much rather be home with my roses," she said.

Maon swung his glance around to the rest of the group. "Mother grows award-winning roses. She has two new tea roses and a climbing rose to her credit."

Amid the general murmurs of appreciation, his mother held forth on the joys of breeding new rose strains. Maon leaned back in his seat to focus once again on Selina. She knew he was watching her because her gaze kept flicking toward him.

Finally, she said in a heated whisper, "Stop staring."

"Was I?"

"You know you were."

Maon bumped Filip's arm. "You have to agree she's worth staring at."

"Why yes. Everyone watched while we entered the room, and I'm sure I heard people saying what a lovely couple we made." With that said, Filip scooped up Selina's hand. Maon rolled his eyes, imagining the puppy-dog expression Filip must have on his face. The man was a self-centered idiot. Short with a scrawny physique and hair that could best be described as pale, Filip Patinka did not draw an admiring eye. No matter what he believed.

Conversation was interrupted when their salads arrived. Soon everyone was busy eating. When the entrees were placed before them, a small kerfuffle was instigated by Filip over the chicken and the fish. It seemed the chicken was dry, and the fish looked ever so much better. Selina solved the problem by switching her plate with Filip's. Maon bit back several remarks he was dying to say, grinning broadly at Selina and saying nothing. When he looked at Audrina and raised his eyebrows, she smothered a chortle, whispering one word. "Precious." Maon clamped his lower lip between his teeth to hold back his laugh.

17

The last of Maon's berry cream cake stared up at him while he decided whether he was too full for one more bite. The others were positioning their forks on their plates and pushing them away. In the lull between dessert and the start of the program, Maon's father said, "Maon, I was sorry to hear that you were shot. Your Aunt Sarah and I were away on Plymouth in the Chiardi section of the Federation. Friends told us on our return. You've fully recovered?"

Maon ignored the sound of contempt that came from his mother and responded, "I am, sir. I spent time in rehab, regrowing the muscles and skin on my side and part of my arm. I'm good as new now."

"That's good. And your latest encounter with a gunman. How did that come about?" Johnathan asked.

Maon had placed what happened on Gallarda in a special, private compartment of stored memories between him and Selina. Although he didn't want to share the story, Maon reluctantly responded, his gaze focused on the ornate light sconce on the wall behind the head table. "It was a line-of-duty thing. Someone took a shot at Ms. Shirley while we were on Gallarda investigating a problem at her company mill. I got us under cover. Marshals and local police arrived to whisk us away."

Audrina scowled and snorted. "It was more than that. Maon's not telling the half of it. But we have Selina here to give us a firsthand account." She directed her gaze at her daughter. "Selina, tell us what a hero Maon really is."

Selina shifted in her chair and let the fingertips of her right hand fall on the fork she'd abandoned on her plate. "Yes. There is much more to the story." Maon watched Selina, tightly focused on each word she said. "The gunman was using a high-powered sniper rifle. I had turned to face Maon a second before the first shot hit my seat back. I would have been killed otherwise. An odd noise sounded by my ear, and then the stuffing started coming out of the headrest. Even after Maon had shoved me to the floor of the air car, it took me a minute to figure out someone was firing at us."

Audrina had shut her eyes and was fanning herself with the evening's program. Maon took her other hand and brought it to his lips to kiss. While Fitzgerald was oh-mying, Filip placed limp fingers over his heart and affected a mortified expression. Maon's father was listening with his eyebrows drawn together while his mother glared at Selina. His parents' faces were a contrast between concern and contempt.

After looking around the table members, Selina continued, "As you can imagine, I fell apart. I huddled on the floor of the car, shaking in terror while Maon did his best to evade more shots from the gunman. He was really quite amazing. So calm while I was a quivering puddle." The look she directed at Maon conveyed her gratitude and awe. "The next thing I knew, he was pulling me out of the door." With a glance to Chief Fitzgerald, she said, "I learned later that the car had been disabled and Maon was forced to make an unexpected landing. He brought us down between two warehouses, which must have blocked the gunman, because there were no further shots." She covered her mouth for a moment and shook her head. "Everything he did seemed methodical, as though he had encountered this exact situation many times before and knew exactly what to do. I wanted to hide in the car." With a rueful smile, she said, "That would have been a bad idea. Maon was smarter. He made it appear we had entered one warehouse before locking us into a different building. It was dark and there were plants everywhere. We went to the far side to wait for the marshal's men to arrive. Then we heard someone break open the door we'd used to enter the building."

"Oh my goodness," Filip said.

Selina gave him a slight smile. "Yes. It was frightening." While she scanned her audience, she said, "But I had Maon with me. He went to confront whoever it was. It turned out to be the gunman. Maon ordered him to surrender. They exchanged gunfire, and Maon wounded him. The marshal's air car arrived, and we jumped in and were driven to safety."

"I am so grateful you were there to protect Selina, my dear boy," Audrina said.

"It was my honor," Maon said. He met Selina's gaze, the sense of connectedness washing over him until she abruptly smiled and turned to Filip.

"I've never told you the story before, Filip," she said.

Maon sat back, tightening his midsection to overcome a rush of nausea.

Filip responded with his hand patting his chest. "Oh, Selina. That story makes my heart seize in fear. You poor dear. However did you manage to endure such an ordeal? And you were injured. A broken elbow, wasn't it?"

Fitzgerald said, "Oh my, yes. Marshal Gage immediately drove her to the Federation Enclave's emergency trauma clinic." He turned to Felicity, Maon's mother. "She received the best care we on Gallarda could provide her."

As Fitzgerald was speaking, the director of the marshals' service rose at the head table to thank the guests for attending and to introduce the guest speaker. Maon let the man's voice buzz in his ears without listening. Instead he observed the individuals seated at the table with him. Filip constantly leaned in to whisper to Selina. Each time he did, she put up her hand as though she wished to shush him, but she never corrected him. His mother had tilted her face aside with her arms held tight across her chest. His father maintained his focus on his hands in his lap, except for moments when he would take a fleeting glimpse at Felicity and wince. Maon sighed. Truth and falsehood were such a jumble to him. What did Selina want? What was the truth about his parents? He was friggin' well going to get the answers he needed.

Polite applause followed the end of the speech. The night was nearly over. Maon was ready to get Selina alone and talk to her. But first, the awards. When he heard his name called as one of three others to receive the Purple Heart, he made his way forward to accept the award. Reseated at the table, he handed the medal to Audrina. She made a big deal over it while his mother glanced at it and passed it on. His father looked at it and then directly at Maon with a smile. The smile touched something that had long been frozen inside him.

Maon relaxed, assuming his stint in the limelight was over. Until he once again heard his name called. Openmouthed, he looked around. When the director, who was handing out the awards, smiled at him and nodded, Maon realized his name had been called again. After he strode to the front, the director shook his hand with a firm grip. The tale of his heroic deeds on Gallarda was recounted. A flush crept onto his cheeks, and he narrowed his focus to the tips of his boots.

The magnitude of what was happening hit him. The goal had been to become a good, solid marshal. Somehow he'd done better than he'd hoped. The marshals' service was honoring him for going above and beyond. For a few moments, he was deeply humbled, and then joy filled him. He had proof he could hand to his mother that he wasn't the failure she had always said he was. Light-headed with happiness, he thanked the director and held up the Special Achievement Award to show it off. Face split wide, he beamed while his fellow marshals and the elite of Tallavan society applauded him. He caught Shane's eye and gave him a nod. Then Maon turned to Selina and winked at her, his smile transforming into his impish half grin.

AS MAON RECEIVED approval from his peers, Selina swallowed. He was so damn beautiful. She struggled to rein in the rush of desire to run to him and hug him close. The emotions she'd kept banked in her chest flared as though kindled to life by the joy that shone from Maon. Her mind knew that what her heart felt was more than pride and happiness. Even if she chose not to dwell on it. Here and now, it couldn't be denied. She loved that brave, protective, kindhearted man. Without thinking how Maon might perceive her actions, she rose from her seat, went to him, and kissed his cheek. The response from the crowd intensified. Maon walked her back to the table arm in arm. When he assisted her to sit, he nuzzled her ear and said, "I love you."

Selina froze. Oh no! What had she done? Yes, she loved Maon, but that didn't change what she had to do. Although he would never understand and would probably hate her, she had to crush all hope they could ever be together. Emotion could not rule her. The need to protect Maon from the inevitable destruction she would bring to him was paramount. She didn't want to be responsible for the death of another man who loved her to his own detriment. Filip was perfect. Weak, unreliable Filip wouldn't stir her to depend on him. Ha! He was far too self-involved to allow Selina to exploit him. Not like Maon. Love had not been enough to stop her from exploiting her father's love for her. She'd taken everything he offered without thought to his needs or concerns. He'd died because she couldn't see past her own selfish interests, hadn't looked after him like she should have because she was too wrapped up in her work, her plans. It was her fatal flaw. She couldn't trust herself with Maon. If she loved him—and she'd just admitted that she did—she had to distance herself from him.

The table was noisy with congratulations when Maon sat. Selina's mother beamed, exclaiming her delight, while Fitzgerald babbled on about how he'd recognized what a top marshal Maon was from the very start. Filip patted Maon on the arm, leaning in to say something in Maon's ear as though they were close friends. Johnathan Keefe quietly radiated pride. Maon's mother had said Maon did the Keefe name proud. The woman had even deigned to smile at him. The glow on Maon's face at her words made the back of Selina's eyes tingle. *Damn her. It takes others acknowledging her son's heroism for her to tell him he's done well.*

Maon's voice interrupted her thoughts. "Selina, may I speak with you privately before you leave?"

Her hand came unbidden to her throat, fingers fluttering. "Of course."

Everyone grew quiet then while the director announced the meritorious service awards. When the last applause had died out and the director had wished them all a good evening, Selina sighed. It did little to ease the regret that was making her chest ache.

"Filip, will you wait for me at the club entrance? I won't be long."

"Yes, darling. I'll be waiting as patiently as I can. You know how I hate to be parted from you." He pouted, pursing his lips for a kiss, which she gave him with a perfunctory peck.

"Thank you." When she turned to Maon, she realized he'd been watching them with a smirk on his face. She scowled and said, "Shall we?"

He stepped up until his imposing body was standing over her. *Damn him.* His attitude always made her want to discipline him. His muscular grace cried out for her to caress him. Neither was on the agenda. No, she was about to break his heart for the final time. She knew what that would feel like to him. Her own heart was cracked and bleeding. One final strike and it would shatter.

MAON HAD ASKED Audrina to wait for him, so she'd requested a dance from Johnathan. With her in good company, Maon went to offer Selina his hand in rising from her chair. While he watched her give Filip a quick kiss, it came to him that Filip resembled a needy lapdog. *Wonder if he's house trained? He certainly has an irritating yippy bark.* With Filip out of the way, Maon looked down on Selina. It was time they had this talk, but the blank expression on her face roiled his stomach. She gave no hint what she was thinking, but the acid in his throat told him it couldn't be good.

With his hand held out to her, he said, "Come. Let's go to the club bar. We can talk there."

Selina accepted his assistance and allowed him to guide her through the half-deserted tables. Their pace was slowed by other guests stopping to congratulate Maon and wish Selina well. When they reached the door, Maon ushered her to a junction of hallways and left toward the bar. After seating her at a table in a darkened corner in the back, Maon made his way to the bartender and ordered himself a Beachum's neat and a light dessert wine for Selina. While he waited for the order to be filled, he observed Selina, his stomach queasy. Her rigid posture didn't bode well.

As he returned, drinks in hand, he decided to be direct. When he set Selina's wine before her, it clinked on the glass-top table. Before settling into his own chair, he took a sip of his whiskey and winced when the burn hit the back of his throat.

Face-to-face with her, he didn't smile. The shield of charm he usually hid behind would hinder him. This was a serious moment. Perhaps the most serious moment of his life.

Selina's fingers were twitching around the stem of her glass. He pulled one of her hands into his own, giving it a gentle squeeze before bringing it to his lips. His gaze settled on Selina's; he watched while a series of emotions passed over her. Desire. Regret. Worry.

"Selina, I love you." She attempted to speak, but he put up his other hand to stop her, not letting her pull her hand from his grip. "Let me say this, and then you may speak." When she nodded, he said, "I love you. And I'm convinced you love me. More than that, I'm certain we want the same thing. Family. Children. Someone to spend our lives with during good and bad times, in sickness and in health, for richer or for poorer." He paused for a moment, letting his eyes do the imploring. "Please, Selina. Tallavan custom says I'm not the one who should do the asking. Please, marry me. Don't make me go back to the superficial life I led before. You make me a better man, and in a small way, I make you better too. I could make a long list of all the things I love about you, but it's not the transitory things, the color of your hair or your eyes, that matter. When I look at you, I see little boys and little girls. Visits with Grandma Audrina. You holding our first grandchild. Please marry me. Please."

While he spoke tears dropped from Selina's eyes. She snuffled, her nose reddening. Maon wiped a tear from her cheek and then found a paper napkin to hand to her. She blew, and while she was mopping up the damp side effects, he said, "You are so beautiful."

The hand holding the rumpled napkin fell to the table with a light *thud*. Disparaging eyes told him she didn't believe him. He smiled. "To me you are always beautiful, even when you wear those colorless sacks you seem to prefer."

A trace of embarrassment pinked her cheeks. "Thank you."

"So?" Maon leaned closer, the smell of Selina's spicy perfume flooding his senses. He took a deep breath, inhaling the fragrance, and found his chest had gone rigid and he couldn't release the air from his lungs. He watched while Selina's delicate eyebrows knit together, and her gaze drifted to their joined hands. She kept them linked but didn't look up when she spoke.

"Maon, you spin an enchanting dream, but I've learned things about myself that would tarnish and spoil the enchantment. If I really had a fairy godmother, I would ask her to wave her magic wand and fix me. Fix me, so I could join you in that happily ever after." She flicked her gaze toward him and then back to her hands before she spit out the words he'd never expected to hear. "I can't marry you. I'm going to marry Filip."

Maon pulled back, letting her hand drop from his. His assumption that Filip was a temporary hurdle easily jumped was wrong. He pinched his fingers to his nose and took several deep breaths.

"Why would you marry that narcissistic asshole? Can't you see he will bleed any happiness from your existence?" Maon scowled at her while she fingered her wineglass. "Look at me and tell me you love him." The grit of his voice brought her eyes up to meet his.

"I don't love him. That's the point." She glowered back at him.

He shook his head. "I don't understand." To hide his anger, he dropped his clenched hands to his lap.

Tears again welled on Selina's eyelashes. "Don't you get it? I use the people I love. I drain them dry. People have died because of me. My father…" She waved her hand in dismissal. "If I don't love Filip, I won't hurt him."

"That is the craziest rubbish I've ever heard. You're not like that."

Thrusting a finger at him repeatedly, she said, "You don't know. You haven't been around me enough to know. It has to be this way. I'm sorry, but your dream of happily ever after is impossible."

"Open your eyes, Selina. You can't drain me dry or use me up. Don't you understand? You're the conflagration that inflames me. You turn me into a blazing inferno, but not one that consumes me. You're the fire of life. Why would you settle for a cold lump of porridge like Filip Patinka when you can have an ever-burning passion with me? I'll tend you, and you'll fuel me, and together we'll never go out."

Selina wiped her streaming nose with the napkin, shaking her head. "It's not that way. It isn't. I'm sorry. There can be no us. I can't let there be."

Maon curled his arms above him, wanting to grab hold of his hair and pull until that pain overwhelmed the agony in his chest. With a thud he brought his fists to the table, making both glasses clatter. Selina jerked up. Maon stared at her. "I'm leaving in four days for my new duty station on Beta Tau. This offer remains open until then. Please reconsider your position. It is absolutely senseless. If you don't contact me before I go, then I will accede to your wishes and get on with my life."

Selina's lip trembled. "I have a business trip to Qingdao in two days. Filip is accompanying me. I won't be contacting you. My decision is final. Find someone else to share your dream." With that she slipped from her chair and nearly ran from the bar.

Maon sat stunned before slumping forward, covering his face with his hands. *Shit.* He could smell her spicy fragrance on his hand. Was this the last time he would be near enough to her for her scent to rub off on him? What else could he have done? She'd thrown his love back at him as the very reason to deny him. *Damn her.* How could he get on with his life without her? He scrubbed his eyes and then sat up. The cool of his glass of Beachum's was warm compared to the iciness of his fingers. He downed the rest of the whiskey, grimacing before carefully placing the short tumbler on the table. He rose to go find Audrina.

He found her laughing with his father to one side of the dance floor. When she caught sight of Maon, her smile fell away. She stepped toward him.

"I'm ready to leave," Maon said. He nodded to his father.

"Let's be off, then." She turned to Johnathan. "Thank you for the dance."

His father smiled at her. "Thank you." His gaze shifted to Maon, concern etched in his eyes.

Maon whisked Audrina from the room and out to the drive to await the car. He didn't speak. He had no words.

Once they were seated, the car pulled away from the club with smooth precision. In the backseat next to Audrina, Maon dropped his head against the cushioned elegance. Eyes shut, he let out a long sigh that struggled past the tight constriction of his chest. His recent experience with physical pain was nothing compared to the agony he was currently suffering. He'd lost her. Given it his best shot and still lost her.

"Maon. Tell me what happened," Audrina said, taking hold of his hand.

"I can't," Maon said in a barely audible voice.

"She's confused. Give her time."

"She didn't sound confused." He grimaced. "No, she knew exactly what she was saying and why. She wants Filip for some reason only she can understand. No uncertainty about it. 'My decision is final.' Those were her exact words."

"I'll speak with her."

"It won't do any good. I gave her four days to contact me. I'm leaving for Beta Tau for my new assignment. She's leaving in two with Filip for Qingdao."

Audrina patted the hand that was holding hers. "Don't give up on her."

"I won't pursue her when she's not willing. It... I won't. With the one person who could change her mind dead, how will she ever—"

"Don't decide now. Your heart is raw. Selina is not a stupid girl. She's always seen through foolishness. She'll come around."

Maon sighed. Despite the confused look on Audrina's face, he didn't want to explain Selina's belief that she'd caused her father's death. "You're coming to Beta Tau soon?"

"Yes, I'll be doing the preparation for the runway show. Selina will arrive a few days before the actual show. The trip to Qingdao is a little over a week. With what she needs to accomplish and the length of the trip, she'll be pushed to get to Beta Tau any sooner."

"Comm me when you get there. I'll take you to dinner." A wistful smile played along his lips while caressed her hand with his thumb. "You're still one of my best girls."

"I'm holding you to that." The smile Audrina gave him was equally pensive. Maon watched it change to a look of grim determination when she turned to gaze out the window.

18

udrina let herself into Selina's apartment with the key code. "Selina? Are you home?" When she paused to listen, she heard the sound of a shower running, so she settled herself on the sofa to wait. Selina had asked her not to stop by tonight, wanting to be alone, assuring Audrina that even Filip had been evicted for the night.

With nothing else to do but fidget nervously, she went through the contents of her evening bag, discarding anything extraneous she'd collected. On her way to dispose of two used tissues and a hard-candy wrapper, she was stopped by the brusque voice of her daughter.

"How did I know you would come here anyway?"

Audrina turned to face Selina. "I couldn't wait. If you had seen how distraught Maon was after you left him tonight, you'd understand."

Selina's head dropped, damp hair falling loosely around her face as she slumped onto the sofa. "I'm sorry I had to do that to him."

Audrina stood before her, posture rigid while she resisted the impulse to berate her daughter. "He loves you, Selina. Why are you rejecting him for that egotistical fop? Filip isn't even half the man that Maon is. Filip will use you. I can't imagine he'd be any kind of father to your children."

Selina squeezed her eyes tight while her face reddened. "Please, Mother!"

"Explain it to me, Selina. Explain it to me, and I'll leave you be."

Selina threw her head back and stared at the ceiling. "It's for the best. I don't want to hurt Maon."

"Selina, do you care for him?"

A burst of air whooshed from Selina's lungs. "Yes. Which is exactly why I have to let him go." She sat up and glared at her mother.

Sadness settled over Audrina like a pall. "Darling, if you have feelings for him, whatever you're concerned is the problem, it can be surmounted."

All evidence of Selina's anger fell away when she crumpled inward, wrapping her arms around herself. A tear trickled down her cheek. "No, no, it can't."

Audrina sat beside Selina, drawing her close, allowing Selina's head to nestle on her shoulder. "Tell me."

"I hurt those I love. I hurt Daddy. I'd hurt Maon." Selina sobbed.

"What are you talking about? You never hurt your father."

"I did. I'm the reason he died." Selina snuffled, accepting the tissue her mother handed her.

"Your father died from an aortic aneurysm. You had nothing to do with that."

Selina's breathing hitched in a hiccup. With the tissue covering her mouth, she said, "I asked too much of him. Audrina business kept him so busy, but I repeatedly went to him for help with my projects."

"You're still not making sense."

Selina's hand dropped, a forlorn look blanketing her face. Her lower lip trembled. "If he hadn't been so absorbed in helping me, he would have taken better care of himself. Did he even visit a doctor regularly?"

Audrina eased back, gripping Selina's fingers tightly. "Of course he did. Selina, your father didn't neglect his health. What happened to him was bad luck."

Selina pulled out of her mother's embrace, fists balled on her lap. "Mother, people don't die from aneurysms anymore. Routine scans catch those."

Audrina stroked Selina's knee. "Oh, darling. Your father's aortic aneurysm was caused by a disease he caught a year after you were born. He'd been living with and surviving the condition since then."

Selina's head came up with a jerk. "What?"

The ache that had been growing in Audrina's throat made it almost impossible for her to speak. "Your father... Your father had the bad luck to encounter an individual with Seilao. It's a very rare blood-borne disease. Your father was seated next to him on a shuttle flight. The man had a bloody nose. Your father assisted him."

Selina ran her fingers through the damp strands of her hair. "Seilao. Why was I never told?"

"I'm sorry we didn't tell you. Your father didn't want to burden you. His disease was controlled by nanites that repaired any blood vessel damage the disease created."

"Then how did he develop the aneurysm?"

"He was due in about a week to receive his regular nanite infusion. Under ordinary circumstances, the nanites can last weeks longer than the transfusion period. In his case, unknown to anyone, his body had been fighting off a major attack on his abdominal aorta. He was home at Etting-ton. While cutting a salad, he sliced his palm open. Badly. He wrapped it up and drove himself into Cahernamon. He came to my office because he wanted me to come with him. The aneurysm ruptured while I was getting ready to leave with him."

Audrina's lips pressed together. With a shake of her head, she contin-ued, "He died before we could get him to the hospital. It was bad luck. His nanites were lower than normal, and the cut allowed the infection to over-take him. The disease could as easily have focused on an artery in his foot. It didn't. It was...bad luck."

"Oh, Mother! Why didn't you tell me this?"

"I don't know. I was so wrapped up in grieving, it didn't seem impor-tant how he died. Just that he had."

Audrina ran her hand up and down Selina's arm. "I can see now it was a mistake. The assumptions you've made are so far from the truth. You didn't cause your father's death. He didn't die because you kept him so busy helping you he didn't take care of himself. It was his joy that you always came to him with problems. We were both in awe of what an amazing businesswoman you were becoming. It humbled him that with your gifts, you asked him for advice. He would be tormented that you're denying yourself true happiness because you falsely believe you had something to do with his death."

Eyes still swimming with tears, Selina said, "I never thought about whether he was taking care of himself. I assumed he was. When he died…"

Audrina put a finger under Selina's chin. "It was never your responsibility to look after him. That was my job. You have always taken on burdens that were not yours. It's your nature. You are so like him. Constantly trying to help others. I've seen you mentoring people the way he mentored you."

Audrina pulled Selina into a tight hug. "Your father might have died young, but I made sure he took care of himself. You need someone like that."

Selina's shoulders slumped in her mother's embrace. "I'm so confused. I need to think. The trip to Qingdao will give me time to do that."

Audrina clasped Selina by the upper arms when she pulled out of the embrace. "Call Maon."

Selina gave her head a slight shake. "No, I can't do that. It would give him hope, and my mind hasn't changed. Maybe I wasn't responsible for Father's death, but I could have been. I just need to think."

"Then leave Filip behind."

Selina avoided looking her mother in the eyes. "I promised to take him. He would be disappointed after bragging to his friends about visiting Qingdao."

Audrina wanted to roll her eyes; instead she said, "He can visit Qingdao anytime."

"His mother doesn't allow him off planet. It's a big deal to him. I can't not take him."

Audrina noted the trembling in Selina's body when she squeezed her daughter's shoulders. "Darling, Maon won't wait forever."

In a quiet voice Selina said, "I know."

～

MAON STOOD outside his father's apartment. He wiped his palms on his slacks, closed his eyes, and took a deep breath. What had really happened years ago between his father and mother?

For years Maon's father had been a figment constructed from Maon's imagination after his memories of the actual man faded. Early on his father was the hero who would come and rescue Maon from his mother's caustic tongue. She'd never physically hurt him, but then she rarely touched him. Her verbal abuse ceased only when she ignored him completely. He'd often cried into his pillow, wishing he were a girl. He'd believed she would love him then, even if his father didn't. When time passed and deliverance never came, he grew angry, agreeing with all his mother's malicious characterizations of his sire and trying his best to please her by doing the exact opposite.

Nothing Maon did changed her mind about him, so in his teens he gave up and took on the role she had always labeled him with. He found he was indeed a natural-born flirt, rowdy and gregarious. The several years he spent away at school were his happiest. He drew girls like a magnet. His male classmates were drawn to his crazy brand of fun. If Shane hadn't decided to befriend Maon and keep him from some of his more dangerous stunts, he might not have made it to eighteen.

His father had been relegated to a cold back burner until he'd approached Maon at the banquet. Watching his parents interact had been a revelation. His father seemed like a nice man. Certainly Audrina and Selina both thought he was. His mother had been rude and mean-spirited.

Since Maon had been shot and nearly died, he'd been rethinking his foundational ideas and assumptions. Selina had shown him, with the right woman it was possible for him to settle down and have a family. The award he'd received from the marshals proved he wasn't a failure in his work. And his father had requested the chance to explain.

It was time, past time, to confront the truth about his father. Maon exhaled and knocked. The door was answered by a woman who bore a close resemblance to his mother, except she was beaming.

"Maon. I'm your Aunt Sarah. Please come in," she said.

Grateful she hadn't attempted to hug him, Maon entered, looking around for his father. He stood motionless while his father approached from the living area.

"Maon. Thank you for coming."

Maon's mouth was dry, making his response gruff. "I have a lot of questions."

His aunt said, "Come, Johnathan. Let's let the boy sit down first."

"Sorry. Where are my manners? Come on in."

"Sure." Maon settled into the corner of the sofa. His aunt and father sat in armchairs opposite. He liked what he saw of the apartment. It was homey and comfortable. The cushions under him had reached the age where they had the right amount of squishiness to lounge on. He brushed a hand over one of the throws available on its arms. Nothing like the austerity of Maon's own place.

"Would you like something to drink?" his aunt asked.

"No, thank you."

"Well, then, I'll leave the two of you alone to talk." Her brows furrowed, she gave Johnathan a slight smile and left the room.

"Son, I know you have questions, but I'd like you to hold on to those until after I tell you what happened twenty years ago."

Maon nodded, commanding his stomach to stop churning.

Johnathan's eyes focused on that distant time as he began his story. "I met your mother when your Aunt Sarah invited me to visit their country house. Sarah and I had been going out, but we were friends more than anything. We both understood our relationship wasn't permanent."

"Your mother was out in the back garden when I first saw her. She looked like the help with a straw hat on her head, wearing work clothes and dirty gardening gloves. She was patting mulch around some flowers she'd planted. When she glanced up, she literally dazzled me with her smile. I was hooked from that instant."

The remembrance brought a slight smile to his lips. He shook his head as though ridding himself of the clinging tendrils of the past. He locked his gaze on Maon. "We married. Had you. Life was perfect."

The sadness Maon had seen in his father's eyes before flooded back. "I wanted to surprise your mother with a trip up into the mountains to a picturesque resort with individual cabins. I asked Sarah to help me prepare the cabin for our visit. So the day before, we drove up with food and other necessities. Sarah insisted on sprinkling rose petals on the sheets. It was going to be like a second honeymoon for your mother and me."

His father's jaw clenched, his face grim. "On the way down we were joking and laughing. I wasn't paying enough attention to the road. The trees were thick, so I didn't see the other car pulled halfway off the road until we'd rounded the curve. I jerked the wheel to go around them, but overdid it. We ended up sliding down off the far lane of the road. The vehicle was canted up on its side, so I crawled out my window. I was helping Sarah out when the car became unbalanced and rolled. Somehow she was pinned underneath."

"Oh my God," Maon said.

"Your aunt should have died that day. But the fellow in the other vehicle was a surgeon. He oversaw getting a med shuttle and her care after the accident. He saved her life. But she was seriously injured. Her lower body had been crushed, and she had brain trauma. It's taken years to restore her body. Our trip to Plymouth was the last visit to her rejuvenation specialist. I've cared for her through all the procedures and physical therapy, although now she looks after me more than I do her."

Maon's confusion must have been obvious to his father. Johnathan threaded his fingers through his hair. "You're wondering how this caused the split between your mother and me." He shook his head. "I'm not sure what I said to her when I called to tell her about the accident and ask her to come to the hospital in Cahernamon. Somehow she got the notion that Sarah and I were returning from a rendezvous in the mountains when the car rolled. When your mother arrived at the emergency room, she was cold, aloof, and very angry. When I suggested we share the duties of staying by Sarah's bedside, she said I could stay with Sarah or go with her. She argued with me adamantly. I refused to let Sarah fend for herself. Your mother told me she wanted nothing more to do with either of us. We'd made the mess we were in, and we could see our way out of it. She hasn't spoken with her sister since that day."

"Oh my God, Father. I've never heard any of this."

"I'm sure you haven't. Your mother made it clear I was not to be a part of your life. Normally she couldn't have withheld visitation privileges, but she held the astronomical cost of Sarah's medical bills over my head. As the head of household, your mother was supposed to settle any remaining costs that insurance didn't cover. She promised to pay the money if I never saw or spoke with you again. I went along with her, hoping I could eventually persuade her to reconsider both the medical expenses and our marriage. She refused to listen to my explanations of what happened that day."

His father paused a moment to collect himself before continuing. "Her payment of the rehabilitation bills allowed Sarah to receive the level of care she did. Standard care would have covered her internal injuries, but she'd have been left without legs. I couldn't do that to her. You can't imagine the guilt I felt for my inattention that caused us to go over the side of the road. And I compounded my mistake by trying to help her from the vehicle. I should have waited for rescue personnel. The car wasn't going down the mountain because of the trees. If she'd been inside when it did its final roll, she wouldn't have…" He winced, his eyes dark with regret.

"Mother made you decide between helping Aunt Sarah and staying with us?"

"Yes," Johnathan said, his voice almost inaudible. "I hoped you would be okay. You would still have your mother. I thought Sarah needed me more."

"I can see how you came to that decision." Maon examined his hands. Sometime during the recitation, they had tightened into fists. The stultifying numbness that had pervaded him while his father spoke was washed away by the heat that now flooded through him. No one could have known his mother would make life hell for Maon. He was her child. Mothers loved their children. Did he pile on more guilt by pouring out the pain he'd endured? He clamped a hand across his eyes when tears pricked. Finally, he fastened tight to his father's agonized gaze. "What's done is done. You're my father. I'm your son. Let's move forward on that basis."

With a choking sound, a dam seemed to break inside his father. Rivulets became steady streams. He brought a fist to his lips to cover the sob escaping. "Thank you, Son."

Maon's father rose, and when Maon stood, Johnathan pulled him into a tight hold. Maon's own face was suffused in tears while the two embraced each other. His father stepped back, placing a palm on Maon's cheek. "I love you, Maon. I always have."

Maon yanked his father back into a hug, his voice breaking while his body shook with his own sobs. "Me too, Dad. Me too."

When Maon regained control, his father called Sarah to come in. At the sight of the two men's damp faces, she burst into tears too.

19

The week before Maon boarded the *Adrasteia* to travel to his new duty station had been the most emotionally draining seven days of his life. He'd been reconciled with his father, received a major award from the marshals' service, and lost Selina. The trip had given him time to get a grip on his response to the changes.

After his arrival on Beta Tau, he deposited the few items he'd brought with him in the apartment he'd be sharing with Shane. After that it hadn't taken long for Maon to immerse himself in his new job. While he wrangled facts and figures on the job, his mind was too engaged to bog down in his personal drama. Although Beta Tau was *the* pleasure planet on the Tallavan side of the Sympallan Drift, he wasn't here to party. He was here to work. Beta Tau was a glittering world, but on the far side of the major dome where Maon would spend each day, life would be a little drabber. Drab was probably for the best, considering the upheaval he'd gone through lately. He needed to put his nose to the grindstone and forget Selina.

At the moment, he was sifting information before him on the screen that covered one wall of his cubicle and muttering under his breath. He'd spent several days pulling together this current data and then mashing, crunching, and massaging it. Nowhere had he found any hint that someone was money laundering via the enormous quantity of liquor imported onto Beta Tau. Not that such a crime was happening. His assignment had been to find out.

With a sigh he let his body fall into the faux-wood plasti-chair that matched the faux-wood plasti-desk that made up the furnishings of his cubicle. So much faux wood cluttered the small space, he'd considered tacking up a poster with the image of a campfire with the big red "don't" slash superimposed and the words, ONLY YOU CAN PREVENT FAUX FIRES.

He rubbed his forehead with his fingers, wishing once again he had a window. But the street outside the marshals' offices was nothing much to look at. Although he would be able to watch anyone who walked by. When he was deeply immersed in following threads through data, he didn't miss people. When he came up for air, he did. The other marshals had welcomed him, but Maon had begged off most of their overtures of friendship. The invitations to get a drink or lunch had stopped when it became clear he was miserable company.

A trip to the automat down the street for a sandwich might be a welcome break, but he'd eaten at the same automat for every meal since he'd come to Beta Tau. Shane had been scarce. The new exec for the station chief, Shane was busy wining and dining all the bureaucrats high and low who would make his job easier. He was making connections among the local Guardia, the planetary corporation, employee organizations, businessmen, and the riffraff that could be found even on a well-policed planet like Beta Tau. Shane intended to make the marshals a career. This position was perfect for him. It was used to groom promising young officers. But it kept him working all the time.

Every evening Maon went home to the apartment he shared with Shane, spent the night reading, and went to bed trying to avoid thoughts of Selina but failing miserably. He'd stayed on this side of the dome, far away from the places he associated with her like the Whip Hand. Randolph would probably be ticked that Maon had been on planet for two weeks and hadn't contacted him.

About to get up and fetch himself a café, Maon heard a familiar voice. Shane was greeting others while he headed along the aisle to Maon's cubicle. Maon rubbed his hands over his face and then stretched his arms wide, arching his back. He attempted to smooth out the wrinkles in his rumpled shirt but gave up when Shane's smiling visage appeared over the top of his cubicle.

"Hey, have we met before?" Shane asked.

"Not sure. You look familiar. Are we married?"

"Nah, just living together."

"That's right." Shane leaned against the cubicle's opening. "Have you heard the latest on Cosmo Bonilla?"

"No. Did they catch him?"

"Not yet. Intel says he came to the Tallavan sector to take over the bliss bead traffic."

Maon thumped a fist on the arm of his chair. "I knew he was up to something, not just hiding here. Why was he on Asturnia, then? Why not Gallarda?"

Shane shrugged. "I don't know, but my guess is he wanted a location not controlled by the drug rings operating on Gallarda. Word is he was interviewing candidates to find the person he'd leave in control of all the operations he planned to consolidate. Most of the smaller organizations were falling in line because he offered them a bigger payout."

"Really."

Shane grunted. "The heads of the three largest organizations were all vying to be top dog. We don't know yet who he chose, but there's been fallout from the takeover throughout the sector. Everyone wants to make a good impression on the big boss. Gallarda's had a spate of hits, and it got me wondering if the attack on Selina was an offshoot of the mayhem."

Maon's forehead wrinkled. "What? Someone trying to make brownie points by taking out an operation that wasn't even dealing in extract? It's not how Bonilla operates. And I'd bet any of the thugs involved in killing their compatriots aren't making Bonilla's good-boy list."

Shane pursed his lips and nodded. "You sound pretty sure of that."

Maon leaned back in his chair, lacing his fingers behind his head. "I spent hours with him while he explained the failings of the various criminals found guilty in drug cases over the last decade. He claimed most of them screwed up because they didn't prune members prone to violence from the organization. As he puts it, selling illegal drugs may be a criminal enterprise, but it's a business like any other. Someone who uses murder as a tool is someone whose business plan has already failed."

Shane smirked. "How do you eliminate a violent man without him coming back at you? Seems like there'd be bloodshed no matter what."

Maon tipped his chin in a quick nod. "He wouldn't say, but he did say a murder-free work environment is better for the bottom line."

"Maybe that's why the Feds have never been able to make a case stick against him."

Maon grimaced. "Maybe." He spread his arms wide and said, "So I'm glad you stopped by to fritter your time away with members of the lower echelons."

"What lower echelons?" Shane extended his leg to tap his foot against Maon's shoe. "I hear you're the up-and-coming new data dink."

"Data crunch. How many times must I tell you the proper term is *data crunch*?" Maon sighed, then grinned at his friend. "If I have to spend my days in this little cage with nothing to do but run on my wheel, I deserve a better title than data dink. Makes me sound like a hamster." Maon scowled and twirled a finger over his head to encompass his surroundings. "They haven't even changed my woodchips in forever."

Shane snorted and slapped him on the shoulder. "Come on. You need a break. Let's go find some food."

Maon pulled at his shirt. "No place special. I'm a little ragged."

"The automat down the street?" Shane quirked an eyebrow.

"Unnh. No, definitely not the automat. I'm trying to end my relationship with the soup machine."

"You always were a fast worker. But a soup machine?"

Maon stood. "What can I say? She made me feel all warm inside."

After a short walk, the pair entered the pub Shane had suggested. It was a short distance from their apartment, but Maon hadn't discovered it. It was perfect. No tourists. Locals only. Cozy in a well-used way with typical bar food high on grease, calories, and taste. The waitress took their orders and brought their drinks. Maon took a long refreshing gulp of his beer, sighing at the flavor. He'd asked for a clean malt, and the bartender hadn't disappointed.

"This is really good."

Shane raised his glass. "Give me a Guinness any day. This isn't Guinness, but it'll do in a pinch."

"You've been busy."

With a whoosh of breath, Shane agreed. "Yeah. Too busy. I now know why exec is a one-year position. I thought I'd have time for rope work at the Whip Hand. Not at this pace."

"Still planning to do that Ball of Beauties rope tie for New Year's Eve?" Maon smirked at memories of all those bare bottoms rising in the air.

"Hell, yeah."

"Ball of bare-bottom beauties. That's what you should call it."

Both men paused when their food orders arrived. A buxom older woman brought Maon his order of hot wings and fried veggies and Shane a basket of ribs and fries. After setting the meals down, she asked, "You both new here?"

"Been here two weeks, darlin'," Maon said.

"Glad you found us. Friday is three-credit pint night. Wednesday is all-you-can-eat wings. Here." She pulled out a slip of paper, wrote a note, and signed it. "Twenty percent off your next visit."

"Thanks." Maon took the coupon. "I'll be back. Don't know about him." He gestured at Shane. "He travels in pretty high circles usually."

"That's not… Well…it's sort of true. It's my job."

Maon looked at the server with eyes wide. "It's his job."

With a laugh and a wink, she said, "You gentlemen have a good time."

The two men didn't speak for a few minutes while they tucked into their respective meals. Maon licked his fingers. "Damn, my grease low-level light has been on for days. This is just what I needed."

"You feeling better?"

Maon fiddled with a fried green bean. "Yes and no. I love being here. The work is great. When I'm busy, I'm fine. I'm… Heck, I've turned into a lovesick boy. Cue violins and heart confetti."

"Sounds like you need female companionship. The Quanthan Queen of Beers Bikini Team is here. You want to try water bombing them again?" Shane asked, quirking an eyebrow and smiling. "Probably isn't even the same team members, so we could get away with it twice."

With a snort, Maon said, "That was fun. But I'm not really up to playing tricks."

"What about the Whip Hand?"

"I don't know." He picked up a wing, looked at it, and thumped it back in the basket.

"Fuck it. You're sure to find someone to play with. You need something to smack some life back into you."

Maon grimaced. "The last time I played there, it was with Selina. Hell, it was the only time I ever played with the damn woman. Once. And the thought of playing with someone else…" He glared at Shane. "It's like she put my cock and balls on ice. Not even a twitch unless I'm thinking about her. I don't know what the crap to do."

"I'm free right now. You're coming with me to the club."

When Maon attempted to demure, Shane said, "You don't have to play. Spend time. Soak in the atmosphere. Besides Randolph won't be happy that we've both been on planet and haven't checked in with him."

"Fine. I'll go."

Shane gestured at Maon's platter. "Finish eating. I need to shower and change first."

Maon looked at the hot sauce he'd dripped on his shirt. "I guess I'll have to too." He ruefully rubbed a napkin on the spot.

After a quick trip to their apartment, the pair took a tram to the other side of the dome where the Whip Hand was located. When his friends walked in his office door, Randolph looked up from the bills he'd been reviewing. "My children! You have returned." He held his arms wide and beamed at them.

"Uh, Randolph, you're younger than both of us," Shane responded, then gave the man a bear hug when Randolph stood.

"I'm glad to see you two," he said, releasing Shane and grabbing hold of Maon. After giving Maon a hearty thump, Shane pulled away and gestured toward the chairs in front of his desk. "Sit."

"Yes, sir." Maon's solemn expression didn't reach his eyes. "I'd say you're not the boss of me, but that wouldn't last." He plopped into the black leather chair.

"Damn straight," Randolph growled back. "How long you two here?"

"Till the marshals send us somewhere else," Shane said.

Randolph leaned forward. "They stationed you both on Beta Tau?"

"Yep."

Randolph's eyes gleamed. "Exceptional! That's the best news I've had all week. Let me cache this, and we can see what's up in the club."

The moment Maon had caught sight of Randolph, he realized he'd missed his friend. The three of them had been close since boarding school. They had an understanding that was made deeper through shared culture and a need for kink. It was a kinship unique to men born and raised on Tallav who chafed at the strictures of its matriarchal society, where women owned and ran everything.

The marshals service was the sole male outlet on Tallav, but a stint in the marshals hadn't suited Randolph. He had created his own haven at the Whip Hand where he could be himself. He was such a scandal on Tallav that he never went home. His mother came to him. Her money had built his BDSM empire on Beta Tau. He loved her, and she loved him. He despised the Tallavan aristocracy that relegated him to living like an off-world pariah.

He led them out to the club's public playroom. "I'll get the two of you set up with staff identities. Then you can use the staff locker room and showers. You'll have plenty of space to store your rope kit, Shane."

"Thanks. That's perfect."

"Maon, I'm short a dungeon monitor in the private playroom. Would you mind filling in?"

"That was fast." Maon shot him a quick smile.

"Tell Shelley at the check-in desk to get you a dungeon manager tank. We have a group coming in from Bingman's Star that has gotten overly rowdy in the past."

"Sure."

"Thanks, bud."

"You owe me."

With a slow, rolling gait, Maon headed toward the door to find Shelley.

"Look at him. He'll have all the female and half the male tourists drooling over him," Randolph said.

"He's a born exhibitionist, but he needs some TLC. He's been through the ringer lately."

"Oh?"

Maon overheard the comments. Even though it meant eavesdropping, if they were going to talk about him, he wanted to hear what they said, especially if they were going to start meddling. He checked over his shoulder. Both men were no longer watching him, so he stopped and slid to the side out of sight of the office door to stay in hearing range.

"He found out his mother lied about his father all these years and kept his father from seeing him," Shane said.

"Damn."

"And Selina—Lasair to you—dumped him."

"Shit."

"Yeah, he seems to be handling it, but he's been quiet, not himself."

"Fuck. He was pretty ecstatic the day they played together here. I thought she might be the one to collar him. I'll find him someone to help him forget."

"He's been avoiding women. He hasn't said it, but he loves Selina."

"Poor broken-hearted boy."

That was enough for Maon; he slipped away. He wasn't going to play the simp for his friends to worry over. Selina had been unequivocal. She wanted nothing to do with him. He needed to get on with his life, do what Shane had said, soak up the atmosphere of the Whip Hand. Maon was perfectly capable of finding female companionship on his own. That he didn't want any right now was just the way it was.

He stripped out of his shirt and pulled on the sleeveless black dungeon monitor shirt, rubbing a hand across the large DM plastered across the chest. This was perfect. He had an obvious excuse for why he couldn't play. The private playroom was reserved for those who were dungeon-approved or being trained by someone who was. Kink groups from off planet often made use of the club while vacationing on Beta Tau.

The atmosphere of the room was what he'd expected. Randolph was efficient and ruthless in dealing with people that created problems in his club. The dim lighting showed that more than half of the room's play equipment was occupied. Muted sighs mingled with groans, gasps, and shrieks all synchronized to pulsing music. In the far corner, with enough space to allow him full range, a whip master was working over identical twins. Greedy boy.

Maon strolled through the room, nodding at the other dungeon monitor. Rick was his name. Or Rich. Maon would have to ask. After acquainting himself with the various scenes being played out, he settled himself in a broad stance, arms over his chest, in position to watch half the room. Rick had stood where he could oversee the other half. Maon allowed himself the enjoyment of watching a pretty little sub being spanked. Perhaps if he kept his mind focused on subs, he wouldn't think about one particular Domme. He could try. *No, for fuck's sake.* He was going to forget her and learn to enjoy life again.

20

The trip by space dart from Tallav to Qingdao had taken Selina eight days, six in hyperspace without the ability to communicate with the outside world. Tales were told of crews going space crazy on long hyperspace jumps. By the time she and Filip had arrived at Qingdao, she knew what could cause mild-mannered citizens to go on killing rampages. All it took was one person like Filip Patinka and the inability to escape from him.

The fifteen hours moving from hyperpoint entry to space dock had given Selina a much needed break while she barricaded herself in the spare stateroom. Her excuse that she had to read and respond to all the messages waiting in her queue was valid, but Filip had still found innumerable reasons to interrupt her.

Once they'd made planetfall and arrived at their hotel, he'd been a constant irritant, fussing to make sure the room was to his satisfaction. His requests to the staff had been couched in ways to make it seem that Selina needed it that way. She'd finally put her foot down when he asked a maid to change a floral arrangement to one of another color that would suit Selina better. The maid had scurried off, happy to escape.

Filip had announced he needed to rest. Selina had been grateful for the respite. She looked at him now and released a slow sigh, not wanting to wake him. Burrowed down in the covers, Filip was making little snuffles and grunts.

It was clear to Selina now that Filip was not working out. But dumping him so far from home wasn't fair to a man who had no experience traveling by himself. She'd wait until just before docking at Tallav on the return flight home. Meanwhile she'd make the best of the situation she'd created for herself.

Ready to scrub away the sterilized grunge of space travel, Selina headed straight for the shower. The spicy-scented toiletries she preferred had been unpacked and were waiting in the bathroom. After washing her hair, she wrapped her long chestnut tresses in a towel and filled the tub with hot water and bubble bath. While she waited for it to fill, she used her sonic hair remover on her legs and underarms. She'd let herself go on the trip. The return to smooth skin was a relief.

By the time she'd soaked away the tension in her muscles, dried herself in the hotel's fluffy towels, and massaged lotion into her skin, she was ready for bed.

Filip was ready too. He was laid out across the huge bed, caressing himself with long strokes. The display was meant to be erotic, but it incited a mental groan rather than a moan. Even the suggestion of sex with Filip was draining. She told him she had business notes to go over before her first meeting the next morning. He pouted and complained, but in the end burrowed back under the covers. He fell asleep quickly, sinking deeper, his previous snuffling turning to outright snores.

Carefully Selina removed her arm from around him and slid out of the bed. She retrieved her robe from the closet and slipped into it. Her desire for sleep had fled. In the suite's main room, she selected tea from the suite's snack tray. With two punches of her thumb, the container heated the tea. From a rack, she picked a bright, floral china mug and poured the hot beverage into it. The steam rose, filling her nose with the soothing scents of a nighttime herbal tea. The midnight-blue sky out the balcony doors beckoned to her, so she took her mug and opened the door. The breeze was gentle, wafting a smell of flowers that reminded her of the lilacs back home. Qingdao was a stunning planet. Unlike Tallav with its uncontrived beauty, Qingdao's beauty was entirely manmade. Sculpted gardens and architecture that emphasized simplicity of line and grace seemed almost natural juxtaposed against the austere mountains that towered above the city.

Under other circumstances she would have enjoyed her visit. Taking slow sips of tea, she turned her mind to the argument she'd had with her mother before leaving Tallav. Her mother's words had never been far from Selina's thoughts. The realization that she had done nothing to cause her father's death was a comfort. Still she missed her father desperately. She drained her mug in one last long, warm swallow and set it aside. Arms wrapped around herself, she stroked the smooth sleeves of her robe.

Her parents had been good together. Never having stopped to analyze what made their marriage special, she did now, hoping to discern the secret they'd shared. They were complete opposites in personality. Her mother was flamboyant while her father was quiet. Business details didn't matter to her. For him, they were the center of his meticulous attention to every facet of the House of Shirley. One thing they had in common: a deep, abiding love for each other and for her.

It had to be more than that. Love faded. At least it did for others. She remembered the arguments she'd overheard between her parents. And they had argued, loudly and robustly. But their fights never devolved to personal attacks. They were strongly worded negotiations over disagreements. Now that she considered it, their quarrels never frightened her. They never signaled a family breakup. Arguments were realignments, putting things back into place. After any particularly heated discussion, they had been extra cuddly and affectionate.

Part of her education on Tallav had been cultural norms and expectations. Women were expected to marry to produce the heirs that would continue their heritage. Whatever other pursuits they engaged in, family was to be paramount in any woman's life, with the head of family also caring for all the extended members. The Shirleys weren't prolific, currently comprising two unmarried great-aunts, her mother's sister and her husband, and her cousin, Ned. When Selina considered the individuals in her circle of friends and acquaintances whose marriages dissolved, she realized most placed their own individual needs first.

That described Filip to a tee. Marrying him would have been the biggest mistake of her life. She would have done her duty, caring for him, sleeping with him, whatever was needed to keep him happy. Was it wrong to want something for herself? She hadn't caused her father's death. Maybe what happened to Kevin hadn't been her fault either?

It had been her first year at university when she was just seventeen. Kevin had been smitten with her, always eager to do anything she asked. Her first real relationship. And she'd reveled in it. Let him follow her everywhere, pampering her. The man would have carried her up twelve flights of stairs if she'd asked. He'd been way over the top, and she'd allowed it, not thinking it would be better if she restrained some of his compulsive behavior.

Then Teandra Wicklow had started her snark campaign against Selina. Teandra was a second-year student and member of the First Daughter's Society, into which every heir to a first family was automatically inducted. Teandra had treated Selina with cold aloofness, which Selina hadn't understood but didn't let worry her. Whatever Teandra's motivation had been for the nasty gossip she aimed at Selina, she got more than her just deserts.

If Selina could take back what she'd done, she would. At first she'd ignored Teandra's snide remarks claiming Selina was nothing without a man. But when Teandra brought Selina's mother into it, accusing Audrina of being a hack who relied on her husband, taking credit for his work, Selina had lost it. In front of Kevin. He'd attacked Teandra. If he hadn't been stopped, he might have killed her. His suicide in prison had been the concluding argument in Selina's self-prosecution. She'd avoided men thereafter. She'd vowed never to be responsible for another man's ruin. Until her duty to marry forced her hand.

Perhaps she should thank Filip. After all, he'd shown her that she didn't want to be with a man who was arguably more self-involved than she had ever been. She'd taken on the blame for Kevin's actions, believing she'd created the situation. But there had been something wrong with Kevin. Something that at seventeen she'd not understood. But his attack on Teandra and his suicide had come from his own troubled mind. If only Selina had talked to her mother back then about what had happened, instead of deciding to protect her from Teandra's nasty remarks. Her mother would have set Selina straight. Audrina's effervescent personality was backed up by a solid core of insight into human motivations. She'd comforted Selina through the horror of the situation but never knew that Selina blamed herself for Kevin's death. Selina had bottled that up inside.

And here she was in another mess, this time truly of her own making. There was no going back. She'd gotten involved with Filip and brought him to Qingdao. She didn't look forward to the drama of breaking things off with him, but then stupidity required its own remuneration.

Her chin dipped to her chest. The sadder consequence was the loss of Maon. Had he moved on as he'd claimed he would? Was she too late to discover that, on the essentials that made a happy marriage, they were in complete agreement? In many ways, as a couple they were the reverse of her parents. Maon was outgoing, and she was quiet. Well, they both liked details. She smiled at memories of him insisting he was a data crunch. Maybe their shared attention to detail would mean fewer arguments between them. Probably not. Maon might be submissive in the bedroom, but not so much outside it.

Why she had ever considered Filip to be submissive was beyond her. He'd proven he wasn't repeatedly. He was a faux sub who topped from the bottom. His veneer of submission covered his self-centered, me-first attitude. *Anything you want, Selina, but could you do this instead of that?* But Filip had also shown her she didn't like to be responsible for every aspect of another person's life. True, Filip was overly needy and resisted everything she told him to do. Still, it was exhausting keeping up with what he ate, what he wore, and what he would do with his day while she was working. Total power exchange was not her answer. That could be summed up in one word. *Maon.* He was her answer, and she would get him back no matter what it took.

SELINA WAS PLEASED WITH HERSELF. She'd accomplished in five days what she thought would take seven. The executive administrator she'd hired to oversee all aspects of House of Shirley business on Qingdao was exceptional. He had anticipated potential problems and dealt with them before her arrival. He'd even convinced the Gallardan mill that had produced her samples to supply them with yarn until their own factory came online. Since things were on track, she'd been able to do more planning than she had expected.

When she stepped off the lift to head toward her hotel room, she had a spring in her step. She'd finished her day early and could return to Tallav ahead of schedule. A celebration was in order. She'd whisk Filip off for one last nice night out.

When she turned the doorknob, she heard groaning sounds that initially worried her. Was Filip ill?

The door swung open, and she had a full view of the suite's main room. Filip was bent over the arm of the sofa, another man thrusting away at his backside. At first too caught up in the sex to notice her arrival, the man, a hotel employee from his uniform, looked up and blanched. When he realized she was there, he hastily pulled his clothes back together.

"Koto! Why did you stop? Keep going!" Filip said.

His head lowered, Koto fled past Selina, muttering, "I'm so sorry. Very sorry."

Filip stood and turned to follow him, and then he saw Selina. He yanked his trousers up and moved toward where she was planted stock-still in the doorway.

"It's not what you think."

Selina crossed her arms over her chest. Wasn't this the icing on the cake? And she had been going to marry this gods-damned self-centered prick. "What am I thinking?"

"It was a little fun while you were away. It means nothing." His eyes were puppy-dog big and pleading for her not to punish him.

Did he imagine she was an idiot? "Do you not understand what the term 'monogamous relationship' means?"

Filip drew himself up in a haughty stance. "Of course, I do. This has nothing to do with that. I love you, only you. This was just sex."

Selina gritted her teeth. She'd put up with a lot from him and yet had still waited to end things with him until their return to Tallav. "Just sex?"

His nostrils flared, and he glared at her. "I wouldn't have to resort to this if you gave me what I needed in bed."

Unbelievable. "So it's my fault you were having sex in our hotel room with another man?" she asked, struggling to control the tone of her voice.

"Yes." He paused, then resumed with a whining tone. "No. I mean, I told you I liked anal sex."

"You told me it was something you wanted to explore. Not that you needed it." Selina sighed, realizing that she was still standing in an open doorway and that anyone could pass by. She stepped inside, slamming the door. Why the hell was she wasting energy on discussing this with him? They had already been finished, and this didn't make them any more or less over. Still, she had no desire for the scene Filip would make if she broke it off with him right now. "That's really not the point. I'm furious with you, Filip. I need time to cool off. Please leave me here alone for a few hours. Go eat in the hotel restaurant. Tell them to bill it to the room. Go calm your boyfriend down. I'm sure he's afraid he'll lose his job. Whatever. Get out of my sight for three hours. Minimum." Three hours should give her time to clear her things from the suite and make arrangements for Filip.

"As you wish, Selina. I only want to make you happy." When he walked past her to leave, he touched her shoulder, gasping when she flinched back. "I'm sorry. I'll do anything to make it up to you."

"Go, Filip."

Selina slumped when she heard the door close. The drama had come earlier than she'd expected, but at least she had a reason he could grasp for dumping him.

When the front desk answered her call, she asked to speak with the manager on duty. With a request for discretion, she booked a new room for herself for one night. She told the manager her companion could remain in their present suite for the duration of the reservation. Put any of his charges on her tab during that period, including restaurant purchases. After that, his bills were his own. He was not to be told where she had gone. The manager promised to send a maid up immediately to assist her in packing.

After she finished the call, Selina sat staring at the desktop. A light tap on the door broke into her thoughts, and she went to let the maid in.

"How may I help you, Ms. Shirley?" she asked.

"Please pack all my clothes in the navy luggage. Mr. Patinka's things stay here."

"Yes, ma'am."

While the maid was busy, Selina considered her options. The thought of Filip's whining entreaties when she told him she was ending things was almost too horrid to contemplate. It might be cowardly, but she didn't want to face Filip's pleading. Especially since it would almost inevitably degenerate into a diatribe on Selina's faults and lack of consideration for him. She would leave him a note.

A sense of relief followed that decision. She paid for an open reservation for Filip for a flight to Tallav and notified the pilot of her private space dart that she wanted to leave the next morning. On notepaper pulled from the desk drawer, she wrote the message that would sever their relationship.

Filip,

What happened today has made it clear we are not compatible. We each have different expectations and to continue our relationship would only lead to more frustration on both our parts.

I am leaving for Beta Tau as soon as possible. This room is paid for the full length of our original plans. In addition, I've notified the hotel staff I will continue to pay for anything you require from the hotel or the restaurant here through our planned checkout date. An open ticket to Tallav is available in your name at Tallav Spacelines should you choose to use it. Please do not contact me. I will not answer or return your calls.

Selina

Selina placed the note on the desk in plain sight and then went into the bedroom. Finished packing Selina's clothes, the maid had started in on the toiletries in the bathroom. She stuck her head out of the door, holding up a bottle, and asked, "Is this lotion yours, ma'am?"

"Yes." Selina checked the drawers and closets, making sure nothing of hers was missed. After the maid brought her toiletry bag out, Selina made certain the only items left in the bathroom belonged to Filip. When she returned to the bedroom, she told the maid, "That's everything. Thank you for your help. I'm adding an extra gratuity for you to my bill."

"Thank you, ma'am. I'm sorry for your distress."

Selina gave her a rueful smile. "I'm not as distressed as you might think. Please do not tell Mr. Patinka where I've gone."

"Of course not, ma'am. He is nothing. Koto wishes to tell you he is sorry for the pain he has caused you and thanks you for not telling the manager on him."

"I'm sure Koto has learned a valuable lesson," Selina said.

"We can only hope," the maid responded.

A knock brought them both out to the main room. The manager entered when the maid opened the door for him and left through it.

"I have your new key code and room number. A porter will assist with your luggage. If there's anything else I can do for you, please don't hesitate to ask."

"Thank you." Selina allowed him to escort her to her new suite after the porter had loaded her bags onto a cart.

21

The past few days Maon had felt more like himself. Spending time at the Whip Hand had done him good. Randolph had been kind enough to allow him to serve as dungeon monitor, so Maon had a reason to stand back and watch. He wasn't ready to pick up his old habits yet. At work, when his mood got better, so had the other marshals' attitudes toward him. While he closed out from the documents he'd been working with on his data screen, he realized he was humming. Audrina had notified him she was on Beta Tau and had been for days with no call from him. She demanded that he meet her at her hotel for lunch today. A smile played across his lips. Lunch would be fun.

If he didn't hurry, he'd be late. He ran his fingers through his hair and checked the front of his shirt. No spills. When he walked through the room that held the work desks of most of the other marshals, Maon nodded and smiled. One group turned to Maon, and Fields asked, "Hey, weren't you the guy that got shot during the Cosmo Bonilla escape?"

"Yeah, that was me." Maon stopped, waiting for an explanation.

"He's turning himself back in."

"Really!" Maon scratched his cheek. "Why?"

Fields shrugged. "Claims he didn't plan or want to escape from prison. Said he thought the shooter was trying to kill him, and the people that grabbed him were rescuing him. He didn't realize, until they'd gotten clean away, they were helping him flee."

"You're kidding?" *That's not what it looked like on the vids.*

Another marshal spoke up. "He made a deal with the Feds. Fingered the head of the third biggest drug cartel on Gallarda in exchange for not charging him with flight and reducing his sentence to two years on his bribery conviction."

Fields added, "Bonilla maintains it was the Gallardan that planned the escape, trying to impress Bonilla, so he could get in good and join Bonilla's organization."

Burns said, "Also Bonilla claims the same guy is behind all the recent hits on Gallarda, the murder of the Shirley employee on Gallarda, and the attempt on Selina Shirley's life. You were there for that too, weren't you?"

Maon brought his hands to his hips. "Yeah, I was. Did they already bring the Gallardan in?"

Fields shook his head. "Not yet. You may want to watch yourself. Bonilla told the marshals when he turned himself in that this guy, Cardo Green, is a loose cannon, big into revenge. Killing people is apparently his favorite way of eliminating problems. Sometimes just because he's pissed."

"It looks like Bonilla's used the time since his escape to finish his takeover of the Gallardan cartels," Burns said.

"He wouldn't have turned himself in if he hadn't." Maon nodded. "Cardo Green's not the kind of guy Bonilla would keep in any organization he ran. Bonilla's subtle. He doesn't like to attract attention. Part of why no one's gotten enough evidence to convict him."

Fields grimaced. "Cardo Green does nothing but attract attention. Probably why he was chosen as Bonilla's sacrifice. I wouldn't want Green after me, though. He's like a wild boar. Even if you get him backed into a corner, he's going to throw everything he has at you to savage his way out. Glad I'm not one of Bonilla's guards."

Maon's scalp prickled while he swiveled his glance away from Fields to the office door and back to Fields. Could Green go after Selina again? Maon forced himself to relax and asked, "Do they know where Green is? Are they close to apprehending him?"

"They're not sure where he is, but it looks like he made it off Gallarda. My guess is he's lying low," Burns said.

"Where's Bonilla now?" Maon asked. Bonilla would be Green's first target.

Fields grunted. "Right here on Beta Tau. He was hiding out in one of the private domes rented to a corporation that tracks back to Furzine."

Burns growled the name that flashed through all their minds. "The Benefactor. I'd bet a hundred credits that bastard is the one that got Bonilla here in the first place so he could take out the rest of his competition. Being dictator for life on Furzine and the power behind the biggest Gallardan drug cartel wasn't enough for the Benefactor. He had to be in charge of it all. Fucking diplomatic immunity."

"Who knew three years ago that the Benefactor would expand his criminal enterprise off Furzine after overthrowing the Furzian dictator for life," said Fields.

Burns responded. "It'll only get worse. That bastard has more ambition in his little finger than all the past Furzian dictators put together."

Fields shook his head, a scowl on his face. "If the Benefactor has taken over and merged all the Gallardan drug cartels, catching these SOBs just got harder."

Maon agreed, but how long Bonilla remained on Beta Tau was a more important issue to him. "Are they transporting Bonilla back to Tallav right away?"

Fields looked at Maon. "No. The Feds are bringing in a transport from Tallav to take him back to Fed Central. It's due here in about three days. They intend to do a fast turnaround and get Bonilla off world as quickly as possible. Meanwhile, he's being held in a secure location."

Maon's dropped his chin to his chest and ran a hand through his hair. *Shit.* In his gut, he knew where Green was headed if he wasn't already on Beta Tau. He looked at the group of marshals and then at the door. "Um. Thanks, guys. I'm late for a lunch date, but I appreciate the heads-up."

"Sure."

"No problem."

While Maon walked to the tram station to hitch a ride to the hotel where the House of Shirley had set up camp, he couldn't shake the sensation that someone was watching him. He shrugged, attempting to relax, knowing his paranoia for what it was, a visceral response to memories of the day he was shot. *Thank you, Cosmo Bonilla.* At least Selina was in hyperspace for the next five days. Plenty of time to catch Cardo Green, especially if he made a play for Bonilla at the spaceport.

Maon had never paid attention in the past to the events that took place in Beta Tau's shopping dome. He'd heard of fashion week but had never been interested in the runway shows that were the heart of it. When he walked into the hotel conference room marked House of Shirley, he caught sight of Audrina immediately. Vivid colors were indispensable to her personal style. Today was no different. Her bright aqua slacks were topped by a white tunic with matching dots. She was tapping her index finger on each of her other hand's fingers while she talked to a young woman.

"And last, make sure that customs gets the authorizations for the pyantha plants. I want them down here in our care, not sitting up on the space station." A smile washed across Audrina's face. "If I haven't told you yet, you're keeping up admirably." She patted the woman's back and turned. "Maon, darling. Just in time! I'm famished, and my feet need a break."

Maon took her outstretched hands in his. "Gorgeous as ever, even when you're hungry."

She stood on her toes and kissed him on the cheek. "Flatterer. I'm harried and harassed." She hooked her arm in his and led him to the door. "Let's try the bistro across the way."

He looked into her face, noting the dark circles under her eyes. "Are things not going well?"

"No, no. The show is right on track. The usual problems." Her smile was wan. "I'm another year older. That's all. You don't look so perky yourself."

"No, I heard some disturbing news. I'll share once we're settled."

The automatic doors of the hotel slid open. Audrina gestured toward a restaurant that offered indoor seating as well as alfresco in a pretty nook decorated with hanging flower baskets. "It's across the way." They didn't speak until after they'd crossed the paved courtyard and been seated at a small outdoor table. The flowers added a delicate scent to the gentle breeze that stirred their leaves. It always amazed Maon that although they were technically indoors under a dome, the Beta Tau planners had made weather an integral part of the experience. Nice weather only. After a short discussion about the salads on the menu, they placed their order.

"So tell," Audrina said.

"The man who escaped when I was shot, Cosmo Bonilla, has worked out a deal with the Feds that involves testifying against a Gallardan drug mogul. His name is Cardo Green. They don't have Green in custody. He could be on Beta Tau and may try to silence Bonilla. It might be a good idea if you can keep your people off the space station three days from today. That's when the Fed ship arrives to secure Bonilla and transport him to Fed Central." No sense worrying Audrina with the remote possibility that Green could go after Selina.

Audrina shook her head. "Oh my. Well, Selina planned to arrive here in five days, so all the fuss will be over before she gets here."

Maon rubbed a finger on the plasti-glass tabletop. "Yeah. We'll all be pulling special duty until the Feds get him off Beta Tau."

"I'm sure this reminds you of when you got shot," she said, her brow furrowed. "That is not going to happen again."

The waiter arrived with their food and drinks, and once everything was set before them, Maon raised his iced tea and said, "Here's to no one getting wounded this time."

"Here, here," Audrina responded, raising her glass of water.

Maon savored the taste of his cold pasta salad. He bit into a slice of salami, creamy sauce coating his tongue. "I heard something about pyantha plants when I walked in."

Between mouthfuls of her own salad, Audrina filled him in on the particulars for the coming show. When she finished both her food and her description, she said, "I sent a ticket for you to the show. Will you come?"

Maon rubbed a hand across his mouth. "I don't know. I'd love to see Selina in her moment of glory, but I don't want it to seem like I'm pursuing her." He paused, fiddling with his fork. "Besides, it would stir up something that's better left alone."

"Well, the ticket's available."

A smile tugged at Maon's lips. "You are good to me."

"Ha!" She grinned at him. "I'll pay the bill. Then let's take the long way back to the hotel, so I can show you off to more people. As my own dear mother used to say, 'never let arm candy go to waste.'"

"Grandma Shirley was a vamp?" Maon smirked.

Audrina looked down her nose at him. "Certainly not. All the Shirley women are ladies. Now let's go, jelly bean."

∾

WHY DID the alteration of Fed plans surprise him? It made perfect sense to create the impression that the Feds were moving Bonilla under tight security when the real strategy was to sneak him off world on a diplomatic craft. Yet when the order came to stand down because the ship carrying Bonilla had entered hyperspace, Maon was surprised. He never credited the Feds with that much intelligence or the ability to keep a secret like that long enough to complete the plan. What about Cardo Green? Had the man even been on Beta Tau?

Maon's feet ached from a day spent walking the concourse ring of the private passenger level of the space station. He calculated that he'd trudged a grand total of twelve miles the nine times he walked the circle. His focus had been on scrutinizing the docking ports of the various private ships and the people he met.

From vidscreens along the outer wall of the ring, he could observe the ships berthed at this level and those that were coming and going from the station. Simulated picture windows, they looked out on space from one of the largest hyperspace facilities in the sector. One even brought the hyperpulse point into view. Although the scene would have been the same from a vidscreen down world, it was unnerving to place your hand against the wall and know that on the other side lay the vacuum of space. It was unsettling to realize you were an infinitesimal heartbeat in an elongated tin can that orbited one of hundreds of inhabitable planets in an arm of an unexceptional galaxy in a teeming universe.

At least this level was quiet compared to the many public passenger levels above that serviced the larger liners that brought the bulk of Beta Tau's tourists to the planet. Patrolling a passenger level was far better than walking the concourse ring on the loading level below. There the chilly air settled into your bones. The scrubbers never seemed to rid it of the noxious smell of C-trol and other fumes. Yeah, walking the private passenger level was much nicer duty. When he got the message the operation was concluded, he headed straight for the lifts to take him to the shuttle docks at the bottom of the station.

When he exited the lift, as expected, tourists clogged the corridor leading to the concourse ring. Despite his need for food and sleep, there was no use hurrying, so he took his time working his way toward the shuttles. A large space liner of sex tourists, middle-aged men all well dressed and jovially leering at one another, discussed what they hoped to experience once they made planetfall. An annoyed mother glared at them and pulled her children to the side to avoid them while her husband sauntered on, unaware he'd left his family behind. Farther on a band of elderly women were toddling along, keeping to the pace of the slowest member of their group.

As Maon stopped to allow a rushing businesswoman to speed around him, he received an urgent message on his EBC. Mentally opening it, he listened while Audrina, in a panicked voice, told him that Selina was coming in early and docking at the private docking level, berth eleven. Maon sent a ping back to let her know he'd gotten the heads-up. His heart raced while he wove his way back through the crowded concourse to the corridor with the lifts. Selina was arriving on the same level the decoy Fed ship was supposed to dock, the ring he'd spent the whole day guarding. No one had seen a sign of Green, but if he were on the station, Maon didn't want to take any chances of Selina running into him.

Maon dodged people, ignoring those who stopped to turn and watch him while he kept jogging. In front of the lift doors, he slid to a stop. After punching the Up button, he sent a message to berth eleven. No response. He drummed his fingers against his thighs, the wait jangling his already strained nerves. Lift number four opened, revealing a full load of people. He brusquely motioned the passengers to exit. One young man attempted to enter, but Maon shoved him back. When Maon stepped backward into the lift, he blocked the opening with his arm, showing his badge to the others waiting. The disgruntled looks on their faces dissolved into surprise, curiosity, and concern. With a punch of his finger, he jabbed the button for the private passenger level. When the doors closed, he messaged Selina, asking her to wait on the ship for him or find a marshal or guardia and wait with them until he could get to her. Once again he fidgeted, thumping fingers in a chaotic dance beat.

Once the door opened, he stepped out, looking both ways along the lengthy corridor that led to the concourse. He searched for Selina, but it was impossible to determine who the people were in the distance. The corridor was too friggin' long. He'd walked this level all day, but here at the center by the lifts, he wasn't sure which way to take for berth eleven. When he turned to check the sign behind him for the direction, the motion of the doors of the third lift drew his attention. It had appeared empty, but now he glimpsed the front half of a shoe. Pink. When he darted toward it, Selina came into view. She had the faraway look of someone receiving an EBC message. "Selina!" She looked up at him and smiled.

The man next to her eyeballed her and then Maon. The instant before the doors sealed, the man sneered and said, "Marshal Keefe."

Everything in Maon froze. Then his stomach dropped and his hands went icy. Cardo Green. Selina was in an elevator with Cardo Green. Maon slammed his hand against chilly metal and looked at the arrow above. They were going down.

Adrenaline sluiced through him. How could this have happened? While he turned full circle, he scanned the dock for another marshal, federal officer, or local guardia. When he found none, he riveted his eyes on the numbers over the lift, watching while one number stayed lit. It was stopped at the loading and maintenance level one tier below, and then it continued on to the next level and stopped again. Green had probably hit all the buttons to hide where he intended to exit. Maon jammed the Down button and, while he waited, sent an urgent flagged message to the marshal's emergency list with the little information he could give.

Cardo Green in the down lift from the private docking level, with Selina Shirley. Green dressed in a space station maintenance shipsuit.

Chest heaving, with his lungs working double-time sucking in air, Maon brought his hands to his head while he waited. The ping of the fourth lift sent him skittering toward it and prying at the doors while they slowly opened. Inside, he punched the button for the loading dock below. The walls seemed to close in on him. He muttered curses under his breath. It made sense that Green had disguised himself as a maintenance worker. He must have positioned himself before the Feds enhanced security and then come out of hiding when he realized they were leaving. Green must have wondered why the Feds had dropped their expanded security.

Now that Maon had seen him, he was either heading for the transport he'd used to get to Beta Tau or returning to where he'd hid before, using Selina as a human shield. *Fuck, don't let him get Selina off station.* His hiding place could be on any level. *What if I chose wrong? No. Start with the next level. It stands to reason Green would have wanted to be close to where Bonilla was supposed to board the Fed transport.*

Shit, couldn't this lift go faster? While resisting the urge to batter the metal doors with his hands, Maon prayed that he was right, and that he wasn't making a mistake by pursuing Green to the private loading level. Those marshals who hadn't taken a shuttle down world were probably scurrying to secure the spaceport and the lifts. Green backed into a corner with Selina as his hostage... *Fuck, no.*

Maon's heart was thumping as though the staccato beat could hasten the lift doors opening. When they began their slow slide apart, he squeezed himself through. His footsteps sounded odd, clattering when he took several steps into the wide access way that split the loading level in half. A pink handbag lay on the floor between the first and second lifts. The flap was open, and all the contents were spilled out in disarray. When he bent to get a closer look, Maon noticed the bottom half of a picture partially hidden by a hairbrush. A swipe of his finger dislodged the vidshot from under the brush. It was Audrina and Selina. Green had definitely brought her to this level. With the image pinched between his thumb and forefinger, Maon sent a quick message to the marshals, letting them know that Green and Selina were on the private loading level.

Maon scanned both directions of the access way, attempting to see Selina and Green, but it was impossible to distinguish the people or objects in the distance, especially those toward the far ends. *Shit.* The level was cavernous. Maon clenched and unclenched his fists at the sounds of normal activity that ricocheted and echoed throughout it, each reverberating clang adding to his tension. On the wall opposite the passenger lifts, were two much larger freight lifts. Two workers were jockeying a floating platform loaded with luggage into the closest one.

Maon rushed across to them, showed his badge, and asked, "Did you see a man dressed in a maintenance suit with a young woman in the last few minutes?"

"Nah," the older man replied.

The younger man nodded and said, "I saw them get out of the lifts."

"Did you notice where they went?" Maon asked while he shifted his weight from one foot to the other.

"Sorry, no. I only looked up for a second." The younger man's mouth twisted in a show of regret. "But I'm sure they didn't go past us this way." His arm rose to point in the direction they'd come from. "I would have remembered that. She was pretty."

Maon gave him a quick cuff on his upper arm and said, "Thanks. That helps." While he headed away from them, he visually scoured the storage platforms along one side for gaps a person could squeeze through. The lower racks were all solidly filled, which made sense. They were the easiest to store crates on. No one could hide there. A series of overhead and regular room doors lined the access way on the other side. Some were open, exposing maintenance bays where mechanics could repair or rebuild broken ship parts. So many friggin' doors, but that was where logic dictated he focus his search. The slow work of trying each door, moving on from those that were locked, and inspecting any he found open was frustrating. Maon reined in his need to rush. If he missed something... *No. Don't even think it.*

In one maintenance bay he encountered a worker who told him he'd seen a man rushing a woman along but hadn't thought much about it. Maon released a frustrated breath. He was on the right track, but it was taking too long. Panic was playing tricks with his ability to behave rationally. He fought back an urge to pummel the man for not stopping Green.

Without thanking the worker, Maon charged back out of the bay and looked as far as he could down the access way. He still had two hundred meters or more before he arrived at the dock's concourse. A short distance ahead, something was lying against the wall. What was that? Maybe Selina dropped something else. Unwilling to continue his slow door-by-door search, he ran toward the speck. When he drew closer, he recognized a woman's shoe, pink like that handbag. It was Selina's shoe, positioned next to a door.

With a twist of his wrist, he attempted to wrench it open. It was locked. Hand against the barrier, he slumped while accessing his EBC. A message from Marshal Fields told him reinforcements were on their way. While Maon listened, he scanned the door and surrounding wall for its designation. When he spotted it, he sent a request, asking station security to unlock it remotely. Almost at once he received a response. *"Will do."*

Time stalled while Maon waited for the chunking sound that would signal the lock was disengaged. Despite being poised expectantly, when it came, he jumped. The next instant he threw open the door. Before him stood nothing but shelves with cleaning supplies and tools, a rack of wet and dry mops, and bins for sorting different refuse. The smell of the cleaners and oily rags jarred his sinuses. Lights illuminated the closet the minute the door opened, fully exposing everything from ceiling to floor. The only free space was a wide aisle that ran through the center. Another set of shelves, full of maintenance paraphernalia, covered most of the back wall. Besides himself, no one else occupied the closet. *Fuck no!* Had he been wrong?

22

If she hadn't been wearing new pink heels rather than her comfortable flats, Selina might have skipped along the concourse. The trip to Beta Tau had been restful. She had taken full advantage, spending long hours sleeping and drawing ideas in colored pencil on one of the large pads she carried with her. The tactile sensation of the pencil, the drag of the point while color was applied to the paper, appealed to her. Her high-tech sketch tablet was useful for creating the exacting files needed to turn her drawings into actual articles of clothing. But pad and pencil were an integral part of her creativity.

Freedom from Filip was a blessing. Why had she ever considered him a viable marriage candidate? Her attempt to avoid drama had been foiled when she found him waiting at the berth where the space dart was docked. Tears and pleading had ensued. Brusque rebukes from Selina hadn't quelled him. She'd been afraid he'd follow her onto the ship if she opened the access tube until a security guard had arrived and escorted Filip away. Still the rest and escape from Filip didn't account for her lighthearted mood. Not completely.

After entering hyperspace from Qingdao, she realized she hadn't told her mother she'd be arriving on Beta Tau early. Selina had planned to surprise her. But now they were docked, she changed her mind. Dropping in unexpectedly during the hectic preparation for a show wasn't such a good idea. Her luggage had been off-loaded and sent to the hotel. With just a shoulder bag, she prepared to exit the space dart, pausing first to send her mother a message.

The walk along the access tube from her small ship to the dock always disconcerted her. She was convinced she could detect a wobble although station safety info claimed they didn't move. Irritated at her own skittishness, she pushed hard against the tube wall. Nothing. *Hummph.* She jumped, and then, certain she'd felt something, pelted toward the docking port, releasing the breath she'd been holding when she stood outside on the concourse. That was stupid and proved nothing. A giggle bubbled up, changing into a snort when she tried to suppress it.

The walkway along the dock was quiet. This level was designated for small private ships like the space dart. The shops, bars, and food kiosks lining the interior walls were designed to tempt more sophisticated and wealthier customers. The corridor to the lifts was one-third of the way along the ring to her left. She moved in that direction at a brisk pace. A smile lit her face while she reveled in her sense of freedom like a nightingale released from a cage. A cage made from her own false beliefs about herself. The floaty trapeze dress she wore with the linear blues, greens, and pinks of a Renoir landscape was vibrantly sexy. She'd even opted to wear killer heels as any smart, young, attractive designer would. Her fashion week debut would take the design world by storm, and Maon Keete would be hers if she had to cuff him and tie him to her bed. Not that she'd need to go that far. No. With a sway of her hips, she imagined the impression she would make on him in this outfit. The sweet man wouldn't be able to resist.

The new shoes were pinching the toes of her left foot. She gratefully took the auto walk, easing from the shoe until she reached the end. Outside the lifts a maintenance worker stood waiting. He was a bear of a man who looked like someone had been stroking his fur the wrong direction. When the lift bell pinged, Selina glanced up at him. His gaze slithered over her before he held a hand out, offering her the opportunity to enter first. Selina wasn't sure she wanted to be in a cramped space with him, but she scolded herself for being paranoid. He was probably having a bad day.

With a nod, she entered, followed by the man. When she did, an urgent message arrived on her EBC. It was Maon. How did he know she was here? Only her mom knew she was here early, and she'd just messaged her. He must have been watching the ship arrivals. Pleasure transformed into a tingle of desire. One quick step forward to push on the button for the shuttle level brought her that much closer to seeing him. As the doors to the lift opened, Selina focused on listening to Maon. She heard her name called. With a glance up, she caught sight of Maon outside the lift while the doors were closing. She grinned, but then confusion struck her. Something was wrong. Maon's face was drained of color, a wash of utter panic in his eyes. A malicious chuckle splattered the enclosed space. Her knuckles turned white from the rigid grip she had on the handle of her handbag. An overwhelming urge to run flooded her. Slowly she turned her head and looked up at the bulky man beside her. His sneer told her everything, even before he said, "Selina Shirley. We meet at last."

Green fastened her arm in his grip and leaned to snarl who he was in her ear. What did he want with her? Was this the person who had sent someone to shoot at her on Gallarda? Why? Why now? Selina tried to control her panic. She was shaking uncontrollably, but she couldn't fall apart. Not now. Maon knew she was in an elevator with this psychopath. He was coming for her, but this time she was determined to help herself.

A gasp escaped her when the solid wall of the lift smacked against her spine. Green's body plastered against her. The pungent smell of unwashed male came close to gagging her when she turned her head away from his lips, which were looming toward her own.

"You owe me, bitch," he growled.

"What did I do to you?" Her voice shook.

"I lost everything because of you. You and your pathetic drug operation. I did the right thing. Took it down. Set up Bonilla's escape, but he turns on me. Says violence ain't the way. Says I shoulda left you alone. Gives me up to the Feds. I couldn't get him today, but I've got you. And you're gonna pay."

His hot breath puffed in her ear as he spoke, and then he found her earlobe and bit hard. At her gasp, he latched his mouth to her neck and sucked his way down to her shoulder, slurping and tonguing. "You like that? Maybe you like it rough?" His teeth clamped down. Pain lanced from her neck to her collarbone as though a chunk of flesh was being torn out. For a moment she lost control. A scream tore from her lungs. His thick hand slapped her face, knocking her head into the wall. "Shut up!" His tongue slathered over the wound, and he said, "Gonna bite you all over, bitch." He pressed something cold and metallic to her temple. The telltale that showed her EBC was powered on winked off. Without her EBC she couldn't message.

Selina's stomach churned with nausea. How could she escape this brute? Physically he was overpowering her. The lift pinged, and the doors opened one level below their starting point. Green had punched every button to make it hard to determine where they got off. Maon wouldn't know where to go. Bread crumbs. She needed to leave him bread crumbs to follow.

Green backed off, holding her upper arm tight. "Don't do anything stupid, or I'll break your neck right here." Selina gave a shaky nod, her cheek throbbing and her head aching from the slap.

As he pushed her forward out of the lift, her handbag slipped on her shoulder. Yes. She let the bag slide to the ground, giving it a little kick to ensure the contents spilled out. "Oh!" She pulled against his hold to reach to pick it up.

Green yanked her back up. "Leave it." Two men were struggling with a luggage float ten meters past the lifts to the left. One looked up, and Selina stared at him intently, but he returned to fixing the gravity belt on the platform.

Green led her to the right, away from the workers. Walls of solidly packed crates lined one side, and doors of varying sizes the other. Even if she could break free of his hold, Green would probably shoot anyone she asked for help. *Break free. Ha.* She could barely keep up with his long strides by trotting with little bursts of speed to prevent him from dragging her. Except for the sounds of the two men behind them, this level was undisturbed. No one else moved along this part of the access way.

The pace had Selina panting hard. She worked to catch her breath when Green stopped outside one of dozens of matching doors. When his attention was distracted while he entered the pass code in the lock pad, she cautiously slipped a shoe off and pushed it to the side against the wall.

When the locking mechanism clunked, he swung the door open and propelled her inside. Lights burst on overhead, illuminating the room. She was in a maintenance closet.

The tang of industrial cleaners assaulted her nose. While Green secured the entrance, he held on to her with one hand. She looked for something she could use as a weapon, taking stock of the stored items, but the moment was over before she found anything suitable. He pushed her down the narrow central aisle toward the back of the closet. Along the right wall, a rack of wrenches hung neatly, smaller to larger. When they passed the tools, she reached out to grasp one.

A hard thrust from Green sent her stumbling forward. "Hands to yourself." At the rear, shelves covered most of the wall.

Green pushed her to the side. His lips contorted into a smirk when he noticed her eyeing the door to the access way. "Even if someone comes in here, they aren't gonna find you." With an evil laugh, he twisted and pulled a knob on the shelf. It moved open like a gate on hinges, revealing darkness beyond. "Smugglers' safe hole. We'll have plenty of time to get acquainted." He sneered, shoving her forward. She lost her footing, tripping and falling into a heap of soft bedding. Unable to see, she quickly flipped herself over, drawing her knees to her chest and wrapping her arms around them.

From her right came the sounds of Green rummaging. An emergency lantern glowed to life, painting the hiding place with a sickly yellowish cast. The space wasn't large, but tall enough for Green to stand. Besides the bed of blankets on which she sat, stacks of food and beverage containers lined a wall. A pile of refuse filled a corner along with bottles of straw-colored liquid she finally realized were urine. The stench of body odor and human waste permeated the air.

With one long stride, Green was towering over her, lust filling his eyes. He had a nasty smile on his lips as he pulled the zipper halfway down and unfastened the belt on his shipsuit. Unable to suppress the mewling sound she was making, Selina scrambled backward like a crab until her back hit a solid obstacle. With her hand, she searched around her for a makeshift weapon but came up empty. While Green was pulling his arms from the suit, Selina realized she was still wearing one shoe. She slipped it off and held it hidden in the folds of her dress by her side. Green removed his boots and then slid the shipsuit down his thighs, kicking free. His erection jutted from a mass of curling dark brown hair.

Nausea returned full force. He squatted, reaching out to grab her ankle. The blankets under her slipped when she tried to brace herself, making it easy for him to pull her closer. With inexorable slowness he dragged her toward him until she fell back. She tried to catch herself from being pulled flat, banging her elbows into the synthsteel floor. His tongue lashed out to swipe the insole of her foot. Saliva seeped between her toes as he sucked them. Revulsion flooded her. As soon as he got within range, she would hit him with the heel of her shoe. If she could stand it that long. He leered at her, chuckling, and moved on to her other foot. Time stalled while Selina endured the torture of his mouth on her body, relentlessly moving up her leg. The snuffling sound he made while he licked and sucked was punctuated by small pinching bites. She whimpered.

"Like that, huh? How about this?" He bit her inner thigh, his teeth sinking in deep enough to draw blood.

Selina cried out in pain. Green's face was suffused with sadistic hunger, but then it went blank while he listened. She hadn't heard anything, but apparently, he had. Then she caught what sounded like the door to the closet banging open. *Oh, please God, let it be Maon.* Green covered her with his body, clamping a hand across her mouth. "Not a sound, bitch."

Selina wanted to scream, but she could barely breathe with Green's grimy palm covering her lips and part of her nose while the full weight of his torso compressed her lungs. When his penis, softening now, pressed into her thigh, she attempted to escape from under him. The useless effort made him roughly shake her head. With her feet and right arm the only parts of her body she could move, hysteria was on the verge of engulfing her. She had to let Maon know she was here. Futilely opening and closing the fingers, she touched something. The shoe! She'd dropped it, but it was near her right hand. When she fumbled, searching for it, she grazed the edge. While she strained against Green's crushing bulk, she stretched toward the shoe. Able to clamp the side between her first and second finger, she dragged it close enough to grab and fling at the wall with the hidden door. The shoe hit the partition with a decisive *thump*.

Green brought the hand he'd pinioned her shoulder with to her throat. "Bitch!" The word hissed into her ear. He squeezed her neck while still holding her mouth shut. Without oxygen she grew light-headed. *Maon, please find me.* Her vision tunneled into blackness.

tumped, Maon looked around the closet. Shit, he was wasting time. The shoe hadn't been a marker for this closet. Green must have taken her farther along the access way. Even now he might be forcing her aboard a ship. Maon wanted to roar out the anguish that filled his chest. Where was she?

When he turned to continue searching outside, a muffled *thump* sounded somewhere in the back of the closet. He whirled to face the rear again. The equipment on the shelves sat motionless, mocking him. Crouched, he tapped on the wall. A hollow thud sounded. Hope surged in him. *That wasn't synthsteel.* A void was behind it. He wrinkled his nose at a faint whiff of feces. In order to scan the lower shelves, he shifted objects to get a better look. The surface of the back of the shelves was smooth under his fingers. No cracks gave evidence of a hidden door. Maybe the whole rack moved?

He steadied himself by grasping a small knob attached to a shelf above his head when he levered himself up. His grasp slipped when it turned unexpectedly. His pulse sped up, and his gut clenched. He staggered onto unsteady feet, his hand shaking while he twisted it again. The shelf made the slightest movement before he quickly released the knob. It was a latch for a hidden door. If Green had Selina in the space beyond, he must be aware someone was in the closet looking for him. Holding his breath, Maon listened, but no other sounds came from beyond the wall.

Maybe he could still surprise Green. With that in mind, he raised his voice. "Damn it. I'm wasting time," he said, turning toward the open entrance. When he strode along the aisle, he picked up a large monkey wrench, hefting its solid weight in his hand while moving on to slam the access way door. The banging sound reverberated through the closet after Maon doused the lights. In the dark, his fingers tightened around his improvised weapon. He couldn't risk using his gun. Selina could be hit. As quietly as possible, he moved to the back of the closet. To override his jittering nerves, he took several cleansing breaths, employing a four count to breathe in...hold...breathe out...hold. As prepared as he could be for what awaited him, he brought the wrench up across his thighs, found the knob, twisted, and pulled.

Green burst out of the opening, thrusting a knife toward Maon's gut. His responses automatic, Maon stepped back and countered with the wrench, bringing it into play to drive Green's knife hand away. He snapped his left arm up and seized Green's wrist, struggling to keep his opponent's greater size from overpowering his hold. The force of the attack pushed Maon into the aisle of the closet while Green maneuvered the blade nearer Maon's chest. Maon attempted to strike Green, slamming the metal tool down, aiming for his shoulder, but the blow didn't fully connect and slid away, ineffective. Green continued to shove the sharp tip of his weapon relentlessly at Maon.

Equipment and cans clanged to the floor when Maon's hold on Green weakened, forcing him to backpedal up the aisle to avoid being stabbed. Green tried grappling Maon closer by grasping his shirt. His fingers slid until he latched on to Maon's belt. Finally overcoming Maon's resistance, he sliced the knife across Maon's shoulder.

With adrenaline surging through his body, Maon didn't even feel the blade when it struck him. He twisted out of Green's grip on his belt. When Green pulled back for another strike, Maon brought the wrench between them and thrust him away with it, creating a gap. He took advantage of the opening, slamming the wrench down on the arm of Green's weapon hand. The shock of the blow and the sudden give when the bone broke were followed by his scream. The knife clattered to the floor. Before Maon could strike again, Green grabbed the tool and pulled. It slid through Maon's sweaty palm. His fingers tightened, and he yanked it free from Green, stepping back while he did.

Green squatted, scrabbling for his weapon, babying his broken arm against his chest. Before he could find it, Maon rushed him, striking him in the side. The force of the blow juddered up Maon's arm. With a dull thump, Green slumped to the floor, his head smacking into the synthsteel. The knife lay gleaming dully, inches from Green's good hand. Maon stomped on it when Green reached for the blade. A backward sling with his foot sent it skittering toward the door. Maon threw his own weapon behind him.

Green was nude. The fury that pulsed in Maon grew exponentially along with his fear for what this monster had done or planned to do to Selina. Rape and then murder. Everything within Maon burned to destroy this malignant creature. Green's eyes jerked around, looking for something to use as a weapon. In a weak attempt to protect himself, he brought his shoulder up to his face and cringed. Maon's left arm hung useless, and blood soaked his shirt. Given an opportunity, Green would come at him again. Maon needed to take him out so he could get to Selina. With one punch he shattered Green's nose. The white-hot rage that had boiled inside him ever since the lift doors had closed on Green and Selina surfaced. His second and third punches broke his jaw. Shock removed any vestige of resistance in Green while blood streamed bright red from his nose and mouth. His eyes rolled back in his head, and he passed out. The sight brought Maon to his senses. He scrambled past Green and rushed through the hidden door.

Selina lay limp and unconscious on the floor. Maon bent over her. Was she dead? He wanted to scoop her into his arms and cradle her to him, but he was afraid of hurting her. With gentle fingers he brushed the side of her face, anguished that he was too late to keep Green from hurting her.

Hands latched on to Maon's shoulders and pulled him backward. He rose and turned, prepared to fight Green again. But the face before him wasn't Green's.

"Maon! Are you okay?"

It was Marshal Fields. Maon shuddered from the pain lancing through his shoulder. "O-okay. I'm okay." His voice was a hoarse stutter.

"You sure?" asked Fields.

"Yeah. I'm sure."

"Help him out of here," Fields told the marshal standing outside in the closet.

Maon's guts twisted. "Selina. She's hurt." He couldn't bring himself to say she might be dead. He tried to turn back to her, but insistent hands caught him.

"Let us get her. You go on ahead." When Maon resisted, Fields said, "I mean it. We'll restrain you if we have to."

Maon allowed himself to be moved through the closet and into the access way, his breathing rapid, heart pounding. Images of the terrible things Green could have done to Selina looped through his mind. She'd been so pale, so limp and unmoving. An eternity later Fields popped out of the door and announced, "She's alive. We need stretchers for both of them."

Maon's feet went out from under him while tears slid down his cheeks. She was alive. He sat with his head buried in the crook of his arm, sobbing. A presence settled beside him, waiting. When Maon gained control of himself, he asked the marshal next to him, "What did he do to her?"

"Fields says she's got a bruise on her face and marks on her throat from where he tried to strangle her."

Maon grimaced.

The marshal continued, "But nothing else. She's still wearing her underwear."

With a shudder, Maon said, "Thank God!"

"They're waiting to bring her out until after they remove Green. Don't want her to endure that."

Maon grunted.

"You look like hell. Is that Green's blood? Or is some of it yours?"

Maon reached up to touch his shoulder, grimacing at the pain slicing through his knuckles. "Mine."

"Let me," the marshal said. "Looks like you might have broken your hand." He moved in front of Maon and pulled open his shirt, popping buttons. Maon grunted when the marshal slid the shirt back. "Knife wound. Still bleeding."

Maon looked at the blood trickling from his shoulder. "I'm fine. Just cold."

"You're in shock. Lie down."

The marshal took hold of Maon when the world slid out from under him. The last thing he heard were the words, "I need some help over here."

DARK FIGURES LOOMED over Selina while she gradually returned to consciousness. One in particular was bent down, his hand nearing her throat. With a harsh raspy cry, she thrashed out with both hands. The figure, male, leaned back from her and wrestled to take hold of her wrists to keep from being clawed by her nails.

"Ms. Shirley. I'm Marshal Fields. You're safe. No one is going to hurt you."

Selina stopped resisting for a moment, examining the man before her but ready to resume her struggle if needed. "A marshal?" she asked, her voice hoarse.

"I'm going to let your wrist go so I can get my badge. It's on my belt. Will you remain calm? Let me show it to you?"

Her head dipped in a brief nod. When he released her wrist, she swallowed, sending a ripple of pain down her throat. After eyeing the badge and then the man, she croaked, "Marshal Fields." Her hammering pulse ebbed and then spiked. Where was Maon? Why wasn't he here? "Maon?" Her breathing sped up in ravaging, harsh gasps.

Fields took her hand. "Marshal Keefe is fine. Only slightly worse for wear." When she struggled to rise, he curbed her movement, pressing gently against her shoulder. "Stay still. You'll see him soon. We're keeping you here until we can move Cardo Green."

Involuntarily her body tensed and her fingers tightened to a white-knuckle hold on Fields. The return squeeze reassured her she was safe.

"Don't worry. He won't hurt you again. Marshal Keefe made sure of that."

"Oh, thank God." She sobbed in dry rough heaves, clutching his hand in a frozen grip.

When her sobs subsided and the hitching of her breathing quieted,

Fields said, "A med tech is here. She has something to relax you. We'll have you out of here as soon as we can."

With that, he released her and eased out of the way. The med tech smiled at her in sympathy. "I'm giving you *feurtumenol*. It will make you feel less jangly. Close your eyes. In a little bit you'll become sleepy. Don't fight it. A nap is the best thing for you right now. If you can sleep in this stench. Whew." She waved her fingers in front of her nose. "I'll be here the whole time."

Selina nodded, one corner of her mouth quirking up in as much of a smile as she could muster. "Thanks." Within minutes she felt drowsy, her eyelids heavy. When they fell shut, she didn't have the energy to open them again.

A touch on her arm startled Selina awake to find the medic looking down on her.

"We're moving you to a gurney. Relax and let us do the work," she said.

The move was quick. While the medics strapped her in place, she noticed that the hidden door of shelves was totally gone. The gurney emitted a faint hum when the gravity field was turned on. Medics at both ends brought it to waist height and steered it along the closet aisle and out to the access way.

Selina lifted her head, looking for Maon. Unable to find him, she sank back and asked, "Where is Maon? I can't see him." Her throat throbbed when she spoke.

The female medic said, "He's gone ahead of you to the clinic. You'll be able to check on him there."

Maon wouldn't have left her unless he had to. Was he seriously hurt? Were they waiting to tell her? If they'd let her climb off, she could get there in half the time this stupid stretcher was taking. "Can't this thing go faster?" She lifted her head to examine the straps holding her in place. "Let me loose. I'll walk."

"No, ma'am. We need to keep you on the gurney," the male medic responded.

Her head grew heavy, so she thumped back down, flinching at the pain that lanced through her skull at the jolt. Why wouldn't they listen to her? Oh gods. It couldn't be. "What are you not telling me? Is Maon hurt?" She was losing her voice, and tears were puddling in her eyes, ready to brim over and spill onto her cheeks.

The medic spoke in a soothing voice. "His hand was hurt from hitting the suspect. And there's a problem with his shoulder. Nothing life-threatening. If I understand it correctly, he got a little woozy, so they took him to the clinic."

Selina released the breath she'd been holding. "Oh."

"Try to relax. We'll be there soon."

The tears that had been clinging to her lashes trickled down her temples when she shut her eyes. It wasn't until she relaxed that Selina realized she'd tightened the muscles of her chest. Maon was going to be okay. Cardo Green was in custody. The nightmare that had started with her decision to request assistance from the marshals was over. She kept her eyes closed while the medics moved her gurney to the cargo lift and onto the station's medical facility.

When she arrived, the ordered efficiency of the clinic's emergency center was shattered by the sound of something crashing to the floor and the bellow of a man. "I need to see her!"

Maon! Selina's eyes flew open. That was Maon. "Let me up!" Any authority her demand might have held was ruined by her whispering rasp.

The medic placed a hand on her shoulder when they approached the alcove where medical personnel were trying to subdue Maon.

His angry yell reverberated. "Don't you put me to sleep!"

Selina struggled against the straps holding her to the gurney. The medic looked away from the scene Maon was making and focused on Selina.

"Let me talk to him."

"Lie still. We need to get you to a doctor for evaluation." the medic said. He was interrupted by a yelp of pain from Maon's alcove.

"Stop kicking, sir, or we will sedate you."

"Please!" Selina said. "It's just my throat."

The medic looked uncomfortable. But with Maon continuing to loudly resist, the man said, "All right." He released the straps and lowered the gurney so Selina could hop off.

Maon went still the moment he saw her, his chest heaving in rapid breaths. "You're okay."

Selina raised her fingers to touch the tender skin of her neck. "A little worse for wear, but I'll be fine."

Maon squinched his eyes and clenched his jaw, struggling to contain his emotions. Selina wanted to take his hand, but the closest one was packed in chill foam. She settled for stroking his arm. When he was able to look at her again, he said, "You dropped your shoe."

"You found it."

"Puce."

"Hmmm?"

"It was puce."

With a slight smile Selina said, "It was pink. Pink for you."

"Oh." Maon's irises darkened.

"I was coming to find you."

"Yeah?" Raw need shot from him like an arrow to her heart.

"Yeah. Let them do what they have to do. I'll be right back." Selina glared at the staff around the bed.

The doctor in charge said, "We're taking him down planet. He needs surgery to reconnect the tendons sliced by the knife."

"Can you wait until I'm free to go with him?" Selina's eyes drilled into the doctor's.

"That shouldn't be a problem."

"Good." With a stroke to Maon's arm, she said to him, "I'll be back. Rest."

Maon gave her a shadow of his half smile. "Yes, ma'am."

Selina's heart skipped a beat. That was her sweet Maon.

The doctor conducted a quick examination and asked the med tech to do a series of scans on Selina. The tests showed no structural damage to her neck other than contusions and swelling. After administering a booster of repair nanites, commonly known as speedheal, she was released with packs of chill foam for her throat and cheek.

When she returned to Maon's alcove, he was already on the gurney sound asleep. The shuttle ride was uneventful. With her EBC still out, she asked a medic to message her mother. Audrina responded that she would meet them at the hospital.

When they arrived, Maon was taken to surgery prep, and Selina was shuffled off to the waiting room. She found Audrina already waiting.

Seeing her mother was a tipping point. Tears streamed down Selina's face when she rushed to Audrina. Her mother's arms wrapped Selina in the security that had always made things better.

A hoarse cry burst from deep inside Selina where all the fear, anger, and horror had been stuffed. "Mommy."

Audrina rocked Selina, stroking her hair. "Hush, baby girl. Everything's going to be fine."

Selina allowed herself to be comforted, letting the consolation act as a balm.

MAON WOKE to find Audrina peering at him with a satisfied smile. "Welcome back."

Maon attempted to speak, but he was so dry all that came out was a raspy croak.

"Here." Audrina held a cup with a straw. "Take a drink of water."

The cool liquid slid down. Several swallows dispelled the sensation that his throat was cracking apart like drying mud.

"Thanks." He took another sip. "Is Selina…?"

"She's napping." Audrina tipped her head to the left.

Stretched out on a sofa, Selina was sleeping peacefully. The last puzzle piece snapped into place with a snick inside his chest. Selina was safe. And she was here. With him.

"You're both going to be fine. They want you to stay through tomorrow to make sure the reconstruction is progressing well."

Maon dragged his gaze away from Selina. "And Selina?"

"She has contusions to her throat and cheek. The speedheal is already working on those."

Maon grimaced. "Good."

"You saved her life, you know. Again."

"I wish—"

"No, you can't change what happened. You did your best. And Maon…" Audrina gave him a fierce look. "Your best is really damn good."

Maon nodded. "Take her to the hotel. She's gonna want to wash away that filthy slimeball's touch."

"I will. When she wakes up. You should rest."

Maon rolled his eyes, and then he chuckled. "I will if you tell me a story."

Audrina smiled affectionately at him. "A story? All right." She settled into the chair next to him. "Let's see." After a brief pause, she began. "Once upon a time there was a beautiful princess."

"Did she have long brown hair?"

"Naturally."

"And topaz eyes?"

"Of course."

Maon settled himself with a sigh. "I like this story already."

A twinkle in her eye, Audrina smiled and continued.

24

Maon woke the next morning to the aroma of breakfast. Never picky about food, he ate everything they brought him. After that, a steady stream of visitors had come to see him, interrupted briefly by the tech running scans on his shoulder and hand. His doctor was due by shortly to sign Maon's release. It was impossible to sleep well in the hospital. Tired, he needed to go home and rest.

"Hey, buddy."

Maon opened his eyes. "Shane."

"Did I wake you?" His forehead furrowed, Shane balanced his weight on one foot, prepared to leave.

"No. At least I don't think so. I was resting my eyes." Maon shot him a weary grin.

Shane scrutinized Maon before he settled into the chair next to the bed. "You don't look too much worse for wear. Sorry I took so long to get here."

"Flesh wound."

Shane grunted. "Yeah. I hear you broke your hand too."

"Nah. They scanned it. Cracked a knuckle. Should have seen the other guy." Maon's grin was cocky.

"I have. You did some damage. Broken arm, nose, jaw."

"Three punches. I'm considering fighting for money."

Shane frowned at Maon's attempt at humor. "The Feds were looking at you for striking a subdued prisoner. One more punch and they would have. Collapsing afterward helped."

Maon shrugged his good shoulder. "Yeah. The chief came by and told me. I thought Green raped Selina. Turns out, I interrupted that." He blew a breath out. "I came really close to completely losing it, but when I realized he'd passed out, I had to get to Selina."

Shane's lips pressed in a tight line, his nostrils flaring. "I'm glad you stopped, but I'm also glad you put him out. He'd have kept coming until he slaughtered you."

Maon ducked his head, staring at where his toes were twitching the sheet.

Shane shifted in the chair. "I saw Selina this morning."

Maon transferred his gaze to Shane. "Yeah."

"She was in the office to give her official statement. Fuck, she can be a hard-ass. They insisted she wait for the Feds. Then she told them what they could do with their demands." Shane chuckled. "Said she was a busy woman and if they needed more, they could wait until her show was over."

Maon smirked. "That's Selina. Bossy."

"How are things?" Shane's eyes pierced Maon.

A gentle smile suffused Maon's face. "She left Gallarda early to come find me."

"Huh."

"Yeah."

"What are you gonna do?"

Maon groaned out a sigh. "Get the hell out of here and throw myself at her feet."

"Sounds like a plan." Shane slapped his hands to his thighs and rose. "Can't stay. You need anything?"

"Nah. I'm good. I'll be out of here today. Thanks for coming."

"Sure. I get to go liaise with the Feds. Seems a marshal apprehended one of their most wanted. As if I needed more work." Shane grinned down at Maon.

Maon's lips twitched. "Probably give that guy a medal when you're the one does the heavy lifting."

"Probably. See you later."

MAON TAPPED in the entry code for his apartment with his pinky finger. Despite being unable to lift his left arm or use his sore right hand, he was grateful for modern medicine. How did people in the past get along without nanites and shortened recovery times?

The trip home had required three tram changes. Bed called. His body ached with exhaustion, but his back itched from the steri-wipes they'd used to clean him. Despite the necessity, taking a shower would be interesting. After ten minutes of wrestling with his clothes, he was nude except for the foam on his right hand that braced the broken knuckle. At last he was standing under the hot water, one arm over his head to keep the foam dry and the other limp at his side. Crap, he couldn't soap himself. *Who cares?* The spray felt good, the heat working to relax his muscles. When he stepped out, he scooped a towel across his elbow. The rough surface quickly absorbed the moisture from his hair and skin. Still, it was a halfhearted effort to dry himself. Too tired to worry about getting the sheets wet, he climbed beneath the covers, shutting his eyes and sighing when he sank into the welcoming softness. Within moments he was gently snoring.

A sharp rapping woke him. Disoriented, he took a moment to remember why his shoulder was throbbing. Pain meds had worn off. Why face the challenge of getting up? He sneered. *Getting decrepit, old man.* The staccato tapping continued unabated. His EBC was flagging an urgent message. Selina. Worried about him. He replied, sending her the pass code to his apartment. No more knocking. Instead the door opened and shut. Footsteps ran toward his bedroom. Selina's feet in pink shoes. He smiled. Selina burst into the room, rushing to his bedside.

"What color are your shoes?" he asked, gazing up at her.

"Brown." Her face, etched with worry, took on an added note of concern when she lifted one eyebrow.

"Fuck's sake. I was hoping for pink. I'll always find you if you leave a trail of pink shoes."

Selina's shoulders relaxed. "You are an idiot. Are you stuck in bed?"

"No. Planning my dismount. Would a triple somersault be showing off?" He flashed a slight grin, followed by a wince of pain.

"You're hurting."

"Yeah."

"Where are your pain meds?"

Maon's brow furrowed, and his mouth twitched to the side. "I don't know."

"I'll find them."

Maon watched her while she searched the bedroom and then went into the bathroom. A minute later she was back out and on her way to the living room. If he was going to get up without Selina there to witness it, it was now or never. *Come on. Man up.* Teeth clenched, he levered himself up with his abdominal muscles, grunting and jerking his arm up when he inadvertently pressed it against the bed. *Shit.* When the pain slowly subsided, he slid his legs off and sat swaying with his eyes shut.

A small, firm hand grasped his good shoulder. "I found them."

He forced his eyelids to open, discovering her standing in front of him, her breasts filling his vision. He dragged her forward, careful to avoid pressing his sore hand against her, and buried his face in the softness of her cleavage.

"You should take your meds."

"Mmmph."

Her body twisted against him, and he heard the clunk of a glass on his bedside table. Then her arms came around him, gently holding him. He released a sigh, sinking into the peace and security that her embrace wrapped about him.

When at last they broke apart, the tightness that had held his heart prisoner since their angry parting at the marshals' banquet unknotted. With a kiss to the top of his head, Selina said, "Take your meds. I'll help you get dressed. Then I'm taking you out to eat."

"Yes, ma'am." He allowed her to pop the pill into his mouth and hold the glass while he drank. Air gurgled up his throat and out in a hearty belch. With a twinkle in his eye and a half smile on his lips, he said, "Maybe we should go back to bed."

"Sweet man, you'll need stamina when you get me there. That means food. Wait here."

The process of getting him dressed was made longer by Maon nuzzling, kissing, and nibbling her when the opportunity arose. After she knelt before him and pulled his boots on his feet, he stood, smirked, and waggled his eyebrows.

"Don't even go there," she said, quickly standing.

Need burned through him. He wrapped his good arm around her, pulling her to him. Her lips were parted slightly. He nipped and lifted his gaze. A fiery response flickered in the golden brown of her eyes. A groan welled within him while he traced her lips from one corner to the other and back with the tip of his tongue. She opened to him, and he claimed her, exploring and savoring. When he paused for a breath, another groan rumbled out of his core, and he resumed where he'd left off with a hardening urgency. He invaded her mouth, tangling his tongue with hers in a heated dance, overloading his senses with a taste and texture like hot-spiced wine. More. He craved more of this woman. All she had to give. Gradually reality reclaimed him, and he eased away, resting his forehead against hers, waiting for the rapid rise and fall of his chest to slow. "I've wanted to kiss you like that for a long time."

"Was the wait worth it?"

A short laugh choked from him, and he pulled her head to rest against him. "You friggin' well know it was."

Her hand brushed along his collarbone, exciting his cock, which was stridently demanding follow-through. "If you're good, I'll let you do it again." She pinched his nipple through his shirt. His erection twitched. "But first we go eat."

Maon loosed a lingering sigh. "Yes, ma'am." He released her from his arm, something his heart never would do.

SEATED ACROSS FROM SELINA, Maon drank in his fill of her. Why had she changed her mind? He was friggin' lucky. While he admired the grace of her slender arms when she handed the menus back to the waiter, it occurred to him that the dress she wore accentuated her beauty.

"So, Cinderella, when did your fairy godmother show up?"

Selina's forehead wrinkled. "Fairy godmother?"

Deadpan, Maon said, "Fairy godmother waves her wand." He waved his foam-encased hand in demonstration. "Turns you from a mouse to a princess."

"Cinderella was never a mouse," she responded.

"I was speaking metaphorically."

She smirked. "Ah." A flush bloomed on her cheeks. "That's all part of what I need to tell you."

Maon realized the depth of her embarrassment when she turned her head to the side to collect herself. "A lot has happened since the banquet."

"Mmm." Her lips pressed together for an instant, and then she looked him in the eyes. "Yes. I left Filip. On Qingdao. To put it bluntly, he was a pain in the ass." She bit back a snicker. "Or his ass was in pain." The chortle escaped her hold.

Maon quirked an eyebrow at her, which made her laugh harder.

Her palm over her mouth, she snorted.

Maon blinked. Selina Shirley had just snorted. With a tentative smile, Maon waited for the joke to be explained.

"Sorry. I caught Filip with his bum filled by a member..." She snorted again. "Oh goodness." She held up a hand and worked to recover her composure. "A hotel staff person was having his way with Filip."

Maon tilted his head to the side. "And this is funny because..."

"I don't know," Selina said through breathy attempts to control her laughter.

Maon's throat went dry, and his chest tightened. Was this the only reason she'd come to him? Because Filip had cheated. "You weren't mad?"

Her shoulders relaxed after she inhaled deeply and then smiled serenely at him. "No. I'd already decided to end things with him when we returned to Tallav. It was like a soap-opera vid." In a singsong voice, she said, "What's Filip up to now that Selina's planning to dump him? Will heartbreak leave him drowning in loneliness or will he find new arms to soothe the hurt away?"

"Oh." The spot in Maon's chest that had tightened released, and he went light-headed, unable to catch hold of the string that trailed from his helium-infused brain. Glibness deserted him.

Her face grew serious. "After the banquet my mother and I had a talk about my father's death. I blamed myself."

Maon reached out and brushed his fingertips over her hand.

"She told me details she'd left out. I'd made assumptions that weren't true and decisions based on them that...that I shouldn't have." She shook her head. "It was such a mess." Selina stopped speaking when their food arrived.

Twirling the spaghetti carbonara on her plate, she said, "Let me explain."

Maon, fork balanced precariously in his fingertips, took a bite of his own pasta but found it hard to swallow.

"I thought my father hadn't gone for a health analysis because I was selfishly taking up his spare time. He was my sounding board and the person I turned to when I needed help with a project. I believed that if he'd not focused on me and my issues, he'd have taken better care of himself. You have to understand. A man I was involved with when I was nineteen committed suicide in jail. He'd attacked someone who was spreading vicious rumors about me and my mother. I blamed myself for his death. And when my father died, I took responsibility for his death too."

If anyone was worth dying for, it was Selina. *Keep that opinion to your-self, idiot. Not what she wants to hear right now.*

"I was wrong. Kevin was mentally ill. And my father's death had nothing to do with me. Mother hadn't told me the details before." She grimaced, twisting her head to the side. With a sigh she turned back and looked at the swirl of uneaten food on her plate. "When my father died, it became important to me to marry and produce the next Shirley heir. But I was afraid that I'd selfishly use my spouse as I'd used my father. I was so confused. And then I met Randolph."

A slight smile lit her mouth when she said the name. Maon attempted to cross his arms over his chest, but pain stabbed through his shoulder. He bit back the urge to curse and asked, "So Randolph helped you?"

Selina lifted her gaze. "He approached me to design the costumes for the staff at the Whip Hand. On a tour of the club, he explained dominance and submission. Something clicked in me. I offered to supply the designs if he would mentor me as a Domme."

Maon's lips pressed together, a flush of jealousy reddening his cheeks. Randolph always began his mentoring with a session in submission. That didn't have to include sex, but with Randolph and a female student, it usually did. *Asshole. He's your friend. You didn't even know Selina then.*

Selina raised one eyebrow and peered intently at him. "We didn't have sex, Maon."

Maon blew a puff of air from his nose. "Good."

Selina smirked at him. "I discovered I had definite dominant tendencies."

"Mmmm. I love your tendencies."

His groin grew heavy when her tongue whisked across her lip before she continued.

"Yes. Well, I decided I needed a Tallavan man, submissive so I could control him, who was somewhat useless except for maybe some domestic skills."

"Useless describes Filip."

"Yes. It does. Useless, yes. As a novice, I mistook his subservience for submission." She shook her head. "Not the same thing at all."

"He's a self-centered little prick."

"It took a while to realize that. I was so concerned with doing the right thing with him." She cleared her throat. "Two people I love dearly told me loud and clear what an ass I was." Her smile brightened, her eyes shimmering with affection. "Thanks."

"You're welcome." Maon grinned.

"My time with Filip made me aware I don't want to control another person's life completely. He was so draining. A narcissistic fool." She reached across the table and covered Maon's hand with her own. "I want a strong man who will protect me when I need it. A man who loves me as much as I love him. A man who's smart and capable. A man who will submit but can also tell me to stop. I want you, Maon Keefe."

25

In that instant, Maon became more acutely alive. The sturdiness of the chair under him was more solid. The textured pattern of the white tablecloth beneath his fingers was more distinct. The aroma of the creamy garlic sauce that coated the tortellini on his plate was more fragrant. No vid could capture this vivid moment full of brilliant shards like a masterpiece of stained glass. It was a living, breathing epiphany that memory alone could hope to retain. At the center was this exquisite woman. Selina Shirley. He would gladly offer his life to this woman. And she wanted him.

Before he realized what he was doing, he found himself on the floor, head in her lap. Emotion choked his throat, making speaking impossible. *Yes. Please, yes.* While he breathed in her fiery scent, he willed this moment to continue forever. Soon, however, desire swelled. Her fingers lightly stroked his hair, running across his forehead to his cheek and along his jawline. With a slight turn of his head, he brushed her thigh with his lips. She was warm and soft beneath the fabric of her dress.

Her voice drifted to him. "Sit beside me."

"Yes," he said and rose to take the seat, his knee brushing hers.

Selina gestured for the waiter to move his place setting so he could sit beside rather than across from her. Satisfied, she picked up Maon's fork and offered him a mouthful of his pasta, watching when he accepted it. She alternated a bite for him and a bite of her own spaghetti carbonara for herself. Selina was his entire world. Observing her while she slid a creamy twist of food into her mouth and chewed kept him mesmerized. She was so beautiful, full of fire and life. Her kindness shone through eyes that glistened in the light from the candle on their table. But desire glittered there too. No words were spoken. None were needed. He was hers, bound by an unseen web she'd spun around his heart. When they'd eaten and drunk their fill, she patted his lips with a napkin, stood, and flicked her finger at him in a gesture to follow.

As though an invisible leash connected him to her, Maon rose and kept pace with her shorter stride. From behind her, he admired her curves, artfully revealed by the folds of her dress. Her legs were slim and gorgeous despite her return to wearing flats. The shoes were part of her business persona. Since he was the business tonight, he didn't mind them. His erection was growing uncomfortable in the confines of his slacks. *Have to get roomier pants. Maybe she'll want me nude all the time.* He strolled after her, his hips rolling in an instinctive way that caught the eye of every female he passed.

Part of him wanted to hurry, to reach the moment where they would be behind closed doors. A greater part reveled in the present and the feel of her pull on him while she purposefully led him to the lift. The thrill that she was claiming him accompanied the anticipation in his groin and chest that was almost painful. He was a bundle of clenching need for desire fulfilled.

The lift was empty when the doors opened. Selina pointed to where she wanted him. Again he was behind her, but the mirrored walls allowed him to look at her face. Their eyes met, and his breath caught at memories of the first time they'd been tangled in each other's gaze. That instant was when this journey to become hers had begun. The gods, the universe, something had thrown them together. He was so friggin' thankful. She'd save him, was saving him. Passion must have flared from his eyes, because the force of it reflecting from hers nearly dropped him to his knees. A smile brushed her lips. "Lower your eyes, sweet man, before you combust."

With each step they took from the lift to her hotel room, Maon's heart seemed to speed its pace, with his cock throbbing in time to the harsh beat.

Outside her hotel room, Selina winked at him over her shoulder. Then she opened the door and led him inside.

"Sit on the sofa. I'll be right back."

Maon complied, meeting her gaze, fierce longing smoldered inside him. A flicker of something—it couldn't be doubt—flashed in her eyes. *She's a new Domme, still learning.* Her mistake with that worm of a man she'd thought to marry proved that. Whatever worry had given her pause, he had no reservations. She had none of the personality traits he'd avoided when playing with dominant women. She wasn't oppressive or bullying. He couldn't see her trying to terrorize someone. She was his perfect match, and she was the hottest woman he'd ever met.

She offered him a smile, love pouring through it, and turned to stride into the bedroom. He kept his gaze riveted on the door frame, striving to determine what she was doing by the whispers of sound that came from the room. When she reappeared, he went completely still. The thumping of his heart ceased. His lungs refused to function. His brain had but one thought. *Mine.*

She returned to stand before him, hands on her hips, her eyes, full of flaming heat, studying him from head to foot. The pink baby-doll nightgown she wore was opaque, keeping her tempting breasts from view. His body rebooted and his mind exploded. *Naked. You need to be naked.* Pink was great, but there were other pink things he wanted to feast on. And yet he sat before her, his breathing rapid, the fingers of his foam-covered hand twitching. She eased her knees on either side of his thighs, climbing onto his lap. She cupped his cheek in her hand, brushing against the rough prickle of his two-day stubble, her spicy scent enveloping him, pushing him to a fiercer level of need.

He held his arms motionless but caressed the silken skin of her legs with his fingertips. Someday he would use those fingers to grip her tight, but not tonight. For now, his injuries wouldn't allow it.

She brought her face close, keeping her eyes locked on his. Desire had blown her irises wide, leaving a rim of golden brown. The instant before her lips touched his, their breath mingled in a hint of moist warmth. The kiss became hungry when, hands clutched to the sides of his head, she pressed in harder. With the tip of her tongue, she traced his mouth before sliding it between his teeth to explore deeper. While she delved, tasting his sweetness, Maon luxuriated in an intimacy he'd never experienced. And then he bit gently, holding her tongue immobile for a moment before releasing it.

When she pulled away, Maon chuckled softly. "I told you I wasn't submissive."

Selina smiled back. "We'll see about that."

Her lips vibrated on his, humming a moan when he captured her mouth, fervently exploring, flicking and savoring the hot cinnamon fire that freshened her breath. His erection was now a painful presence, throbbing and desperate to be set free from his clothing. He pulled back from the kiss, resting his forehead against hers, his gasps coming faster. Need was overwhelming him.

Selina's lips curled in a seductive smile while she swirled her hips over his lap, rubbing against his trapped erection. The desire to pull her into a close embrace, locking her softness against him, was hard to resist. Her fingers feathered through the hair at his nape and down to the buttons on his shirt. One by one, she released each, pulling his shirt from his slacks to undo the last two. After easing it apart, she ran her tongue up his chest to the pulse below his jaw. She sucked, licked, and kissed every spot from behind his ears to his collarbones. Maon tipped his head back, determined to stay still and enjoy the sensations of her questing mouth. When she nipped at the juncture of his neck and shoulder, he hissed. "Yes."

A tweak to his nipple made him jump. Selina laughed softly. "Sweet man, I need you naked."

"Absolutely," he responded. Selina slid from his lap, and Maon stood awkwardly.

"Hold still." She swept his shirt off his shoulders and down his arms, letting it drop to the floor. With a palm to his crotch, she leered at him.

"A little snug in there, isn't it?"

"And getting snugger."

Her slender fingers deftly undid his belt and opened his slacks. With a tug she pulled them around his thighs and slid to her knees in front of him. She nuzzled her face into his groin, her breath searing his skin through his briefs. A twinge of pain and a pulse of pleasure shot along his cock when she bit its length through the cloth. Memories of her talented mouth sucking him when he climaxed made his thoughts clamor for him to thrust his way past her lips again. Not tonight. Tonight he would come inside her, hammering into her depths. *Please let her want that too.*

Selina patted his calf. "Lift your foot." He did, and she pulled off his boot and sock, and then repeated the process with the other. Anticipation pounded in his chest when his slacks slumped farther down. He jerked when she slid her hands under the bottom of his briefs, letting her thumbs massage the juncture between his hips and his abdomen. Then she scratched all the way along his outer legs, leaving his underwear and pulling the pants to his ankles, helping him step out of them. She grabbed his cock through his shorts and said, "We'll finish this in the bedroom. Follow me."

When she released him, he heaved a long sigh. At last, Selina Shirley was claiming him. He sauntered after her, a bulge throbbing in his briefs. A hint of Selina's ass showed when she swayed her hips. "Fuck's sake, you are gorgeous, sweet cheeks."

She stopped and turned to face him, laughter in her eyes. "Sweet cheeks?"

He aimed his sexy half smile at her. "The sweetest."

She sent him a look of mock sternness. "On the bed. Lie on your back."

His grin flashed wide. "Mmmmm. Gotta love a hard-ass with sweet cheeks." He flopped down, gritting his teeth at the stab of pain that shot through his shoulder.

The pressure of Selina's knees against his side distracted him. Gentle fingers reached over and stroked around the healing wound. "You need to be careful. I want you fully functional as soon as possible. Why didn't they give you a sling?"

"Physical therapy starts tomorrow. I didn't want a sling. And that's enough about my shoulder. It's fine. And so are you." His voice deepened with an underlying growl as he spoke. He slipped his good arm around her, crushing her to him, relishing the way his forearm glided along the satiny, thin layer of her lingerie. His arousal returned full force when her hip covered his and one supple leg draped along his crotch and between his legs. She took his mouth, and what little room his brain still had for thought was overwhelmed by wanting, needing to have this woman. The kiss became aggressive with the longing he poured into it. When she bit his lower lip and pulled it slowly through her teeth, he groaned from his core. "I need to be inside you more than anything I've ever needed."

Flashes of fire glimmered in her eyes, piercing him, igniting his soul. Without saying a word, she communicated the deep-seated want within her own heart and body. She slid down his body, her hands heating his already flushed skin. With a quick movement, she straddled both his legs, rubbing his cock through his briefs and adding to his scorching desire.

"Please. Selina…"

"Soon, beloved."

Time crawled. Each moment seemed three times longer. The air around Selina seemed to become thick and syrupy, slowing her movements while she rolled his underwear down. His cock sprang forth, and his hips jerked upward when she kissed the tip. "Please." He groaned.

Selina's smile spoke of her plan to initiate him into blissful mysteries. His gaze riveted, he watched her ease off him, draw his briefs from his lower legs, and throw them aside. Her enigmatic expression remained when she once again straddled him. This time, she stayed on her knees, her hands reaching to the hem of her pink satin babydoll, fingering it while she watched him.

"Let me see, please."

Her lips quirked from mysterious to wicked.

"Please, baby. Let me see."

As her arms rose, peeling the lingerie over her head, Maon feasted on his first sight of her naked body. "Exquisite," he whispered. Everything about her was proportioned perfectly for her size. Breasts like ripe peaches, succulent with the blush of pale pink nipples, made him long to take hold and squeeze their velvety lushness. The rounded curve of her abdomen drew his gaze when Selina's hands dropped to her sides. Sometime he had to nestle on that perfect cushion while his fingers plunged into the folds of her pussy.

When she dragged her moist opening along his cock, the intense sensuality of her movements overcame him. His head fell back while he clenched his eyes shut and gritted his teeth tight. "Unngh! Selina, please. I need…" Words failed him.

"I love you, Maon Keefe." Her words beckoned him to a better place. A place where *as long as we both shall live* was possible. His own astonishing happily ever after.

He forced his eyelids to rise, searing her with a look that branded her as completely his. "Selina Shirley, I love you more than I could ever say."

Finally, she raised his cock to nestle against her entrance, the plump crown leaking precum, and then slowly sank onto him. When the silky warmth of her slid over his cock, Maon nearly shattered. He clamped his eyelids down. With short gasps of breath, he clung to control until the need to come eased. Selina must have realized he was on the edge, because she stilled until his eyes opened. A brilliant smile lit her face while she rocked her hips, gradually increasing the tempo until she was grinding against him at a pace that sent rivulets of sweat trailing between her breasts. Her head tipped back, her hair brushing his thighs while her body swayed to a rhythm that Maon soon matched. He thrust his pelvis up, driving his cock deep inside her. He reveled in the tight, smooth glide in and the even tighter sensation when she clenched her muscles while she lifted. Selina's delicious little moans were a musical accompaniment to the beat their linked bodies created.

He wanted to flip her over, to thrust long and hard while he fiercely claimed her until finally exploding in repeated bursts. His injuries made that improbable, but his inner desire to please her kept him still except for the implacable need to shove his hips upward while she drove him closer to release.

"Fuck's sake, Selina. I'll come if you keep that up."

Her cheeks flushed, hair billowing around her in a crackling mass, her mouth open, face straining, she said one word between tiny puffs and moans. "Yes." Then she dropped onto his chest and fiercely kissed him. The raging fire within him roared into an inferno when her sweat-slickened skin slid across him, the softness of her breasts massaging his chest. The thrust of her tongue between his lips was hot with spice and a burning need. He claimed it, sucking it in to rub against his own, wanting as much of her as he could consume. The pulsating clench and release of her hands circling his throat, thumbs nestled into the hollow above his collarbones, matched the rhythm she maintained on his erection.

He gave a low, growling cry of ecstasy when his balls drew up forcefully and his cum shot into her heat-soaked core in one sustained stream after another. Selina followed his shout with her own, sharp and sweet, her body taut, clinging to him while her muscles pulsed around his cock. His good arm clamped to her waist, he held her tight, relishing the oneness, their naked bodies searing each other. The long drafts of air he sucked into his lungs were filled with her glorious spicy scent. He never wanted to free her. The top of her head lay nestled against his cheek. When his breathing slowed, he brushed his lips against her forehead.

"I love you," he whispered. She tipped back to kiss his jaw.

"I love you too."

26

The day of the first fashion show under her own name had arrived. Selina lay on her side, watching Maon while he slept. The last few days had been exhausting for both of them. In the past Selina had avoided this part of the business. Her mother's experience had been invaluable, but even with her help there had been so many decisions to make and minicatastrophes to fix. Maon had been through intense physical therapy. Multiple sessions each day, with nanite infusions after each, incrementally brought his sliced shoulder muscle back to normal. Yesterday, after one final longer-acting nanite infusion, he was released to strengthen his shoulder on his own.

Despite falling into bed exhausted, they had still spent time exploring and loving each other. Selina was determined to take Maon to the Whip Hand tomorrow and play with him. For now, it was enough to contemplate his face, almost boyish in its relaxation. Eyelids fringed with brown lashes hid the naughty twinkle of his dark-blue eyes. His lips smushed open against the pillow added to the aura of innocence.

With one finger she lightly touched the side of his head, stirring a tawny hair or two. Maon slept on. She did it again a bit longer. This time he twitched. When she did it a third time, his hand darted up to scratch the itch. His eyes opened, and a smile bloomed across his face.

"I have an itch," he said.

"So I see," Selina responded, grinning back at him.

"No, you can't see it."

Before she could respond, she found herself enveloped by the warmth of his body when he covered her, sweeping his arms beneath her to cradle her bottom and bring her firmly against his groin.

"Can you feel it?"

The hard length of his erection was impossible to miss.

"I think so." She loved playing with him.

"Hmmm." His lips gently skimmed hers before he trailed kisses up to her ear. "I need to scratch it." His voice was hoarse. The warm moistness of his breath sent tingles along her spine.

"Would you like me to scratch it?" she asked, twisting her neck to allow him greater access.

"Would you?"

Selina spread her legs and wrapped them around him, clutching his lean, muscular body to her own. "I think I have an itch too."

"Maybe this will help us both." He pulled back until his cock tip hovered at her opening and paused.

Oh no. He was not going to torment her by stalling. When she lifted her hips to take him, she pressed her heels into his backside, forcing his hips forward. The effort caused his cock to slide several inches inside her. It was not enough. Maon obviously felt the same because he thrust his erection in as far as it could go. Then he stopped again. The fullness was wonderful but still insufficient.

With a disapproving look, she said, "If you don't keep going, I will punish you."

"Promises. Promises." His eyes sparkled with mischief, but he began sliding in and out. His strokes, steady with an easy rhythm, were building layer upon layer of pleasure inside her despite the languorous pace.

"Mmmm. That feels so good." Selina sighed. "Just like that."

Maon nipped her lips. "Your wish is my command."

"Kiss me."

He brought his mouth to hers, tenderly brushing his lips over hers. *Nice but not enough.* Hand wrapped around the back of his neck, she forced him closer, kissing him in an intense battle of lips, tongues, and teeth. His thrusts came faster, harder. When the need to breathe became essential, she broke away and said, "Slow down. Make this last."

"Fuck's sake, woman."

"Like this." She began a leisurely swirl of her hips.

He arched, pushing up on straightened arms, and matched her, circling his pelvis so his cock raked her at just the right angle. His face strained above her. He wouldn't come until she did, but holding back was taking its toll. The thought of him on the brink and the delicious sensations of his erection stroking and stroking sent her arcing into a brilliant orgasm. When she spasmed around his cock, he followed her with a deep groan and one word, "Fuck."

He dropped onto her for a moment, panting hard, before rolling them over. Her cheek nestled into the crook of his shoulder, she stroked his chest and abdomen, tracing the well-defined muscles. If only they could stay like this, drowsy and replete, but today was too important to linger in bed. Although this had been a perfect start.

"Time to get up. We have a long day ahead, and I have a present for you,"

"A present?"

"Yes. But you can't open it until you take a shower."

"There really is a present? You're not just saying that to get me out of bed?"

Selina pinned him with stern eyes after flipping on top of him. "Maon Keefe, you are a naughty man. If I say there is a present, there is a present."

Maon responded with a look of solemnity, but it was obvious by the shaking in his midsection he was having trouble maintaining it. "Okay. There is a present."

"You are incorrigible."

His expression changed to one of innocent virtue. "I'm trying to be good. I'd get up, but someone has me pinned down."

Selina slapped his hip.

"Ouch."

With a quick peck to his lips, she slid off him. "Enough. Shower."

A full smile spread across his face. "Yes, ma'am."

～

THE BUSTLE and clamor backstage at the fashion show kept Maon stuck to the director's chair Selina had pointed to as his. Around him an efficient maelstrom whirled while each model went through hair, makeup, and dressing. When the girls queued for a final check, Audrina motioned for Maon to follow her out to their reserved seats.

His gaze sought Selina. Just when he spotted her, she looked up, and he gave her a wink and big smile. To his surprise, she winked back.

"Come on, jelly bean," Audrina said.

Maon took her hand and gave it a squeeze. From the front row the energy that filled the room was palpable. Heads turned toward them. Audrina waved at people, blowing kisses to a few before settling into her seat. It was obvious from the stares directed his way; he was an object of curiosity. His notoriety for being the marshal who saved Selina twice was one reason for the attention. His attire was a close second, the gift Selina had given him this morning. She had designed what he was wearing. One other gentleman wore a similar outfit. Seated on Audrina's other side was Mr. Kowloon, the trade rep from Gallarda.

Maon leaned forward and offered his hand.

Kowloon met him with a broad grin and firm handshake. "Marshal Keefe, you look resplendent," he said, brushing an invisible piece of lint from the sleeve of his jacket. "I am so honored that Ms. Shirley created this lovely ensemble for me. She told me I was her inspiration for its design."

"Yes, sir." Maon smiled in response when Kowloon preened his enjoyment. "I'm looking forward to speaking with you at the after-party." He twirled a finger in the air when he said, "It's loud in here right now."

Kowloon waved a hand and nodded in agreement. "Absolutely."

This morning, when Selina had shown Maon the brilliantly patterned Nehru jacket, peacock-blue slacks, and pale yellow shirt she wanted him to wear to the show, Maon had hesitated for a moment. He was an exhibitionist at heart, but he preferred people to stare at him, not what he was wearing. Selina's shining eyes restrained his objections. For her, he'd dress in a clown suit. Kowloon's jacket was brighter and the pattern wilder than Maon's. With the addition of bright turquoise slacks and a pink shirt, Kowloon easily upstaged Maon.

Other than the lighting and music, the event seemed low-tech to Maon. When he had said as much to Audrina, she explained what he wasn't seeing. Most of the audience had visual data links and subvocal micro-phones. They would broadcast vid and commentary throughout the sector after the show. Several journalists had come from beyond the Sympallan Drift, including one from Fed Central. A data feed accompanied the presentation, so when each model walked into view, details and images of the clothing she was wearing went out to subscribers.

In addition, a shot of the runway was broadcast to visitors on a giant vidscreen erected in the fashion dome's main courtyard and to select buyers throughout the sector. Imagery and audio fed into a booth from remotely controlled cameras. The technical director melded the input into the compelling narrative going out live. It was tempting to watch her work, but not enough to pass up his front-row seat.

Lights over the spectator areas dimmed, and the center backdrop showed a sepia-toned vid, a nostalgic presentation of pyantha fields growing, the crop being harvested, and happy workers turning the plant into yarn and then fabric. The film was in stark contrast to the Gallarda he remembered. When the vid ended, the music segued into a more upbeat tune. The backdrop changed to the logo Selina had adopted, and the first of the models walked out of the wings to wind her way along the catwalk.

While model after model walked by him, the clothing went from casual, to business dress, to party wear, and finally evening wear. The men in the party-wear section sported long Nehru jackets made with vivid prints, like the ones Maon and Kowloon wore. From what he could gather while listening to those around him, people loved the collection. When the models returned for one last single-file turn along the catwalk, Maon watched for Selina to appear. When she did, walking out with the featured model for the show, Maon jumped to his feet, applauding. When the rest of the crowd joined him, satisfaction hummed through him. Selina's smile flashed bright while she accepted the accolade. Then she pinned him with her eyes and blew him a kiss. Maon laughed, caught it, and followed it with a wink. His attention captivated by her, he locked his gaze on her until she went backstage.

Spell broken, excitement bubbled up in him in a wide smile when he scooped Audrina into a hug, lifting her off the floor.

He whooped and said, "Magnificent. She was just magnificent."

Audrina laughed, nodding. "Magnificent. And the show was good too. Now put me down."

Unable to stop grinning, Maon set her back on her feet.

People pressed in tightly around them, invading their personal celebration. Maon suppressed the desire to shove them away, fisting and releasing his hands. With a roll of his shoulders, he reset a smile on his face.

Audrina pushed a hand against one overly aggressive journalist. "Give the man some room. He can handle being shot at, but you reporters are terrifying."

The tension in Maon's chest eased when they edged back, laughing at Audrina's statement. He took his cue from her, forcing himself to be charming and flirtatious until his natural ebullience restored itself. By the time Audrina declared they were leaving, his relaxed stance matched the ease with which he kept the focus on Selina and her accomplishments.

Audrina walked arm in arm with him backstage, leaning in and saying, "Nicely done."

With a slight tilt of his lips, Maon said, "Piece of cake."

SELINA'S SHOW was next to last of the day. Many of the attendees went straight to the hotel venue for the after-party. As much time and effort had gone into planning the party as the show itself. The outdoor patio was transformed into a fantasy Gallardan landscape. Pyantha plants were scattered throughout, growing in large tubs or displayed in arrangements with other greenery and flowers. The pyantha flowers' light golden-yellow color was replicated in darker tones in the cushions strewn along the low sandstone walls that enclosed the courtyard and divided it into sections. Guests were met by a tableau of the models still wearing Selina's designs.

Maon spent the first hour of the party standing with Selina while she greeted her guests, thanked them, and spoke of the inspiration she had drawn from visiting Gallarda and learning more about pyantha fiber. Mr. Kowloon had made the most of his introduction as a Federation representative overseeing Gallardan pyantha development, pointing out the different fabrics in the room that were made from pyantha.

Maon stayed near Selina while she moved from group to group, but the fawning adulation he received grated on his nerves. This was Selina's night. His responses had grown shorter as time went on until Selina suggested Audrina looked tired. Maybe he could escort her somewhere she could sit and rest. Grateful for Selina's awareness of his discomfort, he made his escape.

Now, seated with Audrina in a semiprivate niche along the outer wall, he heaved a sigh.

"Exhausting. I know," Audrina said.

"Yes. I feel like I've spent the day in ambush training."

Audrina laughed. "Hmmm. You did well today when the reporters surrounded you."

Maon snorted. "Ha. I did once I pictured them naked."

Audrina narrowed her eyes. "Not all of them, I hope."

With a smirk, he responded, "Well, maybe not all of them."

Audrina chuckled and gave him a light punch. "So. You and Selina."

"Yeah."

"Don't go mum on me now. We're leaving Beta Tau in a couple of days."

"Sorry." He reached up and ran a hand through his hair. "She hasn't asked me to marry her. So I don't know what's next. I'm stationed here and not due for a transfer for at least two years. I could quit and go back to Tallav, but I'm not keen on relying on my mother for my income again. We could live together, but she hasn't asked me to do that either."

Audrina patted his arm. "I'm sure she has a plan. It's her nature to be methodical. I have one suggestion. What about working part-time for the marshals?"

Maon's forehead wrinkled when he shook his head. "I don't see how that would help."

"I mean on Tallav. Part-time on Tallav."

"They won't let me do that. Everyone wants to be stationed on Tallav. New data analysts don't get posted to Tallav." Maon sighed. "I don't want to pressure Selina. You're right. She's got a plan. I can be patient." He took Audrina's hand in his. "I'll wait years if I have to."

"Good Lord, I hope not. That would mean years until I have grandchildren. I'm not as long-suffering as you are." Audrina kissed his cheek. "Come on. Let's hit the buffet table. I'm hungry."

Maon rose and offered Audrina his arm. While he escorted her across to where a member of the catering staff was carving slices of various roast meats, his gaze found Selina. The yearning that had vanished once they had consummated their relationship reappeared. His throat thickened when wistfulness choked him. He'd wait, but it would be hard.

27

The morning after Selina's show, Maon lay on the bed, hands laced behind his head, watching Selina. Her fingers wiggled in the air while she ticked off items from her mental to-do list.

"Enough of that." With a swift lunge, he grabbed her and pulled her to lie beside him. "You've got a producer, a director, and untold other minions competently taking care of things. Time to relax and enjoy your victory."

The firm grasp of her fingers and thumb holding his chin held him in place while she offered him a quick caress of her lips. "You're right." The hope she would continue to touch him fled when she released him and scooted away. "We're going out."

"Do we have to?" Spending the day in bed with Selina sounded perfect to him.

"Definitely." The one word and a mysterious smile were her only response.

Maon studied her for a moment and then lurched up when she said, "Get moving. Now!"

After a quick shower, he was dressed and waiting on her to finish. Was she finally going to tell him her plans, ask him to move in with her, ask him to marry her? It was impossible to tell. "Where are we going?" He raised his voice so she could hear him at the bathroom vanity where she was finishing applying her makeup. He purposefully stayed out of her line of sight, so she couldn't determine his eagerness to know, but the question hadn't sounded as casual as he'd hoped it would.

Her response was full of unvoiced laughter. "You'll like it." The next moment she strode out of the bathroom and looked him up and down. "You'll do. Let's go."

It soon became apparent they were headed to the Whip Hand. She wanted to play. Which was great, but…she'd be leaving in another day, and they hadn't yet discussed their specific future. Surely she wasn't planning a long-distance relationship. Quick glances at her face revealed pleased serenity. She must have already decided. Audrina hadn't known Selina's plans either and now couldn't be quizzed since she'd boarded a flight back to Tallav late last night. Selina would tell him sometime today. If she wanted to play first, he could do that. His cock twitched. Fuck's sake, he could do that.

Inside the Whip Hand their first stop was the changing room. Maon kept his eyes focused on Selina's, now Lasair's, delectable bottom. She had eliminated the hood from her fiery costume, but otherwise, she was the Lasair of his memories. The rub of the thick leather collar constraining his throat was a welcome sensation. She held the leash attached to it indolently against her side, an unnecessary prop. At this moment the only thing that would keep Maon from following her was a command to stay. Even then she might need to say it twice.

When they made their way from the Whip Hand's changing room, Randolph stepped toward them. While offering his arm to Selina, he said, "Lasair, our table awaits."

Maon growled. *What the hell?*

Lasair cast a glance at him over her shoulder. "Hush."

Eyes narrowed, Maon glared at the back of Randolph's head. If Randolph thought he was sharing Selina, he was dead wrong.

Without turning around, Randolph said, "You can turn the laser beams off, Maon. Lasair and I have business to discuss."

Maon's jaw twitched, and he gritted his teeth, but he dropped his gaze. *Business? What business?*

Randolph led them to a small table toward the rear of the club's bistro.

Maon waited until they were seated and Lasair had pointed to the floor, commanding him to kneel. Lasair's preferred pose was becoming second nature to him: butt on his heels, spine straight, arms to his sides, thighs spread, gaze lowered. She tapped his shoulder twice, which meant he was free to change his position as needed.

"Thank you for meeting me, Randolph."

"You're welcome. So you think you're ready to take the next step?"

"Yes."

"I agree." Randolph summoned a server. A delicious odor wafted around Maon when the waiter appeared. "I'd like you to sample a new item the chef is adding to our menu. It's a risotto made with the little grub snakes native to Beta Tau."

Maon could imagine the look on Selina's face. "Grub snakes?"

Randolph chuckled. "Really, they add an unbelievable flavor to the risotto."

A smile twitched along Maon's lips when he heard Lasair moan. "Oh my goodness. This is heavenly."

Randolph chuckled again. "I told you so. I ordered Maon coconut water."

"Thank you. That's perfect."

Lasair lowered the glass in front of Maon. "Drink this."

Maon accepted it, unable to ignore the aroma of the risotto despite his best efforts. *Fuck's sake, that smells good.* At least the sweet, nutty flavor of the coconut water was refreshing.

Lasair's fingers brushed his when she took the empty glass from him. His breathing hitched at the tingle that flashed up his arm. She was better than any risotto, no matter how heavenly. Her hand stroked his hair, and satisfaction flooded him, spiraling warmth though his body. Lasair's voice interrupted his pleasure when she said, "Up, Maon. Time to go."

Once again he trailed behind Lasair and Randolph into the Whip Hand's public play area. Players here were limited to those who had met Randolph's standards or were on staff. Even now with his gaze set on Lasair, Maon could determine the scenes being played out from the sounds coming his way. The cracking report of a bullwhip was ubiquitous to the room. Paid whip masters provided demos, instruction, and question-and-answer sessions round the clock. During prime evening hours, the main stage presented choreographed shows that were more like circus acts than BDSM play scenes. The public play area paid the bills. The private play area and rooms were for those wanting real scenes rather than watching a performance. Lasair stopped in the public room, surprising Maon.

A tug on his leash forced him forward. Lasair turned to face him. His heartbeat kicked up a notch. With his gaze lowered in submission, the curve of her breasts, pushing up from the tight constraint of her flame-orange corset, came into view. A small sting bit his cheek when she drew the handle of the leash down the side of his jaw and then slapped him with it.

"Look at me."

He leaned toward her while his eyes snapped to hers. "Yes, Lasair."

"Randolph plans to use me in a bullwhip demo tonight."

Maon's mind raced. *Was she going to let Randolph use his whip on her? No. Not happening. What was Randolph thinking?*

The leash handle tapped his cheek again. "Randolph has been teaching me to work with a whip. He wants me to demonstrate basics. He'll talk. I'll crack the whip. Slow walk-throughs. That kind of thing. But we're finishing with me using it on a person. It's my first time. I'd like to share the experience with you."

Maon's face broke into a wide smile. "Sweet cheeks, I'm up for anything you're up for."

"Of course you are." One eyebrow rose in a sardonic expression. "You'll wear head and eye gear."

"If you insist."

"I do."

"As long as you don't permanently harm my baby-making apparatus, I'm good. For the sake of our future progeny." He winked and enjoyed the way Lasair's chin ticked up higher.

"Watch it. I may not feel comfortable punishing you with a whip, but the night is young, and a private room awaits us." She spun back around to face Randolph, who was hiding a smile. "He agrees. Let's do this."

Once onstage Randolph and Lasair covered the basics of using a whip. They were a good team. Now the crowd's attention was riveted on Maon strung up by his wrists and stripped of his clothing. Lasair brought the handle of her whip firmly up between his legs while her other hand stroked his back and sides. He shuddered at the sensation of silky finger-tips skimming up the taut stretch of his muscles to the soft hair of his armpit. There was no doubt Randolph had trained her. He was an expert on keeping a sub off balance and guessing at his next move.

Slowly she dragged the handle away from Maon and moved to face him. "Your eyes are dilated, sweet man. That alone would tell me you're aroused by thoughts of my whip on your skin." She brushed the curled whip down his chest to his belly, then repositioned it to stroke him from his balls to the tip of his cock. He spasmed with a slight shudder. She laughed, low and husky. "Your cock says the same thing."

Maon groaned. She would doubtless use the discoveries she'd made about his body over the last few days to prolong the sexual torment. On one knee she nuzzled his groin, flicking a drop of precum from the plump head of his aching erection.

A sexy laugh slipped out when she rose before him. The tip of her tongue played along her lips. "You taste perfect."

Maon groaned again. "Please, Lasair. The whip."

Lasair sent him a placid smile. "Patience, Maon." With one hand, she brought the whip to his mouth while with the other, she caressed his balls. She wanted him to kiss the whip. Quickly compliant, he pressed a pucker to it, his eyes locked on hers.

"Good boy."

Heels clicking, she strode behind him. He tried to relax by regulating his breathing. Her scrutiny wouldn't miss his struggle. The sound of her shoes tapping against the floor was accompanied by the swish of the lash and fall sliding along the floor's cushioned tiles. When she finally swung, letting the cracker snap to the right of him, he jumped. Surprise reverberated from the crowd behind them. With a quiet, self-deprecating laugh, Maon adjusted his stance. He heard Randolph snort.

"Did I startle you, Maon?" Lasair's question was sharp, pointed.

Maon's response was to shuffle his feet. She flicked the whip out and gave his ass a quick stinging pop.

"Ahhh!"

"I asked you a question."

"Yes, Lasair. You startled me." Fuck's sake. This wasn't a game. She was really going to demand his full immersion in the scene. And why not? She was his Domme. All lingering thoughts of maintaining his control fled his brain. He sank deep into his submissive nature, letting her build the connection between them and forge a unity where they could read each other's hearts and minds.

The crowd watched, spellbound, quietly voicing their sympathy for him or approval at a particularly well-aimed strike. Lasair's placement was precise, her timing just right, driving his sense of self into a winding spiral where pleasure and pain blurred together and his every feeling of and need for control was obliterated. Heat radiated from the skin on his backside, which must be a pleasing shade of pink. Finished with the whip, Lasair caressed that heat, fingering the welts she'd placed on his ass.

"You have a gorgeous bum."

Maon's words were breathed out with a puff of air. "Thank you, Lasair."

With a smack to his right butt cheek, she said, "Let's get you down. I have more delicious fun planned for us."

Maon's legs were unsteady when she released his wrists. Giddiness suffused him. The whip play had been amazing. More awaited. Was it possible to be this happy? Selina steadied him until he could stand alone. He stretched, flexing the muscles in his arms, and then assumed a standing pose that allowed her to reattach his leash. His Selina. His Lasair. After scooping up his folded clothes, he followed her off the stage, looking with foggy satisfaction at Randolph, who gave him an indulgent nod.

Along with the physical arousal and happiness rising to a painful ache inside him, Maon was content. It was an odd emotion for him to feel at the Whip Hand. It was an odd emotion for him to feel anywhere. His experience with contentment had come in fleeting bursts when he relaxed with close friends like Shane and Randolph. But there it was. Solid. Foundational. Selina had given him this gift. He suppressed the urge to pick her up and swing her around. Not appropriate behavior for a sub. Not that he was a sub. No. Not completely. But Selina—Lasair—was his Domme. For her, he was as near to a total submissive as he could ever be.

INSTEAD OF TAKING him to the noir room they'd used before, Lasair led Maon into the dark-out room. Suffused white light gave a measure of visual clarity to the room's inky color scheme. Everything inside was pitch-black: walls, ceiling, floor. The sole furnishing, a padded bench with extensions for both arms to be tied at right angles to his body, was also black, down to the leather binding straps.

"Knees."

In instant obedience, Maon dropped, lacing his hands behind his neck, keeping his gaze lowered and spreading his knees wide. When she took a step closer, she felt his body tense. He flicked his tongue out and licked his lips. She reveled in how hyperaware she had become of him already, and they hadn't yet reached the more intense part of their play.

"Climb on the bench. Lie faceup. Stretch out your arms. I'm uncertain how you'll react, so I'm restraining you tonight."

Heat radiated from Maon while she moved around him, securing his arms and legs. She resisted the urge to stroke him, preferring to fuel the growing sexual tension that a more clinical approach to cuffing him produced. In the mirror positioned directly over the bench, Selina watched his face while he responded to her tugs and the slap of leather on wrists, ankles, and midsection. His gaze followed her ministrations, his nostrils flaring from time to time. She loved him in this state, and she loved being the one to take him there.

In the low light, the fiery orange of her corset seemed to pulse. She hadn't planned that visual addition to their play. Happy serendipity. She did intend their play to affect all five senses. They were already well into seeing and touching. And hearing. Sounds, in this darkened space with its matte-black walls, were amplified. The rustle when she moved, the faint click of the hidden cupboard closing, and the clink when she tapped the two bottles in her hands.

It worked both ways. The *thut* of skin pulling away from leather and the creak of the bench when Maon stirred. Her fingertips and nipples tingled. This man was her erotic match. They were made for each other.

She positioned the bottles in Maon's line of sight. His eyes widened slightly. She bit her lip to hide her smile.

"Goodness. You seem uneasy." She waggled the bottle of massage oil. With a flick of her thumb, she opened it and then moved it under his nose. "Smell. Spice oil. Mmmm. Lovely. It can't be this bothering you."

Maon smirked and narrowed his eyes.

Closing the lid, she placed it in his right hand. "Don't let it drop."

"It must be this." Gripping the other bottle by its lid, she dangled it over his face. Inside neon-green liquid churned as though it was alive.

Maon's gaze darted from the bottle, to Lasair, and back to the bottle. "Are we playing horror vid?"

She chuckled softly. "No, sweet man. But that's a good idea for the future. I'll put it out of eyesight for now. But I promise; you're going to love it." She tucked the bottle into his left hand. "Don't let it drop either."

"Yes, Lasair."

When he said her name, he drew out the last syllable, ending with a roll of the *r*. Before they were done, she'd have him using that tongue to trill more than letters. She cupped her breast through the corset, squeezing her nipple to release some of the pent-up need rumbling inside her.

The leather straps binding Maon slapped against the table when he flexed his arms and chest. His gaze was glued to her while he waited to see what she would do. He was solemn, save for a brief smirk when she had tweaked her own nipple. He looked as though he was preparing to endure rather than enjoy.

"Let's take care of that tension." She removed the oil bottle from his hand and drizzled a trail of the slippery liquid over his shoulders and chest. Despite the soothing sensation of her fingers twirling a pattern through the oil, he was much tighter than he should be. *Ahhh.* She moved his face with a finger to his chin so he no longer looked to his left at the pulsing chartreuse goo in the bottle he held.

"Focus on me."

Their gazes locked. A shadow that had lurked in Maon's eyes since he'd seen the green bottle dissipated to be replaced by an expression of quiescent hunger. He released a long sigh, and the muscles of his chest relaxed. She gave his nipple a gentle pinch and a quirky smile. "Very good."

She dribbled more oil, massaging along his arms, devoting attention to his hands and fingers. He had such agile hands with long fingers perfect for stroking across the keys of an interface or bringing ecstatic responses from her body. She moved on to his collarbones, working her way to his abdomen and each leg before finishing with toes. He was strength and power personified, and he placed those aspects of his nature in her charge to be used only at her direction. Today he didn't need to be strong. Before she was finished with him, he'd be a puddle at her feet. By the time she was done applying the oil, his muscles were so slack she questioned whether he could get to his feet or even sit.

One part of his body was rock hard. His gaze had followed her while she stroked and caressed every bit of him except his cock, which stood stiffly at attention. Despite the erotic beauty of that rigid salute, Maon's cock would have to wait. First she would engage the last of his five senses, taste. She bent over, covered his lips with hers, and claimed it in a long, sultry kiss. His tongue tangled with hers, thrusting in rhythmic penetration. Perfect. When she broke the kiss, he groaned. She gave a low chuckle. "I have another use for that mouth of yours."

"Your pussy?" His voice had grown dark and heavy, plucking at the cords of arousal deep inside her.

"If you ask nicely."

"Please, may I lick your sweet pussy, Lasair?"

Instead of verbally assenting, she toggled the foot pedal that lowered the bench, and when it had reached the desired height, she threw her leg over him. She'd trimmed her hair with this moment in mind. Now, positioned a scant inch above where he licked his lips, she swiped down, dragging her labia across his mouth. His tongue immediately darted out to lap up the slickness of her arousal while he moaned his pleasure. Each time the tip touched her clit, she savored the flash of blissful sensation. She ground against him, and he began sucking.

"Shit yes. Just like that." She collapsed forward, grasping the sides of the bench by the top of his head. The upward spiral toward orgasm came hard and fast until the peak hit, and she shuddered, her pussy squeezing tight in a climax that thrust deep through her core. When clarity returned, Maon was moaning beneath her, using his tongue to stroke her clit, sending zinging pulses through her that made her twitch. Then he chuckled.

She panted and with a huff of air said, "Sweet man, you do that very well."

When she swung her leg over and away, Maon licked his lips. "That was fun."

"I have just the reward." Her inner cat was purring but showed its teeth in a wicked grin.

Desire blazed from his eyes. "Please use your pretty mouth on me."

"On no. Not this time," she said while prying the green bottle from his hand. When she brought it up, Maon's stomach tightened.

"This is a gift from Randolph. He's thinking of calling it Ecstasy in a Bottle." She unscrewed the cap and set the slim container next to Maon's hip. With the attached brush, she painted his cock with short strokes, starting at the base just above where her fingers firmly gripped him. Fizzing. Swirling. Churning. The bubbling stuff had an immediate effect. Unable to lie still, Maon writhed to the extent the leather straps allowed. His jaw clenched, he sucked in air between his teeth.

She continued to paint his penis, finally reaching the top and twirling a large blob in the hole at the tip. His eyes rolled back in his head.

She put the bottle in the cupboard.

"Lights off."

With the bottle hidden away, his glowing green cock was the only thing visible in the pitch-black. The slime moved with a life of its own. She stroked his body. Lax muscles had tightened, stiffening until his body was as rigid as the table beneath him. In the mirror, his erection was rippling fluorescent green. The scent of the spicy oil she used on his skin wafted around him. With a whisper in his ear, she said, "Breathe." She chuckled at his attempt to suck air into a chest tight with tension.

His hips undulated in a rhythm of their own, thrusting up, pushing to attain some impossible pinnacle. With her fingers, she shared in his erratic twitches, watching while the goo assaulted every nerve fiber in his long cock. He was incredibly beautiful in his ecstasy, control shattered, voicing his abandon in gasps and moans, until with a long undulation he cried, "Lasair."

When she caressed his balls with her finger, they pulled up hard.

"Lights on low."

The point of no return arrived when hundreds of tiny bubbles burst at the base of his cock. The pinprick pops moved up his erection, reaching the tip, and he came in an exquisite rush of overwhelming pleasure. Cum shot in long streams, falling in warm stickiness on his chest and stomach. It was the most erotic sight she'd ever seen. His breath coming in quick pants, he lay undone and unmoving, unable to relax the upward thrust of his pelvis. She stroked his side, restoring his grip on reality, allowing him to settle against the table. With a heated washcloth, she cleaned the green away and then took another to wash his body.

Maon chuckled to himself. His eyes shone like moonlight reflected off the still water of a deep lake, and his lips formed a placid, silly smile.

"I think you're a little drunk."

"And you're not even wearing puke." Maon laughed at his own joke.

"Uh-huh. You know that you look as dopey as you sound. Right?" Gods, she loved this man.

Forehead furrowed, he considered his reflection. "I look exceptionally handsome. Ecstatically handsome. A man women want to have their way with." He waggled his eyebrows at her. "You weren't planning to ravish me, were you?"

Selina raised one eyebrow at him while she released his ankle from its restraint. When she finished, she helped him sit up and scoot to the end of the table.

Maon swayed but remained upright. "I need a kiss," he said while staring into her eyes. When she moved between his legs, he wrapped his arms around her, dropping one hand to squeeze her bottom. "I like no panties." He smirked at her before covering her mouth, trailing the tip of his tongue along her lips until she opened and let him release his desire in forceful thrusts.

When the need for air broke them apart, she said, "Enough of that. We have a social engagement."

"Can we miss it?"

"No. Hop down." When he did, she reattached his leash and led him out the door. To the sub waiting outside the room, she clicked her fingers and said, "Clean."

28

W hen they stepped out of the club, hand in hand, Maon had recovered his equilibrium to an extent. He was still giddy with happiness. If he and Selina were characters in a children's vid, they'd be skipping, bursting into song, and dancing their way along the path. "Where are we going?" he asked.

"We're almost there."

Selina drew him across a wooden footbridge that took them to a trail between trees into a glade beyond. They were headed into a park. What kind of social engagement was held in a park? Not that Maon had paid attention to the small parks that dotted Beta Tau's main dome. Their manicured precision couldn't compare to the natural beauty of Tallav. This was different. Knee-high grasses sprinkled with wildflowers brushed against him when he yielded to the gentle pressure of Selina's hand pulling him onward. When they reached a low, flat boulder partially hidden by the greens, browns, and golds of the unmown grass, he noticed a picnic basket.

"A picnic? Randolph's not going to show up, is he?"

Selina giggled. It was a sound both incongruous and totally delightful. "No. It's just us."

Maon pulled Selina's warm, soft form against him, picked her up, and swung her. Laughter pealed from her lips while her head tipped and her hair arced behind her. Maon clasped her nape and drew her to him, kissing her with a gentle passion before releasing her to drop back to the ground.

They stood staring into each other's eyes for a moment before Maon asked, "Is there food?"

Selina laughed. The gold that flecked her topaz eyes danced in merriment. "There's food."

With a tug she pulled him toward the basket, but Maon preempted her. "Allow me." Hands on her waist, he set her atop the boulder. His intention to pass the basket to her went astray when the smell of something delectable hit his nose. The aroma intensified when he flung the lid up, propping it open with his head, and inspected the contents of the basket.

"Hey. Over here," Selina called.

The perfectly ripe pingo plum sent a burst of sweetness across his tongue while its juices overwhelmed his mouth and trickled down his chin. He looked up from the basket, smiling at Selina with closed lips lest he lose another drop of the fruit's nectar.

Selina accepted the basket, setting it beside her. Maon polished off the plum and attempted to clean up with the napkin Selina handed him. She was eating her own plum in neat slices.

Maon sent her a lopsided grin. "I'm sticky still."

"I like you sticky." She gave him a cheeky smile.

Maon pulled himself up to sit next to her. With a nod, he said, "Fruit board and knife. So civilized."

"One of us should be."

Maon steadied the platter of meat and cheese sticks she handed to him, adjusting his body to make a space between them for it and the other items she was pulling from the basket. When they'd eaten their fill, Selina packed the refuse away. A full stomach and the heat of the rocky surface beneath them made Maon drowsy. He lay back, munching on one last breadstick, Selina curling against him, snugged into the curve of his shoulder.

"I could stay like this forever," he murmured.

"Forever," Selina repeated. The warmth of her palm settled over his heart. "Your heartbeat is so strong and steady. I can't go one day without feeling it, letting it reassure me that all is right with the universe."

Maon threw the rest of the breadstick to the birds, wiped his fingers on his slacks, and brought his hand up to caress her face. He pushed silky strands of hair behind her ear so he could trail his knuckles down the softness of her cheek. "You make me want to be strong and steady. To keep you safe. To keep our children safe."

He continued to stroke her, his fingertips playing across her lips. After a time he said, "I don't want to smother you. Your fire is what first attracted me." He grinned at the prick of sensation when Selina tweaked his nipple. "You're gifted, Selina. I want to give you the support you need, not weigh you down."

"You could never weigh me down, Maon Keefe. You've brought a lightness to my life that's been missing. You're like an overgrown puppy, slathering happiness on everyone with a big wet tongue."

"Mmmm. Are you asking to be slathered?"

Selina giggled. "No. Maybe later." When Selina grew quiet, Maon basked in the serenity of her body clasped against his.

"You don't seem to realize it, but you're gifted too, Maon."

A gentle snort slipped out, Maon's unvoiced denial.

"You are. Whether you agree or not. I don't want to take you away from something you're really good at. You're an amazing marshal."

"Are you asking me to marry you?"

"I was getting to that. Will you?"

"Will I what?"

Selina sighed. "I love you, you exasperating, sweet man. Will you marry me?"

Maon rose to his side, looking at the woman snuggled into the crook of his arm. "Yes. Absolutely. Name the day." He cocked his panty-melting grin and said, "Never mind, let's do it now."

Selina gazed up at him, her eyes unblinking beacons of love, her cheeks glowing. When her lips parted to speak, Maon claimed them, euphoria washing over him while tingling radiated from every point where his body met hers.

When they broke apart from the kiss, Selina settled glazed eyes on his. "Wedding later. For Mother's sake." She melted into him, reaching for him, only to pull back abruptly. With a stern look, she said, "You're coming home with me now."

Maon laughed against her lips and whispered, "Try to stop me."

SEVEN MONTHS LATER.

Randolph handed Shane another beer before settling in the pool chair beside him. The wedding of their best friend to his perfect woman had been an event the two wouldn't have missed. Rather than the solemn formal affair of most society weddings, Maon and Selina's ceremony had been casual, full of laughter and poignant moments.

Audrina beamed from beginning to end and was now working hard to get Maon's mother to spend the night at Ettington in hopes of broaching a détente between Maon's parents. Maon had warned her it was a pointless effort, but she'd insisted on making the attempt. Shane was on the side of letting Maon's mother continue to live the unhappy life she'd created for herself, but Audrina claimed doing so also kept Maon's dad ensnared in sorrow. Shane would have advised he just get over it because he couldn't understand how anyone could love that harpy. To each his own.

As the cold brew washed down his throat, Shane pointed. He and Randolph had a perfect view of Selina and Maon where they sat chatting with Maon's father and Aunt Sarah beneath a large umbrella. "I'll bet that grin hasn't left his face since Selina claimed him."

"They'll be happy," Randolph said.

"Mmmpf," Shane agreed. "Best of both worlds. Part-time marshal. Full-time husband."

"How did he manage that?" Randolph asked.

"Didn't. Audrina did. Intimate friend of the director."

Randolph lowered his sunshades to look at Shane. "Really. That woman has mad skills."

"Thank the fuck she only uses them for good."

Randolph settled back and took a swig from his beer. "I don't get the puke joke. Something about Selina's pink dress."

"Morning sickness," Shane said.

"God, kids."

"He bought it lock, stock, and barrel," Shane agreed.

"Better him than me," Randolph said. "Just being at a wedding scares the crap out of me."

Shane laughed. "No worries. There's not a Tallavan woman alive that'd marry either one of us. Off planet, we do the asking. We're safe."

"Mmmpf," Randolph agreed.

"Besides we're both safe from needing to provide the family an heir. You have your sister. I have my brother."

Randolph nodded slowly. "How is your brother?"

"Doing good. He's been working on his banking competency. Thinks it will be an asset if he has to take over managing the family financial assets."

"Doesn't that require a commitment of several years to the marshals?"

Shane squinted from the glare on the pool where Selina's great-aunts were cautiously dipping their toes. "Yeah."

"Is your mom happy about that?"

Shane snickered. Thomas had really stepped in it with her. "Huh. She was pretty put out when he told her. He's only twenty-nine, so she wasn't pressuring him to marry yet."

"He's still plenty young."

"That's what he says. Plans to wait until he's thirty-five. I can't blame him for that. But Mother doesn't like it. As soon as his commitment is up, she'll be after him for a granddaughter."

"Like I said about Maon, better him than me."

The two watched while Selina rose and twitched a finger at Maon to follow her. Which he did with a combination of besotted smile and sexy saunter.

"Fuck." Shane waved his hand in Maon's direction. "That's what you get when you cross an exhibitionist with a lovesick fool."

Randolph laughed. "I need another beer if I'm going to have to watch all this unadulterated happiness. My sadistic side needs sedation."

Shane raised an eyebrow and glanced at Randolph. "If you need me to, I can tie you up." Then he smirked. Life was good. His career was flourishing. Women were falling all over themselves to be bound in his rope. His friends and family were doing well. The future looked bright. Knock wood that wouldn't change.

∽

MAON SLID his hands up Selina's hips, bunching the skirt of the pale pink silk dress she'd worn for their wedding up to her waist. He pulled her closer, wrapping his arms around her. The sensation of her body rubbing against his when she lifted on her toes to place a hand at his nape was nearly perfect. Her lips touched his. The kiss, their first on this first night of their married life, was seismic. Maon was certain the ground beneath his feet rocked. Or maybe the earthquake was internal, and he was the one shaking.

There had been so many guests to accommodate for the wedding that Selina had decided they would spend their wedding night in one of Ettington's guest cottages. She'd chosen the one farthest away from the main house. It had been a good idea because he had no intention of being quiet as he and Selina physically expressed their love for each other.

Selina pulled back and gazed at him. He was mesmerized by the hints of fire that sparked in her topaz eyes. His fiery Domme. His Selina. His wife.

"I love you, Maon Shirley."

"I love and adore you, Selina Shirley."

"You're not a Keefe anymore. You're mine. And I'm never letting you go."

Maon's lips twitched. "Sweet cheeks, I'm shackled to you for life." He dropped to his knees. "You and little Thor." He kissed her belly through the fabric.

She thumped him on the head. "We are not calling our son Thor."

"Zeus?"

"Sweet man, if you don't stop, you're going to be punished on your wedding night."

Maon chuckled. "I'll be good." He stood and drew her into his arms.

She fisted both sides of his shirt collar. "I expect better than good." With a yank she pulled herself up so their lips met and claimed his mouth.

Thoroughly addicted to her spicy taste, Maon's whole body responded with rampant need. He pressed himself to the softness of her breasts while their tongues tangled and teeth nipped. When she brought her hand down to his butt and squeezed, he moaned into her mouth. *Fuck's sake.* He needed to be buried inside her.

With her lips playing over his, she said, "Clothes off."

He pulled her dress over her head to reveal the lacy white bra and garter belt beneath. Trust Selina to do the unexpected. He'd envisaged red-orange lingerie. It was her signature color, but she'd chosen sexy-as-hell virginal white. He stood, stunned, soaking up the erotic sight of her.

"I meant your clothes too."

Maon raised his gaze to see her smirking at him. She knew the effect she had on him. He shed his clothes as rapidly as possible and then planted his hands on his hips, displaying his body and his rigid cock for her to inspect. The fire she ignited in him flared as her gaze swept up and down, finally resting on his erection. He moved, making his cock sway, and shot his panty-melting half smile at her. Her shoulders pushed back, and her chest pressed out. Bull's-eye! He'd hit the target center mass.

"Get on the bed, faceup, legs spread, knees up, feet flat on the mattress."

For a moment he lost the ability to breathe. That tone of voice always immobilized him in the split second before he obeyed. He climbed onto the bed and positioned himself exactly as she had directed. His cock bobbed in anticipation when she slid between his legs, brought her mouth down, and huffed warm air on his balls. Then she licked them, and it was all he could do to lie still. All part of the game they played. His role was to remain immobile no matter what she did to him. Her goal was to break his composure and force him to respond physically. Unlike Randolph's challenges, Maon always lost to Selina. But then Selina's prize went to the loser. The longer he resisted, the better the reward. It guaranteed he'd make it a long match.

Tonight she'd started with his balls, but before he gave up the struggle, she would have to apply her skill to all his erogenous zones. She knew every one of them. The tip of her tongue gently flicked each of his nuts, and then she dragged the flat of her tongue up them.

"Fuck's sake! Yes!" He could be as loud as he wanted.

She chuckled while licking him again, and his hips nearly came up. *Gods, this was hard.* But tonight of all nights he would hold out. Selina wouldn't let him fail. Sure enough, she bit his inner thigh. The pain helped him center again.

He didn't know how much time she spent tormenting and pleasuring him. His nipples were sore from her attention to them. Love marks dotted his body. His belly was damp from the pre-cum his cock had wept nonstop. Finally, she straddled him, dragging her pussy along his erection. He released a long, tortured cry, shuddered, and thrust his hips up to grind against her.

"Sweet man, you lose."

"Thank the gods."

She positioned his cock and sank onto him. Her body softened at the same time his relaxed into the completeness that their joining always created. They were yoked together, linked emotionally, mentally, and spiritually. Bodily union mirrored that invisible bond, brought it into the open where they could touch it and affirm it.

The physical connection was ephemeral. You couldn't rest in it for long before desire reestablished itself, demanding they move and begin the spiral climb to oblivion. And so they did in a slow rhythm of thrust and retreat that gradually increased in speed and force. Hot skin slid against straining muscle. Lips met. Teeth nipped. Hands clutched. Sensation united them and strummed the cord that made them one.

"Gods, Selina. I've got to come."

"Yes. Sweet man. Sweet husband. Now."

An instant before his release hit him, Selina came, squeezing his erection in the satiny vise of her pussy and crying out inarticulate sounds of pleasure. He shouted her name as his whole body responded in a massive orgasm. He was barely aware when she slipped off him and curled up next to him with her head on his chest.

His wits returned slowly to the warmth of her hand stroking his abdomen. He let his fingers wander over her, fiddling with her hair, caressing her shoulder, smoothing along her side. Satisfaction, thorough and complete, filled him. They were one. United. He was hers, and she was his. How had he gotten so lucky to find the only woman in the entire universe who fit him so perfectly?

"Mars."

"Hmm," Selina responded.

"I really think we should call our firstborn Mars."

"If we're going with Greek and Roman gods, Apollo would be perfect. He's the god of poetry and music. Right? And he was very pretty."

Maon grunted and flipped her off him and onto her back. He scowled at her.

"Not Apollo?" Her eyes twinkled with mischief.

He growled at her.

"How about Devon?"

Maon considered for a moment, smiled, and said, "Devon Mars Shirley. Has a ring to it." When she began to sputter her response, he brought his lips to hers and kissed her until she was breathless.

He lifted onto his forearms. "Thank you, Selina Shirley. For saving me. For loving me." He brushed his hand down to the side of her abdomen swelling with their child. "For giving me a family." He smiled at her. "Devon Geoffrey Shirley."

Surprise lit Selina's face. "Oh. For my father."

"Yes."

"It's perfect. Thank you."

"You're welcome." He nipped her lower lip and chuckled hedonistically. "Prepare yourself. Now it's my turn."

Discover more of Cailin's sci-fi romance on her website at
https://cailinbriste.com
Subscribe to her newsletters for monthly updates on her releases, sales, and events.
https://cailinbriste.com/cailins-newsletter-sign-up/

Read on for an excerpt from *Rand: Son of Tallav* book #3 in this series.

RAND: SON OF TALLAV EXCERPT

Briarcliff, Tallav

The slender slice of moon did little to light the edge of the cliff, over which the desperate bleating of a lamb sounded. Rhiannon, Tallav's second moon, had yet to rise and brighten the night sky. Why the gardener's boy sought Penny out on the patio rather than running to get the overseer, she didn't question. He was a child and probably ran for the nearest adult. Peering over, she could make out a patch of dirty white caught in a bush. At least the lamb had slid into the branches, it's fall blocked from the vertical plunge of the cliff to the river below.

How had it gotten here? The early lambs weren't old enough to be out of the lambing shed, which was nowhere near the cliff. She slid carefully down the slight grade of the rim and tried to calm the animal while she waited for help to arrive. She'd sent the boy on to the overseer with a request to bring rope.

Careful to stay out of range of the lamb's thrashing, she spoke to it in gentle, crooning tones. The animal quieted, no longer flailing but still bleating plaintively. The creamy tan color of the lamb's body was more difficult to see in the dark, but the face, white with black speckles, stood out. To her horror, she noticed one of those dark marks was in the shape of a heart. This was the orphan lamb the overseer had allowed Sophie to help feed. That lamb was bedded down every night by the overseer himself in the enclosure built next to his office in the main barn. Someone had to have brought this lamb out here. She'd damn well find out as soon as she rescued it from its precarious predicament.

Above her, loose rock skittered with the sound of someone descending. She tipped her head back and shouted, "Don't come down. Just drop the end of the rope."

"We won't need a rope."

The low, throaty words confused her. That wasn't the overseer. She lost sight of the darkened form above her when she sat up to roll over on the clumps of rock and grass beneath her to get a better look. A solid thud struck her back, sending pain lancing along her spine and around her rib cage. The lamb renewed its thrashing when she slid into it, knocking it backward. Squealing in terror, it tumbled out of view.

Heart pumping, Penny windmilled in a futile attempt to keep from falling forward. She straddled the bush with her legs, the sharp ends of broken stems lacerating her exposed face and hands, snagging in the long-sleeved pajamas she wore. For an instant, her momentum stopped. In desperation she clamped her fists onto the bush's base, ignoring the sting of abrasions.

A second strike from her assailant's booted foot hit her high to one side of her backbone.

Something snapped inside.

Pain flooded her shoulder.

Jarred forward, she began a slow-motion tumble headfirst over the bush.

Fingers and palms tore while branches slid through her grasp until the strain on her good shoulder from the somersault forced her to let go.

Oh God. I'm falling. Sophie. Oh God. I can't die and leave Sophie.

Her temple struck a jutting rock, and darkness claimed her.

Above, a figure scrambled to the top of the cliff, humming a cheery tune. The wordless melody stopped at the sound of someone rushing toward the precipice. By the time the overseer arrived, the spot was empty. No lamb. No Penny. Just moonlight casting the side of the cliff in shadow in the waning heat from a late summer day. With an exclamation of frustration and an oath that he'd see to that boy for pulling pranks, the overseer left.

It wasn't until the next day, when no one could find Penny, that the overseer mentioned his fruitless trip to the cliff edge. Her body lay on the rocks, half in and half out of the river. Officially she was a casualty of misadventure.

∾

The Whip Hand, Beta Tau

Randolph stroked the disheveled softness of Eva's hair before firmly gripping the back of her neck. "You did very well, Eva." A shudder and sob were her only response. The time he'd spent with Eva over the last week had been a refreshing change from the business expansion consuming him for over a year. Although he might not have taken on Eva's remedial training if her master hadn't been a member of the Beta Tau board of directors.

Her body writhed when he drew a finger over the marks he'd left on her back. One or two spots were seeping blood. He swirled the tip in the fluid before scraping his nail across the abrasion. The sight of Eva, arms shackled above her head, undulating before him, sent a jolt of pleasure through him.

"Your master doesn't hurt you often, Eva. Perhaps that's why you believed you could manipulate him. He brought you to me to break that habit."

"Yes, Sir." A whimper escaped her lips.

Randolph threaded his fingers into her hair and pulled her head back, noting the tears inching down her cheek. "This is our last session before I return you to your master. The pain you've experienced was not a punishment. You've learned your lesson and learned it well." He brushed his finger through the damp trail on her face. "This was for me. Your tears are your gift to me. I'm a sadist, Eva. I enjoy hurting you. But I haven't taken you over the edge of what you could bear. If your master sends you again, I will break you. Do you understand?"

"Unnnhhh." The sound flew from her.

Randolph jostled her head. "Say you understand."

"I understand, Sir." The words came out with a squeak.

"Good," he said, unwinding his fingers from her hair. He allowed the chain attached to her shackles to lengthen with a flick of his wrist before again engaging the locking mechanism. Gripping both her hips, he pulled her back until she was bent before him. He smacked her bottom. "Do not come. Your orgasms belong to your master. Correct?"

"Yes, Sir."

"Say it," he ground out.

"My orgasms belong to my master."

Randolph stepped away, allowing her master to step forward and take over. He didn't watch the happy reunion when he exited the scene. He made his way to his office, brushing his fingertips through his neatly trimmed smoky brown hair. His cock had gone semihard, but Eva wasn't his type and she wasn't his. If she were, he would have taken her much deeper before fucking her.

His type. He had to smirk at that. His type hadn't really been doing it for him lately. Probably the stress, which in theory should be diminishing. The addition of a private play space to his new suite had been a gift to himself a long time in coming. He'd finally indulged himself. The combination of play space, office, and apartment allowed him a level of privacy he'd never had. Perfect on days like today when he was too tired to face the onslaught of those seeking a personal moment with the celebrity owner and top sadist of the Whip Hand. He rarely entered the main play floors anymore, so when he did, the clamor was more strident.

After keying open his office door, he strode to the bar and a bottle of high-priced bourbon, pouring himself two fingers. He settled into his desk chair, downed a swallow of the liquor, and set the glass on the black coaster that protected his expensive desk.

He leaned back, eyes closed, waiting for the ripples of the chair adjusting to end, and then tapped the button that started his personal massage program. Heat soothed his tired back before the chair switched to a gentle overall kneading. A wince tightened his face when it began pummeling the knots in his shoulders.

The yearlong renovation had included an upgrade to the Whip Hand's business offices. His new office was larger, including a sitting area and many other luxuries that put his old one with a desk and two chairs to shame. This desk was a work of art. The surface was black and white ebony inlay over black ebony. Its thick legs and panels were carved reliefs of tormented bodies struggling to free themselves from the wood. It made an impression on anyone who entered the room.

Yet he preferred his old office. Except for this chair. His old office with this chair would be just right, but the Whip Hand had evolved light-years beyond its original concept.

The expansion and renovation moved it well past its simpler days when he'd spent as much time on the floor as in his office. Now, a week could pass without him ever setting foot in any of the club's venues. He'd passed oversight of the club's subs to Tom. He was good at the job, but doing so still gave Randolph the sense that he'd allowed something to slip away.

As the chair resumed the previous gentle kneading, he realized what he missed: the immediacy. His own whip demos and playtime on the floor had evaporated, replaced by more and more meetings. Damn, he was a stodgy businessman now.

The chair's program ended. Randolph drained the glass of bourbon and was about to retire to his apartment, shower, and climb in bed. When he sat forward, the red light that signaled an emergency comm winked at him from the touch bar on his desk. He sighed and brought up the message viewer. His forehead creased when he noted the comm was from his mother. Tabbed open, the static image showed her, shoulders drooped, no makeup, face puffy, and eyes red.

Randolph's chest tightened. The last time he'd received a message with his mother looking this distraught was when she'd announced she was divorcing his father. He touched the start button.

"Randolph. I have bad news. Dear, I don't know how to say this, so I'll... Your sister died. She was trying to save a lamb. She fell from the cliff above the river." Tears streamed down her face. "It's awful, Rand. She lay there all night." She reached for a tissue offscreen and blew her nose. "Please come home as soon as you can. We've had her cremated. The memorial service will be held when you arrive." Pain was written in every line of her face. "Please, I need you here. I need you to stay."

Stunned, a lump forming in his throat, Randolph sat immobile, unable to assimilate what he had heard. Penny couldn't be dead. Both his beloved sister and nemesis, she, more than any other person, had driven him away from home, family… Tallav. How could the avenging angel, the destroyer of his life, be dead?

A replay of his mother's comm did little to answer the questions swirling in his mind. She fell from the cliff? A ripple of nausea hit him. Fuck all. Penny knew the cliffs along the river at Briarcliff too well to have fallen from them. Not until he'd replayed the message a third time did he apprehend his mother's last statement. Come? He would absolutely come. But stay? His mother just needed to get her feet under her. No way would he stay on Tallav longer than required to help her settle his sister's affairs.

His fingers drifted to rub the inscribed heart on the pewter bead tied to his wrist by a leather cord. Penny was dead. It wasn't possible. Someone so full of bullheaded life couldn't die. Not the sister he'd never stopped loving even through the slinging vitriol they'd both flung at each other over the last twenty-one years. The sister who clung to distorted facts. Refused to listen each and every time he'd tried to reconcile. She couldn't be gone. The hope he'd clung to that his big sister would once again be his best friend couldn't be shattered. Every bitter word he'd spoken to her in anger hammered at him. If only…

He dropped forward, head in his hands, while searing pain flooded his soul.

Purchase Rand: Son of Tallav, Book #3
https://books2read.com/rand

ALSO BY CAILIN

ABOUT CAILIN BRISTE

Cailin Briste is a USA Today Bestselling author who writes erotic, science fiction, suspense, and fantasy romance. She and her husband are vagabonds, living in an RV named Floyd pulled by a beautiful monster of a truck, Fiona.

Her Sons of Tallav series is set in a sector of Federation space far off the beaten path. The Tallavan marshals are tasked with keeping the peace while coming to terms with the matriarchal system of their home planet, Tallav. Tricky because each is heavily involved in the BDSM lifestyle.

A Thief in Love Suspense Romance series, begins with a cat burglar who steals priceless art and antiquities from other thieves. Sebastian is a Robin Hood character whose Maid Marion is his equal on the rooftops of their futuristic city. Each book in the series focuses on a member of his crew.

The Guardians of the Vale series, starting with *A Prince of Her Own*, will be published sometime in the future.

Subscribe to her newsletter at http://cailinbriste.com/cailins-newsletter-sign-up/ for information about her latest releases, exclusive giveaways, and special prices.

www.ingramcontent.com/pod-product-compliance
Lightning Source LLC
Chambersburg PA
CBHW021225250626
47155CB00008B/2936